HIDDEN

HIDDEN

A House of Night Novel

P. C. CAST and **KRISTIN CAST**

ST. MARTIN'S GRIFFIN

NEW YORK

HIDDEN. Copyright © 2012 by P. C. Cast and Kristin Cast. All rights reserved. Printed in the United States of America. For information, address St. Martin's Press, 175 Fifth Avenue, New York, N.Y. 10010.

www.stmartins.com

The Library of Congress has cataloged the hardcover edition as follows:

Cast, P. C.
    Hidden / P.C. Cast and Kristin Cast. — 1st U.S. ed.
        p. cm. — (House of Night ; 10)
    ISBN 978-0-312-59442-8 (hardcover)
    ISBN 978-1-250-01415-3 (e-book)
1. Redbird, Zoey (Fictitious character)—Fiction. 2. Teenage girls—Fiction. 3. Vampires—Fiction. 4. Paranormal fiction. 5. Occult fiction. I. Cast, Kristin. II. Title.
    PS3603.A869H53 2012b
    813'.6—dc23

                                                                        2012036195

ISBN 978-1-250-04174-6 (trade paperback)

St. Martin's Griffin books may be purchased for educational, business, or promotional use. For information on bulk purchases, please contact Macmillan Corporate and Premium Sales Department at 1-800-221-7945, extension 5442, or write specialmarkets@macmillan.com.

First St. Martin's Griffin Trade Paperback Edition: April 2014

10 9 8 7 6 5 4 3 2 1

This is for those of you who have made mistakes,
and who are brave enough to correct them,
and wise enough to learn from them.

ACKNOWLEDGMENTS

Kristin and I would like to thank our St. Martin's family. We so appreciate that our team loves the House of Night world as much as we do! A special THANK-YOU to our hard-working production staff for meeting those tight deadlines! You guys are awesomesauce!

Once again we'd like to voice our appreciation for our Tulsa community. Your support and enthusiasm for the House of Night humbles and moves us. We are proud to call Tulsa home.

Thank you, CZ. You know why. XXXOOO

As always, we thank our friend and agent, Meredith Bernstein, without whom the House of Night would not exist. We heart you!

HIDDEN

CHAPTER ONE

Lenobia

Lenobia's sleep was so restless that the familiar dream took on a sense of reality that overstepped the ethereal realm of subconscious outlets and fantasies and became, from the beginning, all too heartbreakingly real.

It began with a memory. Decades, and then centuries fell away leaving Lenobia young and naïve again, and in the cargo hold of the ship that had carried her from France to America—from one world to another. It was during that journey that Lenobia had met Martin, the man who should have been her Mate for his entire life. Instead he had died too young and had taken her love to the grave with him.

In her dream Lenobia could feel the gentle roll of the ship and smell the scent of horse and hay, sea and fish—and Martin. Always Martin. He was standing before her, gazing down at her through eyes that were olive and amber and worried. She had just told him she loved him.

"It is impossible." The dream memory replayed in her mind as Martin reached out, took her hand, and lifted it gently. He raised his own arm until the two were side by side. *"You see the difference, you?"*

The dreaming Lenobia made a small, wordless exclamation of pain. The sound of his voice! That distinct Creole accent——deep, sensual, unique. It was the bittersweet sound of his voice and its beautiful accent that had kept Lenobia away from New Orleans for more than two hundred years.

"No," the young Lenobia had answered his question as she gazed

down at their arms—one brown, one white—where they pressed together. *"All I see is you."*

Still deeply asleep, Lenobia, Horse Mistress of the Tulsa House of Night, moved restlessly, as if her body was attempting to force her mind to awaken. But this night her mind did not obey. This night dreams and what might have been ruled.

The sequence of memories shifted and changed to another scene, still in the cargo hold of the same ship, still with Martin, but days later. He was handing her a long string of leather tied to a small pouch dyed a deep sapphire blue. Martin put it around her neck saying, *"This gris-gris protect you, cherie."*

In the space of a heartbeat the memory wavered and time fast-forwarded a century. An older, wiser, more cynical Lenobia was cradling the crumbling leather pouch in her hands as it split and spilled it contents—thirteen things, just as Martin had told her—but most of them had become unrecognizable during the century she'd worn the charm. Lenobia remembered a faint scent of juniper, the smooth feel of the clay pebble before it turned to dust, and the tiny dove's feather that had crumbled between her fingers. But most of all Lenobia remembered the fleeting rush of joy she'd felt when, in the midst of the disintegrating remnants of Martin's love and protection, she'd discovered something that time hadn't been able to ravage. It had been a ring—a heart-shaped emerald, surrounded by tiny diamonds, set in gold.

"Your mother's heart—your heart—my heart," Lenobia had whispered as she'd slipped it over the knuckle of her ring finger. *"I still miss you, Martin. I've never forgotten. I vowed it."*

And then the dream memories rewound again, taking Lenobia back to Martin, only this time they weren't at sea finding one another in the cargo hold and falling in love. This memory was dark and terrible. Even dreaming, Lenobia knew the place and the date: New Orleans, March 21, 1788, not long after sunset.

The stables had exploded in fire and Martin had saved her, carrying her from the flames.

"Oh, no! Martin! No!" Lenobia had screamed at him then, now

she whimpered, struggling to awaken before she had to relive the horrible end of the memory.

She didn't wake. Instead she heard her only love repeat the words that had broken her heart two hundred years before, feeling it again as if the wound were raw and fresh.

"Too late, cherie. This world too late for us. I see you again, though. My love for you don' end here. My love for you, it never end . . . find you again, cherie. That I vow."

As Martin captured the evil human who had tried to enslave her, and then walked back into the flaming stables with him, saving Lenobia's life, the Horse Mistress was finally able to wake herself with a wrenching sob. She sat up in bed, and with a trembling hand brushed her sweat-soaked hair from her face.

Lenobia's first waking thought was for her mare. Through the psychic connection they shared, she could feel that Mujaji was agitated, almost panicked. "Shhh, my beauty. Go back to sleep. I am well." Lenobia spoke aloud, sending soothing feelings to the black mare with whom she had a special bond. Feeling guilty for upsetting Mujaji, she bowed her head and cradled her hand, twisting the emerald ring around and around her finger.

"Stop being so foolish," Lenobia told herself firmly. "It was just a dream. I am safe. I am not back there. What happened then cannot hurt me more than it already has," Lenobia lied to herself. *I can be hurt again. If Martin has come back—really come back—my heart can be hurt again.* Another sob tried to escape from Lenobia, but she pressed her lips together and forced her emotions under control.

He might not be Martin, she told herself firmly, logically. Travis Foster, the new human hired by Neferet to assist her in the stables, was simply a handsome distraction—him and his big, beautiful Percheron mare. "Which is probably exactly what Neferet intended when she hired him," Lenobia muttered. "To distract me. And his Percheron is just an odd coincidence." Lenobia closed her eyes and blocked the memories that lifted from her past, and then repeated aloud, "Travis might not be Martin reincarnated. I know my reaction to him is unusually strong, but it has been a long time since I have taken a lover." *You have never taken a human lover—you vowed not to,* her conscience reminded her. "So it's simply past time I took a vampyre lover, even if briefly. And *that* type of distraction will be good for me." Lenobia tried to busy her imagination with considering and then rejecting a list of handsome Son of Erebus Warriors, her mind's eye not seeing their strong, muscular bodies, but instead envisioning whisky brown eyes tinged with familiar olive green and a ready smile . . .

"No!" She would not think of it. She would not think of *him*.

But what if Travis could really hold Martin's soul? Lenobia's errant mind whispered enticingly. *He gave his word he would find me again. Perhaps he has.* "And then what?" Lenobia stood and began to pace restlessly. "I know all too well the fragility of humans. They are too easily killed, and today the world is even more dangerous than it was in 1788. My love ended in heartbreak and flame once. Once was too much." Lenobia stopped and put her face in her hands as her heart knew the truth, and pumped it through her body and soul, becoming reality. "I am a coward. If Travis is not Martin I do not want to open myself to him—to take a chance on loving another human. And if he is Martin returned to me, I cannot bear the inevitable, that I will lose him again."

Lenobia sat heavily in the old rocking chair she'd placed beside her bedroom window. She liked to read there, and if she couldn't sleep her window faced east so she could watch the rising of the sun and look out at the grounds beside the stables. Though Lenobia appreciated the irony, she couldn't help but enjoy the morning light. Vampyre or not, at her core she would eternally be a girl who loved mornings and horses and a tall, cappuccino skinned human who had died long ago when he had been far too young.

Her shoulders slumped. She hadn't thought of Martin so often in decades. His renewed memory was a double-edged sword—on one side she loved recalling his smile, his scent, his touch. On the other his memory also evoked the void his absence had left. For more than two hundred years Lenobia had grieved for a lost possibility—a wasted life.

"Our future was burned away from us. Destroyed by flames of hatred and obsession and evil." Lenobia shook her head and wiped her eyes. She must regain control over her emotions. Evil was still burning a swath through Light and goodness. She drew in a deep, centering breath and turned her thoughts to a subject that never failed to calm her, no matter how chaotic the world around her had become—horses—Mujaji, in particular. Feeling calmer now, Lenobia reached out again with that extra special part of her spirit that Nyx had touched, and gifted with an affinity for horses, the day sixteen-year-old Lenobia had been Marked. She found her mare easily, and instantly felt guilty at the mirrored agitation she sensed in Mujaji.

"Shhh," Lenobia soothed again, repeating aloud the reassurance she was sending through her bond with the mare. "I am only being foolish and self-indulgent. It will pass, I give you my vow, sweet one." Lenobia focused a tide of warmth and love on her night-colored mare, and, as always, Mujaji regained her own calm.

Lenobia closed her eyes and released a long breath. She could envision her mare, black and beautiful as the night, finally settling down, cocking a back leg, and falling into a dreamless sleep.

The Horse Mistress concentrated on her mare, shutting out the turmoil that the young cowboy's arrival at her stables had caused within her. *Tomorrow,* she promised herself sleepily, *tomorrow I will make it clear to Travis that we will never be more than employer and employee. The color of his eyes and the way he makes me feel, all of that will begin to ease when I distance myself from him. It must . . . it must . . .*

Finally, Lenobia slept.

Neferet

Even though the feline was not bonded to her, Shadowfax came willingly at Neferet's call. Thankfully, classes were over for the night, so when the big Maine coon met her in the middle of the field house it was dimly lit and empty—no students were about; Dragon

Lankford himself was also absent, but probably only temporarily. She had seen only a few red fledglings on her way there. Neferet smiled, satisfied at the thought of how she added the rogue reds to the House of Night. What lovely, chaotic possibilities they presented—especially after she ensured Zoey's circle would be broken and her best friend, Stevie Rae, would be devastated, grieving the loss of her lover.

The knowledge that she was assuring future pain and suffering for Zoey pleased Neferet immeasurably, but she was too disciplined to allow herself to begin gloating before the sacrificial spell was complete and her commands were set into motion. Though the school was unusually quiet tonight, almost abandoned, the truth was anyone could happen into the field house. Neferet needed to work quickly and quietly. There would be ample time to revel over the fruits of her labors later.

She spoke softly to the cat, coaxing him closer to her, and when he was near enough she knelt to his level. Neferet had thought he would be leery of her—cats knew things. They were much harder to fool than humans, fledglings, or even vampyres. Neferet's own cat, Skylar, had refused to relocate to her new Mayo penthouse suite, choosing instead to lurk in the shadows of the House of Night and watch her knowingly with his large, green eyes.

Shadowfax wasn't as wary.

Neferet beckoned. Shadowfax came to her, slowly closing the last bit of distance between them. The big cat wasn't friendly—he didn't rub against her and mark her affectionately with his scent—but he came to her. His obedience was all that concerned Neferet. She didn't want his love; she wanted his life.

The Tsi Sgili, immortal Consort of Darkness, and former High Priestess of the House of Night, felt only a vague shadow of regret as her left hand caressed the long length of the Maine coon's gray tiger striped back. His fur was soft and thick over his lithe, athletic body. Like Dragon Lankford, the Warrior he'd chosen as his own, Shadowfax was powerful and in the prime of his life. Such a shame he was needed for a greater purpose. A higher purpose.

Neferet's regret did not equate to hesitation. She used her Goddess-given affinity for felines and channeled warmth and reassurance through her palm and into the already trusting feline. While her left hand caressed him, encouraging him to arch and begin to purr, her right hand snaked out and with her razor-edged athame, she quickly, cleanly, slashed Shadowfax's throat.

The big cat made no sound. His body spasmed, trying to jerk away from her, but her hand fisted in his fur, holding him so close that his blood sprayed, hot and wet, across the bodice of her green velvet dress.

The threads of Darkness that were always present around Neferet throbbed and quivered with anticipation.

Neferet ignored them.

The cat died faster than she'd imagined, and for that Neferet was glad. She hadn't expected him to stare at her, but the Warrior cat held her gaze even after he had collapsed into the sandy field house floor and could no longer fight her, but lay breathing shallowly, twitching silently, and staring.

Working quickly, while the cat was still living, Neferet began the spell. Using the blade of her ritual athame, Neferet drew a circle around Shadowfax's dying body, so that as blood pooled around him it poured into it, and a miniature moat of scarlet was formed.

Then she pressed one palm of her hand into the fresh, warm blood, stood just outside the circle, and lifted both hands—one bloody, one holding the scarlet-edged knife, and intoned:

> *"With this sacrifice I command*
> *Darkness controlled by my hand.*
> *Aurox, obey me!*
> *Rephaim's death it will be."*

Neferet paused, allowing the sticky threads of cold blackness to brush against her and gather all around the circle. She felt their eagerness, their need, their desire, their danger. But above all else, she felt their power.

To complete the spell she dipped the athame into the blood, and wrote directly into the sand with it, closing the incantation:

> *"Through payment of blood, pain, and strife*
> *I force the Vessel to be my knife!"*

Holding an image of Aurox in her mind, Neferet stepped inside the circle and plunged the dagger into Shadowfax's body, pinning him to the field house floor while she loosed the tendrils of Darkness so that they could consume their feast of blood and pain.

When the cat was thoroughly drained and absolutely dead, Neferet spoke, "The sacrifice has been made. The spell cast. Do as I command. Force Aurox to kill Rephaim. Make Stevie Rae break the circle. Cause the reveal spell to fail. Now!"

Like a nest of seething snakes, the minions of Darkness slithered into the night, heading away from the field house and toward a lavender field and the ritual that was already underway there.

Neferet gazed after them, smiling in satisfaction. One particular thread of darkness, thick as her forearm, whipped through the door that opened from the field house to the stables. Neferet's attention was pulled its way by the muffled sound of breaking glass.

Curious, the Tsi Sgili glided forward. Being careful to make no noise, and cloaking herself in shadow, Neferet peered into the stables. Her emerald eyes widened in pleased surprise. The thick thread of Darkness had been clumsy. It had knocked one of the gas lanterns from its resting place on a peg that hung not far from the piles of neatly stacked hay Lenobia was always so meticulous about choosing for her creatures. Neferet watched, fascinated, as first one tuft of hay caught fire, sputtered, and then with a renewed surge of yellow, and a mighty *whoosh!* it fully caught.

Neferet looked down the long line of closed, wooden stalls. She could see only the faint, dark outlines of a few of the horses. Most were sleeping. Some were lazily grazing, already settled down for the approaching dawn and the rest the sun would bring them until it set and students arrived for their never ending classes.

She glanced back at the hay. An entire bale was engulfed in flame. The scent of smoke drifted to her, and she could hear crackling as, like a loosed beast, the fire fed and grew.

Neferet turned away from the stable, closing the thick door between it and the field house securely. *It seems likely that Stevie Rae may not be the only one who will be grieving after tonight.* The thought satisfied Neferet, and she left the field house and the carnage she'd caused there, not seeing the small white cat who padded to Shadowfax's motionless body, curled beside him, and closed her eyes.

Lenobia

The Horse Mistress awakened with a horrid feeling of forboding. Confused, Lenobia rubbed her hands over her face. She'd fallen asleep in the rocking chair near her window and this sudden awakening seemed more nightmare than reality.

"This is foolishness," she muttered sleepily. "I must find my center again." Meditation had helped quiet her thoughts in the past. Resolutely, Lenobia drew a deep, cleansing breath.

It was with that deep breath that Lenobia smelled it—fire. A burning stable to be specific. She clenched her teeth together. *Begone, ghosts of the past! I am too old to play these games.* Then an ominous cracking sound had Lenobia shaking off the last of the sleep that had clouded her mind as she moved quickly to the window and drew aside the heavy black drapes. The Horse Mistress looked down at her stables and gasped in horror.

It hadn't been a dream.

It hadn't been her imagination.

Instead it was a living nightmare.

Flames were licking the sides of the building and as she stared, the double doors just at the edge of her vision were thrown open from the inside and against a backdrop of billowing smoke and consuming flames was the silhouette of a tall cowboy leading a huge gray Percheron and a night black mare from within.

Travis let loose of the mares, shooing them into the school grounds and away from the flaming stables, and then he ran back into the flaming mouth of the building.

Everything within Lenobia came alive as the sight extinguished her fear and doubt.

"No, Goddess. Not again. I am no longer a frightened girl. This time his end will be different!"

CHAPTER TWO

Lenobia

Lenobia bolted from her chamber, raced down the short stairwell that led from her quarters to the ground floor and the stables. Smoke was seeping snake-like from under the door. She controlled her panic and pressed her palm against the wood. It wasn't warm to the touch, so she yanked open the door, assessing the situation rapidly as she moved into her stables. The fire burned most fiercely at the far end of the building in the area where the hay and feed were stored. It was also the area closest to Mujaji's stall as well as the large foaling stall the Percheron, Bonnie, and her Travis had taken up residence in.

"Travis!" she shouted, lifting her arm to shield her face from the heat of the growing flames as she raced down into the stables and began opening stalls, freeing the horses closest to her. *Out, Persephone—go!* Lenobia nudged the roan mare, who was frozen from fright and refusing to leave her stall. When she darted past her and through the exit, Lenobia called again, "Travis! Where are you?"

"Gettin' the horses out that are closest to the fire!" he yelled as a young gray mare bolted from the direction of Travis's voice and almost trampled over Lenobia.

"Easy! Easy, Anjo." Lenobia soothed, steering the terrified horse to the exit.

"East exit is blocked by flames and I—" Travis's words broke off as the tack room windows exploded and hot glass shards flew through the air.

"Travis! Get out of there and call 911!" Lenobia yelled as she opened the closest stall and freed a gelding, hating that she'd not grabbed her phone and made the call herself before she'd run from her room.

"I just did!" replied an unfamiliar voice. Lenobia looked through the smoke and flames to see a fledgling jogging toward her, leading an utterly panicked sorrel mare.

"All is well, Diva," Lenobia calmed the horse automatically, taking the rope from the girl. At her touch the mare quieted, and Lenobia unhooked her lead rope, encouraging her to gallop through the nearby doorway after the other escaping horses. She pulled the girl back with her, away from the increasing heat, saying, "How many more horses are—" Lenobia's words broke off as she saw that the crescent on the girl's forehead was red.

"I think there are only a few left." The red fledgling's hand was shaking as she wiped sweat and soot from her face, gasping the words. "I—I grabbed Diva 'cause I always liked her and thought she might remember me. But even she was scared. Real scared."

Then Lenobia recognized the girl—Nicole. She'd had an aptitude for horses and a natural seat, before she'd died and then undied and joined Dallas's rogue group. But there was no time to question the child. No time for anything except getting the horses—and Travis—to safety. "You did well, Nicole. Can you go back in there?"

"Yes." Nicole nodded jerkily. "I don't want them to burn. I'll do whatever you tell me to do."

Lenobia rested her hand on the girl's shoulder. "I just need you to open the stalls and get out of the way. I'll guide them to safety."

"Okay, okay. I can do that." Nicole nodded. She sounded breathless and frightened, but without hesitation she followed Lenobia and they jogged back into the swirling heat of the stables.

"Travis!" Lenobia coughed, trying to see through the increasingly thick smoke. "Can you hear me?"

Over the crackling flames he yelled. "Yes! I'm back here. Stall stuck!"

"Get it open!" Lenobia refused to give in to her panic. "Get them all open! I can call the horses to me, to safety. I can get them out. Follow them. I can guide you all out!"

"Got 'em open!" Travis yelled a moment later from the pit of the smoke and heat.

"These are all open, too!" called Nicole from much closer.

"Now follow the horses and get out of the stables! Both of you!" Lenobia shouted before she began sprinting, backward, away from the fire and to the double doors of the exit she'd left open wide behind her. Standing in the doorway she lifted her arms, palms open, and imagining she was pulling power directly from the Otherworld and the mystical realm of Nyx, Lenobia opened her heart, her soul, and her Goddess-given gift and cried, "Come, my beautiful daughters and sons! Follow my voice and my love and live!"

Horses seemed to explode from out of the flames and the inky smoke. Their terror was so palpable to Lenobia it was almost a living being. She understood it—this terror of flames and fire and death—and she channeled strength and serenity through herself and into the horses that galloped past her and into the school grounds.

The red fledgling staggered, coughing, after them. "That's it. That's all the horses," she said, collapsing into the grass.

Lenobia barely spared Nicole a nod. Her emotions were focused on the restless herd behind her, and her eyes were focused on the thickening smoke and the licking flames before her from which Travis did not emerge.

"Travis!" she shouted.

There was no answer.

"The fire's spreading fast," said the still-coughing red fledgling. "He might be dead."

"No," Lenobia said firmly. "Not this time." She turned to look at the herd, calling out to her beloved black mare, "Mujaji!" The horse nickered and trotted toward her. Lenobia put up a hand, halting her. "Be calm, sweet one. Watch over the rest of my children. Lend them your strength and serenity, as well as my love," Lenobia said. The mare reluctantly but obediently began moving around the clusters of frightened horses, herding them together. Satisfied, Lenobia turned away, drew two deep breaths, and sprinted into the mouth of the burning stables.

The heat was terrible. The smoke was so dense it was like trying to breathe boiling liquid. For an instant Lenobia was transported back to that terrible night in New Orleans and another burning barn. The thick ridges of the scars on her back ached with a phantom memory of pain, and for a moment panic ruled, rooting Lenobia in the past.

Then she heard him cough, and her panic was shattered by hope, allowing the present and the true strength of Lenobia's will to overcome her fear. "Travis! I can't see you!" she shouted as she ripped off the bottom of her nightgown, stepped into the closest stall, and dunked it in the water trough.

"Go—back—" he said between hacking coughs.

"Like hell I will. I've watched a man burn because of me. I do not like it." Lenobia pulled the soaking cloth over her like a hooded cloak and moved farther into the smoke and heat, following Travis's coughs.

She found him next to an open stall. He'd fallen and was trying to pull himself up, but had only made it to his knees where he was bent over gagging and coughing. Lenobia didn't hesitate. She stepped into the stall and dunked the ripped cloth into the stall's water trough again.

"What the?" Another cough raked him as he squinted up at her. "No! Get—"

"I have no time for arguing. Just lay down." When he didn't move quickly enough, she kicked his knees out from under him. He fell onto his back with a grunt and she spread the wet cloth over his face and chest. "Yes, like that. Flat," Lenobia commanded, as she reached into the water trough, and quickly splashed the liquid over her face and hair. Then, before he could protest or foil her plan by moving around, she grabbed Travis's legs and began pulling.

Did he have to be this big and heavy? Lenobia's mind was getting fuzzy. Flames were roaring around her and she was sure she could smell burning hair. *Well, Martin had been big, too . . .* Then her mind stopped working. It was as if her body was moving on automatic with no one piloting it except a primal need to keep dragging this man from danger.

"It's her! It's Lenobia!" Strong hands were suddenly there, trying to take her burden from her. Lenobia fought. *Death would not win this time! Not this time!*

"Professor Lenobia, all is well. You made it out." The coolness of the air registered, and then her mind was able to put sense to what was happening. She gasped, breathing in the clean air and coughing out heat and smoke as gentle hands helped her to the grass and put a mask over her nose and mouth, through which even sweeter air flooded her lungs. She sucked in the oxygen and her mind completely cleared.

Human firemen swarmed the grounds. Powerful water hoses were being turned to the flaming stables. A pair of paramedics was hovering, staring at her, looking lost and obviously surprised at how quickly she was recovering.

She ripped the mask from her face. "Not me. Him!" She yanked the smoldering cloth from Travis's too still body. "He's human—help him!"

"Yes, ma'am," one of the EMTs mumbled and they started working on Travis.

"Lenobia, drink this." A goblet was thrust into her hands and the Horse Mistress looked up to see the two vampyre healers from the House of Night infirmary, Margareta and Pemphredo, crouching beside her. Lenobia drained the wine that was heavily laced with blood in one long swallow, instantly feeling the life energy it carried tingle through her body.

"You should come with us, Professor," Margareta said. "You will need more than that to completely heal.

"Later," Lenobia said, tossing the goblet aside. She ignored the healers, as well as the sirens and voices and general chaos around her. Lenobia crawled to Travis's head. The EMTs were busy. The cowboy already had a mask of his own, and they were starting an IV in his arm. His eyes were closed. Even under the soot smudges, she could see that his face was scalded and red. He was wearing an untucked T-shirt that had obviously been thrown on hastily over his jeans. His strong forearms were bare and already blistering. And his hands— his hands were burned bloody.

She must have made an involuntary noise—some small outward sign of the horrible heartache she was feeling—because Travis opened his eyes. They were exactly as she remembered—whisky brown tinged with olive green. Their gazes met and held.

"Is he going to survive?" she asked the paramedic closest to her.

"I've seen worse, and he is gonna scar, but we need to get him to St. John's ASAP. The smoke inhalation is worse than his burns." The human paused, and even though Lenobia hadn't taken her gaze from Travis's, she could hear the smile in his voice. "He's a lucky guy. You almost didn't find him in time."

"Actually, it took me two hundred and twenty-four years to find him, but I am glad I was in time."

Travis started to say something, but his words were drowned in a terrible, hacking cough.

"Excuse me, ma'am. The gurney's here."

Lenobia moved to the side as Travis was transferred to the gurney, but their gaze never broke. She walked beside him as they rolled him to the waiting ambulance. Before they loaded him within, he pushed off his mask, and in a gravelly voice asked, "Bonnie? Okay?"

"She's fine. I can feel her. She's with Mujaji. I'll keep her safe. I'll keep all of them safe," she assured him.

He reached out to her, and she carefully touched his burned, bloodied hand. "Me too?" he managed to rasp.

"Yes, cowboy. You can bet that big, beautiful mare of yours on that." And not giving a damn that she could feel everyone staring at her—humans, fledglings, and vampyres—Lenobia leaned down and kissed him softly on his lips. "Look for happiness and horses. I'll be there. This time making sure *you* are safe."

"Good to know. My mamma always said I needed a keeper. Hope

she rests better knowin' I got me one." He sounded like his throat was full of sandpaper.

Lenobia smiled. "You've got one, but I think it is *you* who needs to learn to rest."

The tips of his fingers touched her hand and he said, "I believe I can now. I was just waitin' to find my way home."

Lenobia stared into his amber and olive eyes that were so familiar, so very, very much like Martin's, and imagined she could see through to that also familiar soul—to the kindness and strength, honesty and love that somehow had fulfilled his promise to return to her. Deep within her Lenobia knew that even though the rest of the tall, wiry cowboy looked nothing at all like her lost love, she'd found her heart again. Emotion clogged her voice, and all she could do was smile, nod, and turn her hand so that his fingertips rested on her palm—warm, strong, and very much alive.

"We need to get him to St. John's, ma'am," said the EMT.

Lenobia took her touch reluctantly from Travis, wiped her eyes, and said, "You can have him for a little while, but I'll want him back. Soon." She turned her storm cloud gaze on the white-jacketed human. "Treat him well. This barn fire is small in comparison to the heat of my temper."

"Y-yes, ma'am," the EMT stammered, quickly lifting Travis into the ambulance. Before they closed the doors and, with lights flashing, drove away, Lenobia was sure she heard Travis's chuckle turn to a wracking cough.

She was standing there, staring after the ambulance and worrying about Travis, when someone nearby cleared his throat rather obviously, and Lenobia's attention instantly shifted. Turning, she saw what her tunnel vision-like focus on Travis had caused her to ignore. The school seemed to have exploded. Horses milled nervously as close to the east wall as they could get. Fire trucks were parked on the grounds beside the stable, spraying enormous hoses filled with rushing water on the still burning structure. Fledglings and vampyres had gathered in frightened groups, looking helpless.

"Calm, Mujaji . . . calm. All is well now, my sweet one." Lenobia closed her eyes and concentrated on using the gift her Goddess had granted her more than two hundred years ago. She felt the beautiful black mare respond instantly, releasing her agitation and blowing out the last of her fear and nervousness. Then Lenobia's connection shifted to the big Percheron, who was pawing the ground fretfully, ears flicking wildly as she searched for Travis. "Bonnie, he is well. You have nothing to fear." Lenobia spoke softly, echoing the waves of emotion she was transmitting to the anxious mare. Bonnie quieted almost as quickly as had Mujaji, which pleased Lenobia immensely and allowed her to spread her attention easily to the rest of the herd. "Persephone, Anjo, Diva, Little Biscuit, Okie Dodger"— she picked through the herd, sending special warmth and reassurance to individual horses—"follow Mujaji's lead. Be calm. Be strong. You are safe."

The nearby throat cleared again, breaking her concentration. Irritated, Lenobia opened her eyes to see a human standing in front of her. He was dressed in a fireman's uniform, and he was watching her with raised-brow, open curiosity. "Are you talking to those horses?"

"Actually, I am doing much more than that. Take a look." She made a gesture at the herd behind him. He turned, and his face registered surprise. "They've calmed down a bunch. That's bizarre."

"Bizarre has such negative connotations. I like the word magickal instead." Dismissively, Lenobia nodded to the fireman and then began striding toward the group of fledglings that were clustered around Erik Night and Professor P.

"Ma'am, I'm Captain Alderman, Steve Alderman," he said, almost jogging to keep up with Lenobia. "We're working to get this fire under control, and I need to know who's in charge here."

"Captain Alderman, I would like to know that myself," Lenobia said grimly. Then, she added, "Come with me. I'll get this sorted out." The Horse Mistress joined Erik, Professor P, and their bunch of fledglings, which included a Son of Erebus Warrior, Kramisha, Shaylin, and several fifth and sixth former blue fledglings. "Penthesilea, I know Thanatos is with Zoey and her circle, completing the ritual at

Sylvia Redbird's farm, but where is Neferet?" Lenobia's voice was a whip.

"I-I simply do not know!" The literature professor sounded shaken, staring over her shoulder at the burning stables. "I went to her quarters myself when I saw the fire, but there was no sign of her."

"How 'bout her phone? Didn't nobody try to call her?" Kramisha said.

"Not answering," Erik said.

"Wonderful," Lenobia muttered.

"Can I assume that due to the absence of the others you just mentioned, you are in charge here?" Captain Alderman asked her.

"Yes, it appears, by default, I am," she said.

"Well, then, you need a school roster, ASAP. You and the teachers should check immediately to be sure all of your students are present and accounted for." He jerked his thumb toward a bench not far from where they stood. "That girl—the one with the red moon on her forehead, is the only kid we found anywhere near the barn. She's not hurt, just shook up a little. The oxygen is clearing her lungs unusually fast. Still, it might be a good idea for her to get checked out at St. John's."

Lenobia glanced over to where Nicole was sitting, breathing deeply from an oxygen mask while a paramedic checked and rechecked her vitals. Margareta and Pemphredo hovered close by, glaring at the EMT like he was a particularly disgusting insect.

"Our infirmary is better equipped to take care of injured fledglings than a human hospital," Lenobia said.

"Whatever you say, ma'am. You're in charge here, and I know you vamps have your own unique physiology." He paused and added, "No offense meant by that. My best friend in high school was Marked and Changed. I liked him then. I still like him."

Lenobia managed a smile. "No offense taken, Captain Alderman. You were only speaking truth. Vampyres do have different physiological needs than humans. Nicole will be fine here with us.

"Good. Guess we'd better send some of our boys into that field house and look for any other kids that might be close by," said the captain. "Looks like we can keep the fire from spreading, but best search the adjoining parts of the school."

"I think the field house is a waste of your men's time," Lenobia said, following what her instinct was telling her. "Have them focus on putting out the stable fire. The fire didn't start by itself. That needs to be investigated, as well as being sure none of our people were trapped in the blaze. I'll have our Warriors search the adjoining parts of the school, beginning with the field house."

"Yes, ma'am. It does look like we got here in time. The field house will have smoke and water damage, but it's going to look a lot worse than it really is. I think the structure has remained sound. It's a nice building made from good, thick stone. It'll take some rebuilding, but its bones were made to last." The fireman tipped his hat to her and went off, shouting orders at the nearest men.

Well, at least that's some good news, Lenobia thought, trying to avert her eyes from the smoldering mess that was her stables. She turned back to her group. "Where's Dragon? Still in the field house?"

"We can't find Dragon, either," Erik said.

"Dragon's missing?" The stables had been built with a shared wall of the large, covered field house. Until then she'd been too preoccupied to think about it, but the absence of the Leader of the Sons of Erebus during a time of school crisis was highly unusual. "Neferet and Dragon—I do not like that neither are here. It bodes ill for the school."

"Professor Lenobia, um, I saw her."

Everyone's eyes turned to the petite girl with cascades of thick, dark hair that made the delicate features of her face seem almost doll-like. Lenobia put a name to her face quickly, Shaylin—the newest fledgling at the Tulsa House of Night, and the only fledgling whose original Mark was red. Lenobia had thought there was something rather odd about her from the first moment she'd met her just days before. "You saw Neferet?" She narrowed her eyes at the fledgling. "When? Where?"

"Only an hour or so ago," Shaylin said. "I was sitting outside the dorm, looking at the trees." She shrugged nervously and added, "I used to be blind, and now that I'm not anymore I like to look at stuff. A lot."

"Shaylin, what about Neferet?" Erik Night prodded her.

"Oh, yeah, I saw her walking down the sidewalk to the field house. She, um, she looked very, well, *dark*." Shaylin paused, looking uncomfortable.

"Dark? What do you mean by—"

"Shaylin has a unique way of seeing people," Erik interrupted. Lenobia watched him put a calming hand on Shaylin's shoulder. "If she thought Neferet looked dark, then it's probably a good thing you kept the human firemen from poking around the field house."

Lenobia wanted to question Shaylin further, but Erik met Lenobia's gaze and shook his head, almost imperceptibly. Lenobia felt a chill of foreboding shiver down her spine. That premonition decided her. "Axis, go with Penthesilea to the administrative office. If Diana isn't awake, wake her. Get the school roster and distribute it among the Sons of Erebus Warriors. Have them account for each student and then have the students report to their mentors before they return to their dormitory rooms." As the professor and the Warrior hurried away, Lenobia met Kramisha's frank gaze. "Can you get these fledglings"—Lenobia paused and her gesture took in the random, lost-looking students that were milling around the area— "to report to their mentors?"

"I'm a poet. I can figure out some serious iambic pentameter. That means I can boss around a few scared, sleepy kids."

Lenobia smiled at the girl. She'd liked her even before she'd died, and then come back as a red fledgling who had such prophetic poetic skills that she'd been named the new Vampyre Poet Laureate. "Thank you, Kramisha. I knew I could count on you. Be sure you hurry. I don't need to tell *you*, but dawn is getting too close."

Kramisha snorted. "You tellin' me? I'll be crispier than that barn if I'm not inside and under cover soon."

As Kramisha hurried off, calling to the scattered fledglings, Lenobia faced Erik and Shaylin. "The three of us need to search the field house."

"Yeah, I agree," Erik said. "Let's go."

Shaylin held back, though, and Lenobia noticed she shook his hand off her shoulder. Not in an irritated or mean way, but in a distracted way. She watched the young red fledgling gaze skyward and sigh. Lenobia caught a sense of importance—a sense of waiting or wanting.

"What is it?" Lenobia asked the girl, even though the last thing she should have been doing was giving attention to a distracted, strange, red fledgling.

Still gazing upwards, Shaylin said, "Where's the rain when you need it?"

"Huh?" Erik shook his head at her. "What are you talking about?"

"Rain. I really, really wish it would rain." The girl looked from the sky to him and shrugged, appearing a little embarrassed. "I swear I could smell it in the air. It would help the firemen and make double sure the fire didn't spread to the rest of the school."

"The humans are handling the fire. We need to check out the field house. I don't like that Neferet was seen going in there."

Lenobia began heading toward the field house, assuming the two of them would follow her, but she hesitated when Shaylin still resisted. Turning on her, ready to call the fledgling to task for either insolence or ignorance, Erik beat her to it by saying something.

"Hey, this is important." He spoke in a low, urgent voice to Shaylin. "Let's go with Lenobia and check out the field house. The firemen can get the rest of this stuff under control." When Shaylin continued to hold back and resisted going toward the field house, he said, more loudly, "What's going on with you? Since Thanatos and Dragon, and even Zoey and her group aren't here, we need to be careful about not letting everyone know what we might—"

"Erik, I *do* think Lenobia's right," Shaylin cut him off. "It's just, I want to know what's going to happen to her."

Lenobia followed Shaylin's gaze to see Nicole, still sitting on the bench, between the two infirmary vampyres, looking soot-smudged and pink-skinned.

"She's one of Dallas's red fledglings. I wouldn't be surprised if she had something to do with the fire," Erik said, clearly annoyed. "Lenobia, I think you should make Nicole go to the infirmary, and then keep her locked in there until we figure out what the hell really happened here."

Before Lenobia could respond, Shaylin was speaking. She sounded firm and much wiser than her sixteen years. "No. Have her go to the infirmary to be sure she's okay, but don't lock her up."

"Shaylin, you don't know what you're talking about. Nicole is with Dallas," Erik said.

"Well, she's not with him right now. She's changing," Shaylin said.

"She did help me get the horses out," Lenobia said. "If she was involved in the fire it would have been a lot easier for her to slip away in the smoke. I would have never known she was there."

"That makes sense. Her colors are different—better." Then Shaylin, firmness and wisdom dissipating, looked big-eyed at Lenobia and said, "Ah oh. Sorry. I said too much. I need to learn to keep my mouth shut."

"What atrocity has been committed on the school grounds this night!" The voice thundered over Lenobia. Across the school grounds, moving quickly toward them, was a phalanx of vampyres and fledglings with Thanatos in their lead, Zoey and Stevie Rae on either side of her and, bizarrely enough, Kalona, wings unfurled defensively, striding along with them just behind Thanatos, as if he had suddenly become Death's Guardian Angel.

It was at that moment that the night sky opened and it began to rain.

CHAPTER THREE

Zoey

I'd known it before we saw the fire trucks and the smoke. I'd known all hell had broken loose at the House of Night the moment Thanatos had witnessed the truth of Neferet's crimes. That night it had been proven beyond all doubt that Neferet was on the side of Darkness. Thanatos hadn't wasted any time outing her. On the way back to the school from Grandma's lavender farm, the High Priestess of Death had made the emergency call to Italy and officially informed the Vampyre High Council that Neferet was no longer a Priestess of Nyx—that she'd chosen Darkness as her Consort. Neferet had been seen for who she really was, something I'd wanted since I'd first realized her disgusting truth. Only, now that I'd gotten my wish, I had a terrible feeling that outing Neferet would serve more to free her than to force her to pay the consequences for her lies and betrayals.

Everything seemed so awful and so confusing, like the entire night had been the last half of a terrible slasher horror movie: the ritual, rewatching images of my mother's murder, what had happened with Dragon and Rephaim and Kalona and Aurox . . . Aurox? Heath? *No, I can't go there! Not now.* Now the stables were on fire. Seriously. At our school horses were neighing and clustering nervously by the east wall. Lenobia looked singed and soot-covered. Erik and Shaylin and a bunch of other fledglings were standing there, shell-shocked and soggy because, of course, it had started to pour buckets of rain. And Nicole, as in the Nicole who was a super mean red fledgling and Dallas's skanky, hateful girlfriend, was collapsed on a bench with a couple of human EMTs hovering around her like she was the gold-winged baby Jesus.

I wanted to punch a button, turn off the scary movie, and drift to sleep safely curled up next to Stark. Hell, I wanted to close my eyes and go back to a time when the worst stress I had was triple boyfriend stress, and that had been really, really bad.

I mentally shook myself, did my best to shut out the chaos that surrounded me inside and out, and focused on Lenobia.

"Yes, the stables caught fire," she was explaining to us. "We don't know who or what caused it. Have any of you seen Neferet?"

"We have not seen her in person, but we have seen her image in the recorded spirit of Zoey's grandmother's land." Thanatos lifted her chin, and in a strong, sure voice that carried through the rain pronounced, "Neferet has allied herself with the white bull. She sacrificed Zoey's mother to him. She will be a powerful enemy, but enemy she is to everyone who follows Light and the Goddess."

I could see that the announcement shook Lenobia, although I knew the Horse Mistress had been aware that Neferet had become our enemy months ago. Still, there was a big difference between thinking something, and knowing the worst you had imagined was true. Especially when that something was so horrible it was almost beyond comprehension. Then Lenobia cleared her throat and said, "The High Council has shunned her?"

"I have reported what I have witnessed this night," said Thanatos, acting High Priestess of our House of Night. "The High Council commands Neferet appear before them where they will mete out justice upon her for her betrayal of our Goddess and of our ways."

"She had to have known what you would find if your ritual was successful," Lenobia said.

"Yeah, which is why she sent that thing of hers after us—to kill Rephaim and mess up our circle and stop the reveal ritual," Stevie Rae said, sliding her hand within Rephaim's, who stood tall and strong by her side.

"Doesn't look like that worked," Erik Night said.

He was standing close to Shaylin. Now that I thought about it, it seemed Erik had been spending a lot of time standing close to Shaylin. Hmmm...

"Well, it would've worked," Stevie Rae said, "but Dragon showed up and stopped Aurox for a while." She paused and looked back at Kalona. She actually sent him a warm, sweet, Stevie Rae smile before continuing, "Kalona is really who saved Rephaim. Kalona saved his son."

"Dragon! That's where he is—with you guys," Erik said, his eyes searching around behind us, obviously expecting to see Dragon.

I felt my gut clench and blinked hard so that I wouldn't start bawling. When no one said anything I drew in a deep breath and delivered the really crappy, sad news. "Dragon *was* with us. He fought to protect us. Well, us and Rephaim. But..." I trailed off, finding it hard to say the next words.

"But Aurox gored Dragon to death, breaking the spell that had sealed the circle and setting the rest of us free so we could get to Rephaim and protect him," Stark had no problem finishing for me.

"It was too late, though," Stevie Rae added. "Rephaim would have died, too, if Kalona hadn't shown up in time to save him."

"Dragon Lankford is dead?" Lenobia's face had gone still and white.

"He is. He died a Warrior, true to himself and to his Oath. He has been reunited with his Mate in the Otherworld," Thanatos said. "We all served witness to it."

Lenobia closed her eyes and bowed her head. I could see her lips were moving, as if she was murmuring a soft prayer. When she lifted her head her face was set in angry lines and her gray eyes looked like storm clouds. "Burning my stables was a distraction which allowed Neferet to escape."

"It seems likely," Thanatos said. Then the High Priestess paused as if listening carefully through the rain and firemen and horse noises. Her eyes narrowed and she said, "Death has been here—recently."

Lenobia shook her head. "No, the firemen are clearing the stables. I do not believe anyone died there."

"I am not sensing a fledgling or a vampyre spirit," Thanatos said.

"All the horses got out!" Nicole spoke up suddenly. I was surprised at her tone. I mean, until then I'd only heard Nicole sneer or say something nasty. This Nicole sounded like a regular kid—one who was normal and upset by stuff like horses on fire and evil loosed on the world.

But Stevie Rae, like me, knew a very different Nicole.

"What the hell are you doin' here, Nicole?" Stevie Rae said.

"She was helping Lenobia and Travis get the horses out," Shaylin said.

"Yeah, I'm sure she was—right after she set the fire!" Stevie Rae said.

"Bitch, you can't talk to me like that!" Nicole sneered, her voice becoming way more familiar.

"Watch yourself, Nicole," I said, stepping up beside Stevie Rae.

"Enough!" Thanatos lifted her hands and power surged, crackling through the rain and making all of us jump. "Nicole, you are a red fledgling. It is past time you gave your allegiance to the only High Priestess of your kind. You will *not* curse at her. Is that understood?"

Nicole crossed her arms and nodded, once. She didn't look sorry at all to me, and her attitude, on top of everything else that had happened that night, really pissed me off. I faced her and told her exactly what was on my mind. "You need to get that no one's going to put up with your crap anymore. From here on things are going to be different."

"For one, you'll have to get through me to hurt Zoey," Stark said.

"You used me to try to kill Stevie Rae once. That will never happen again," Rephaim spoke up.

"Zoey, Stevie Rae," Thanatos said sharply. "To be respected as High Priestesses you must act accordingly, and so must your Warriors."

"She tried to kill us. Both of us!" Stevie Rae said.

"Not recently!" Nicole shouted at Stevie Rae.

"How can we battle the great and ancient Darkness that has been newly loosed upon this world if we are no more than bickering children?" Thanatos spoke quietly. She didn't sound powerful or wise or strong. She sounded tired and hopeless, and that was way scarier than the zapping thing she'd done before.

"Thanatos is right," I said.

"What are you talkin' 'bout, Z? You know what Nicole's really like." Stevie Rae pointed at her. "Just like you knew what Neferet was really like, even when no one else believed you."

"What I'm talking about is that Thanatos is right about the bickering. We can't even begin to beat Neferet if our team isn't strong and together." I looked at Nicole. "Which means either get on our team, or get the hell off."

"If she's cussing, she's serious," Aphrodite said.

"I am in agreement with her," Damien said.

"As am I," Darius added.

"Me, too," Shaunee spoke up, and close behind her Erin said a quick, "Yep."

"I chose my side," Kalona spoke solemnly. "I believe it is time others do, too."

"I'm new here, but I know which side is right, and I choose their side." Shaylin stepped over to stand with us. Erik followed her. He didn't say anything, but he did meet my gaze and nod. I smiled at him and then turned to face Thanatos, supported by my group's solidarity. "We're not bickering kids. We're just tired of being pushed around by people who say they know what's best, but who seem to keep messing up—even more than we do."

"Which is a lot," Aphrodite said dryly.

"You're not helping," I responded automatically. To Nicole I said, "So choose your team."

"Fine. I choose Team Nicole," she said.

"Which really means Team Selfish," Stevie Rae said.

"Or Team Hateful," Erin said.

"Or Team Unattractive," Aphrodite added.

"Thanatos is leaving," Lenobia spoke quickly, gesturing to the High Priestess's back.

"As I originally thought," Kalona's voice seemed to dry up the rain with his anger. "She returns to her civilized High Council and leaves us to battle evil."

Thanatos stopped, turned, and skewered the winged immortal with her dark gaze. "Oathbound Warrior, be still! My word is no less binding than yours. Where I am going is to follow Death. Sadly, that does not take me from this school, nor will it in the foreseeable future." Without another word Thanatos continued walking away from us and toward the smoldering entrance to the field house.

"Jeesh, she's so damn dramatic." Aphrodite rolled her eyes. "She already said it's not a vamp or a fledgling or a horse. So, what the hell? If a gnat dies are we all going to freak the fuck out?"

"What is your problem?" Nicole shook her head at Aphrodite. "Goddess, you're always such a hag. Why don't you think instead of running your mouth? Thanatos isn't talking about bugs and shit like that. She has to be talking about a cat. That's the only other animal spirit here she'd care about."

That shut up Aphrodite, creating what seemed like a giant silent vacuum while we all realized Nicole had to be right.

I sucked air. "Oh, Goddess no! Nala!"

Frowning at Nicole, Aphrodite said, "Relax, our cats are at the depot—even that smelly dog. It's not one of ours."

"Duchess is *not* smelly," Damien said. "But, oh, I'm so glad she and Cammy are safe."

"I'd just die if something happened to Beelzebub," Shaunee said.

"I would, too!" Erin added, sounding more defensive than worried.

"I love Nal." Stevie Rae met my eyes and we both blinked back tears.

"Our familiars are safe." Darius's deep voice seemed to anchor me, until Erik spoke.

"Just because the cat wasn't one of yours doesn't make its death any less awful." Erik sounded way more mature than usual. "Wonder who's on Team Selfish now?"

I sighed, and was going to agree with Erik when Nicole made an exasperated sound and started walking away from us—following the path Thanatos had just taken.

"Where do you think you're goin'?" Stevie Rae called after her.

Nicole didn't pause. She didn't turn around, either, but her voice trailed back to us. "Team Selfish is going to help Thanatos with the dead cat—*whosever* dead cat it is—because Team Selfish likes animals. They're nicer than people. The end."

"I don't know what she's talking about," Aphrodite said.

I rolled my eyes at her.

"This is all some kinda act she's puttin' on. That girl can't be trusted." Stevie Rae glared after Nicole.

"Well, I can tell you that Nicole almost succumbed to smoke inhalation helping me free the horses," Lenobia said.

"Her color's changing," Shaylin whispered.

"Shhh," Erik said to her, touching her shoulder.

"She tried to kill me!" Stevie Rae sounded like she was getting ready to explode.

"Oh, for shit's sake, who *hasn't* tried to kill you? Or Zoey. Or me for that matter. Get over it," Aphrodite clipped, and before Stevie Rae could answer back, she raised her hand, palm out and continued, "Save it. Unless you and Stark and the rest of the burn-up-in-daylight-red-fledglings are planning on spending the day here and under cover, we'd better be reloading the short bus and getting back to the depot. Oh, and birdboy is gonna be one hundred percent bird and zero percent boy pretty soon, too, which I'm sure is awkward in public."

"I really hate it when she's right," Stevie Rae said to me.

"Tell me about it," I said. "Okay, why don't you guys gather up everyone who is supposed to go back to the depot? I'll find out what's going on with Thanatos and Death and whatnot, and then meet you at the bus. Soon."

"You mean you and I will find out what's going on with Thanatos and Death and whatnot, and then meet them at the bus. Soon," Stark corrected me.

I squeezed his hand. "That's exactly what I mean."

"And I," Kalona said. "I will follow Thanatos with you as well, though I will not be returning to the depot." His lips turned up just a little as his gaze shifted from me to his son. "Soon, though. I will see you all again soon."

Stevie Rae let loose of Rephaim's hand long enough to hurl herself into Kalona's arms, squeezing him in a giant hug, which seemed to surprise him as much as it did the rest of us, though Rephaim looked on with a humongous grin. "Yeah, we'll see you real soon. Thanks again for showin' up for your son."

Kalona awkwardly patted her back. "You are welcome."

Then she had a hold of Rephaim's hand again and was retracing our path to the parking lot. "'Kay, we'll wait for y'all, but remember, sure as sugar, the sun's gonna rise real soon."

Aphrodite shook her head and hooked her arm through Darius's. "What the hell does 'sure as sugar' mean, anyway? Do you think she even graduated from the eighth grade?"

"Just help her get the kids on the bus," I said.

Thankfully, the wind had picked up along with the rain, and both swallowed Aphrodite's reply as she and Darius and the rest of my circle, plus Shaylin and Erik, walked off—in theory doing what I asked of them. Which left me alone with Stark, Lenobia, and Kalona.

"Ready?" Stark asked me.

"Yeah, of course," I lied.

"The field house it is then," Lenobia said.

Following Thanatos and Nicole, I tried to ready myself for something terrible, but my terrible quota had been filled for the night, and all I could do was wipe the rain from my face and put one foot in front of the other. I wasn't really ready for anything but bed.

It was warm and dry inside the field house, but it smelled like smoke. The sand under our feet was damp and dirty. *Dragon would hate to see his place messed up like this,* was what I was thinking when Kalona pointed to the center of the dimly lit arena where I could just make out the vague shapes of Thanatos and Nicole.

"There—out there," he said.

"We should have lit the torches," Lenobia was murmuring as we walked across the soggy sand. "The humans extinguished almost all the lanterns along with the stable fire."

I didn't want to say anything, but the truth was that I was glad it was hard to see because I knew whatever it was Thanatos and Nicole were gathered around was not going to be pretty. I kept that thought to myself, though, and grabbed Stark's hand, borrowing strength from his firm grip.

"Have a care where you walk." When we got close to where she and Nicole were, Thanatos spoke to us without looking up from where she had knelt on the field house floor. "There is evidence of spellwork here. I'll want it saved and examined so I can discover who is responsible for this atrocity."

I peeked over her shoulder, not really understanding what I was seeing. A circle had been drawn in the sand. The sand looked weird and dark inside it. In the center of the circle were a couple of furry blobs. To the side of the blobs there were words scratched into the sand. I squinted, trying to make them out.

"What the heck is it?" I asked.

Red vampyres saw way better in the dark, so I knew when Stark's arm went around me that whatever it was, it was bad. Real bad. Before I could repeat my question, Nicole reached into her pocket and took out her phone. "I got a flash on this thing. It'll hurt your eyes, but at least it'll take a picture."

She was right. I was blinking tears and spots from my vision in the next second. Kalona, whose immortal vision was less susceptible to being messed with by light than any vampyre, spoke solemnly. "I know whose work this is. Can you not feel her lingering presence?"

My vision blinked clear and I moved closer, even though Stark's grip on me tried to pull me back. Too late, I understood what I was looking at. "Shadowfax! He's dead!"

"Sacrificed in a dark ritual," Thanatos said.

"And Guinevere, too," Nicole added.

I felt like I was going to puke. "Dragon's cat *and* Anastasia's cat? Both of them have been killed?"

Thanatos reached out and gently stroked her hand down Shadow-fax's side, moving from his body to the much smaller cat that was curled up beside him. "This little one did not die sacrificially. She was not part of the ritual. Grief stopped her heart and her breath." The High Priestess stood and turned to Kalona. "You say you know whose work this is."

"I do, as do you. Neferet sacrificed the Warrior's cat. It was done as payment. Darkness obeys her, but the price of its obedience is blood and death and pain. That price must be paid over and over again. Darkness is never sated." He pointed to the words. "That proves what I say."

In the dim light I could see the sad, dead bodies of the cats, but the words written to the side of them were hard for me to make out. I didn't have to ask. Holding me close to him, Stark read them aloud.

> *"Through payment of blood, pain, and strife*
> *I force the Vessel to be my knife."*

"The Vessel is what Neferet calls Aurox," Kalona explained.

"Oh, great Goddess, this proves more than that this is Neferet's work." Thanatos's dark gaze met mine. "Your mother's death wasn't simply a random sacrifice to Darkness. It was the payment required to create Neferet's creature, the Vessel, Aurox."

My knees turned to rubber and I moved even closer to Stark. It felt like his arm was all that was keeping me standing.

"I knew that damn bull kid was bad news," Stark said. "No way was he some kind of gift from Nyx."

"The Vessel is the opposite. He is a creature fashioned from pain and death by Darkness, and controlled by Neferet," Thanatos said.

I couldn't tell them what I thought I'd seen in the Seer Stone. How could I, with Stark's arm around me, Dragon newly dead, and the awfulness of the cats? But I was too raw—too tired and hurt and confused to guard my words anymore to keep from blurting Heath's name, so instead, like a moron, I babbled. "There has to be more to Aurox than that! Remember what he asked you about after class? He wanted to know who he was—*what* he was. You said he could decide that for himself and not let his past control his future. Why would a creature who was totally made of Darkness, totally nothing but Neferet's Vessel, care to question anything about himself?"

"You have a point. I do remember Aurox came to me." Thanatos nodded. Her gaze moved back to the bodies of the cats. "Perhaps Aurox isn't completely an empty vessel. Perhaps his interaction with us, and in particular you, Zoey, touched some piece of a conscience within him."

I felt a rush of emotion that had Stark sending me a startled, questioning look. "He was telling the truth!" I explained. "Tonight, just before Aurox ran off he said 'I chose a different future. I chose a new future.' He meant that he hadn't wanted to hurt Rephaim or Dragon, but he couldn't help it if Neferet had control of him."

"It makes sense." Thanatos nodded, speaking slowly as if working her way verbally through a maze. "The sacrifice of Dragon Lankford's familiar was needed because Neferet was losing control of her Vessel. We all saw Aurox shift from the bull creature, to the boy, and then begin to shift back to the bull again as he ran off."

"You also had to have seen how freaked he was when he was Aurox again and he saw what he'd done to Dragon," I said.

"That doesn't change the fact that Aurox killed Dragon," Stark said. I could feel the tension coming from him and I hated that his face had turned into a hard mask.

"What if he only killed Dragon because of Neferet's awful sacrifice of Shadowfax?" I asked, trying to get Stark to see that there might be more than one right answer.

"Zoey, that doesn't make Dragon any less dead," Stark said, dropping his arm from around me and making a small movement away from me.

"Or Aurox any less dangerous," Kalona said.

"But perhaps less of a threat than we firstly believed," Thanatos spoke reasonably. "If Neferet must perform a sacrificial ritual, one of this extent, each time she wants to control him, she will have to choose carefully and selectively about how and when she uses him."

"He said it over and over that he chose a different future," I insisted.

"Z, that does *not* make Aurox a good guy," Stark said, shaking his head at me.

"You know, people can change," Nicole suddenly spoke up. We all blinked at her. Obviously I wasn't the only one of us who had forgotten she was there.

I hated to agree with Nicole, so I just chewed my lip silently and worried.

"Aurox is not a person, nor a guy, good or bad." In the dark field house, Kalona's deep voice seemed bomb-like, blasting against my already battered nerves. "Aurox is a Vessel. A creature created to be Neferet's weapon. Could he have a conscience and the capability to change?" He shrugged. "We can only guess at that. And truly, does it matter? It makes no difference whether a spear has a conscience. What is important is who is wielding the weapon. Neferet, clearly, wields Aurox."

"How long have you known this?" I rounded on Kalona. Stark was staring at me like I was being irrational, but I didn't stop myself. Even if I couldn't figure out how to tell them, I believed I had glimpsed Heath's soul within Aurox through the Seer Stone. "If you knew what Aurox was, why didn't you say something before now?"

"No one asked me," Kalona said.

"That's crap," I said, totally displacing my anger and frustration and confusion from myself and the Aurox/Heath puzzle and smacking Kalona with it. "What else have you kept from us?"

"What else would you like to know?" he replied without hesitation. "Just be careful, young Priestess, that you truly want to hear the answers to the questions you ask."

"You're supposed to be on our team, remember?" Stark said, stepping between Kalona and me.

"I remember more than you realize, red vampyre," Kalona said.

"What the hell is that supposed to mean?" Stark shot back at him.

"It means you haven't always been all goody-goody!" Nicole shouted.

"Don't you dare talk about him!" I hurled my words at her.

"Again you fight yourselves!" Thanatos shouted, the passion in her voice stirring the air around us. "Our enemy has wreaked havoc on our own house. She has committed murder not once, not twice, but over and over. She has allied herself with the greatest evil this world has ever known. Still you strike out at one another. If we cannot unite she has already defeated us."

Thanatos shook her head sadly. She turned from us back to the bodies of the two cats. The High Priestess knelt beside them and, once again, swept her hand gently over each of them. This time the air above the cats began to shimmer and the glittering outlines of Shadowfax and Guinevere materialized—only they weren't the adult cats that lay so still and cold on the area floor. They were kittens. Plump, adorable kittens. "Go to the Goddess, little ones," Thanatos spoke softly, warmly to them. "Nyx and those you love best await you." Young Shadowfax reached a fuzzy paw out to bat playfully at the edge of Thanatos's billowy sleeve before both kittens disappeared in a puff of glitter. I could swear I heard the distant sound of Anastasia's musical laughter, and I imagined she and Dragon must be having a blast welcoming their kittens to the Otherworld.

The Otherworld . . .

My mom was there, along with Dragon and Anastasia and Jack and, if I'd been wrong about what I'd seen within Aurox, Heath was there, too. I'd been there. I knew the Otherworld existed as surely as I knew I existed. I also knew it was an amazing, magickal place, and even though it hadn't been my time to die and stay there, the beauty of it still lingered in my mind and my soul, forming a little bubble of wonder and safety that was the complete opposite of what the real world around me had become.

"Would it be so bad if we lost?"

I hadn't realized I'd spoken aloud until Stark shook my shoulder. "What are you talking about, Z? We can't lose because Neferet can't win. Darkness can't win."

I could see his worry and feel his fear. I knew I was freaking him out, but I couldn't stop myself. I was just so damn tired of everything being a struggle between death and Darkness, love and Light. *Why couldn't it all just end? I'd give anything if it all would just end!* "What's the worst thing that can happen?" I heard myself asking and then kept right on babbling the answer to my own question. "Neferet will kill us. Well, being dead doesn't seem so awful." I flailed my hand in the direction of where the kittens had so recently manifested.

"Jeesh, give up much?" Nicole muttered under her breath in disgust.

"Zoey Redbird, death is far from the worst thing that could happen to any of us," Thanatos said. "Yes, Darkness seems overwhelming now, especially after all we have discovered this night, but there is love and Light here, too. Think of what sadness your words would bring Sylvia Redbird."

I felt a jolt of guilt. Thanatos was right. There were worse things than dying, and those worse things happened to the people you left behind. I bowed my head and stepped closer to Stark, taking his hand in mine. "I'm sorry. You guys are right. I should never have said that."

Thanatos smiled kindly at me. "Go back to your depot. Pray. Sleep. Find comfort and guidance in the words Nyx spoke to us: *Hold to the memory of the healing that happened here this night. You will need that strength and peace for the upcoming fight.*" She hesitated, sighed heavily, and added, "You are so very young."

I wanted to scream *I know! I'm way too young to save the world!* Instead I stood there silent, feeling stupid and useless while Thanatos bent and gathered the bodies of Shadowfax and Guinevere to her, wrapping them in her voluminous skirts and holding them closely and gently, as if they were sleeping babies. Then she motioned to Kalona saying, "Come with me. I must tell the Sons of Erebus the sad news of the death of their Sword Master. While I do that I would have you begin building a pyre for Dragon and these little ones. It is at the lighting of that pyre that I will officially proclaim you Death's Warrior." Without another look at me, Thanatos walked from the field house. Kalona followed her without glancing at Stark or me.

"Your team, by the way, *sucks*." Shaking her head, Nicole walked away, too.

I could feel Stark's eyes on me. His hand seemed stiff in mine. I looked up at him, sure that he was going to shake me or yell at me or at the very least ask what the hell was wrong with me. Again.

Instead, he opened his arms, said, "Come here, Z," and he just loved me.

CHAPTER FOUR

Aurox

Aurox ran, not knowing or caring where his body took him. He only understood he had to get away from the circle, from Zoey, before he committed another atrocity. His feet, fully morphed into cloven hoofs, tore the fertile ground, carrying him with inhuman speed through the winter dormant lavender fields. Like the breeze flowing over his body, emotions surged through Aurox.

Confusion—he hadn't meant to harm anyone, yet he had killed Dragon and perhaps even Rephaim.

Anger—he had been manipulated, controlled against his will!

Despair—no one would ever believe that he hadn't intended to harm anyone. He was a beast, a creature of Darkness. Neferet's Vessel. They would all hate him. Zoey would hate him.

Loneliness—and yet he was *not* Neferet's Vessel. No matter what had happened that night. No matter how she had managed to control him. He did not, *would not* belong to Neferet. Not after seeing what he'd seen tonight . . . feeling what he'd felt tonight.

Aurox had felt Light. Even though he had not been able to embrace it, he'd known the strength of its goodness in the magickal circle, and recognized the beauty of it in the invocation of the elements. Until the sickening threads had claimed and controlled the beast within him, he'd watched, mesmerized, the soul-moving ritual that had culminated in Light washing the touch of Darkness from the land, and from him, though for him that purification had lasted only a moment. Only long enough for Aurox to realize what he'd done. Then the just anger and the understandable hatred the Warriors had felt for him had overwhelmed him, and Aurox had only humanity enough left to flee and to *not* kill Zoey.

Aurox shuddered and moaned as the change from beast back to boy rippled through his body, leaving him bare footed and bare chested, clothed only in ripped jeans. A horrible weakness overwhelmed his body. Breathing hard and trembling, he slowed, stumbling to a walk. His mind was a war. Self-hatred filled him. Aurox wandered aimlessly in the predawn, not knowing or caring where he was, until he could no longer ignore the physical needs of his body and he followed the scent and sound of water. At the edge of the crystal stream Aurox knelt and drank until the fire within him was sated and then, overcome with exhaustion and emotion, he collapsed. Dreamless sleep finally won the battle within him, and Aurox slept.

Aurox woke to the sound of her song. It was so soothing, so peaceful, that at first he did not open his eyes. Her voice was rhythmic, like a heartbeat, but it was more than the rhythm that touched Aurox. It was the feeling that filled her song. Not that he felt with her the way he channeled violent emotions to fuel the metamorphosis that changed his body from boy to beast. The feeling in her song came from her voice itself—joyful, exhilarating, grateful. He didn't feel those things with her, instead it brought to him images of joy and allowed the possibility of happiness to play through his waking mind. He couldn't understand any of the words, but Aurox did not need to. Her voice soared, and that transcended language.

Waking more fully, he wanted to see the owner of the voice. To question her about joy. To try to understand how he could create that feeling for himself. Aurox opened his eyes and sat up. He'd collapsed not far from the farmhouse, near the bank of the little stream. It was a winding ribbon of clear water that drifted softly, musically, over sand and stone. Aurox's gaze followed the stream down, to his left, where the woman, wearing a sleeveless dress fringed with long strands of leather decorated with beads and shells, stood. She danced gracefully, beating out the rhythm of her song with bare feet. Even though the sun was just lifting over the horizon and the early morning was cool, she was flushed, warm, alive. Smoke from the bundle of dried plants in her hand drifted around her, seemingly in time with her song.

Just watching her made Aurox feel good. He didn't need to channel her joy—it was palpable around her. His spirit lifted because the woman was so filled with the emotion that she overflowed. She flung back her head and her long hair, silver streaked with black, easily reached her slender waist. She raised her bare arms, as if embracing the rising sun, and then began to move in a circle, keeping time with her feet.

Aurox was so caught up in her song that he didn't realize she was turning to face him, and would see him, until their eyes met. He recognized her then. This was Zoey's grandmother, who had been in the center of the circle the night before. He expected her to gasp or scream at the sight of him suddenly appearing there in the long grass at the edge of her stream. Instead her joyous dance came to an end. Her song ceased. And she spoke in a clear, calm voice. "I see you, *tsu-ka-nv-s-di-na*. You are the shapeshifter who killed Dragon Lankford last night. You tried to kill Rephaim as well, but you did not succeed. You also charged my beloved granddaughter as if you meant her harm. Are you here to kill me, too?"

She lifted her arms again, drew a deep breath of the cool, clean morning air and concluded, "If so, then I will tell the sky that my name is Sylvia Redbird, and today is a good day to die. I will go to the Great Mother to meet my ancestors with joy filling my spirit." Then she smiled at him.

It was her smile that broke him. He felt himself shatter and in a trembling voice he barely recognized as his own, Aurox said, "I am not here to kill you. I am here because I have no other place to go."

Then Aurox began to weep.

Sylvia Redbird hesitated for only a small heartbeat of time. Through his tears Aurox watched her tilt her head up again and nod, as if she'd received an answer to a question. Then she walked gracefully to him, the long leather fringe on her dress rustling musically with her movements and the touch of the cool morning breeze.

She did not hesitate when she reached him. Sylvia Redbird sat, folding her bare feet beneath her, and then she put her arms around him and drew his head to her shoulder.

Aurox never knew how long they sat like that together. He only knew that as he sobbed she held him and rocked him gently, back and forth, softly singing a chant and patting his back in time to her heartbeat.

Finally, he pulled back, turning his face away in shame.

"No, child," she said, taking his shoulders and forcing him to meet her gaze. "Before you turn away, tell me why you wept."

Aurox wiped his face, cleared his throat, and in a voice that sounded young and, he thought, very foolish, said, "It is because I am sorry."

Sylvia Redbird held his gaze. "And?" she prompted.

He blew out a long breath and admitted, "And because I am so alone."

Sylvia's dark eyes widened. "You are more than you appear to be."

"Yes. I am a monster of Darkness, a beast," he agreed with her.

Her lips tilted up. "Can a beast weep in sorrow? Does Darkness have the capacity to feel loneliness? I think not."

"Then why do I feel so foolish for weeping?"

"Think on this," she said. "Your spirit wept. It needed to mourn because it felt sorrow and loneliness. It is for you to decide whether or not that is foolish. For me, I have already decided there is no shame to be found in honest tears." Sylvia Redbird stood and held one small, deceptively frail hand out to him. "Come with me, child. I open my home to you."

"Why would you do that? You watched me kill a Warrior last night, and wound another. I could have killed Zoey as well."

She cocked her head to the side and studied him. "Could you have? I think not. Or at least I think the boy I see at this moment could not kill her."

Aurox felt his shoulders slump. "But only you believe that. No one else will."

"Well, *tsu-ka-nv-s-di-na*, I am the only person here with you at this moment. Is my belief not enough?"

Aurox wiped his face again and stood, a little unsteadily. Then he took her delicate hand very carefully in his. "Sylvia Redbird, your belief is enough at this moment."

She squeezed his hand, smiled, and said, "Call me Grandma."

"What is it you call me, Grandma?"

She smiled. "*Tsu-ka-nv-s-di-na* is my people's word for bull."

He felt hot and then cold. "The beast I become is more terrible than a bull."

"Then perhaps naming you *tsu-ka-nv-s-di-na* will take some of the horror from what sleeps within you. There is power in the naming of something, child."

"*Tsu-ka-nv-s-di-na*. I will remember that," Aurox said.

Still feeling shaky, he walked with the magickal old woman to the little farmhouse that rested between sleeping lavender fields. It was made of stone and had an invitingly wide porch. Grandma led him to a deep leather couch and gave him a hand-woven blanket to wrap around his shoulders. Then she said, "I would ask you to rest your spirit." Aurox did as she asked while Grandma sang a song softly to herself, built a hearth fire, boiled water for tea, then retrieved and gifted him with a sweatshirt and soft leather shoes from another room. After the room was warm and her song was finished, Grandma motioned for him to join her at a small wooden table, offering him food from a purple plate.

Aurox sipped the honey-sweetened tea and ate from the plate. "Th-thank you, Grandma," he said haltingly. "The food is good. The drink is good. *Everything* here is so good."

"The tea is chamomile and hyssop. I use it to help me be calm and focused. The cookies are my own recipe—chocolate chip with a hint of lavender. I've always believed chocolate and lavender are good for the soul." Grandma smiled and bit into a cookie. They ate in silence.

Aurox had never felt so content. He knew it couldn't be, but somehow he had a sense of belonging here with this woman. It was that odd but wonderful sense of belonging that allowed him to begin speaking to her from his heart.

"Neferet commanded me here last night. I was to disrupt the ritual."

Grandma nodded. Her expression was not surprised but contemplative. "She wouldn't have wanted to be revealed as my daughter's murderer."

Aurox studied her. "Your daughter was murdered. You witnessed the record of it last night, yet you are serene and joyful today. Where do you find such peace?"

"From within," she said. "It also comes from the belief that there is more at work here than what we can see—what we can prove. For instance, at the very least I should fear you. Some would say I should hate you."

"Many would say that."

"Yet I neither fear nor hate you."

"You—you are comforting me. Giving me sanctuary. Why, Grandma?" Aurox asked.

"Because I believe in the power of love. I believe in choosing Light over Darkness—happiness over hatred—trust over skepticism," Grandma said.

"Then it is not me at all. It is simply that you are a good person," he said.

"I don't think being a good person is ever very simple, do you?" she said.

"I do not know. I have never tried to be a good person." He ran a hand through his thick blond hair in frustration.

Grandma's eyes wrinkled with her smile. "Have you not? Last night you were commanded by a powerful immortal to stop a ritual, and yet, miraculously, the ritual was completed. How did that happen, Aurox?"

"No one will believe the truth about that," he said.

"I will," Grandma said. "Tell me, child."

"I came here to follow Neferet's command—to kill Rephaim and distract Stevie Rae so that the circle would break and the ritual would not succeed, but I could not do it. I could not break something that was so filled with Light, so *good*," he spoke in a rush, wanting to get the truth out before Grandma stopped him, shunned him. "Then Darkness took possession of me. I did not want to change! I did not want the bull creature to emerge! But I could not control it, and once it was present, it only remembered its last command: kill Rephaim. It was only the washing of the elements and the touch of Light that halted the beast long enough for me to regain some control to make it flee."

"That's why you killed Dragon. Because he tried to protect Rephaim," she said.

Aurox nodded, bowing his head in shame. "I did not want to kill him. I did not intend to kill him. Darkness controlled the beast, and the beast controlled me."

"Not now, though. The beast is not here now," Grandma said softly.

Aurox met her gaze. "He is. The beast is always here." He pointed to the middle of his chest. "It is eternally within me."

Grandma covered his hand with hers. "That may be, but you are here as well. *Tsu-ka-nv-s-di-na*, remember that you *did* control the beast enough to flee. Perhaps that is a beginning. Learn how to trust yourself, and then others may learn to trust you."

He shook his head. "No, you are different than everyone else. No one will believe me. They will only see the beast. No one will care enough to trust me."

"Zoey shielded you from the Warriors. It was because of her protection that you were able to flee."

Aurox blinked in surprise. He hadn't even thought of that. His emotions had been in such turmoil that he hadn't realized the extent of Zoey's actions. "She did protect me," he said slowly.

Grandma patted his hand. "Do not let her belief in you be wasted. Choose Light, child."

"But I already tried to and failed!"

"Try harder," she spoke sternly.

Aurox opened his mouth to protest, but Grandma's eyes stopped his words. Her gaze said that her words were more than a command—they were a belief.

He bowed his head again. This time not in shame, but in response to a tentative glimmer of hope. Aurox took one small moment to savor the new, wonderful feeling. Then, gently, he took his hand from under Grandma's and stood. In answer to her questioning look he said, "I must learn how to prove you right."

"And how will you do that, child?"

"I must find myself," he spoke with no hesitation.

Her smile was warm and bright. Unexpectedly, it reminded him of Zoey, which made the tentative glimmer of hope expand until it warmed the center of him. "Where will you go?"

"Where I can do the most good," he said.

"Aurox, child, know that as long as you control the beast, and do not kill again, you may always find sanctuary with me."

"I will never forget it, Grandma."

When she hugged him at the door, Aurox closed his eyes and breathed in the scent of lavender and the touch of a mother's love. That scent and that touch stayed with him as he drove slowly back to Tulsa.

The February day was bright and, as the man on the radio said, *warm enough to start wakin' up the ticks.* Aurox parked Neferet's car in one of the empty spaces at the rear of Utica Square, and then he let instinct guide his steps as he walked from the busy shopping center along the backstreet called South Yorktown Avenue. Aurox smelled smoke before he reached the great stone wall that encircled the House of Night.

This fire was Neferet's work. It reeks of her Darkness, Aurox thought. He didn't allow himself to consider what that fire might have destroyed. He focused only on following his instinct, which was telling him he had to return to the House of Night to find himself and his redemption. Aurox's heart was beating hard as he slipped within the shadow of the wall and made his way silently and swiftly around the east boundary of the school until he came to an old oak that had been split so violently that part of it rested against the school's wall.

It was a simple thing, really, to scale the rough wall, grasp the winter nude branches of the shattered tree, and then drop to the ground on the other side. Aurox crouched in the shadow of the tree. As he'd hoped, the brightness of the sun had emptied the school grounds, keeping fledglings and vampyres within the stone buildings, behind darkly curtained windows. He moved around the split base of the tree, studying the House of Night.

It was the stables that had burned. He could see that easily. It didn't seem that the fire had spread, though it had left an exterior wall to the stables collapsed. That damaged opening had already been draped by a thick black tarp. Aurox pressed closer to the tree. Picking his way over the splintered fragments of its broken base, and its tangled mess of limbs, Aurox wondered why no one had thought to clear the wreckage of the tree from the otherwise meticulously cared for grounds. But he didn't have time to wonder for long. A huge raven suddenly landed on a drooping limb right before him and began a terrible and loud series of croaks and whistles and oddly disturbing clucks.

"Go! Be gone!" Aurox whispered, making shooing noises at the big bird, which only made the creature explode in more of the croaking noises. Aurox lunged forward, intent on throttling the thing and his foot caught on an exposed root. He fell forward, hitting the ground heavily. To his shock, he kept falling as the earth opened under the weight of his body and he hurled, headfirst, down . . . down . . .

There was a terrible pain in his right temple, and then Aurox's world went black.

CHAPTER FIVE

Zoey

I'd fallen asleep wrapped in Stark's arms, so waking up to him shaking me while he glared and almost shouted, "Zoey! Wake up! Stop it! I mean it!" was totally confusing.

"Stark? Huh?" I sat up, dislodging Nala, who'd made herself into a fat orange donut on my hip. *"Mee-uf-ow!"* Nala grumbled and padded to the end of the bed. I looked from my cat to my Warrior—they were both staring at me like I'd committed mass murder. "What?" I said around a big yawn. "I was just sleeping."

Stark grabbed his pillow and wadded it behind him so that he was propped up in bed. He crossed his arms, shook his head, and looked away from me. "I think you were doing a lot more than *just sleeping.*"

I wanted to strangle him.

"Seriously, what is wrong with you?" I asked him.

"You said his name."

"Whose name?" I blinked, having a flashback to that creepy old movie *Invasions of the Body Snatchers* and wondering if Stark had turned into a pod person.

"Heath's!" Stark scowled. "Three times. It woke me up." Still not looking at me, he said, "What were you dreaming?"

What he'd said had shocked the hell out of me, making me mentally scramble. What the hell had I been dreaming? I thought back. I remembered Stark kissing me before I went to sleep. I remembered the kiss was super hot, but I'd been super tired and instead of doing more than kissing him back, I'd put my head on his shoulder and totally passed out. After that I didn't remember a thing until he was shaking me and yelling at me to stop it.

"I have not one clue," I said honestly.

"You don't have to lie to me."

"Stark, I wouldn't lie to you." I brushed my hair from my face and then touched his arm. "I don't remember dreaming about anything."

He looked at me then. His eyes were sad. "You were calling Heath. I'm sleeping right here next to you, but you were calling for him."

The way he sounded made my heart squeeze. I hated that I'd hurt him. I could have told him it was ridiculous of him to be mad at me for something I'd said when I was asleep—something I hadn't even remembered, but ridiculous or not, Stark's hurt was real. I slid my hand in his.

"Hey," I said softly. "I'm sorry."

He threaded his fingers with mine. "Do you wish he was here instead of me?"

"No," I said. I'd loved Heath since I was a kid, but I wouldn't trade Stark for him. Of course, the rest of the truth was that had Stark been the one killed, I wouldn't have traded Heath for him, either. But that was definitely something Stark didn't need to hear—not now—not ever.

Loving two guys was a confusing mess, even when one of them was dead.

"So, you're not calling out for him because you want to be with him instead of me?"

"I want you. Promise." I moved forward and he opened his arms to me. I fit perfectly against his chest and breathed in his familiar smell.

He kissed the top of my head and hugged me. "I know it's stupid of me to be jealous of a dead guy."

"Yep," I said.

"Especially when I actually liked the dead guy."

"Yep," I agreed.

"But we belong together, Z."

I leaned back so that I could look into his eyes. "Yes," I said seriously, "we do. Please don't ever forget that. No matter what amount of crazy is going on around us—I can handle it, but I need to know my Warrior is here for me."

"Always, Z. Always," he said. "I love you."

"I love you, too, Stark. Always." I kissed him then and showed him that he absolutely didn't have to be jealous of anyone else. And, at the same time, for just a little while, I let the heat of his love burn away the memory of what I'd seen when I'd looked through the Seer Stone that night . . .

Next time I woke up it was because I was way too hot. I was still in Stark's arms, but he'd shifted a little and thrown his leg over me, cocooning me in my fuzzy blue blanket. This time he wasn't being Crazy Boyfriend. He looked cute and little-boy young and out cold.

As per usual, Nala had made her bed on my hip, so before she could grumble I scooped her up, and slid both of us as gently and quietly as I could to the other, cooler, side of the bed. Totally asleep, Stark made a vague motion with his sword hand, as if reaching out for me. I focused on happy thoughts—brown pop, new shoes, kittens that didn't sneeze in my face—and he relaxed.

I tried to relax, too—for real. Nal stared at me. I scratched behind her ears and whispered, "Sorry for waking you up. Again." She butted her face against my chin, sneezed on me, and then jumped back on my fuzzy blue blanket, circled three times, and returned to being a sleeping fur donut.

I sighed. I needed to do like Nala—curl up and go back to sleep, but my mind was too awake. With awakeness came thinking. After we'd made love, Stark had sleepily murmured, "We're together. Everything else will work itself out." I'd fallen asleep feeling secure that he was right.

Now that I was, sadly, fully conscious, I couldn't avoid the whole think-too-much-worry-too-much thing. Although, my guess was if Stark knew what I'd imagined I'd seen through the Seer Stone last night, he'd take back his *everything else will work itself out* comment, and turn back into Mr. I'm Jealous of a Dead Guy.

I put my hand over the small round stone that hung on a slender silver chain around my neck and dangled innocently between my breasts. It felt normal—like any other necklace I could have worn. It wasn't radiating weird heat. I pulled it from under my T-shirt and slowly lifted it. I drew a deep, fortifying breath, and peeked through it at Stark.

Nothing strange happened. Stark stayed Stark. I turned the necklace a little and took a peek at Nala. She stayed a fat, sleeping, orange cat.

I put the Seer Stone back under my shirt. What if I had imagined it? Seriously. How could Heath be in Aurox? Even Thanatos said he'd been created by Darkness through the sacrifice of my mom. He was a Vessel—a creature under the control of Neferet.

But she'd needed to kill Shadowfax to *totally* control him, and he had asked those questions about what he really was to Thanatos.

Okay, but does any of that make a difference? Aurox wasn't Heath. Heath was dead. He'd gone on to a deeper realm of the Other-world that I hadn't been able to go *because Heath was dead.*

Reflecting my restlessness, Stark stirred, frowning in his sleep. Nala cat grumbled again. No way did I want either of them awake again, I got quietly out of bed and tiptoed from the room, ducking under the blanket Stark and I used as a door.

Brown pop. I needed a serious dose of brown pop. Maybe I'd get lucky and there would be some Count Chocula and uncurdled milk left, too. Yum, just thinking about it made me feel a little better. I could seriously heart me some breakfast cereal.

I shuffled down the dimly lit tunnel, following it past turn-offs and other blanket-covered doorways behind which my friends rested as we waited for the sun to set, until I entered the alcove which was the common area we used as a kitchen. The tunnel sorta dead-ended there, making room for some tables, laptops, and a few full-sized fridges. "There's gotta be some brown pop left in here somewhere," I muttered to myself, as I rummaged through the first fridge.

"It's in the other one."

I made a stupid-sounding squeak and jumped. "Jeesh, Shaylin! Don't lurk like that. You almost scared the pee outta me."

"Sorry, Zoey." She went to the second of the three fridges, and pulled out a can of fully leaded, totally loaded with sugar and caffeine brown pop, handing it to me with an apologetic smile.

"Shouldn't you be sleeping?" I sat in the closest chair and sipped my pop, trying not to sound as grumpy as I felt.

"Yeah, well, I'm tired and all. I can feel the sun hasn't set yet, but I got a lot on my mind. Know what I mean?"

I gave a little snort. "I super know what you mean."

"Your color's kinda off." Shaylin made the comment as nonchalantly as if she'd just said something as normal as mentioning the color of my shirt.

"Shaylin, I don't really get this color stuff you talk about."

"I'm not sure how much of it I really get, either. All I know is that I see it and if I don't think about it too much it usually makes sense to me."

"Okay, give me an example of how it usually makes sense to you."

"That's easy. I'll use you as my example. Your colors don't change very much. Most of the time you're purple with silver flecks. Even when you were getting ready to go to the ritual at your grandma's place, and you knew it was gonna be a hard thing to watch, your colors stayed the same. I checked because . . ." Her voice trailed off.

"You checked because?" I prompted.

"Because I was curious. I checked the nerd herd's colors before you left, but, well, I just realized how invasive that sounds."

I furrowed my forehead at her. "It's not like you're reading our minds or anything like that. Is it?"

"No!" she assured me. "But the longer I have this True Sight stuff, and the more I practice it, the more real it gets for me. Zoey, I think it tells me things about people—things that they sometimes would rather keep hidden."

"Like Neferet. You said she's dead-fish-eye color on the inside, and on the outside she's gorgeous."

"Yeah, like that. But also like what I'm seeing with you. It's like Kramisha would say, I'm not keeping to my own business."

"Why don't you tell me what you're seeing with me, and then I'll tell you whether I think you're poking too much into my business."

"Well, since you've been back from the ritual at your grandma's house, your colors are darker." She paused, stared at me, shook her head, and then corrected herself. "No, that's not totally accurate. It's not that they're just darker—it's that they're murkier. Like the purple and the silver got swirled together and muddied."

"Okay," I said slowly, starting to understand what she meant by *violation*. "I get that you see a difference in me, and that's kinda strange, especially when you said my colors don't usually change. But what does it mean to you?"

"Oh, yeah, sorry. I think it means you're confused about something—something serious. It's bothering you. Really messing with your head. Is that kinda right?"

I nodded. "That's kinda right."

"And does it make you feel weird that I know that?"

I nodded again. "Yeah, a little." I thought about it for a second and then added, "But here's the truth—I'd feel less weird if I knew I could trust you not to blab to everyone that my colors are murky and I'm real confused about something. That's the violation part."

"Yeah." She sounded sad. "That's what I thought, too. I want you to know that you can trust me. I've never been a blab-er. Also, this gift Nyx gave me when I was Marked, well, it's totally incredible. Zoey, *I can see again.*" Shaylin looked like she could burst into tears. "I don't want to mess it up. I'm going to use the gift the way Nyx wants me to."

I could tell she was seriously upset, and I felt bad for her—I especially felt bad that I had had something to do with her being upset. "Hey, Shaylin, it's okay. I understand what it's like to have a gift you feel a big responsibility for and don't want to mess up. Hell, you're talking to the Queen of Mess Up." I paused, and then added, "It's part of what I'm confused about right now. I do *not* want to make one more immature, stupid, wrong decision. What I do and say affects way more people than just me. When I make crappy decisions it's like a domino mess up. Fledglings, vampyres, and humans can all be screwed. That sucks, but it doesn't change the fact that I do have a gift from Nyx, and I am responsible for how it's used."

Shaylin thought about that for a while, and I sipped my brown pop. I was actually liking talking to her. It was way better than brooding about Aurox and Heath and Stark and Neferet and—

"Okay, how about this," Shaylin interrupted my internal non-brooding brood. "What if I see colors change for a person? Is it my responsibility to tell someone—someone like you?"

"What do you mean? Like come to me and say 'Hey, Zoey, your colors are all murky. What's up?'"

"Well, maybe, but only if we're friends. What I was thinking about was more like today when I saw Nicole. Her colors were like the rest of Dallas's group—all blood-like, swirled together with browns and blacks—like something bleeding in a sandstorm. Last night, at the stables, hers had changed. There was still a rusty red there, but it looked clearer, brighter, but not in a bad way. More like in a getting cleaner way. It's weird, but I swear I saw some blue in her. Not like sky blue, though. More like the ocean. That's what made me think that the bad in her might be washing away, and after I thought it, it felt right."

"Shaylin, what you're saying is really confusing," I said.

"Not to me it isn't! It's getting less and less confusing. I just *know* things."

"I get that, and I believe you're telling me the truth. The problem is that your *knowing* is so subjective. It's like you're grading life, and people are the answers, but instead of your people answers being true-false, where it's easy to judge whether what you're getting is right or wrong, they're essays. And that means your response could depend on lots of different things. None of it is black and white." I sighed. My own analogy was making my head hurt.

"But, Zoey, life isn't black and white or true and false, and neither are people." She sipped her pop, which I noticed was clear. I was thinking that I really didn't understand clear pop—it had no caffeine in it and never seemed sweet enough—when she continued, "I understand what you're trying to say, though. You believe I see people's colors. You just don't believe in my judgment of them."

I started to deny it, and say something that would make her feel better, but a nudge from within had me changing my mind. Shaylin needed to hear the truth. "Basically, yes, that's it."

"Well," she said, straightening her shoulders and lifting her chin, "I think my judgment is good. I think it's getting better and better, and I want to use my gift to help. I know we have a fight coming. I heard what Neferet did to your mom, and how she's chosen Darkness over Light. You're going to need someone like me. I can see inside people."

She was right. I did need her gift, but I also needed to know I could trust her judgment. "Okay, so, let's start. How about you keep your eyes open? Let me know if you see anyone's color changing."

"The first one I want to report is Nicole. Erik told me about her. I know she's been real bad in the past. But the truth is in her colors, and they say she's changing."

"All right. I'll keep that in mind." I raised my brows at her. "Speaking of keeping stuff in mind—I'm not being mean or anything like that, but you need to keep an eye on Erik. He's not always—"

"He's arrogant and selfish," she interrupted me, meeting my gaze steadily. "He's gotten by on how hot he is and how talented he is. Life's been easy for him, even after you dumped him."

"Did he tell you I dumped him?" I couldn't tell if she was being bitchy or not. She didn't sound like it, but then again, I didn't know her very well. It did seem like every time I saw her, I saw Erik. Not that I cared. Seriously. It wasn't jealous. It was more like I felt responsible for warning her.

"He didn't have to tell me. About a billion other kids beat him to it," she said.

"I don't have any hard feelings toward Erik. I mean, he can be with whoever he wants. If you like him, that's no problem at all with me." I realized I was having a bout of verbal IBS, but I couldn't seem to stop talking. "And he doesn't want to be with me anymore, either. That's way over. It's just that Erik—"

"Is a dickhead." Aphrodite's voice saved me. She walked past us, yawning, and stuck her head in one of the fridges. "And now you've heard it from two of his ex-girlfriends. Ex being the most important part of that sentence." She came over to the table and put a jug of orange juice and a bottle of what I guessed was super expensive champagne down in front of the empty chair beside me. "Of course, Z didn't call him a dickhead. She was being nice." As she spoke, Aphrodite went back to the fridge and got into the freezer. There was the sound of glasses clanking against each other. When she came back to the table she was holding a frosty crystal glass that was long and slender, like you see people drinking out of at New Year's Eve parties on TV. "Me, I'm not so nice. Dick. Head. That's our Erik." She popped the champagne cork, sloshed a tiny bit of orange juice in the glass, and then filled it to almost overflowing with bubbly champagne. She grinned at the glass and said, "Mimosa—as my mom would say, *breakfast of champions.*"

"I know what Erik is," Shaylin said. She didn't sound pissed. She didn't sound pleased. She sounded sure of herself. "I also know what you are."

Aphrodite raised one blond brow at her and took a long drink of her mimosa. "Do tell."

Uh-oh, I thought. I suppose I should've done something to stop what was going to happen, but it was a little like standing on train tracks and trying to push a car out of the way. I was more likely to get smashed than to get the car out of trouble—so I gawked and drank my brown pop instead.

"You're silver. That reminds me of moonlight, which tells me you've been touched by Nyx. But you're also a buttery yellow color, like the light of a small candle."

"Which tells you what?" Aphrodite studied her well-manicured fingernails, clearly not caring about Shaylin's answer.

"Which tells me that, like a little candle, you could be easily blown out."

Aphrodite's eyes narrowed and she slapped her hand against the tabletop. "That's it, new kid. I have been through too much battle-against-Darkness crap to put up with your mouth *or* your know-it-all attitude." She looked like she was getting ready to go for Shaylin's throat. I was considering running and trying to find Darius when Stevie Rae bubbled into the room.

"Hey, y'all! 'Mornin'!" she said around a big yawn. "Man, I'm tired. Is there any Mountain Dew left in the fridge?"

"Oh, for shit's sake, it's not morning. It's sunset. And why the hell is everybody awake?" Aphrodite threw up her hands.

Stevie Rae frowned at her. "It's polite to say mornin' to people, even if it's not technically correct. And I like to be up early. There's nothin' wrong with that."

"He's a bird!" Aphrodite said, pouring herself some more champagne.

"Are you drinkin' already?" Stevie Rae asked.

"Yes. Who are you? A bumpkin version of my mom?"

"No, if I was any version of your momma I'd be okay with you drinkin' your breakfast, 'cause your momma is seriously messed up." Stevie Rae put the can of Mountain Dew back in the fridge. "And now that I think about it, drinkin' pop for breakfast probably isn't a great idea, either. I'll bet there's some Lucky Charms around here somewhere."

"They're magically delicious," Shaylin said. "And if you find them I'll have some, too."

"Count Chocula." Since it didn't look like Aphrodite was going to kill anyone (at that moment) my voice was working again. "If you see a box of that, I'll take it."

"What the hell's wrong with mimosas?" Aphrodite was saying. "Orange juice is for breakfast."

"What about the champagne part? That's alcohol," Stevie Rae said.

"It's pink Veuve Clicquot. That means it's *good* champagne, which cancels out the alcohol part," Aphrodite said.

"Do you really believe that?" Shaylin asked.

Looking at me and pointedly ignoring Shaylin, Aphrodite said, "Why is it speaking to me?"

"I have a headache, and we haven't even left for school yet," I told Aphrodite.

"The stables almost burned down and our High Priestess was outed for being a murderous demi-goddess. I think we can all miss school today," Aphrodite said.

"Nuh uh," Stevie Rae said. "We *gotta* go to school because of all that. Thanatos is gonna need us. Plus, Dragon's got to have his funeral pyre. That's gonna be bad, but we have to be there for it."

That even shut up Aphrodite. She continued to drink while Stevie Rae poured herself and Shaylin some Lucky Charms (which is a lesser cereal than Count Chocula, even though it does have marshmallows), and we all just looked generally gloomy.

"I'm gonna miss Dragon," I said. "But it's really cool that he's with Anastasia again. And the Otherworld is awesome. Really."

"You got to actually see them reunited, didn't you?" Shaylin asked, wide-eyed.

"We all did," I said, smiling.

"It was beautiful," Stevie Rae said, sniffling and wiping her eyes.

"Yeah," Aphrodite said softly.

Shaylin cleared her throat. "Look, Aphrodite, I didn't mean to sound so bitchy before. What I said was wrong. I shouldn't use my gift like that. You do have a flickery yellow light inside your moonlight light, but that's not because you're going to blow out. It's part of your uniqueness—your warmth. Here's the truth—it's small and hidden, because you keep how warm and good you really are hidden most of the time. But that doesn't change that it's still there. So, I'm sorry."

Aphrodite turned cool blue eyes to Shaylin and said, "It puts the lotion in the bucket."

"Oh, boy," I said. "Aphrodite, just drink your breakfast. Shaylin, that's a good example of what you and I were talking about before. I don't question your gift. I don't doubt it. I do have an issue with your judgment in deciphering it."

"I deciphered it perfectly," Shaylin said, sounding upset and defensive. "But Aphrodite pissed me off. So I messed up. I said I was sorry."

"Apology not accepted," Aphrodite said, and turned her back on Shaylin.

Which was when Damien came rushing into the room, holding his iPad and looking more disheveled than he usually looked when he emerged from what he liked to call his beauty rejuvenation period. He hurried straight to me, lifted his iPad, and said. "You guys have to watch this!"

I was only mildly curious at first as I saw the Fox 23 evening news anchor, the totally to-die-for gorgeous Chera Kimiko talking. We hearted us some Chera. Not only was she vampyre-level beautiful, but she was actually a real person, versus the usual plastic talking heads news anchor types.

Aphrodite peeked over my shoulder at Damien's iPad. "Kimiko is classic. I'll never forget that time she spit out her gum right in the middle of the news. I thought my dad was gonna shit kittens because—"

"Chera's great, but this is *bad*," Damien cut her off. "And serious. Neferet just gave a press conference."

Ah, hell . . .

CHAPTER SIX

Zoey

We all huddled around Damien's iPad. He pressed play and the Fox 23 video began. Along the bottom of the screen blazed the caption: *CHAOS AT THE TULSA HOUSE OF NIGHT?* Then the screen was filled with Neferet and a bunch of guys in suits. She was standing someplace really pretty—lots of marble and art deco. I felt a little start of recognition. Chera Kimiko was speaking off camera.

"Vampyres and violence? You'd be surprised at who is saying yes. Fox 23 exclusively has breaking news tonight from a former High Priestess at Tulsa's House of Night."

A stupid commercial came up and while Damien tried to skip it I said, "The picture looks like she's someplace downtown."

"It's the lobby of the Mayo," Aphrodite said dryly. "And that's my dad standing behind her."

"Ohmy*goodness!*" Stevie Rae's eyes were giant and round. "She's giving a press conference with the mayor?"

"And some of the city council. Those are the rest of the suits with him," Aphrodite said.

Then the video started to play and we all shut up and gawked.

"I am here to officially and publicly sever my ties with the Tulsa House of Night and the Vampyre High Council." Somehow Neferet managed to look regal and victimized at the same time.

"She's so full of shit," Aphrodite said.

"Shhh!" the rest of us shushed her.

"High Priestess Neferet, why would you sever ties with your people?" asked one of the reporters.

"Can we not be considered one people? Are we all not intelligent beings with the capacity to love and understand one another?" Apparently she was speaking rhetorically because she didn't wait for an answer. *"Vampyre politics have become distasteful to me. Many of you know that recently I opened employment at the House of Night to the Tulsa community. I did so because of my conviction that humans and vampyres can do more than just uneasily co-exist. We can live and work and even love together."*

Stevie Rae made gagging noises. I kept shaking my head back and forth in disbelief.

"I received so much resistance from the Vampyre High Council that they sent their High Priestess of Death, Thanatos, to Tulsa to intercede. The current vampyre administration promotes violence and segregation—just look at the past six months and the record of increasing violence in Midtown Tulsa. Do you really believe all of the attacks, especially those involving bloodletting, were human gang related?"

"High Priestess, are you admitting that vampyres have attacked humans in Tulsa?"

Neferet's hand flew dramatically to her neck. *"If I knew that with one hundred percent certainty, I would have gone to the local police immediately. I only have suspicions and concerns. I also have a conscience, which is why I have left the House of Night."* Her smile was luminous. *"Please, you no longer need to call me High Priestess. From here on I am simply Neferet."*

Even through the video I could see the reporter blushing and smiling at her.

"There have been rumors of a new kind of vampyre, one with red Marks. Can you substantiate that rumor?" asked another reporter.

"Sadly, I can. There is, indeed, a new type of vampyre—and fledgling. Those who are Marked in red are damaged in some way."

"Damaged? Can you give us an example?"

"Certainly. The first that comes to mind is James Stark—a fledgling

who came to us from Chicago after he accidentally caused his mentor's death. He has become the first Warrior red vampyre."

I gasped.

"That bitch is talking about your boyfriend!" Aphrodite said.

"Just last night the school's longtime Sword Master, Dragon Lankford, was killed. Gored to death by a bull. Lankford was in James Stark's company when the accident"—she emphasized the word, making it clear she didn't believe it—*"happened."*

"Are you saying this Stark vampyre is dangerous?"

"I'm afraid he could be. Actually, many of the new fledglings and vampyres could be. After all, the new High Priestess of the Tulsa House of Night is Death."

"Can you give us more specifics about—"

One of the suits stepped forward, cutting Neferet off. *"I, more than most, am highly concerned about these developments in the vampyre community. As many of you know, my beloved daughter, Aphrodite, was Marked almost four years ago. I understand all too well that vampyres do not like humans to meddle in their personal, political, or criminal affairs. They have long policed their own. But, let me assure you, and our local House of Night, that by Tulsa Council resolution, we will be creating a committee to look into vampyre-human relations. I'm afraid that is all the time we have for questions today."* The man who stepped forward and spoke into Neferet's microphone was Aphrodite's dad—the mayor of Tulsa. *"I do have one more short announcement to make. Beginning immediately, Neferet has been added to the City Council committee under the title of Vampyre Liaison. Let me reiterate, Tulsa intends to partner with vampyres who wish to live peacefully with humans."* When the reporters all started speaking at once, he raised one hand, smiled a little patronizingly (which weirdly reminded me of Aphrodite). *"Neferet will be authoring a weekly column in the Tulsa World's Scene insert. For now that will be the forum through which she will answer your multitudes of questions. Keep in mind that we are at the very beginnings of a partnership here. We must move slowly and gently so as not to upset the delicate balance of vampyre-human relations."*

I was watching Neferet's face instead of the mayor and I saw the way her eyes narrowed and the hardening of her expression. Then Mayor LaFont waved at the camera and the video shifted back to Chera Kimiko and the studio. Damien tapped the screen, and it went blank.

"Oh, for shit's sake! My father has lost what living with my mother had left of his mind," Aphrodite said.

"Hey, thought I heard someone call my name." Stark walked into the room, running his fingers through his bed head and giving me his sexy, cocky, half smile.

"Neferet just had a press conference and told everyone you're a dangerous killer," I heard myself telling him.

"She did what?" He looked as shocked as I felt.

"Yeah, and she did more than that," Aphrodite said. "She got with my dad and has the city making her look all good-guy-like, and us all blood-sucker-like."

"Uh, newsflash of our own, Aphrodite," Stevie Rae said. "*You're* not a blood-sucker anymore."

"Oh, please. As if my parents know anything about me. I haven't spoken to either one of them for months. I'm only their daughter when it's convenient for them—like now."

"If it wasn't so scary it'd be funny," Shaylin said.

"Neferet is making it look like *she* broke with the High Council and the school, versus being kicked out for killing my mom," I explained to Stark.

"She can't do that," Stark said. "The Vampyre High Council won't let her do that."

"My dad is loving this," Aphrodite said. I noticed she'd set the champagne aside and this time was refilling her glass with just orange juice. "For years he's wanted to figure out how he could get in with vampyres. After they got over me not turning into a clone of my mom, they were actually pleased when I was Marked."

I was watching Aphrodite closely and remembering the day that seemed so long ago now when I had overheard her parents being really pissed at her for having the leadership of the Dark Daughters taken away from her and given to me. Aphrodite was looking like her usual ice queen self right now, but in my memory I could still hear the sound of her mother's hand slapping her face and see the tears she had had to choke down. It couldn't be easy for her to have her dad call her a "beloved daughter" when the truth seemed like all he'd ever wanted was to use her.

"Why? What do your parents want with vamps?" Stevie Rae asked.

"To get access to more money—more power—more beauty. In other words, being part of the cool crowd. It's all they've ever wanted—to be cool and powerful. They use whoever they can to get them what they want, including me, and, obviously, Neferet," Aphrodite said, weirdly echoing what I'd been thinking.

"Neferet is not the way for them to get any of that," I said.

"No kiddin', Z, she's crazier than a rat in a tin shithouse," Stevie Rae said.

"Well, whatever that means, yeah, but not just that. Did anyone else notice Neferet's look when Aphrodite's dad was talking? She definitely didn't like how things ended," I said.

"A committee, a newspaper column, and going slowly and gently doesn't seem like something the Consort of Darkness would be particularly interested in," Damien agreed.

"And she definitely didn't like it when the mayor avoided the question about you being dangerous," I said.

"I'd like to be dangerous to Neferet!" Stark blurted, still looking kinda shell-shocked.

"My dad is very good at promising one thing and delivering another," said Aphrodite. "I can tell you right now that he thinks he can play that game with Neferet." She shook her head. No matter how callous she sounded, her expression was strained.

"We need to go to the House of Night. Now. If Thanatos doesn't know about this, she needs to," I said.

Neferet

Humans were so weak and boring and so terribly plain, Neferet thought as she watched the mayor, Charles LaFont, simper and placate and continue to avoid any direct questions about danger and deaths and vampyres after their press conference. *Even this man who the whisperings of rumor said was next in line for a senatorial seat, and was supposedly so charismatic and dynamic*... Neferet had to hide her sarcastic laughter in a cough. This man was *nothing*. Neferet had expected more from Aphrodite's father.

Father! A voice echoed from her past, startling her and causing Neferet's grip on the filigreed iron banister to tighten suddenly, spasmodically. She had to cough again to hide the cracking sound that came from the wrought iron as she pried her hand from it. This was when her patience ended.

"Mayor LaFont, would you escort me to my penthouse." The words should have been a question, but Neferet's voice did not frame them as such. The four city councilmen who had joined the press conference and the mayor turned in her direction. She easily read each of them.

They all found her beautiful and desirable.

Two so much so that they would be willing to forsake their wives, their families, and their careers to mate with her.

Charles LaFont was not one of those two. Aphrodite's father lusted after her—of that there was no doubt—but his foremost desire was not sexual. LaFont's greatest need was to feed his wife's obsession with status and social acceptance. It was a pity, really, that he couldn't be more easily seduced.

All of them feared her.

That made Neferet smile.

Charles LaFont cleared his throat and nervously adjusted his tie. "Of course, of course. It would be my pleasure to escort you."

Neferet nodded coolly to the other men and ignored their hot eyes on her as she and LaFont got into the elevator and headed up to her penthouse suite.

She didn't speak. Neferet knew he was nervous and much more unsure of himself than he pretended to be. In public his façade was one of easy charm and entitlement. But Neferet saw the scared, simpering human that crouched below his surface.

The elevator doors opened and she stepped out into the marble foyer of her suite.

"Join me for a drink, Charles." Neferet gave him no opportunity to decline. She strode to the ornate, art deco bar and poured two glasses of rich red wine.

As she knew he would, he followed her.

She handed him one of the glasses. He hesitated and she laughed. "It is only a very expensive cabernet—not laced with blood at all."

"Oh, indeed." He took the glass and chuckled nervously, reminding her of a small, skittish lapdog.

Neferet loathed dogs almost as much as she loathed men.

"I had more to reveal today than just the information about James Stark," she said coldly. "I think the community deserves to understand just how dangerous the House of Night vampyres have become."

"And I think the community does not need to be panicked needlessly," LaFont countered with.

"Needlessly?" She spoke the one word question sharply.

LaFont nodded and stroked his chin. Neferet was certain he believed he looked wise and benevolent. To her eyes he appeared weak and ridiculous.

It was then that Neferet noticed his hands. They were large and pale, with thick fingers that, for all their size, looked soft and almost feminine.

Neferet's stomach heaved. She almost gagged on her wine as some of her cool demeanor slipped.

"Neferet? Are you well?" he asked her.

"Quite well," she spoke quickly. "Except that I am confused. Are you saying that by alerting Tulsa of the dangers of these new vampyres you would be needlessly panicking them?"

"That is exactly what I'm saying. After the press conference Tulsa will be on alert. Continuing violence will not be tolerated; it will be stopped."

"Really? How do you intend to stop vampyre violence?" Neferet's voice was deceptively soft.

"Well, that is quite simple. I will continue to carry on with what we began today. You have alerted the public. With you acting as liaison on our newly established committee between the City and the High Council, you will be a voice of reason speaking for human-vampyre coexistence."

"So it is with words that you will stop their violence," she said.

"Spoken *and* written words, yes," he nodded, looking very pleased with himself. "I do apologize if I spoke out of turn when I mentioned the newspaper column. It was a last-minute notion of my good friend, Jim Watts, senior editor of the *Scene* insert of the *Tulsa World*. I would have spoken to you about it first, but since you appeared at my office this afternoon with your alert, things spiraled quickly and publicly."

Because I arranged them that way—because I goaded your inept system into action. Now it is time I push you into action just as I did the journalists and the councilmen.

"Reticence and writing were not what I planned when I sought you out," she said.

"Perhaps not, but I have been in Oklahoma politics for almost twenty years, and I know my people. Slow and easy prodding is what works with them."

"Like herding cattle?" Neferet said, not hiding the disdain in her voice.

"Well, I wouldn't use that analogy, but I have found that forming a committee and researching, polling the community, getting sample feedback, all of that does make for a well-greased wheel in the cog of city politics." LaFont chuckled and sipped his wine.

Hidden in the folds of her velvet dress, Neferet closed her hand into a fist and squeezed until her talon-like fingernails punctured her palm. Warm drops of scarlet pooled under her fingernails. Unseen by the ignorant human, the tendrils of Darkness slithered up Neferet's leg, seeking . . . finding . . . drinking . . .

Ignoring the icy heat of the familiar pain, Neferet met LaFont's gaze over his wineglass. Quickly, she dropped her voice to a soothing singsong.

> *"Peace with vampyres is not what you desire.*
> *They burn too bright, too fierce, you envy their fire.*
> *Reticence and writing be damned!*
> *You must do as I—"*

LaFont's cell phone began to ring. He blinked and the glassy expression that had lidded his eyes cleared. He put his wineglass down, took the phone from his pocket, squinted at the screen, and then said, "That's the police chief." He punched the screen and wiped a hand down his face as he said, "Dean, good to hear from you." LaFont nodded and then glanced up at Neferet. "You will forgive me, I'm sure, but I need to take this. I'll get back with you soon about the specifics of the committee and the Q and A column."

The mayor retreated quickly to the elevator, leaving Neferet alone except for the hungry tendrils of Darkness.

She allowed them to drink from her only for a few more beats of her heart, and then she brushed them away and licked the fresh wounds on her palms so that the cuts would close.

The threads pulsed around her, hovering in the air like a nest of floating snakes, eager to do her bidding. "Now you owe me one favor," she told them before picking up the penthouse phone and punching in Dallas's number.

When he answered he sounded angry, "Someone better fucking be dead to call me this early!"

"Shut up, boy! Listen and then obey." Neferet smiled at the silence that followed her command. She could almost smell his fear through the phone. Then she spoke quickly, gaining more certainty and more control over her temper as she instructed the red vampyre. "The school will soon know that I have broken with the House of Night and joined the Tulsa City Council. You know, of course, I only plan to use these humans to ignite conflict. Until I return openly to you, you will be my hands and eyes and ears at the House of Night. Act as if you want to get along with the rest of the school now that I am gone. Gain the confidence of the professors. Make friends with the blue fledglings, and then do what teenagers do best: stab each other in the back, spread rumors, create cliques."

"That nerd herd of Zoey's ain't gonna trust me."

"I told you to shut up, listen, and obey! Of course you cannot gain Zoey's confidence—she is too close to Stevie Rae for that. But you can disrupt that tight knit circle of hers; it is not as strong as you think. Look to the Twins, particularly Erin. Water is more easily manipulated and more changeable than fire." She paused, waiting for him to acknowledge her command. When he did not, she snapped, "Now you may speak!"

"I understand, High Priestess. I'll obey you," he assured her.

"Excellent. Has Aurox returned to the House of Night?"

"I haven't seen him. At least he wasn't rounded up with the rest of us and taken to the dorm after the fire. Did—did you set the fire?" Dallas asked hesitantly.

"Yes, though it was more fortuitous accident than purposeful manipulation. Did it cause much destruction?"

"Well, it burned up part of the stables and caused a big mess," he said.

"Were any horses or fledglings killed?" she asked eagerly.

"No. That human cowboy was hurt, but that's about it."

"How disappointing. Now, go about what I have commanded. When I return and control the House of Night and rule as Tsi Sgili Goddess of all Vampyres, you will be richly rewarded." Neferet punched the end call button.

She was sipping her wine and contemplating a slow, painful death for Charles LaFont when a noise from the bedroom tugged at her attention. She'd forgotten the young bellboy who had brazenly flirted with her when she'd arrived earlier that night. He'd been very willing to feed her then. He would be less willing now that he realized how close to draining him critically she had come. She stood and carried her half empty wineglass with her as she headed to her bedroom. She would be able to taste his fear in what was left of his blood.

Neferet smiled.

CHAPTER SEVEN

Zoey

Stevie Rae and I were supposed to meet Thanatos in her classroom. I'd called her while we were in the short bus on our way to campus. We hadn't spoken much. All she'd said was that she knew about Neferet's press conference and to come to her room right away.

The House of Night smelled like smoke.

The whole school reeked. As we pulled into the parking lot I realized that it didn't just stink like smoke. Sadly I'd had enough experience to recognize the sharp scent of fear.

The normal school day hadn't started, that much was super obvious. There were fledglings milling all around in gossipy little groups. They definitely weren't heading to first hour. That should have been cool. I mean, what kid doesn't love a snow day or a random water leak or whatever? But somehow it didn't feel cool. It felt confusing and not safe.

"Okay, so, I realize it's totally not normal for me to say this, but I think Thanatos should have made everyone go to classes today." Aphrodite creepily echoed my thoughts again as we unloaded from the bus. "What's going on instead is bullshit and a recipe for holy-fuck-we-can't-make-it-without-Neferet panic." Aphrodite made a sweeping gesture that took in the clusters of whispering fledglings as well as the vampyres and fledglings who were working at one of two grim jobs—clearing the rubble from the stables or adding to the enormous network of wooden beams and planks that would become Dragon Lankford's funeral pyre.

"I am in agreement with you, my beauty," Darius said grimly.

Silently, I sent up a quick but fervent prayer: *Nyx, help me to say and do the right thing—and help my circle, my friends, to be strong and sure.* Then I faced my group and followed my gut. "Okay, as much as I hate to admit it out loud, well, or even not out loud, Aphrodite's right."

Aphrodite tossed back her long blond hair. "Of course I am."

"This school needs a big dose of normal and, sadly, I think we're the best part of normal they're gonna get right now."

"That mean they's fucked," Kramisha said. She had on her yellow bobbed wig and stacked heels that had to have been five inches of black patent leather. Her skirt was short and super sparkly. Somehow she pulled off the crazy look, making me consider (for about 2.5 seconds) wearing heels more often.

"I'm being serious, Kramisha," I said.

"So am I," she said.

"Look, y'all. We can be normal. A new normal. One that's more interestin'," Stevie Rae said with a big grin up at Rephaim.

Aphrodite snorted. I ignored her, smiled at Stevie Rae, and kept talking. "We're going to split up. Part of you guys go to the stables. Part of you go to Dragon's pyre. *Remember, be normal,*" I said sternly. "Act like you would regularly act. We need to get a grip and help guide things back to something that seems manageable. Look, right now it feels like we've been attacked from everywhere. The stables were on fire. Cats were killed. Dragon's dead. And now Neferet isn't just an evil nutjob. She's an evil nutjob who has involved the human community in stuff that's way beyond their understanding or their ability to deal. We gotta be strong and visible. We gotta keep the House of Night together. Like I told Thanatos last night—we're a lot more than bickering children and it's about time we stand up, stand together, and get the respect we deserve."

"Wise counsel, Priestess," Darius said, making me want to hug him. "I will go to Dragon's pyre and spread calm there." He smiled warmly at Aphrodite. "Come with me. Your influence will be good for the Warriors who are bereft over the Sword Master's death."

"Usually, I'd say, wherever you go, I go, handsome," Aphrodite said. "But I need a little Z time, so I'm gonna go with her to talk to Thanatos. How 'bout I meet you at the pyre afterward?"

Her words surprised me, and I thought about the fact that, except for Shaylin earlier that day, I hadn't really talked to anyone since the reveal ritual. The bus ride back with Dragon's body had been silent and difficult. Then there had been the fire, the dead cats, and—thankfully—sleep, though not enough of it. All of that meant no one had backed me into a corner about Aurox. Was Aphrodite getting ready to? I glanced at her. She'd tiptoed and was giving Darius a kiss. She looked like she always did—crazy about her Warrior and kinda bitchy about everything else.

"I'm gonna go with Z, too," Stevie Rae's voice broke into my neurotic study of Aphrodite. "When we get done talkin' to Thanatos I'll be out by the funeral pyre. You're gonna be needin' some serious grounding there, and earth is the right element for that." She gave Rephaim a quick kiss. "Will you meet me out there?"

"I will." He kissed her back, touching her cheek gently. Then he glanced at me. "If no one has an objection, I would like to patrol around the wall of the school, especially the eastern wall. If Neferet's threads of Darkness are slithering around we need to know about it."

"That sounds like a good idea. You guys okay with that?" I asked, looking to Stark and Darius for input. The two Warriors nodded. "Okay, great." Then I turned my attention to Stevie Rae. "I think invoking your element is a really good idea, too, Stevie Rae. Damien, Shaunee, and Erin—you guys keep your elements close. If they can help strengthen or support, call on them. Just don't be totally obvious and . . ." My words trailed off as I fully realized what I was saying. "No. That's wrong. If you need to use your element *do* be obvious."

"I get your point, Z," Damien said. "It's about time the House of Night is aware that there are prodigious forces of good working on our side against all that Darkness."

"Prodigious means real big," Stevie Rae translated.

"We know what it means," Kramisha said.

"I didn't," Shaunee said.

"Me, neither," Erin said.

I wanted to grin at the Twins and say it was nice to have them making twin-like comments, but as soon as Erin had spoken she'd blushed bright pink and turned away from Shaunee, who was looking super uncomfortable, so I gave up—temporarily—and made a mental note to light a red and blue candle for the two of them and ask Nyx to give them some extra help. If I could find the time. Hell, if Nyx could find the time.

I stifled a sigh and kept talking. "Okay, good. So, separate into groups. Go do normal things—like get some study books and go to the library."

"That's not *my* normal," I heard Johnny B mutter, and a bunch of the kids around him laughed.

I liked the sound of their laughter. It was normal.

"Then go grab a basketball or something boy-like in the field house," I said, not able to *not* grin at them.

"I'm goin' to the cafeteria. The kitchen at the tunnels looks like locusts been through it. Z, we need to make a run to the grocery before we head back there," Kramisha said.

"Yeah, well, that's normal. Go ahead. Anyone who didn't get to eat before we left go with her. And, guys, spread out. Don't just eat in clumps. Talk to the other kids," I said.

The fledglings made noises of agreement and organized themselves, breaking into little groups around Darius, the Twins, Damien, and Kramisha. Rephaim headed off by himself. I watched his back for a little while, wondering if he'd ever really fit in, and if he didn't what that would do to his relationship with Stevie Rae. I glanced at her. She was gazing after Rephaim, too, with a look of total adoration. I chewed my lip and continued to worry.

"You okay, Z?" Stark's voice was pitched low, and he put his arm around my shoulders.

"Yeah," I said, leaning into him for a moment. "I'm just obsessively worrying, as per usual."

He squeezed me. "That's cool, as long as you don't start bawling. The whole snot cry thing you do is seriously unattractive."

I punched him playfully. "I never cry."

"Oh, yeah, that's right, and you never snot, either," he said, smiling his cocky, cute grin at me.

"I know! Amazing, right?" I teased.

"Riiiight." He drew the word out and kissed me on the top of my head.

"Hey," I said, still nestled safely in his arms. "Would you go to the stables and give Lenobia a hand? I'm going to meet with Thanatos, then I'll come to the stables and find you."

He hesitated for just a moment and I felt his arms tighten around me. Stark didn't like to separate from me, especially when crazy stuff was going on, but he nodded, said a quick, "I'll be there, watching for you." Then he kissed my forehead, let me go, and started off toward the stables. I shivered, chilled after the warmth of his touch. The other kids began to drift away in their groups, with Stevie Rae and Aphrodite hanging back with me.

"I'm going with you two, but wait a sec. First I'm gonna give my mom a call. She needs to know Neferet isn't just full of bullshit, but full of danger."

"Do you think she'll listen to you?" I asked.

"Absolutely not," she said without hesitation. "But I'm gonna try anyway."

"Why don't you just call your daddy? I mean, he's the mayor and not your momma," Stevie Rae said.

"In the LaFont household Mother is boss. If there's any chance of Mr. Mayor getting a clue about Neferet, it'll come from her."

"Good luck with that," I said.

"Yeah, whatever," Aphrodite said, before taking out her phone and moving away from us.

Surprising me, Shaylin stepped away from one of the departing groups and walked to my side. "Can I come with you guys?" Her voice was soft, but she'd spoken clearly and her chin was lifted as if she was ready for a fight.

"Why do you want to?" I asked.

"I want to ask Thanatos about my colors. I know you guys told me to keep quiet about my gift, and I understand why. It was definitely something Neferet didn't need to know. But she's not High Priestess here anymore, and I have questions that I need to find answers to. Like Damien said, it's been a long time since anyone has had True Sight. Well, Thanatos is smart. And old. I figured she could maybe give me some answers. If either of you don't mind, that is," she added quickly.

I looked at Stevie Rae. "You're her High Priestess. Are you okay with that?"

"I dunno for sure. What do you think?"

"I think if we can't trust Thanatos we're totally screwed," I said honestly.

"Well, then I think it's time to circle the wagons, and believe Thanatos is one of the good guys. So, I suppose I'm okay with it."

"Yeah, okay," I said.

"Thanks," Shaylin said.

"Well, that was a waste of time." Aphrodite joined us as she put her phone back into her super cute sparkly gold Valentino purse. "At least it wasn't a waste of *much* time."

"She wouldn't listen to you at all?" I asked.

"Oh, she listened. Then she said that she had two words for me: Nelly Vanzetti. Then she hung up."

"Huh?" I said.

"Nelly Vanzetti is my mom's shrink," Aphrodite said.

"Why would your momma give you her name?" Stevie Rae asked.

"Because, bumpkin, that's my mom's way of telling me she thinks I'm sounding super crazy. Not that she cares whether I'm actually crazy—she's just letting me know she doesn't care to listen to me, but she'll pay her shrink to." Aphrodite shrugged. "Same old thing."

"That's really mean," Shaylin said.

Aphrodite narrowed her blue eyes. "Why are you here?"

"She has a gift," Stevie Rae said.

"My give-a-shit level is very low about that," Aphrodite said.

"I have questions for Thanatos," Shaylin said.

"So she's going with us," I said.

"Whatever." Aphrodite gave her a dismissive look. "Go on, then. Ahead of us. I gotta talk to these two, without colorful ears listening."

"Go ahead of us, Shaylin," I said before the two of them could start arguing. Again. "We'll meet you in Thanatos's office."

Shaylin nodded, frowned at Aphrodite, and then walked away.

Aphrodite held up her hand. "Yeah, I know, I should be nicer, blah, blah. But she bugs me. She reminds me too much of a mini-Kim Kardashian, which means she's useless, irritating, and way too visible."

I looked at Stevie Rae, expecting her to argue. All she did was shake her head and say, "I am tired of beating a dang dead horse."

"Dead horse? That's all you've got? Really?" Aphrodite said.

"I'm not speakin' to you at all ever again," Stevie Rae told her.

"Good. Now, on to the important stuff. You two aren't gonna like either of the things I have to say, but you need to listen up—unless you want to be like my mom."

"We're listening," I said.

Stevie Rae kept her lips pressed together, but nodded.

"First, bumpkin, I know you've gone all goo-goo-eyed about Kalona since he dropped water on your birdboy and resurrected him—"

"He cried immortal tears on his son and magickally brought him back from near death. Jeeze Louise, you were there! You saw it," Stevie Rae said.

"You're not speaking to me, remember? But you just made my point for me. Up until a few hours ago we believed Kalona was as batshit crazy and dangerous as Neferet. Now he's Death's Warrior. The school's gonna slobber all over him, just like they did after he broke out of the ground. We're going to show more sense. Or, at least *I'm* going to show more sense. It'd be nice if you two joined me."

"I'll never trust him." I spoke quietly, saying words that came from deep in my heart.

"Z, he gave Thanatos his oath," Stevie Rae said.

I met her gaze. "He killed Heath. He killed Stark. He only brought Stark back because Nyx forced him to pay a life debt for Heath.

Stevie Rae, I was in the Otherworld with him. Kalona asked when Nyx would forgive him. She told him he could only ask when he was worthy of her forgiveness."

"Maybe that's what he's working toward," she said.

"And maybe he's a manipulative, lying, rapist and murderer," Aphrodite countered. "If Zoey and I are wrong, then great. You can say 'told ya so' and we'll all smile and throw an effing party. If we're right we will *not* have been caught off guard when a fallen god goes on *another* rampage."

Stevie Rae sighed. "I know—I know. You're makin' sense. I'm not gonna trust him one hundred percent."

"Fine. But keep an eye on your birdboy, too. He trusts his dad one hundred percent, which means Kalona can use him. Again."

Stevie Rae's expression tightened, but she nodded. "Yeah, I will."

"Second"—Aphrodite shifted the bulk of her attention to me— "explain the weird shit that went through your mind when you called that fucking bull by Heath's name last night."

"What?" Stevie Rae blurted. "That's not true. Is it, Z?"

Okay, lying would be easy. I could just say that Aphrodite had obviously lost her mind and had been hearing things. I mean, there had been a crapload of Crazy happening all at once last night—not to mention all of the elements manifesting so powerfully that nothing was totally clear except my mom's murder by Neferet and the fact that she was the Consort of Darkness.

And I almost did lie.

Then I remembered what lying to my friends had cost me before—not just their trust for a while, but it had cost me respect for myself. I didn't feel good when I lied. I felt out of sync with the Goddess and the path I believe she wanted me to walk.

So, I drew a deep breath and told the truth in one burst of words: "I looked through the Seer Stone at Aurox and I saw Heath and it freaked me out and I called his name and Aurox turned and looked at me before he started changing back into that bull thing and that's why when he charged me I just stood there and told him he wouldn't hurt me. The end."

"You have lost your fucking mind. Shit, and I think I threw away my mom's shrink's number too soon. You need to medicate and evaluate."

"Well, I'm gonna be nicer than Aphrodite, but it just doesn't make any sense, Z. How could Heath be around Aurox?"

"I don't know! And he wasn't around him. It was like Heath glowed *on* Aurox. Or at least shadowed him with a moonstone shine." I wanted to scream my frustration at not being able to describe what I'd glimpsed.

"Was it like a ghost?" Stevie Rae asked.

"That might make a little bit of sense," Aphrodite said, nodding to Stevie Rae, as if the two of them were figuring through it. "We were in the middle of a ritual evoking Death. Heath's dead. Maybe we snagged his ghost."

"I don't think so," I said.

"But you don't know for sure, right?" Stevie Rae said.

"No, I don't know anything for sure except that the Seer Stone is old magick, and old magick is strong and unpredictable. Hell, it's not even supposed to be anywhere except the Isle of Skye, so I don't know what's going on with me seeing stuff through it here." I threw up my hands. "Maybe I imagined it. Maybe I didn't. This is weird, even for me. I thought I saw Heath, and then Aurox changed completely into that bull thing and ran off."

"Things were happenin' real fast," Stevie Rae said.

"Next time you see Aurox you need to look through that damn stone at him, that's for sure," Aphrodite said. "And don't be alone with him."

"I'm not planning on it! I don't even know where he is."

"Probably back with Neferet," Aphrodite said.

I should've kept my mouth shut, but I heard myself speak up. "He said he'd chosen differently."

"Yeah, right after he killed Dragon and almost killed Rephaim," Aphrodite said.

I sighed.

"What did Stark say about it?" Aphrodite asked. When I didn't answer she raised a blond brow. "Oh, I get it. You haven't told him, right?"

"Right."

"Well, I can't blame you for that, Z," Stevie Rae spoke gently.

"He's her Warrior—her Guardian," Aphrodite insisted. "However annoying and arrogant he can be, he needs to know that Zoey has a thing for Aurox."

"I do not!"

"Okay, not Aurox, but Heath and you think Heath might be Aurox." Aphrodite shook her head. "Do you see how Crazy Town that sounds?"

"My life is Crazy Town," I said.

"Stark needs to know that you might be vulnerable to Aurox," Aphrodite said firmly.

"I am not vulnerable to him!"

"Tell her, bumpkin."

Stevie Rae wouldn't meet my eyes.

"Stevie Rae?"

She sighed and finally looked at me. "If you think there's even a little chance that Heath is haunting Aurox or whatever, that means you're not gonna think clear 'bout him. I know. If I lost Rephaim and then thought I saw him around some other guy, even if it seemed crazy, that guy would be able to get to me. Here." She pointed to her heart. "And most of the time that overrules here." She pointed to her head.

"So tell Bow Boy what you think you saw," Aphrodite said.

I really hated it, but I knew they were right. "Fine. It's gonna suck, but fine. I'll tell him."

"And I'm telling Darius," said Aphrodite.

"Well, I'm tellin' Rephaim," Stevie Rae added.

"Why!" I wanted to explode.

"Because the Warriors around you need to know," Aphrodite said.

"Fine," I repeated through gritted teeth. "But that's it. I'm sick of people talking about me and my boy issues."

"Well, Z, you do got you some boy issues," Stevie Rae said lightly, hooking her arm through mine.

"We need to tell Thanatos, also," Aphrodite said as the three of us started to walk toward her classroom. "Her affinity is Death. It makes sense that she understands ghosts or whatever."

"Why don't we just put it in the *Tulsa World* and have Neferet write a damn Q and A about it?" I said.

"That's almost a cuss word. Watch yourself. Damn is an entry word. Next thing you know, fuck will be flying out of your mouth," Aphrodite said.

"Flying fuck? That just sounds wrong," Stevie Rae told her, shaking her head.

I picked up the pace, practically dragging Stevie Rae along with me and making Aphrodite jog to catch up with us. I didn't listen to them as they argued about cuss words. Instead I worried.

I worried about our school.

I worried about the Aurox/Heath issue.

I worried about telling Stark about the Aurox/Heath issue.

And I worried about my clenching stomach and the possibility of my IBS acting up in the middle of everything. Again.

CHAPTER EIGHT

Shaunee

"Damien, I think I should stay way away from the stables. Lenobia has had a massive overdose of fire lately." Shaunee looked from Damien to Erin. The three of them had moved off with each other when Z had told them to scatter, but instead of actually scattering they hung together, trying to figure out where each of them, with their elements, would do the most good.

"That is a good point," Damien agreed. "It makes more sense for you to go over by Dragon's pyre. You'll be needed there soon."

Shaunee's shoulders slumped. "Yeah, I know, but it's not something I'm looking forward to."

"Just get into your element and it'll be easy," Erin spoke up.

Shaunee blinked at her, not just surprised that she'd spoken— Erin had definitely been avoiding speaking to her since they'd un-Twined—but surprised at her off-handed tone. She was talking about burning Dragon's body as if it were no more than lighting a match. "Nothing about Dragon's funeral will be easy, Erin. With or without my element."

"I didn't mean *easy* easy." Erin looked annoyed. Shaunee thought that it seemed these days Erin always looked annoyed. "I just meant that when you really get into your element other things don't bother you so much. But maybe you're just not that into your element."

"That's bullshit." Shaunee felt the heat of building anger. "My affinity for fire isn't any less than yours for water."

Erin shrugged. "Whatever. I was just trying to help you out. From now on I'll quit trying." She turned to Damien, who was looking from one to the other of them as if he wasn't sure whether he should jump in between them or run in the opposite direction. "I'm gonna go to the stables. Lenobia will be glad to see water, and I don't have an issue with using *my* element." Without another word, Erin walked away.

"Has she always been like that?" Shaunee heard herself asking Damien the question that had been circling around in her mind for days.

"You'll have to define *that.*"

"Heartless."

"Honestly?"

"Yeah. Has Erin always been so heartless?"

"That's really difficult for me to answer, Shaunee." Damien was speaking softly, as if he thought he needed to be careful his words didn't bruise her.

"Just tell me the truth, even if it is hard," she said.

"Well, then, *honestly* until the two of you broke up it was mostly impossible to tell what each of you was like individually. I'd never known one of you without the other. You two finished each other's sentences. It was like you were two halves of a whole."

"But not now?" Shaunee prodded when he hesitated.

"No, now it's different. Now you're individuals with your own personalities." He smiled at her. "The nicest way I can put this is that it's pretty obvious to most of us that your personality is the one *with* the heart."

Shaunee stared after Erin. "I knew it before, and it bugged me. You know, the way she could be so sarcastic and gossipy and mean. But she could also be so funny and cool to hang out with."

"Funny usually at other people's expense," Damien said. "Cool because she excluded others to make herself seem better than every-one else."

Shaunee met his gaze. "I know. I see it now. Back then all I could see was that we were best friends, and I needed a best friend."

"What about now?" he asked.

"Now I need to be able to like myself, and I can't do that if I'm only one half of a whole person. I'm also tired of always having to say something sarcastic or witty or just downright hateful." She shook her head, feeling sad and really old. "That doesn't mean I think Erin's awful. Actually, I want her to be as cool and funny and great as I used to believe she was. I guess I've just come to realize that she has to either be, or not be, those things on her own. It doesn't have anything to do with me."

"You're smarter than I thought you were," Damien admitted.

"I'm still crap at school."

He smiled. "There are other kinds of smart."

"That's good news for me."

"Hey, don't underestimate yourself. You might actually be good at school if you tried a little."

"I know that sounds like a good thing to you, but I'm fine with the 'other kinds of smart' part." Damien laughed, and Shaunee added, "I'm gonna head to the pyre. Maybe hanging around there will help."

"Help you or the Warriors?"

"Either. Both. I don't know," Shaunee said with a sigh.

"I'm going to believe that it'll help both," he said. "I'm going to move around—like air. I'll try to blow away some of the Darkness that's clinging to this place."

"You feel it, too?"

He nodded. "I can feel that the energy here is bad. Too much negative has happened in too short a time." Damien cocked his head, studying Shaunee. "Now that I've considered it more, I don't think you should stay away from the stables. Fire isn't bad. *You're* not bad. Lenobia knows that. Remember how you made the horses' hooves heat up so that we could ride them through the ice storm?"

"I remember." Shaunee did, and the memory made her feel lighter.

"Then go to the pyre—help there—but go to the stables, as well. Remind everyone that fire can do a lot more than destroy. It's how it's wielded that's important."

"I'm guessing you mean something like it's how fire is used that's important?"

Damien's grin widened. "See, I told you that you might be good at school. Wield is an excellent vocab word: to have or be able to use, as in power or influence."

"You're making my head hurt," Shaunee said, but she also laughed.

"So, I'll see you at the stables later?"

"Yeah, you will."

Damien started to walk away and then turned back to her, giving Shaunee a quick, tight hug. "I'm glad you became your own person. And if you need a friend, I'm here for you," he told her, and then he hurried off in the general direction of the stables.

Shaunee blinked back tears and smiled, watching his fluffy brown hair bounce around in his own little breeze. "Fire," she whispered, "send a little spark with Damien. He deserves to find a hot guy to make him happy, especially because he always tries so hard to make others happy."

Feeling better than she had in weeks, Shaunee walked in a different direction. Her steps were slower, more deliberate than Damien's, but she wasn't dreading where she was going anymore. She wasn't looking forward to the pyre and the burning—she wasn't Erin. She couldn't just shut out sadness and pain by freezing her feelings. *And you know what? I wouldn't want to be cold and frozen inside, even if it meant I didn't hurt as much,* she decided silently.

Shaunee was centering herself and drawing strength from the steady warmth of her element. *Thank you, Nyx. I'll try to wield it well,* was what she was thinking when the immortal's voice intruded.

"I have not thanked you."

Shaunee looked up to see Kalona standing near the big statue of Nyx that stood before the school's Temple. He was wearing jeans and a leather vest, one that looked a lot like what Dragon used to wear. Only this vest was bigger and it had slits through which Kalona's black wings emerged and then tucked against his back. This vest also didn't bear the insignia of the Goddess on it, but that was hard to think about when he was staring at her like that with his otherworldly amber eyes.

He really is absolutely, inhumanly gorgeous. Shaunee shook the thought from her mind and focused instead on what he'd said. "Thank me? What for?"

"For giving me your cell phone. Without it Stevie Rae would not have been able to call me. Rephaim might be dead were it not for you."

Shaunee's face was warm. She shrugged, not sure why she suddenly felt so nervous. "You're the one who came when she called. You could've just not answered and kept being a shitty dad." Shaunee realized what she'd said after she blurted it and pressed her lips together, telling herself *stop speaking!*

There was a long, uncomfortable silence, and then Kalona said, "What you say is the truth. I have not been a good father to my sons. I am still not being a good father to all of my sons."

Shaunee looked at him, wondering exactly what he meant. His voice sounded weird. She would have expected him to be sad or serious or even pissed. Instead he just seemed surprised and a little awkward, as if the thoughts he was thinking were just now occurring to him. She wished she could see his expression, but his face was turned away from her. He was gazing at Nyx's statue.

"Well," she began, not really having a clue what to say to him. "You're fixing your relationship with Rephaim. Maybe it's not too late to fix your relationship with your other sons, too. I know if my dad showed up and wanted to have something to do with me, I'd let him. I'd at least give him a chance." The immortal's head turned and he stared at her. Shaunee felt jittery, like those amber eyes could see too much of her. "What I mean is, I don't think it's ever too late to do the right thing."

"You believe that, honestly?"

"Yeah. Lately I've believed it more and more." She wished he'd look away from her. "So, how many kids do you have?"

He shrugged. His massive wings lifted slightly before settling again. "I have lost count."

"Seems like knowing how many kids you have is a good place to start in the whole I'd-like-to-be-a-good-dad thing."

"Knowing a thing and acting on a thing are distinctly different," he said.

"Yeah, totally. But I said it's a good place to *start*." Shaunee jerked her head toward Nyx's statue. "That's also a good place to start."

"At the Goddess's statue?"

She frowned at him, feeling a little easier under his gaze. "There's more to it than just hanging out at her statue. Try asking for her—"

"Forgiveness is not granted to all of us!" his voice thundered.

Shaunee felt herself begin to tremble, but her eyes shifted to Nyx's statue. She could almost swear that the full, beautiful, marble lips tilted up, smiling kindly at her. Whether it was her imagination or not, it gave Shaunee the burst of courage she needed and the fledgling continued in a rush, "I wasn't gonna say forgiveness. I was gonna say help. Try asking for Nyx's help."

"Nyx would not hear me." Kalona spoke so quietly that Shaunee almost didn't hear him. "She has not heard me for eons."

"During those eons how many times did you ask for her help?"

"Not once," he said.

"Then how do you know she's not listening to you?"

Kalona shook his head. "Have you been sent to me to be my conscience?"

It was Shaunee's turn to shake her head in denial. "I haven't been sent to you, and Goddess knows I have enough trouble dealing with my own conscience. I sure as hell can't be anyone else's."

"I would not be so sure, young fiery fledging . . . I would not be so sure," he mused, and then, abruptly, Kalona turned away from her, took several long, swift steps, and launched himself into the night sky.

Rephaim

He didn't mind all that much that most of the other kids still avoided him. Damien was nice, but Damien was nice to just about everyone, so Rephaim wasn't sure if the boy's kindness had much of anything to do with him. At least Stark and Darius weren't trying to kill him or keep him from Stevie Rae. Recently Darius even seemed a little friendly. The Son of Erebus Warrior had actually helped him when he'd stumbled onto the bus the night before, still weak from his magickally healed injury.

Father saved me and then pledged himself as Death's Warrior. He does love me, and he is choosing the side of Light against Darkness. The thought of it made Rephaim smile, even though the former Raven Mocker was not as naïve and trusting as Stevie Rae and the others believed him to be. Rephaim wanted his father to continue on Nyx's path—wanted it badly. But he, better than anyone except the Goddess herself, knew the anger and violence the fallen immortal had wallowed in for centuries.

That Rephaim existed was proof of his father's ability to cause other's great pain.

Rephaim's shoulders slumped. He'd come to the part of the school grounds where the destroyed oak lay—half against the wall of the school—half on the ground inside. The center of the thick old tree appeared as if it had been struck by a lightning bolt hurled by an angry god.

Rephaim knew better.

His father was an immortal, but he wasn't a god. Kalona was a Warrior, and a fallen one.

Feeling oddly disturbed, Rephaim's gaze moved from the gash that was the destruction at the center of the tree. He sat on one of the downed limbs well toward the edge of the tree's broken canopy, studying the thick boughs that rested against the school's east wall.

"That needs to be fixed," Rephaim spoke aloud, filling up the silent night with the humanness of his own voice. "Stevie Rae and I could work on it together. Perhaps the tree is not a complete loss." He smiled. "My Red One healed me. Why not a tree?"

The tree didn't answer, but as Rephaim spoke he had the strangest sensation of déjà vu. Like he'd been there before, and not just during another school day. Been there before with the wind in his wings and the brilliant blue of the daylight sky beckoning to him.

Rephaim's brow furrowed and he rubbed it, feeling a headache build. Did he come here during the day when he was a raven, when his humanity was hidden so deeply within him that those hours passed as a shadowy, indistinct blur of sight and sound and scent?

The only answer that came to Rephaim was the dull throbbing in his temples.

The wind moved around him, rustling through the downed boughs, causing the sparse, winter-browned leaves that still clung tenaciously to the old oak to whisper. For a moment it seemed the tree was trying to speak to him—trying to tell him its secrets.

Rephaim's gaze shifted back to the center of the tree. Shadows. Broken bark. Splintered trunk. Exposed roots. And it looked like the ground near the center of the tree had already begun to erode in upon itself, almost like there was a pit forming beneath it.

Rephaim shivered. There had been a pit below the tree. One that had imprisoned Kalona within the earth for centuries. The memory of those centuries, and the terrible, semi-substantial existence filled with anger and violence and loneliness that he had lived during that time, was still part of the heavy burden Rephaim bore.

"Goddess, I know you have forgiven me for my past, and for that I will always be grateful. But, could you, perhaps, teach me how to truly forgive myself?"

The breeze rustled again. The sound was soothing, as if the tree's ancient whispering could be the voice of the Goddess.

"I will take that as a sign," Rephaim spoke aloud to the tree, pressing his open palm to the bark beside him. "I will ask Stevie Rae to help me make right the violence that shattered you. Soon. I give my word. I will return soon." When Rephaim walked away to continue his patrol of the school's perimeter, he thought he might have heard a stirring deep beneath the tree, and imagined it was the old oak thanking him.

Aurox

Aurox paced in agitation, covering the small, hollowed-out space beneath the shattered oak in three strides. Then he turned, and took three short strides back. Back and forth, back and forth, he went. Thinking . . . thinking . . . thinking . . . and wishing desperately that he had a plan.

His head pained him. He had not broken his skull when he'd fallen into the pit, but the lump on his head had bled and swollen. He hungered. He thirsted. He found it difficult to rest within the earth, though his body was exhausted and he needed to sleep so that he might heal.

Why had he believed it a good idea to return to this school—to hide on the very grounds where the professor he had killed, as well as the boy he had attempted to kill—lived?

Aurox put his head in his hands. *Not me!* He wanted to shout the words. *I did not kill Dragon Lankford. I did not attack Rephaim. I chose differently!* But his choice hadn't mattered. He had transformed into a beast. That beast had left death and destruction in his wake.

It had been foolish of him to come here. Foolish to believe he could find himself here or do any good. Good? If anyone knew he was hiding at the school he would be attacked, imprisoned, possibly killed. Even though he was not here to do harm, it would not matter. He would absorb the rage of those who discovered him, and the beast would emerge. He would not be able to control it. The Sons of Erebus Warriors would surround him and end his miserable existence.

I controlled it once before. I did not attack Zoey. But would he even get an opportunity to try to explain that he meant no harm? Even have an instant to test his self-control and to prove he was more than the beast within him? Aurox resumed his pacing. No, his intent would not matter to anyone at the House of Night. All they would see would be the beast.

Even Zoey? Would even Zoey be against him?

*"Zoey shielded you from the Warriors. It was because of her pro-
tection that you were able to flee."* Grandma Redbird's voice soothed
his turbulent thoughts. Zoey had shielded him. She'd believed that
he could control the beast enough not to harm her. Her grandmother had offered him sanctuary. Zoey could not want him dead.

The others would, though.

Aurox didn't blame them. He deserved death. Regardless of the
fact that he had, recently, begun to feel, to long for a different life, a
different choice, it did not change the past. He had committed violent, vile acts. He had done anything Priestess had commanded.

Neferet . . .

Even silent, an unspoken word in his mind, the name sent a
shudder through his agitated body.

The beast within him wanted to go to Priestess. The beast within
him needed to serve her.

"I am more than a beast." The earth around him absorbed the
words, muffling Aurox's humanity. In despair, he grabbed a twisted
root and began to pull himself up and out of the dirt pit.

"That needs to be fixed."

The words drifted down to Aurox. His body froze. He recognized the voice—Rephaim. Grandma had told him the truth. The
boy lived.

Aurox's invisible load lifted slightly.

That was one death that did not need to be on his conscience.

Aurox crouched, silently straining to hear to whom Rephaim
spoke. He didn't feel anger or violence. Surely if Rephaim had any
idea whatsoever that Aurox was hidden so close, the boy would be
filled with feelings of vengeance, would he not?

Time seemed to pass slowly. The wind increased. Aurox could
hear it whipping through the dry leaves of the broken tree above
him. He caught words that floated with the cool air: *work . . . tree . . .
Red One healed . . .* All in Rephaim's voice, absent of malice, as if he
just mused aloud. And then the breeze brought him the boy's prayer:
"Goddess, I know you have forgiven me for my past, and for that I will

always be grateful. But, could you, perhaps, teach me how to truly forgive myself?" Aurox hardly breathed.

Rephaim was asking for his goddess's help to forgive himself? Why?

Aurox rubbed his throbbing head and thought hard. Priestess had rarely spoken to him, except to command him to execute an act of violence. But she had spoken around him, as if Aurox had not had the ability to hear her or to formulate thoughts of his own. What did he know about Rephaim? He was the immortal Kalona's son. He was cursed to be a boy by night, a raven by day.

Cursed?

He had just heard Rephaim praying, and in that prayer he had acknowledged Nyx's forgiveness. Surely a goddess would not curse and forgive with the same breath.

Then with a little start of surprise, Aurox remembered the raven that had mocked him and made such a noise that it had caused Aurox to fall into this pit.

Could that have been Rephaim? Aurox's body tensed as he readied himself for the seemingly inevitable confrontation to come.

"I give my word. I will return soon," Rephaim's voice drifted down to Aurox. The boy was leaving, though temporarily. Aurox relaxed against the earthen wall. His body ached and his mind whirred.

That he could not stay in the pit was obvious, but that was all that was obvious to Aurox.

Had Rephaim's goddess, the one who had forgiven him, also led him to Aurox's pit? If so, was it to show Aurox redemption or revenge?

Should he turn himself in, perhaps to Zoey, and take whatever consequences were meted out?

What if the beast emerged again, and this time he could not control it at all?

Should he flee?

Should he go to Priestess and demand answers?

"I know nothing," he whispered to himself. "I know nothing."

Aurox bowed his head under the weight of his confusion and

longing. Tentatively, silently, he mimicked Rephaim with his own prayer. It was simple. It was sincere. And it was the first time in his life Aurox had ever prayed.

Nyx, if you are, indeed, a forgiving goddess, please help me . . . please . . .

CHAPTER NINE

Zoey

"Neferet must be stopped," Thanatos said with no preamble.

"Sounds like good news to me. Finally," Aphrodite said. "So is the entire High Council showing up here to call bullshit on her stupid press conference, or is Duantia coming by herself?"

"I can't wait till the humans hear the real deal about her," Stevie Rae spoke after Aphrodite, sounding as pissed as Aphrodite and not giving Thanatos a chance to reply. "I'm dang tired of Neferet smiling and batting her eyes and making everyone believe she's all sugar and spice and everything nice."

"Neferet does much more than bat her eyes and smile," Thanatos said grimly. "She uses her Goddess-given gifts to manipulate and harm. Vampyres are subject to her spell—humans have little defense against her."

"Which means the Vampyre High Council has to stand up and do something about her," I said.

"I wish it were that simple," Thanatos said.

My stomach clenched. I had one of my *feelings,* and that was almost never good.

"What do you mean? Why wouldn't it be that simple?" I asked.

"The High Council will not mingle humans in vampyre affairs," she said.

"But Neferet's already done that," I said.

"Yeah, talk about closin' the barn door after the cows have already gone out," Stevie Rae said.

"The bitch killed Zoey's mom." Aphrodite was shaking her head as if in disbelief. "Are you saying that the High Council is just going to ignore that and let her get away with murder *and* talk shit about all of us?"

"And what would you have the High Council do? Expose Neferet as a killer?"

"Yes," I spoke up, glad I sounded tough and mature instead of scared and about twelve, which was really how this whole thing was making me feel. "I know she's immortal and powerful, but *she killed my mom*."

"We have no proof of that," Thanatos said quietly.

"Bullshit!" Aphrodite exploded. "We all saw it!"

"In a reveal ritual set in motion by a death spell. Neither can be repeated. The land has been washed clean of that act of violence by all five elements."

"She took Darkness as her Consort," Aphrodite argued. "She's not just in league with evil, she's probably doing the nasty with it!"

"Eeew," Stevie Rae and I said together.

"Humans would never believe any of it, even if they had been there." We all turned to look at Shaylin, who until then had been standing silently and watching the four of us with what I'd thought was a kinda glazed, shocky expression. But her voice was steady. Sure, she looked nervous, but her chin was lifted again and she had what I was coming to recognize as her stubborn face on.

"What the hell do you know about it and why are you speaking?" Aphrodite snapped at her.

"This time last month I was a human. Humans don't trust vampyre magick." Shaylin faced Aphrodite without flinching. "You've been around all this magick too long. You have totally lost perspective."

"And you have totally lost your mind," Aphrodite snarled, puffing up like a blowfish.

"Squabbling children again." Thanatos didn't raise her voice, but her words cut through the almost-girl-fight tension between Aphrodite and Shaylin.

"They don't want to fight," I spoke into the sudden silence. "None of us do. But we're all frustrated and we expected you and the High Council to do something, *anything*, to help us against Neferet."

"Let me show you the truth of who we are, and then you might understand more about this fight you are insisting we take to the humans." Thanatos lifted her right arm, holding her palm up at about chest level away from her body. She cupped her hand, breathed in deeply, and with her left hand, swirled the air above her upraised palm, saying, "Behold the world!" Her voice was powerful, mesmerizing. My eyes were drawn to her palm. On it a globe of the world was taking form. It was awesome—not like those boring globes history teachers/coaches use as dust-gatherers. This one looked like it was made of black smoke. The water rippled and rolled. The continents emerged, carved from onyx.

"Ohmy*goodness*," Stevie Rae said. "It's so pretty!"

"It is," Thanatos said. "And now behold who we are in the world!" She flicked the fingers of her left hand at the globe, as if she were sprinkling it with water. Aphrodite, Stevie Rae, Shaylin, and I gasped. Little sparkles began appearing, dotting the onyx landmasses with tiny diamond lights.

"That's beautiful," I said.

"Are they diamonds? Real diamonds?" Aphrodite asked, stepping closer.

"No, young Prophetess. They are souls. Vampyre souls. They are us."

"But there are so few lights. I mean, compared to the rest of the globe that's all dark," Shaylin said.

I frowned and stepped closer along with Aphrodite. Shaylin was right. The earth looked huge compared to the sprinkling of sparkly dots. I stared and stared. My eyes were drawn to the clusters of shininess: Venice, the Isle of Skye, somewhere in what I thought was Germany. A cluster of light in France, a few splotches in Canada, and several more sprinkled around the continental U.S.—several more, but still not very many.

"Is that Australia?" Stevie Rae asked.

I peered around to the other side of the globe, catching sight of another spattering of diamonds.

"It is," Thanatos said. "And New Zealand as well."

"That's Japan, isn't it?" Shaylin pointed to another tiny splotch of glitter.

"Yes, it is," Thanatos said.

"America doesn't have as many diamonds as it should," Aphrodite said.

Thanatos didn't respond. She met my gaze. I looked away, studying the globe again. Slowly, I walked all the way around her, wishing I'd paid better attention in geography class—any of them. When I completed my circle I met the High Priestess's gaze again.

"There aren't enough of us," I said.

"That is the absolute, unfortunate truth," Thanatos said. "We are brilliant, powerful, and spectacular, but we are few."

"So, even if we could get the humans to listen to us we'd be opening a door to our world that's better left closed." Aphrodite spoke calmly, sounding mature and uncharacteristically non-bitchy. "They start thinking their rules apply to us, that we need them to keep us in line, and that means they start putting out our lights."

"Simply, but well put." Thanatos clapped her palms together and the globe disappeared in a puff of sparkly smoke.

"Then what do we do? We can't just let Neferet get away with her crap. It's not like she's gonna stop with a press conference, a committee, and a newspaper column. She wants death and destruction. Hell's Bells, Darkness is her Consort!" Stevie Rae said.

"We gotta fight her fire with our fire," Shaylin said.

"Oh, for shit's sake. I can't deal with one more kid who uses bad metaphors instead of just saying what's what," Aphrodite said.

"What I mean is if Neferet is involving humans, then we should, too. But on our own terms," Shaylin said. I saw her mouth the word *hateful* afterward, but Aphrodite had decided to ignore the fledgling. Again. And, thankfully, Aphrodite wasn't looking at her.

"Shaylin, you interest me, child. Why is it you have accompanied these two Priestesses and the Prophetess?" Thanatos asked abruptly.

We Priestesses and Prophetess went silent. Personally, I wanted to see how Shaylin was going to handle Thanatos. I liked to think Stevie Rae had shut up for the same reason. I already knew Aphrodite's reasoning, which Shaylin had summed up with the succinct word she'd mouthed: *hateful*.

The little red fledgling raised her chin and looked super stubborn. "I came with them because I wanted to ask you about my gift. And they agreed." Shaylin paused, glanced at Aphrodite and added, "Well, two of the three agreed."

"What gift has Nyx given you, fledgling?"

"True Sight. I think." She glanced nervously from Stevie Rae to me. "Right?"

"We think so," I said.

"Yep. At least that's what Damien's research tells us, and he's almost always right about anythin' he's researched," Stevie Rae said.

"She said Neferet was the color of dead fish eyes. That makes me think she might have something more than simple mental illness or mild retardation going on," Aphrodite surprised me by saying.

"You see auras?" Thanatos asked while she studied Shaylin like she was peering down a microscope and the fledgling was pressed against a glass slide.

"I see colors," Shaylin said. "I don't know what to call it. I—I was blind before the night I was Marked. I had been since I was five. Then, *zap!* I get a red crescent moon in the middle of my forehead, my vision back, and with it I get colors. Lots of colors. Because of them I know things about people. Like I knew Neferet was rotten inside the second I saw her. Even though on the outside she was beautiful." I watched her clench her hands together behind her, and hold still under the High Priestess's scrutiny. "It's the same way I know Erik Night is basically an okay guy, but he's weak. He's always taken the easy road. Your color is black, but not like flat black. It's deep and rich and I can see little lightning bolts of golden light zapping through it." She sighed. "I think that means you're really old and smart and powerful, but you also have a serious temper, which you keep under control. Most of the time."

Thanatos's lips tilted up. "Go on."

Shaylin looked quickly at Stevie Rae and then back at Thanatos. "Stevie Rae's colors are like fireworks. That makes me think that she's the kindest, happiest person I've ever met."

"That's only 'cause you never knew Jack," Stevie Rae said, smiling a little sadly at Shaylin. "But thanks. That's a real nice thing to say about me."

"I'm not meaning to be nice. I'm just trying to tell the truth." Her eyes went to Aphrodite. "Well, most of the time I'm trying to tell the truth."

Aphrodite snorted.

I waited for her to get to me—to tell Thanatos that my colors had gotten darker because I was super worried—but she didn't say anything about me at all. She just gave a little nod of her head, like she'd decided something inside herself, and finished by saying, "That's why I'm here. I need your advice about how to use my gift and to know the truth about it."

I think it was then that I started to respect her. Thanatos wasn't just any High Priestess. She was a member of the High Council and her affinity was for death. Okay, Thanatos was scary. Seriously. Yet here was Shaylin, all less than a hundred pounds of her, less than a month old as a fledgling, standing up to Thanatos, without giving away anything too private about me. She hadn't even said the stuff about Aphrodite's flickery nice spot color. That took guts. Lots of them.

I glanced down at Shaylin's clenched hands and saw that her fingers had gone white. I knew how she felt. I'd had to stand up to a powerful High Priestess shortly after I'd been Marked, too.

I moved closer to Shaylin. "Whatever you want to call what she sees, Shaylin has a gift. I agree with Damien. I think it's True Sight."

"We all do," Stevie Rae said.

"Can you help me?" Shaylin asked.

Thanatos surprised me then. She didn't say anything. She turned and walked over to her desk, gazing down at it as if the answer to Shaylin's question were written on the big daily calendar she used as a desk pad. She just stood there like that, with her head bowed, for what seemed like a super ridiculously long time. I'd decided that I needed to clench my hands behind me to keep from fidgeting, too, when the High Priestess finally turned around and faced the four of us.

"Shaylin, the answer I have for you is the same as the answer I have for Zoey and Stevie Rae and Aphrodite." I heard Aphrodite mutter something about not remembering asking her a damn question, but Thanatos spoke over her. "Each of you has been unusually gifted by our Goddess, and that is fortuitous for us because we will need all of the powers Light can gift us with if we are to battle Darkness."

"You mean *beat* Darkness, don't ya," Stevie Rae said.

I knew Thanatos's answer before she spoke it. "Darkness can never truly be beaten. It can only be battled and exposed by love and Light and truth."

"Losing side. Again," Aphrodite said under her breath.

"I am going to give each of you a task so that you may exercise your gifts. Prophetess, I give the first to you," Thanatos spoke to Aphrodite.

Aphrodite sighed heavily.

"You have been gifted by Nyx with visions that are warnings of dire things to come. Did you have a vision before Neferet's press conference?"

"No." Aphrodite looked surprised by Thanatos's question. "I haven't had a vision for about a week now."

"Then what good are you, Prophetess?" Her words were hard, cold. Thanatos almost sounded cruel.

Aphrodite's face got real pale, and then blazed with pink. "Who are you to question me? You're not Nyx. I don't answer to you. I answer to her!"

"Exactly." Thanatos's expression relaxed. "Then answer to her.

Listen to her. Watch for her signs and signals. Your visions have become increasingly painful and difficult, have they not?"

Aphrodite nodded in a quick tight movement.

"Perhaps that is because our Goddess wishes for you to exercise your gift in other ways. You did so, briefly, before the High Council. Remember?"

"Of course I remember. It's how I knew Kalona and Zoey's souls had left their bodies."

"But you didn't need a vision to tell you that."

"No."

"My point has been made," Thanatos said. She turned to Stevie Rae. "You are the youngest High Priestess I have ever met, and I have lived a very long time. You are the first red vampyre High Priestess in the history of our people. You have a powerful affinity for earth."

"Yeaaah." Stevie Rae drew the word out as if she was waiting for Thanatos's punch line.

"It is your task to practice leadership. You defer to Zoey far too often. You are a High Priestess. Draw strength from the earth and begin behaving as a High Priestess should." Thanatos didn't give Stevie Rae a chance to respond. Her dark gaze skewered Shaylin. "If you have True Sight your gift is only as good as you are. Do not squander it on pettiness and jealousies."

"That's why I'm here," Shaylin spoke quickly. "I want to learn how to use it the right way."

"That, young fledgling, is something you must grow up and teach yourself. Your task is to study those around you. Come to your High Priestess with your results. Stevie Rae will use the power of her element, as well as her growing leadership power, to guide you."

"But I don't know—" Stevie Rae began and Thanatos cut her off. "And you never will know. Anything. Anything important at all. *Unless* you take on the responsibility of being a High Priestess. Learn to rely on yourself so that others may feel secure in relying on you."

Stevie Rae closed her mouth and nodded, looking like she was about twelve and the exact opposite of a High Priestess. But I didn't have time to say anything to her because Thanatos had finally turned her torpedo eyes on me.

"Use your Seer Stone."

"Huh?"

"It frightens you," she spoke as if I hadn't said anything. "The truth is the world should frighten you, should frighten all of you, right now. Fear is not a reason to avoid your responsibilities. You have a piece of old magick that responds to you. Use it."

"How? For what?" I blurted.

"A Seer Stone, a True Color gift, a Prophetess, a High Priestess—all of those powerful things are useless unless you all begin to answer those questions for yourself. You say you are not bickering children? Prove it. You are dismissed." She turned her back to us and strode to her desk.

My friends and I obviously had the same impulse at the same time. As one we began scurrying for the exit door.

"I will light Dragon Lankford's pyre at midnight. Be present for the ceremony. Immediately afterward I need you and the rest of your circle in the school lobby. I have called my own press conference."

Her words hit us like an invisible wall. We all stopped, turned, and gawked at her. I swallowed past the lump of dryness in my throat and said, "But you said we can't stand up to Neferet in the human community. So, what are we press conferencing about?"

"We are continuing in goodwill what Neferet began only to create chaos and conflict. She opened this school to human employees. We are going to announce in the conference that, though we are sad to see Neferet leave our school's *employ,* we are happy to take job applications from the community for more positions at the House of Night. We will smile. We will be warm and open. James Stark will be present and will be charming and handsome and harmless."

"You're going to make Neferet look like nothing more than a disgruntled employee?" Aphrodite said. "That's brilliant!"

"And normal," I said.

"Something humans will totally understand," Shaylin said.

"Hey, if ya really want to be normal and human-like, we need to have an open house job fair thingie." We stared at Stevie Rae.

"Go on," Thanatos said. "What is your idea, High Priestess?"

"Well, my high school used to have a job fair for seniors at the end of the school year. It was kinda like a regular open house at school, what with the bad punch and the baked goods and all. But businesses from Tulsa and Oklahoma City, and even from Dallas would come and take job applications and set up interviews for the seniors while the rest of us hung around and wished we were graduating." Stevie Rae smiled sheepishly and shrugged. "Guess I thought of it 'cause I missed my chance, gettin' Marked and all."

"Actually that is an interesting idea," Thanatos shocked me by saying. "We will mention our willingness to open our school to a *job fair*"—she spoke the words as if they were in a foreign language—"during the press conference later tonight."

"If you're gonna have a real open house we need a bunch of folks here. How 'bout we invite Street Cats and do a whole fund-raising cat adoption thing? That'd be something Tulsa could get behind," Stevie Rae added.

"And it would be normal," Aphrodite said. "Charity events are normal, and they bring out the people with the big bucks, and that's a good thing."

"An excellent point," Thanatos said.

"My grandma can help coordinate with Street Cats. She and Sister Mary Angela, the nun who's their director, are friends," I said.

Thanatos nodded. "Then I will call Sylvia, and ask her if she feels up to coordinating what we shall call an open house evening and job fair for Tulsa. The presence of your grandmother, as well as the nuns, will have a normalizing, calming affect."

"My momma can bake like a ton of chocolate chip cookies and come, too," Stevie Rae said.

"Then invite her. I have faith in you, as does Nyx. Do not disappoint either of us. And now, you are truly dismissed."

We left Thanatos's classroom talking about the press conference and the open house and how it felt good that we had a Plan. It was only later that I realized I hadn't said one single word about the Aurox/Heath situation . . .

CHAPTER TEN

Shaunee

The Sons of Erebus Warriors went grimly about the job of stacking timber and building Dragon's pyre. Shaunee tried to do what she could to help them. She could tell how well wood would burn just by touching it, so she pointed out all of the particularly dry logs, or planks, and guided the Warriors into placing them just right, so that the fire would burn cleanly and quickly.

Shaunee tried to be encouraging. She told them they were doing a good job, and that Dragon would be proud of them, but that only seemed to make them quieter, grimmer. Darius was even silent and almost felt like a stranger. It was only after Aphrodite breezed up, tossing her hair and talking with her usual take-no-prisoners attitude that things started to get better.

"So, handsome, do you remember the lecture Dragon gave you when you and I first started going out?" Aphrodite winked at several of the other Warriors. "I'll bet Stephen and Conner and Westin remember it, don't ya? Wasn't it the three of you who had to pull extra training with Darius after Dragon found out he was *fraternizing with a fledgling*?" Aphrodite had lowered her voice and affected a tone that sounded weirdly like the Sword Master.

The Warriors had actually smiled. "Three days in a row Dragon made each of us have a go at your boy there."

Darius snorted. "Watch yourself, Conner. I have not been a *boy* for decades."

Conner laughed. "I think that's what Dragon was having a problem with."

Aphrodite smiled flirtatiously and ran a hand down Darius's thick bicep. "He was trying to tire you out so that you wouldn't be *energetic* enough to fraternize with me."

"That would have taken an army of vampyres," Darius said.

It was Stephen's turn to snort. "Really? Is that why Anastasia had to intervene?"

Aphrodite's blond brows went up. "Intervene? Anastasia? You didn't tell me that, handsome."

"It must have slipped my mind, as I was too busy fraternizing with you, my beauty."

"Ha!" Westin scoffed. "There is no way any one of us could forget Anastasia, hair flying, descending upon our Sword Master, calling him to task for picking on poor, young Darius."

Shaunee had to join the laughter. "She seriously said Dragon was picking on Darius?"

Conner, who was tall and blond and almost as hot as Shaunee's element, said, "She absolutely did. She even called him Bryan and reminded him that had *she* not fraternized with a fledgling a century ago, his life would be much less interesting."

"I'd known Dragon Lankford for fifty years," Stephen said. "I'd never seen him bested by any other Warrior, but Anastasia could stop him with a single look."

"It is good that they are together," Darius said.

"He lost himself without her," Westin said.

"Something I can well understand." Darius lifted Aphrodite's hand, kissing it gently.

"You truly did see them reunite?"

"Yes." Darius, Aphrodite, and Shaunee spoke together.

"He's happy again," Shaunee said.

"She died first, but she waited for him," Aphrodite said. She was smiling at Darius, but Shaunee could see tears in her eyes.

"She died a Warrior's death," Westin said.

"As did Dragon," Darius said.

"We need to remember this tonight," Shaunee said. "Remember their joy and their oath and that they still have love."

"Always love," Darius said softly, touching Aphrodite's cheek.

"Always love," she echoed. Then she raised a blond brow. "If you're not too tired, that is."

"Ha! So Anastasia was right! We were picking on poor, young Darius." Stephen and the other Warriors laughed and Darius sputtered while Aphrodite teased.

Shaunee backed away from the growing pyre and the group that surrounded it. *Fire, warm this small spark of joy that Aphrodite managed to ignite within them. Help the Warriors to remember that Dragon and Anastasia are together and happy.* She felt the warmth of her element rush from around her and circle the group, invisible to the eye, and almost undetectable to anyone who didn't have an affinity for fire. But it helped. *She* had helped. Shaunee really believed it.

Feeling slightly less awful, she wandered away. Shaunee knew she needed to go to the stables, but that didn't mean she was eager to face the destruction that her element had caused. *I wasn't wielding it, though,* she reminded herself. Still, she meandered, taking a circuitous route and heading toward the courtyard that had the pretty fountain in it. From there she'd walk the back way, by the parking lot, that led more directly to the field house than to the stables.

Shaunee heard water before she heard Erin's voice.

She hadn't meant to be all creeper-like and lurky. She'd only moved quietly into the shadows around the courtyard because she hadn't wanted a scene with Erin—not because she was spying on her.

Then she heard the other voice. Shaunee didn't recognize who it was at first. He wasn't talking loud enough. She only recognized Erin's flirty giggle. Shaunee was trying to decide if curiosity was the same as nosiness when his voice got louder and she realized the guy Erin was aiming her flirty giggle at was Dallas!

Feeling sick to her stomach, Shaunee moved closer.

"Yeah, that's what I'm sayin'. I can't get you off my mind, girl. You know what water and electricity make when they come together, don't you?"

Shaunee stayed completely still, waiting for Erin to call him a douche bag and tell him to run back to nasty Nicole where he belonged; instead her stomach dropped as she heard Erin's flirty answer, "Lightning—that's what electricity and water make. Sounds hot to me."

"That's because it *is* hot. *You* are hot. You're like a sauna, girl—or a steam bath I'd like to soak in."

Shaunee had to press her lips together in a tight line to keep from yelling *eew* and calling Dallas a douche herself. Erin would. No way would she want anything to do with Dallas. He was a total asshole. He hated Stevie Rae and Zoey! Stevie Rae had said he'd tried to kill her! Erin was just setting him up to smack him down and put him in his place.

Shaunee waited for it. Nothing. She heard nothing. Walking quietly, Shaunee moved even closer. Erin was probably gone. She'd probably rolled her eyes and walked away and not even bothered with telling Dallas to get lost.

Shaunee was wrong. Real wrong.

Erin had backed up against the fountain. Water was flowing all over her. Her hair, her clothes, her body. Dallas was staring at her like he was starving and she was a T-bone steak dinner. Erin lifted her arms over her head, making her boobs press against her soggy shirt, which was white and wet and now totally see-through.

"How's this for a wet T-shirt contest?" Her voice was all sexy and she shimmied a little, making her boobs bounce.

"You win. That's the hottest thing I've ever seen, girl."

"I can show you something hotter," Erin said. With one motion she pulled her soaked T-shirt off and then unhooked her lace bra.

Dallas was breathing so hard Shaunee could hear him. He licked his lips. "You're right, girl. That is hotter."

"And what about this?" Erin hooked her thumbs in the waist of her little plaid skirt and pulled it off. She smiled at Dallas as he stared at the little lace thong she was still wearing.

"How 'bout takin' the rest of that off?" His voice had deepened and he'd moved closer to her.

"Sounds good to me. I like wearing nothing but water." Erin peeled off the thong. Now all she had on were her Christian Louboutin boots. She ran her hands all over her body with the water. "Wanta get wet with me?"

"Wet isn't all I wanta get with you," he said. "Girl, I'm gonna open up a whole other world for you."

"I'm ready for it," she said silkily, still touching herself. "'Cause I'm sick of the boring-ass world I've been living in."

"Lightning, girl. Let's make some lightning and some changes."

"Bring it!" Erin said.

Dallas closed the distance between them. The two of them were wrapped together and so into each other that Shaunee didn't have to worry about them hearing her when she rushed away, totally nauseated, her eyes filled with tears.

Zoey

"If you guys don't mind I'm gonna go to the media center. Damien thought there might be some old books on True Sight in the reference section if I dig hard enough. He's probably better at research than I am, but I'm stubborn," Shaylin said. "If there's something to find, eventually I'll find it."

"No problem," I said and Stevie Rae gave a shrug saying, "Sounds good to me."

She started to walk away and then paused. "Hey, thanks for letting me come with you and talk to Thanatos. And thanks for hearing what I had to say in there. And, well, sorry again for that thing with Aphrodite earlier."

"I'm not the one you need to keep apologizing to for that," I said.

"Yeah, well, I think you're the only one who will listen," Shaylin said, glancing in the direction Aphrodite had twitched off.

"Aphrodite'll listen. Just not very well," Stevie Rae said. "You did good in there, Shaylin. I like what you say about people's colors. I think you should focus on following your gut about what you see."

"Huh," Kramisha huffed as she hurried up to us. "I say guts can get you in a shit ton of trouble."

I was thinking, *understatement of the year,* as Stevie Rae was asking, "What's up, Kramisha?"

"It's Dallas's red fledglings. They're actin' like they wanta help clean up the stable."

Stevie Rae frowned. I chewed my lip. Kramisha crossed her arms and tapped her foot.

"Is helping a bad thing?" Shaylin spoke into the uncomfortable pause.

"Dallas's group has been, well . . ." I hesitated, trying to form a phrase that didn't involve using words I tried (pretty much) to avoid.

Kramisha beat me to it, "They's ass bites."

"Maybe they're trying to change," Shaylin said.

"They's *devious* ass bites," Kramisha added.

"We don't trust them," I explained.

"And we have lots of reasons to don't trust 'em," Stevie Rae said. "But I have an idea. Thanatos said I gotta practice being a leader and Shaylin's gotta practice her True Sight thing. So let's do both." Stevie Rae straightened her back and her voice changed from sweet and girl-like to a woman who sounded more confident and lots older. "Shaylin, you can go to the media center later. Right now you'll come with me to the stables. I want you to look at the colors of the red fledglings there and tell me which ones are most dangerous."

"Yes, ma'am," she said.

"Uh, you don't have to call me ma'am," Stevie Rae said quickly, sounding like herself again. "Just lettin' me boss you around is good enough."

"You ain't that bossy," Kramisha said.

"Well, I'm tryin' to be." Stevie Rae sighed, then glanced at me.

I grinned at her. "You can boss me if you want to."

She gave me an *ack!* look. "If I ever try to you can call me a wiener and tell me to slap myself with a bun and mustard."

I laughed. "Well, then, if you don't care I'm gonna take some time by myself. I need to think about this Seer Stone thing. I'll meet you at the stables in a little while, though. If you see Stark, tell him I'm fine and I'll be there soon."

"Okie dokie," Stevie Rae said.

I watched the three of them walk off. I could hear Kramisha asking Shaylin about her color, and before the kid could answer her, she was already explaining to Shaylin that there was no damn way her color could be any kind of orange 'cause she didn't like her no orange. Shaylin was looking confused but interested. Stevie Rae looked thoughtful and determined, like she was trying to reflect on the outside the leadership she was working on on the inside.

Me? I imagined if you put a mirror up to me I'd look confused and tired and see that my mascara was clumping and my hair was frizzing.

I wanted to go with my friends and help them get the stables cleaned up. I wanted to find Stark and have him hold my hand and tease me about over-worrying and Internet health symptom googling. Mostly I wanted to forget about the stupid Seer Stone around my neck and focus on something that made more sense—like hateful red fledglings and homework. But I knew Thanatos had been right. We would need all of our gifts to have a chance at even just keeping Darkness at bay. So instead of following my friends, I walked a different path. I cleared my mind as much as I could, and let my instincts guide me. When it was obvious where my feet were leading me, I whispered, "Spirit, please come to me. Help me not to be too afraid." The element I felt most comfortable with soothed my fear, so that by the time I was standing before the shattered oak tree, it was like my emotions were wrapped in a soft, warm blanket.

I needed the comfort blanket. This place scared me. Professor Nolan had been killed here. Stevie Rae had almost been killed here. Kalona had ripped from the earth here. Jack—poor sweet Jack—had died here.

My gut had taken me here. Worse, my Seer Stone had started to radiate heat.

Yep, I thought. *Like Kramisha said, following your gut can cause a shit ton of trouble.* I sighed and admitted the truth my instinct had followed—if there's old magick at the House of Night, this was an excellent place for it to be hiding. Sgiach had told me that old magick was powerful. It was also unpredictable and dangerous. I remembered her explaining that how it manifested had a lot to do with the Priestess who had called it to her.

So, what did that mean for me? What kind of Priestess was I becoming?

I sighed. *A confused, crappy one who didn't get enough sleep.*

One with potential, drifted through my mind.

One who doesn't know enough, I mentally countered with.

One who needs to believe in herself, the wind whispered to me.

One who needs to quit screwing up, my mind insisted.

One who needs to believe in her Goddess.

And that stopped my mental battle.

"I do believe in you, Nyx. I always will." Resolutely, I pulled the warm Seer Stone from under my T-shirt, took a deep breath, lifted it, and stared through the little Lifesaver-like hole at the broken, battered oak tree.

For a second nothing happened. I squinted, and the tree was just a messed-up old tree. I started to relax and, typically, that's when all hell broke loose.

From the center of the shattered trunk an ugly, terrible whirling vortex of shadows emerged. Within the whirlpool I could see horrible creatures with twisted bodies covered in skin that was mottled, as if they were rotting from disgusting diseases. Their eyes were cavernous sockets. Their mouths were sewn shut. I could smell them. It was a stink like old roadkill mixed with a backed-up toilet. I gagged and must have made a retching sound, because as a group, they turned their sightless faces to me. Their long, skeletal fingers reached toward me.

"No! Stop!" Spirit's comfort was shattered. I was paralyzed by fear. And then from the very center of the vortex a beautiful, full moon-colored light flashed up, burning the horrid creatures into nothingness and knocking me backward on my butt. I dropped the Seer Stone, severing my link to the old magick. As I blinked and gasped, the tree became the tree again. Old and creepy, but mundane and broken.

Not caring about Thanatos or Death's commands I scrambled to my feet and ran like hell.

"I'm not crazy. It's my life that is crazy. I'm not crazy. It's my life that is crazy . . ." Between panting breaths I spoke the words like a mantra, over and over to myself, trying to find my normal—my center, or even just a small measure of calm, but my heartbeat was pounding so loud I could hear it in my ears and I couldn't seem to catch my breath. *Heart attack,* I thought. *This level of crazy is too much for me and I'm having a heart attack.*

I'd just realized that maybe I couldn't catch my breath and my heart was pounding like crazy because I was still running, when strong, familiar hands grabbed me, jerking me to a sudden stop. Like a total girl I collapsed against Stark, shaking so hard that my teeth were chittering.

"Zoey! Are you hurt? Who's after you?" Stark kept me tucked against him while he turned me so that he was staring through the darkness behind me. I'd wrapped my arms around him and I could feel that he'd slung his bow and an arrow holder over his shoulder. Readiness radiated from him. Even through my panic, his presence calmed me. I gulped air, shaking my head. "No, I'm okay. I'm okay."

He held me out at arm's length, looking up and down my body like he was checking for wounds. "What happened? Why are you freaked and running like a crazy person?"

I frowned at him. "I'm not a crazy person."

"Well, you were running like one. And inside here"—he pressed a finger against my chest over my quieting heart—"you were definitely feeling whacked."

"Old magick."

His eyes widened. "The bull?"

"No, no, nothing like that. I looked through the Seer Stone at the tree. You know, the *tree,* by the east wall."

"Why in the hell would you do that?"

"Because Thanatos told me I needed to practice with the stupid Seer Stone in case it could somehow be used to fight Neferet."

"So you saw something that came after you?"

"Well, no. Yes. Kinda. I saw some creepy things inside something that looked like a tornado whirlpooling up from the middle of the tree. Stark, they were seriously the most disgusting things I've ever seen. And they smelled bad. Really, really bad. Actually, they almost made me puke. I did gag, which was when they noticed me, but before they could do anything this bright light zapped them." I paused, thinking through my panic. "Actually, the zapping light was kinda like Sookie's fairy-light-thing. Do you think there's any chance I'm a fairy?"

"No, Z. Focus. *True Blood* is fiction. This is the real world. What happened after the zapping light?"

"I don't know. I ran." I glanced around us and noticed that I'd run all the way along the inside of the wall and I was almost at the stables. "I ran a really long way."

"And?"

"And nothing. Except that you grabbed me. Goddess, I thought I was having a heart attack."

"So you were scared. That's it?"

I frowned at him again. His voice was kind, but his expression was strained, like he was trying to choose between shaking me, or kissing me. "Well," I said slowly. "Yeah, but I was *really* scared."

His grip on my shoulders turned into a giant, squashing bear hug. I felt his body relax. He let out a long breath that ended up being a chuckle. "You scared the bejezzus out of me, Z."

"Sorry," I mumbled against his chest, wrapping my arms around him again and squeezing him back. "Thanks for finding me and being totally ready to save me."

"You don't have to say sorry. I'm your Warrior—your Guardian—

it's my job to save you. Even though you're usually pretty good at saving yourself."

I leaned back so I could see his eyes. "I'm a job?"

His lips tilted up in his cocky, half grin. "Full time. Totally. No benefits and no days off, either."

"Seriously?"

"Okay, no." His cocky grin got wider. "I do remember getting some sick days when an arrow burned me and a few more when a crazy Scotsman cut me up. So, I take that back. I get benefits. They're just crappy ones."

"You're so fired!" I would've smacked him, but I didn't want to take my arms away from around his shoulders.

"You can't fire me. I signed up for life." Stark's smile faded from his lips, but remained in his eyes. "You're my Priestess, my Queen, *mo bann ri*. I'll never leave you. I'll always protect you. I love you, Zoey Redbird." He bent and kissed me so tenderly that I felt the truth of his commitment deep in my soul.

When his lips finally left mine I looked up at him. "I love you, too," I said. "And you know you don't have to be jealous of a dead guy, right?"

He touched my cheek. "Right. Sorry 'bout that last night."

"That's okay. And, um, speaking of—there's something you need to know."

"What?"

I took a big breath and blurted, "Last night at the end of the ritual I looked through the Seer Stone at Aurox and I saw Heath. That's why I didn't let you and Darius hurt him."

I felt the tension level in Stark's body shoot back up to the Danger! Red Alert! range.

"Is that why you were calling Heath in your sleep last night?" He sounded more hurt than pissed.

"No. Yes. I don't know! I was telling you the truth. I don't remember what I was dreaming, but it makes sense that Heath was on my mind after seeing him when I looked at Aurox."

"That bull thing is *not* Heath. How can you even think that?"

"It's not that I'm thinking it. It's what I *saw*."

"Zoey, look, there has to be an explanation for what you saw." He took a step back. My arms slid down from around his shoulders.

"That's why Thanatos wants me to practice looking through the Seer Stone, so I can figure out how it works." I felt cold and alone without his arms around me. "Stark, I'm sorry. I didn't *want* to see Heath in Aurox. I don't want to see or say or do anything that would hurt you. Ever." I was blinking hard, trying to keep from bursting into tears.

Stark ran his hand through his hair. "Z, please don't cry."

"I'm not crying," I said, and then hiccupped a little sob and back-handed a tear that had somehow escaped from my eye.

Stark reached into his jeans' pocket and pulled out a crumpled tissue. He stepped close to me again, and wiped the second tear that had followed the first escapee. Then he kissed me, softly, handed me the tissue, and pulled me back into his arms.

"Don't worry, Z. Heath and I made peace in the Otherworld. I'd be glad to see him again."

"Really?" I had to step out of his arms long enough to blow my nose.

"Well, yeah. Glad to see him again, but not as glad for you to see him again." His honesty made both of us smile. "And I know you wouldn't hurt me on purpose. But, Z, that bull thing is *not* Heath."

"Stark, I knew Aurox had something to do with old magick from the first time I saw him. He made me feel weird as hell." I hated telling him, but he deserved nothing less than honesty from me.

"Of course he made you feel weird. He's a creature of Darkness! And, yeah, he's old magick. He was created by the nastiest kind of that shit when Neferet killed your mom as a sacrifice. I'd worry about you if he *didn't* make you feel weird."

I let out a deep breath. "Well, I guess that does make sense."

"Yeah, and I'll bet if we work on it together we can figure out why that stone showed you Heath last night." When I just chewed my lip he kept on, like he was reasoning aloud. "Think about it, Z. What all have you seen through the stone?"

"Well, on Skye I saw those old sprites—the elementals."

"Were they like the things you saw today?"

I shuddered. "No, not at all. The elementals were unearthly, mysterious, strange, but in a good way. What I saw today was grotesque and terrifying."

"Okay, except for just now at the tree, and last night at the ritual, has the Seer Stone shown you anything else since we've been back from Italy?"

I met his gaze. "Yes. You."

CHAPTER ELEVEN

Zoey

"Me? Z, you're not making any sense," Stark said.

"I know, I know. I'm sorry. It's just that it kinda felt like I was creeping on you when I did it because you were sleeping, and I only did it because it was back when you were having trouble sleeping, and it was actually mostly an accident, so I never said anything to you, and now it seems like I could have made the whole thing up," I finished in a rush.

"Zoey, I can listen in on your emotions. That's way more creeper-like than you peeking through a stone at me while I'm asleep. Plus, you're right. My sleep had been really jacked up. I don't blame you for checking me out with the stone. Just tell me what you saw."

"I saw a shadow over you. I remember thinking that it looked like a ghost Warrior. You opened your hand and the Guardian Sword appeared. Then the ghost-shadow guy grabbed it and it turned into a spear. I think it was bloody. It scared me, so I called spirit and chased the thing away. You woke up then and we uh . . ." My face felt hot. "Well, we made love and I forgot about it."

"Z, I like to think I'm good in bed and all, but even so, how the hell could you forget about seeing a ghost guy with a spear hanging out over me?"

"Seriously, Stark. Right after that we walked into what Stevie Rae called one hot mess of bullpoopie here at the House of Night. *I was busy.*" I crossed my arms and glared at him. "Wait, I didn't totally forget about it. I told Lenobia about the shadow guy."

"Great, so a professor knows but I didn't know."

"You do now."

"Well, what did Lenobia say about it?"

"Basically she told me to keep my eyes open here in the real world, versus gawking through the stone, which is what I did until last night when I saw Heath," I said.

"Look through it at me again."

"Now?"

"Now."

"Fine." I lifted the Seer Stone, took a deep breath, and peeked through it at him.

"Well? How do I look?"

"Grumpy."

"And?"

"Annoying."

"Nothing else?"

"Maybe kinda cute. But only maybe." I put the stone back under my shirt. "Totally just you. I didn't think I'd see anything. The stone wasn't hot."

"It gets hot?"

"Yep, sometimes." I chewed my lip and thought about it. "That's actually why I looked through it at you the first time. It got warm."

"Was it warm when you looked through it at Aurox?" he asked.

"No, but I knew I had to look through it. It was like I was compelled to," I said. "And it'd been warm before when Aurox was around."

"Fucking old magick. It's a pain in the ass," he said. "You'd think there'd at least be a playbook that had the rules for it listed somewhere, but no."

"I should call Sgiach. I mean, she gave me the stone. She deals with old magick. Maybe she'd be able to give me some guidelines."

He gave a little snort. "Didn't you ask her for that on Skye?"

"Yeah," I said.

"If I remember right, she didn't give you any real answers."

"You remember right. She did say that she thought the only old magick left on this earth was on Skye."

"She was wrong," Stark said.

"Yeah, definitely."

"You know what I think?"

Stark moved close to me again and put his arm around me. I rested my head against his shoulder and slid my arm around his waist and said, "That I'm Crazy Town?"

He grinned and kissed my forehead. "You're not Crazy Town. You're Crazy Metropolis. Hell, Z, you're Crazy Universe. But I like me some crazy."

"Now you sound like Stevie Rae." We smiled at each other, relaxing back into the foundation of our relationship—our commitment to each other—our belief in each other. "So, what were you going to say? What do you think?"

"I think that I'm done with deciding what I'm going to do because of what other people say. Especially adult other people who hand us mysteries, or drop us off in the middle of a shitstorm without giving us any real help," he said.

"Yeah, I get that. I've been feeling like that since Neferet lost her mind and I was the only one who knew it."

"Okay, so, let's figure this old magick stuff out ourselves. Z, you have an affinity for all five elements. No one can even remember the last time that happened. You're a different kind of fledgling—a different kind of High Priestess. You're a young warrior queen, and I'm your Guardian. Together there's nothing we can't take on." His cocky smile was back. "We took on the Otherworld and won."

"Yeah, except for the part about you dying and all," I reminded him.

"Just a small detail. It turned out okay."

I squeezed him, pressing myself against his strong side. "It turned out better than okay." He kissed me and I drew strength from his taste and his touch and his love. Maybe Stark was right. Maybe there wasn't anything we couldn't take on together. I sighed happily and snuggled against him.

"Let's go to the stables." Stark jerked his chin forward at the long building not far from us.

"I guess we should. I'll bet Erin's there. Even from here I can see it looks soggy."

"Actually, I haven't seen Erin in a while." Stark shrugged. "Maybe that's because the stables are really better off than you'd think. Most of the damage was from smoke. All that really burned was a bunch of hay and bedding and one stall."

"Persephone's fine, right?" Twining my fingers through his, we started walking slowly toward the stables, letting our arms and hips brush against each other.

"She's good. All of the horses are good. Well, except Bonnie. She's acting pretty nervous. Lenobia put her in a turn-out with Mujaji to settle her down. Apparently the two of them get along. Which reminds me, a bunch of fledglings said they saw Lenobia kissing Travis before the EMTs took him away," Stark said.

My eyes got giant. "Seriously? I can't wait till Aphrodite and Stevie Rae hear that!"

Stark chuckled. "Stevie Rae already has—via Kramisha, who is telling everybody." He bumped my shoulder with his. "All that time you spent at the tree made you miss out on some good gossip."

I looked up at him, confused. "All that time? I was only there for, like, a minute."

Stark stopped. "What time do you think it is right now?"

I shrugged. "I dunno. I'd have to look at my phone, but we got to Thanatos's room at seven-thirty. We were probably there half an hour or less, so it couldn't be any later than eight-thirty-ish."

"Zoey, it's eleven-thirty. We only have time to meet everyone at the stables and then go to Dragon's funeral pyre."

All of my insides went cold. "Stark, I lost more than three hours!"

"Yeah, you did, and I don't like it. Give me your word that you won't look through that damn stone again unless I'm with you."

I was freaked enough not to argue with him. "You got it. I'm totally giving you my word. I'm not looking through that thing unless you're with me."

His shoulders relaxed and he gave me a quick kiss. "Thanks, Z.

Something that can steal time from you is Not Good." He gave the last two words special emphasis. "I know Sgiach said old magick could be good or bad, but I don't care which one it is if it takes without asking."

"I know. I know." We'd starting walking again, but I kept a tight hold on his hand. "No wonder I felt like I was going to have a heart attack. I'd been stuck standing there, staring at those disgusting, smelly things for *hours*." I shuddered.

"It's okay. We're going to figure out this old magick crap. I'm *not* going to let anything happen to you."

Stark squeezed my hand and I squeezed back. I wanted to believe him. I did believe *in* him—his strength and his love. It was the other side that I was worried about. The unknown side that Darkness sat squarely in the middle of. It kept creeping up and picking off people I loved.

I was thinking about how much I didn't want to lose anyone else when the stupid Seer Stone began heating up. I stopped, pulling Stark to a halt with me. I pressed my hand over the spot it was warming on my chest.

"What?" he asked.

"It's getting hot."

"Why?"

"Stark, I have no clue. You're supposed to be helping me figure that out, remember?"

"Okay, right. Yeah. We can do this." He started looking around. "So, let's figure it out."

"How?"

"Well, I'm thinking," he said.

I sighed and tried to think, too. We'd stopped under one of the big trees just outside the perimeter of the east side of the stables. I glanced up quickly, suddenly worried about lurking things with no eyes and sewn shut mouths. But there was nothing above us. Actually, it was really peaceful around us. All I could think of was that there was nothing to think of. Voices drifted to us from the stables and I could hear equipment and stuff running—like tractors and whatnot were being used to drag things away and clear up the debris. I heard the sound of another motor, this one coming from somewhere behind us and getting closer.

"That's weird," Stark said, looking back over my shoulder. "Taxis don't come here."

I followed his gaze and saw the beat-up, maroon-colored car with boxy black letters spelling TAXI on the side of it. Stark was right. It was super weird to see a taxi at the House of Night. Hell, Tulsa wasn't exactly known for its awesome taxi service. I mentally shrugged—the Midtown trolley was cooler anyway.

Then Lenobia stepped from the side entrance to the stables and practically ran to the car. She opened the back door and reached down to help guide the tall, bandaged cowboy out. The taxi sped away. Travis and Lenobia just stood there looking at each other.

My Seer Stone felt like it was going to burn a hole in my shirt. I pulled it out and held it away from my skin. I didn't say anything, though. Stark and I were too busy staring at Travis and Lenobia. They weren't real close to us, but still it felt like an invasion of their privacy to be gawking at them—even though we kept standing there gawking at them.

Then it hit me. I bumped Stark's arm and, keeping my voice low, said, "The stone got super hot as soon as Travis got out of the cab."

Stark looked from Travis and Lenobia to the stone and then to me. He put a firm hand on my shoulder and said, "Do it. Look through the stone at him. I've got you. I'm not going to let anything happen to you. If something tries to suck time from you I'm going to stop it."

I nodded and, like ripping off a Band-Aid in one quick pull, I lifted the Seer Stone, framing Travis and Lenobia within its circle.

It started like what happened at the tree, at first my vision of the two of them remained exactly the same. I watched Lenobia's hands fluttering nervously over Travis's bandaged hands. They looked like big white mittens, and I could see that the gauze wraps went up his forearms. Even from where we stood, his face looked abnormally red and shiny, like he'd gotten a bad sunburn and had put a bunch of aloe gel on it. But he didn't look like he was in pain. He was smiling. A lot. At Lenobia. I was getting ready to drop the Seer Stone and tell Stark that I was, indeed, Crazy Universe, when Travis bent and kissed Lenobia.

Everything changed then. There was a brightness that caused me to blink and when my sight cleared Travis was gone. In his place was a really hot, young, black guy. He had long hair that was pulled back in a low ponytail and shoulders so broad he looked like a linebacker. He was kissing Lenobia as if it were his last kiss in the world. And she was kissing him back—only it was a different Lenobia. She looked young, like she was only sixteen or so. She wrapped her arms around him like she'd never let go. All around them the air wavered and shimmered, like I was watching them over the top of a bubbling pot. Only instead of steam rising, I swear there were robin's egg blue spirits of happiness flitting around them. The happiness swelled within me and started bubbling, as if the pot was my head and the water my emotions. The ground fell away beneath my feet. I was floating in joy and love and blue bubbles.

Then my head got real dizzy and my stomach totally rebelled.

"Zoey! Stop! That's enough. Put! It! Down!"

I realized Stark was yelling at me and pulling at the Seer Stone. I felt the earth under my feet again. The blue bubbles evaporated and the joy went away, leaving me sick and drained and super shaky. I dropped the Seer Stone in time to bend over and puke beside the tree.

"You're okay. You're okay. I got you, Z. Everything's fine." Stark was holding my hair back while I continued to retch and heave up my guts.

"Stark? Zoey?" Lenobia was coming toward us, sounding breathless and worried. I could hear Travis close behind her asking what was wrong. I couldn't answer, though. I was too busy barfing.

"Zoey! Oh, Goddess, no!" Lenobia's concern skyrocketed when she realized I was puking.

"She's not rejecting the Change. She's okay," Stark reassured her while I took yet another tissue he offered me and wiped my mouth.

Finally done puking I leaned against the tree, embarrassed and grossed out. I seriously hate to puke.

"Then what is it? Why are you sick?"

With Stark on one side and Lenobia on the other, they guided me to a wrought iron bench that wasn't far away from the big tree (but far enough away so that we wouldn't smell my puke—eesh).

"Should I get someone?" Travis asked.

"No," I said quickly. "I'm fine. I'm better now that I'm sitting." I glanced at Stark questioningly. He nodded. "Whatever you saw, tell her. We trust her."

I looked from him to Lenobia. "And you trust Travis?"

She didn't hesitate. "With my life."

The big cowboy smiled and stepped closer to her. Their shoulders touched.

"Okay, what happened is my Seer Stone started heating up. When Travis got out of the car it got *really* hot. Stark was here, so we decided I should look through it at, well, you guys and see if that would help me start to understand what it shows me. So I looked through it at you two."

"Seer Stone?" Travis asked. He didn't sound freaked out at all. He just sounded curious.

"It's an old magick amulet given to Zoey by an ancient vampyre queen," Lenobia explained. "What did you see?"

"Well, nothing but you two until you kissed." I smiled sheepishly. "Sorry for watching you while you were kissing."

Travis smiled and put a bandaged arm around Lenobia's shoulders. "If I have my way about it, little missy, you'll be seein' a whole lot me of me kissin' this pretty girl."

I waited for Lenobia to strike him dead with her death-ray vision. Instead she looked adoringly up at him, pressed her hand to his chest over his heart, and rested her head, carefully, against his shoulder. Then she repeated, "What did you see when we were kissing?"

"Travis turned into a big black guy and you turned into a younger version of yourself. And all around you there were these wispy, bubbly, happy things that were blue. I'm pretty sure they were sprites of some sort." My eyes widened. "Actually, now that I think about it, the bubbles reminded me of the ocean. Huh. Weird. Anyway, I got all caught up in it, like it lifted me from the earth and put me in a happy blue ocean bubble. Sorry. I know that sounds crazy." I held my breath, waiting for Lenobia to laugh and Travis to scoff.

They didn't do either. Instead, Lenobia began to cry. I mean, seriously. She did the big, shoulder-shaking, snot bawl that I tend to be prone to. Travis just held her closer to him. He looked down at her as if she was a miracle personified. "I've known you before. That's why you feel like home to me."

Lenobia nodded. Then, through her tears, she told me, "Travis is my only human mate, my only love, returned to me after two hundred and twenty-four years. I vowed never to love another after him, and I have not. We met and fell in love on the ocean in a ship that carried us from France to New Orleans."

"So the Seer Stone showed me the truth?"

"Yes, Zoey. It absolutely did," Lenobia said before she turned her face into Travis's chest and wept while he held her, releasing two centuries of waiting and loss and pain.

I stood and took Stark's hand again, pulling him away so that the two of them could be alone. As we walked into the stables he said, "This does not mean Aurox is Heath come back to you. You know that, right?"

Stevie Rae saved me by rushing up and gushing, "Ohmy*goodness!* Where have you been? I can't wait to tell you 'bout Lenobia and Travis."

"Been there. Done that," Stark said. "Where are Aphrodite and Darius?"

"They're already in front of Nyx's Temple at the funeral pyre," Stevie Rae said. "We're meeting them there real soon."

"I'll go find Erin and Shaunee and Damien. We need to get going."

"What's up with him?" Stevie Rae asked, watching Stark stride away.

"Heath may really be inside Aurox," I said.

Stevie Rae echoed my thoughts exactly by saying, "Ah, hell!"

CHAPTER TWELVE

Kalona

Being on the side of Light wasn't as interesting as he remembered. Truth be told, Kalona was bored. Yes, he understood why Thanatos had told him to stay in the background and not draw attention to himself until after Dragon's funeral. It was then that she was going to announce to the school that he was her new Warrior, and would take the position of Sword Master and Leader of the Sons of Erebus at the Tulsa House of Night. Until then his presence would be confusing, if not insulting to the other Warriors.

The problem was Kalona had never minded being insulting. He was a powerful immortal. Why should he be bothered by the inconsequential feelings of others?

Because those I find most inconsequential sometimes surprise me: Heath, Stark, Dragon, Aurox, Rephaim. The last name in his mental list startled him. Rephaim had seemed inconsequential to him at one time, but he'd been wrong. Kalona had realized he loved his son—needed his son.

What else had he been wrong about?

Probably quite a lot of things.

The thought depressed him.

He paced back and forth along the darkest, most shadowy side of Nyx's Temple. There he was within hearing distance of Dragon's pyre, so he could come when Thanatos called, but he was also out of sight.

Being told what to do annoyed him. It had always annoyed him.

And there was this fledgling who had an affinity for fire, Shaunee.

She seemed to have the ability to prod him, to make him consider things he was unused to spending his time considering.

She'd done it before. He'd meant to manipulate her—to get information about Rephaim and the Red One. What had happened was that she had gifted him with something ridiculously mundane and simple: a cell phone. That small gift had saved his son's life.

Now she'd made him think about all those eons he'd spent apart from Nyx.

"No!" he spoke the word aloud, causing the little grove of redbuds that had been planted on the west side of Nyx's Temple to shake as if a storm threatened them. Kalona focused his thoughts and quieted his temper. "No," he repeated using a voice that was no longer filled with otherworldly power. "I will not think of the centuries I have spent apart from her. I will not think of her at all."

Laughter danced around him, causing the redbud grove to shimmer, shift, and then burst into full bloom as if the summer sun had suddenly beamed down upon them. Kalona clenched his fists and looked up.

He was sitting on the stone eaves of the temple. There was little light on that side of the building, which was why Thanatos had commanded he wait there, but Erebus was a light unto himself.

Erebus—his brother—Nyx's immortal Consort. The one being in this universe who was most like him, and the one being in this universe Kalona hated even more than he hated himself. Here! In the mortal realm after all these eons? *Why?*

Kalona hid his shock with disdain. "You are shorter than I remembered."

Erebus smiled. "Good to see you, too, brother."

"As usual, you put words in my mouth."

"I apologize. I do not need to. Not when your own words are so interesting. *I will not think of her at all.*" Not only was Erebus almost a mirror image of Kalona, he also mimicked his brother's voice perfectly.

"I was speaking of Neferet." Kalona quickly collected his thoughts and lied easily. It had been eons, but he used to be good at lying to Erebus. Kalona found he still had the knack.

"I doubt you not, brother." Erebus leaned forward, spread his golden wings, and floated gracefully to the ground before Kalona. "You see, *that* is exactly why I made this little visit."

"You came to the earthly realm because I was Neferet's lover?" Kalona crossed his arms over his broad chest and met his brother's amber gaze.

"No, I came because you are a liar and a thief. The rape of the last of Neferet's goodness is just one of your many crimes," Erebus said. He, too, crossed his arms over his chest.

Kalona laughed. "You have not been spying well enough if you believe rape had anything to do with what Neferet and I shared. She was more than willing, more than ready for my body."

"I was not speaking of her body!" Erebus's voice had risen and Kalona could hear the sound of vampyres calling, questioning what was happening over by Nyx's Temple.

"As usual, brother, you have appeared to cause problems for me. I was supposed to remain in the shadows, unseen and waiting to be summoned. Though, as I consider more fully, it will be amusing to watch you deal with mortal discovery. A quick word of advice—even vampyres tend to overreact when meeting a god."

Erebus didn't hesitate. He lifted both hands and commanded, "Conceal us!"

There was a rush of wind and a feeling of lightness that Kalona found so familiar, so bittersweet, that only two responses came to his mind—anger or despair. He would not allow Erebus to see his despair.

"You defy Nyx? She has proclaimed that I may not enter the Otherworld. How dare you take me here!" Kalona's night-colored wings were fully extended and he tensed, ready to attack his brother.

"You always play the impetuous fool, brother. I would never go against my Consort's proclamations. I did not bring you to the Otherworld. I only brought a piece of the Otherworld to you to shield us, if only for a few moments, from mortal eyes." Erebus smiled again. This time he did not dim the beauty of his expression. Sunlight glowed from his body. His wings glistened with feathers of gold. His skin was perfect as if he had been fashioned from the rays of the sun.

He had been, Kalona thought with disgust. *He had been fashioned when the sky kissed the sun. Just as I had been fashioned when the sky kissed the moon. The sky, like most immortals, is a fickle bastard who took as he pleased and then paid no attention to the offspring he left behind.*

"How does it feel? Better than when you snuck in, chasing after that little fledgling, Zoey Redbird. Then you were only spirit. You could not feel the magick of Nyx's realm against your skin. And you always were so impressed by anything you could touch, could physically claim as your own."

Good, Kalona thought, *he becomes angry. That will cause his perfection to blur.*

It was Kalona's turn to smile. The light he turned on his brother was not the hot, garish light of the sun. It was the cool, silver luminescence of the moon. "Still jealous that I touched her after all this time? You do remember Nyx is a goddess, do you not? She could not be touched had it not been her will, her desire, to be stroked, caressed, loved by—"

"I did not come here to speak of my Consort!" The words exploded in flashes of golden heat around Kalona.

"Such a display of godly temper!" Kalona chuckled sarcastically. "And they named you the good one. If only the lackeys that choose to remain in the Otherworld could see you now."

"It is not that they named me the good one. They named you the usurper!" Erebus hurled the words at his brother.

"Truly? Ask again. I believe, after eons of careful consideration, they would name me the one who refused to share her," Kalona said.

"She chose me." Erebus's voice was low; his fists were clenched at his sides.

"Did she? My memory differs."

"You betrayed her!" Erebus shouted.

Kalona ignored his brother's temper tantrum. He had witnessed them before. Instead he spoke with the coldness of the moon's surface. "Why did you come? Say what you have to say and then be gone. The mortal world is not much of a realm, but it is mine. I will not share it with you, just as I would not share her with you."

"I come to warn you. We heard your oath in the Otherworld. We know you have pledged to be Death's Warrior and to become Sword Master of this school."

"And Leader of the Sons of Erebus," Kalona added. "Do not forget the rest of my title."

"I could never forget that you intended to blaspheme my children."

"Children? Are you mating with humans now and producing males that grow up to be vampyre Warriors? That is fascinating, especially as I was judged so harshly for creating my sons."

"Walk away." Erebus's golden eyes began to glow. "Leave this place and stop meddling in the lives of Nyx's vampyres and in the lives of the honorable Warriors who have pledged themselves to my service."

"But are you not meddling by commanding me away? I am surprised Nyx allowed it."

"My Consort does not know I am here. I came only because you are, again, causing her turmoil. I live to keep turmoil from her. That is the only reason I am here," Erebus said.

"You live to lick her feet and you are, as always, jealous of me." Kalona couldn't help his surge of joy at what Erebus's words had revealed, *I can still make Nyx feel! The Goddess watches me!* The immortal reined in his emotions. He must hide his joy from Erebus. When he spoke again, his voice was emotionless. "Know this—I did not swear into your service. I am sworn into the service of a High Priestess who personifies Death through her Goddess-given affinity. All your visit has done is to give me cause to make a clear distinction between those Warriors who call themselves your sons, and those who do not. I will not burden your *sons* with my leadership."

"Then you will leave this House of Night," Erebus said.

"No. But you will. Bear this message to Nyx for me: Death does not differentiate between those who follow her and those who follow other gods. Death comes to all mortals. I do not need your permission, or the Goddess's, to serve Death. Now, begone, brother. I have a funeral to attend." Kalona brought his arms forward and slapped his palms together, causing a blast of frigid silver light to shockwave around him, shattering the small Otherworld bubble his brother had created and hurling Erebus up, away, and into the sky.

When the light around him faded, Kalona's feet once more touched the earth and he was, again, standing beside Nyx's Temple.

Aphrodite rushed around the corner. Stopped. And stared at him.

"Am I summoned?" he asked.

She blinked and rubbed her eyes, as if she was having trouble clearing her vision. "Were you messing around with a flashlight over here?"

"I own no flashlight. Am I summoned?" he repeated.

"Almost. Some moron, meaning Kramisha because she was in charge of candle collection, forgot the spirit candle. I need to grab one from Nyx's Temple. You're supposed to follow me back to Dragon's pyre. Thanatos will finish the circle, say some nice stuff about Dragon, and then introduce you."

Feeling oddly uncomfortable under the gaze of the strange, abrasive human Nyx had, for reasons unfathomable to almost everyone, Chosen as her Prophetess, Kalona grunted a wordless response, and turned to open the side door to the temple.

It would not open.

Kalona tried again.

He strained, using all of his vast immortal strength.

It absolutely would not open.

It was then that he noticed the wooden door had disappeared. The handle protruded from thick, solid stone. There was no entryway. Nothing.

Suddenly Aphrodite was pushing him aside. She grabbed the handle, pulled it, and the stone faded, becoming a wooden door again, which opened easily for her. She glanced up at him before she stepped over the threshold of the Goddess's temple. "You are so fucking weird." She tossed her hair and went inside.

The door closed behind her. Kalona pressed his hand against it and, under his palm, it shivered and turned from welcoming wood to stone.

He backed away, feeling a horrible sinking within him.

It was only a few minutes later that Aphrodite emerged through a completely normal-looking door. She was holding a thick purple pillar candle and as she strode past him she said, "Well, come on. Thanatos wants you to stand at the edge of the circle and try not to look conspicuous. Though, you know, that would be a lot easier if you wore more clothes."

Kalona followed her, trying to ignore the empty place inside him. He was exactly what Erebus had named him, impetuous fool and usurper. If Nyx had been watching him, it was with nothing except disdain. She denied him everything—entrance to the Otherworld, entrance to her Temple, entrance to her heart . . .

Centuries should have lessened his pain, but Kalona was beginning to understand that the opposite was true.

Aurox

Nyx, if you are, indeed, a forgiving goddess, please help me . . . please . . .

Aurox didn't flee from his earthen hiding place. Instead he repeated that one sentence, that one prayer, over and over. Perhaps Nyx rewarded diligence. At least he could offer the Goddess that.

It was during the litany of his silent prayer that the magick began to swirl around him. At first Aurox's spirit leapt. *Nyx heard me!* It only took moments to realize how wrong he'd been. The creatures that materialized, oozing from the cool, dank air around him, could not be in the service of a forgiving goddess.

Aurox cringed away from them. Their stench was almost unbearable. Their sightless faces horrible to gaze upon. His heartbeat increased. Fear shivered through him and the beast inside him stirred. Had these things been sent to him as judgment for the deeds he had committed in Neferet's service? Aurox used his own fear and began feeding the beast within him. He did not want it to awaken, but he would fight before he succumbed to the swirling mass of malevolence that threatened to envelop him.

Yet, Aurox was not enveloped. Slowly, the creatures climbed upward, riding in a magickal whirlpool. The higher they arose from the pit, the faster they moved. It seemed as if they had been summoned and were gradually awakening to a soundless call.

Aurox quieted his fear and the beast within him subsided. They did not want him. They paid him no attention whatsoever. The tail of the cylinder was trailing a black, fetid mist. Not sure what compelled him, Aurox reached out and brushed his hand through it.

His hand became the mist, like they were formed of the same substance. The whirlpool felt like nothing, yet it appeared to have dissolved Aurox's flesh. Wide-eyed, he tried to pull his hand free, but it was gone. He had no hand, and then a shudder went through him as the mist began to absorb his flesh. Helplessly, Aurox watched his forearm disappear, then his bicep, then his shoulder. He tried to awaken the beast—to tap into the power that slumbered within him, but the mist buffered his feelings. It numbed him as it drew him. When it absorbed his head Aurox became the mist. He felt nothing except a vast longing—an unfulfilled seeking—an unrelenting need. For what? Aurox could not tell. All he knew was that the Darkness had engulfed him and was carrying him on a tide of despair.

There must be more to me than this! he thought frantically. *I have to be more than mist and longing, darkness and a beast!* But it seemed he was no more than those things. Despair overwhelmed him as he realized the truth. He was all of those things and none of those things. Aurox was nothing . . . nothing at all . . .

Aurox thought the retching sound might be his own. Somewhere, somehow, his body must still be his and it was revolted by what was happening. Then he saw her.

Zoey was there. She held the white stone in front of her. Just like she had the night before, at the ritual where he had tried to make a choice—tried to do the right thing.

He felt the mist shift. It, too, saw Zoey.

It was going to absorb her.

No! His spirit cried deep within him. *No!* Aurox's mind echoed that cry. Instead of despair, he began to feel something else as he watched Zoey. He felt her fear and her strength. Her resolve and her weakness. And Aurox realized something that surprised him. Zoey felt just as unsure about herself and her place in the world around her as he did. She worried about not having the courage to do the right things. She questioned her decisions and was ashamed of her mistakes. Once in a while even Zoey Redbird, gifted fledgling touched by her Goddess, felt like a failure and considered giving up.

Just as he did.

Compassion and understanding flowed through Aurox, and as it did he felt a surge of white hot power. In a blinding flash, he dropped from the center of the disintegrating whirlpool, landing firmly in his reformed body, gasping for fresh air and trembling all over.

He did not rest there long. Still shaking and weak, Aurox found hand and footholds in the gnarled maze of broken roots. Slowly, he pulled himself up to the lip of the pit. It took a very long time. When he finally reached the top, he hesitated, listening hard.

He heard nothing but the wind.

Aurox lifted himself from the ground, using the broken trunk as concealment. Zoey was gone. He studied the area around him and his eyes were immediately drawn to a huge mound of timbers and planks, topped by a figure wrapped in a shroud. Even though it was encircled by what appeared to be the entire House of Night, Aurox had no trouble recognizing what he was seeing. *It is Dragon Lankford's pyre,* was his first thought. *I killed him,* was his second. Like the despair in the magickal mist, the funeral drew him.

It was not difficult to get close to the circle of fledglings and vampyres. Sons of Erebus Warriors were heavily and obviously armed, but everyone's attention was focused within the circle and on the pyre at its center.

Aurox moved stealthily, using the large old oaks and the shadows beneath them as cover until he was close enough to make out the words Thanatos was saying. Then he gathered himself and leaped. Grasping a low-hanging limb, Aurox climbed up and out, which was where he crouched, having an unimpeded view of the macabre spectacle.

Thanatos had just finished the casting of the circle. Aurox could see that four of the vampyre professors were holding candles and representing each of the elements. He expected to see Zoey in the center of the circle, near the pyre, and was surprised instead to see that Thanatos was holding the purple spirit candle in one hand, and a large torch in the other.

Where was Zoey? Had the creatures in the mist captured her? Was that what had caused their dissipation? Frantically, he searched the circle. When he found her standing beside Stark, surrounded by her circle friends she looked sad, but unwounded. She was watching Thanatos attentively. There appeared to be nothing wrong with her except that she mourned the loss of the Sword Master. Aurox became so weak with relief that he almost lost his perch in the tree.

Aurox stared at her. She had begun this internal conflict he felt. Why? He was almost as baffled by her as he was by the feelings she had awakened within him.

He shifted his attention to Thanatos. She was walking gracefully around the circumference of the circle, speaking in a voice that calmed even his frayed nerves.

"Our Sword Master died as he lived—a Warrior, true to his oath, true to his House of Night, and true to his Goddess. There is another truth here that must needs be told. Though we mourn his loss, we acknowledge that he was only a shell of himself without his mate, the gentle Anastasia." Aurox glanced at Rephaim. He knew that, as a Raven Mocker, he had killed Anastasia Lankford. What an irony it was that the Sword Master had died to protect him. Greater irony yet that the boy's face was awash in tears, and that he openly wept over Dragon's death.

"Death was kind to Dragon Lankford. Not only did she allow

him to die a Warrior, but she was a conduit to the Goddess. Nyx has reunited Bryan Dragon Lankford and his beloved, as well as the bright, shining spirits of their two feline familiars, Shadowfax and Guinevere."

Their cats died, too? I do not remember any cats being at the ritual. Confused, Aurox studied the funeral pyre. Yes, now that he was paying closer attention, he could see two small bundles, shrouded with Dragon, nestled close to either side of the fallen Warrior.

Thanatos had paused in her walk around the circle to stand directly in front of Zoey. The High Priestess smiled at the fledgling. "Tell us, Zoey Redbird, as you have actually entered the Otherworld and returned, what is the one constant there?"

"Love," Zoey said without hesitation. "Always love."

"And you, James Stark? What did you find in the Otherworld?" Thanatos asked the young Warrior, who stood with his arm around Zoey's shoulders.

"Love," Stark repeated in a strong, steady voice. "Always love."

"That is a truth." Thanatos continued walking around the circle. "I can also tell you that my closeness with Death has shown me glimpses of the Otherworld. What I have been allowed to see has taught me that though love remains with us when we pass from this realm to another, it cannot exist eternally without compassion, just as Light cannot exist without hope, and Darkness cannot exist without hatred. So with that truth spoken and acknowledged, I would ask you to open your hearts and welcome our new Sword Master and Leader of the Sons of Erebus Warriors, my Oath Bound Warrior, Kalona!"

Aurox mirrored the surprise he saw in many of the faces below him as Kalona, the winged immortal he knew had long sided with Darkness, strode into the circle and approached Thanatos. He fisted his hand over his heart and bowed respectfully. Then he lifted his head and his deep voice filled the air.

"I have sworn to be Death's Warrior, and that I will be. I have sworn to be the Sword Master of this House of Night, and that I will be. But I will not attempt to fill Dragon Lankford's place as Leader of the Sons of Erebus Warriors." Aurox saw that Thanatos was watching him carefully, though her expression seemed pleased. The Warriors that were spaced all around the circle shifted, as if they were unsure of what to think of the immortal's proclamation.

"I will serve as Death's Warrior," Kalona repeated. He was speaking to Thanatos, though his voice carried around the circle and through the crowd that had gathered for the funeral. "I will protect you and this school. But I will not take a title that links me with Erebus."

"I was part of the High Council when you claimed to be Erebus come to earth," Thanatos said. "What say you about that?"

"I claimed no such title. That was Neferet's doing. She strives to be a goddess, and that means she needs an immortal Consort, so she named me Erebus come to earth. I rejected that role when I rejected Neferet."

Whispers soughed through the circle like wind through trees. Thanatos lifted the torch she still held. "Silence!" Voices stilled, but shock and disbelief remained. "Kalona speaks the truth about Neferet. Dragon was killed by her creature, Aurox. He was not a gift from Nyx. Last night, during the reveal ritual at Sylvia Redbird's lavender farm, the earth showed us the terrible truth. Aurox was created by Darkness through the sacrifice of Zoey Redbird's mother. He is a Vessel under the thrall of Neferet. Darkness continues to control him through sacrifice most bloody." She pointed her torch at the three bodies atop the pyre. "I have evidence that Shadowfax's life was taken by Neferet so that Darkness maintained dominion over Aurox. For Anastasia's little Guinevere, that death was one too many. Grief stopped her heart and she willingly followed Shadowfax to the Otherworld to be reunited with those they both loved best."

Aurox's body went still. He could not even find his breath. He felt as if Thanatos had just disemboweled him. He wanted to shout: *It is not true! IT IS NOT TRUE!* but her words continued to bludgeon him.

"Zoey, Damien, Shaunee, Erin, Stevie Rae, Darius, Stark, Rephaim, and I!" she shouted each name. "We bore witness to Neferet's dark deeds. Dragon Lankford died so that our witness could be made public. Now we must take up the battle that felled our Sword Master. Kalona, I am pleased to hear your confession. You attempted to usurp Erebus, though it was only on earth. It is clear to the High Council that you were goaded by the machinations of Neferet. I do accept you as Death's Warrior and the school's protector, but you may not lead the Warriors who have been sworn as his sons. That would be disrespectful to the Goddess as well as her Consort." Aurox saw the immortal's eyes flash with momentary anger, but he bowed his head to Thanatos and fisted his hand over his heart before saying, "So mote it be, High Priestess." Then he backed to the edge of the circle, where anyone near him took small, but conspicuous half steps away.

Thanatos called for Shaunee to invoke fire and light the funeral pyre. As the pillar of fire engulfed Dragon Lankford's pyre, Aurox dropped from the tree and, unseen by anyone, stumbled back to the shattered oak and disappeared belowground where, alone, he sobbed his despair and self-hatred into the torn earth.

CHAPTER THIRTEEN

Zoey

"Is everything okay, Z?" Stark spoke low next to my ear as my circle group and I gathered near the entrance to the school lobby. Thanatos had asked us to wait for her to finish speaking with the professors and Warriors, and then she'd join us for the press conference.

"I'm sad about Dragon," I whispered back to him.

"I didn't mean that." He kept his voice soft, so that I was the only one who could hear him. "I meant is everything okay with the stone? I saw you touch it during the funeral."

"I thought I felt it heat up for a little while, but then it went away. It was probably just because we were standing so close to the pyre. Speaking of"—I raised my voice and said to Shaunee—"good job with the fire part of Dragon's funeral. I know it's not easy to keep lighting funeral pyres, but you help. You make it get over with faster."

"Thanks. Yeah, we're all sick of funerals. At least before this one we got to watch Dragon enter the Otherworld, but seeing the cats up there on the pyre with him made it especially sad." She wiped her eyes and I wondered how she (or anyone) could bawl and still look pretty. "Actually, that reminds me," Shaunee continued, turning so she faced Erin, who was hanging at the tail end of our group, gawking at the kids still by the pyre like she was looking for someone. "Erin, is it cool with you if I move Beelzebub's litter box and stuff to my room? He's been sleeping there most days."

Erin glanced at Shaunee, shrugged, and said, "Yeah, whatever. That litter box smells like shit anyway."

"Erin, cats don't like to use a dirty litter box. You have to clean it every day," Damien informed her with a frown.

Erin gave a sarcastic little snort. "Not anymore I don't have to." Then she returned to checking out the other kids.

I noticed she wasn't crying. I thought about it and realized she hadn't cried once during the entire funeral. At first this whole Twin breakup had seemed to freak Shaunee out the most, but as time passed I was starting to notice that Erin was not acting like herself. Although, I suppose that's normal, since acting like herself used to mean acting just like Shaunee, who was now acting a lot more mature and nicer. I made a mental note to find time to talk to Erin, to make sure she was okay.

"Dang, I wish Thanatos hadn't told Rephaim to wait with the rest of the kids on the bus. He was super upset at the funeral. I hate leaving him alone like that," Stevie Rae said, coming up beside me.

"He's not alone. He's with all the other red fledglings. I watched them walk over to the bus. Kramisha was talking to him about poetry being a way to vent emotions."

"Kramisha will baffle birdboy with her poetry crap. Blah . . . blah . . . rhyming iambic blah," Aphrodite said. "Plus, even you have to understand that letting the human public know about his little 'bird issue'"—she air quoted—"isn't a good idea."

"Hey there, uh, sorry to interrupt, but I'm looking for the school lobby."

As a group, we turned and gawked at the human who was walking toward us down the sidewalk that led from the main parking lot. Behind him trailed a guy holding a camera and a big bag of stuff crammed into a black bag slung over his shoulder and a long gray mic-thing dangling over his head.

Predictably, Damien was the first of us to pull himself together. I mean, Damien really should be crowned Miss Congeniality for the Tulsa House of Night.

"You are absolutely at the correct spot. Well done, you, for finding us!" Damien's smile was so warm that I watched the tense set of the human's shoulders relax. Then he actually held out his hand and said, "Excellent. I'm Adam Paluka, from Tulsa's Fox News 23. I'm here to interview your High Priestess and, I'm guessing, some of you as well."

"Nice to meet you, Mr. Paluka. I'm Damien," Damien said, taking his hand. Then he giggled a little and added, "Oooh, strong grip!"

The reporter grinned. "I aim to please. And call me Adam. Mr. Paluka is my dad."

Damien giggled again. Adam chuckled. They made major eye contact. Stevie Rae nudged me and we shared a *Look*. Adam was cute, seriously cute in a young, up-and-coming metro-sexual guy way. Dark hair, dark eyes, good teeth, really good shoes, and a man satchel, which Stevie Rae and I spotted together. Our eyes telegraphed to each other *potential boyfriend for Damien!*

"Hi there, Adam, I'm Stevie Rae." She stuck out her hand. As he took it she said, "You don't have a girlfriend, do ya?"

His straight-toothed smile faltered, but only a little. "No. I don't, um. No. I absolutely do not have a girlfriend." Then his eyes took in Stevie Rae's red tattoo Mark. "So, you're one of the new kind of vampyres your ex-High Priestess has been talking about."

Stevie Rae gave him a big smile. "Yep, I'm the first Red Vampyre High Priestess. Cool, isn't it?"

"Your tattoo is certainly pretty," Adam said, looking more curious than uncomfortable.

"Thank you!" Stevie Rae gushed. "This here's James Stark. He's the first Red Vampyre Warrior. His tattoo is awesome, too."

Stark put his hand out. "Nice to meet ya. And you don't have to tell me my tattoo is pretty."

Adam's face lost some of its color, but he shook Stark's hand. His smile seemed genuine—nervous, but genuine.

"Hi," I chimed in, shaking his hand. "I'm Zoey."

Adam's gaze quickly shifted from the full tattoo on my face, to the V-neck of my T-shirt and the glimpse of tattooing across my collarbone, down to my palm, which was also covered in the same filigree tattoo. "I didn't know vampyres were getting additional tattooing done. Is your artist here in Tulsa?"

I grinned. "Yeah, sometimes. But mostly she's in the Otherworld." I could see he was trying to process what I'd just said, so I took the opportunity to blurt, "Hey, you said you don't have a girlfriend, but how about a boyfriend?"

"Um, no, I don't have a boyfriend, either. At least not currently." Adam glanced at Damien, who met his gaze.

Success! was what I was thinking when Aphrodite snorted and said, "Oh, for shit's sake, this isn't *The Bachelorette*. I'm Aphrodite LaFont. Yes, the mayor is my father. Whoop-dee-fucking-do." She wrapped her arm through Darius's. "And this is my Warrior, Darius."

Adam's cute brow went up as he took in Aphrodite's school sweater, with the sixth former insignia of the three Fates sewn over her left breast pocket. "Are human beings allowed to attend the House of Night?"

"Aphrodite is a Prophetess of Nyx, a fact proven by the bond she has with Darius, who is a Son of Erebus Warrior and Oath Sworn as her protector." Thanatos was speaking from the shadows as she walked gracefully toward us. I thought her timing was excellent, as was her entrance. She looked tall and powerful, ageless and classically beautiful. Her voice was pleasant and informative, as if she lectured human reporters every day. "I know the inner workings of our society are not common knowledge, but I believe most humans are aware that a Warrior cannot bond to a human with an oath of protection."

"Actually, even though this interview is last minute, I did have time to do some general research, and that is one fact I did uncover."

"That Aphrodite is a Prophetess of Nyx, and is attending school here, as are several red fledglings and vampyres, will be one of the topics of our interview. Although it appears that interview has already begun." Thanatos emerged fully from the shadows, nodding toward the cameraman who was holding up the camera and definitely had been filming us, even though none of us had been paying any attention to him. "I am Thanatos, the new High Priestess of the Tulsa House of Night. Merry meet, Adam Paluka. You are welcome at our school."

"M-merry meet." Adam only bobbled a little. "I didn't mean to offend by filming early."

Thanatos smiled. "You did not offend us. We invited you here. I am pleased that the interview has begun without formalities. Shall we remain out here, under the beautiful Tulsa night sky, and continue?"

"Sure," Adam said after a nod from the cameraman. "The gaslights are actually good lighting. If you give us a sec, we can use a boom mic and get as many of your group on tape as you'd like."

"That sounds lovely. Zoey, Aphrodite, Stevie Rae, Stark, and Damien, please stay for the interview. Darius, would you, Shaunee and Erin, be sure the gathered fledglings have returned to their dormitories? Tonight has been a difficult one for our school." Darius bowed to Aphrodite and Thanatos, then he and Shaunee walked off together. Erin headed in the opposite direction.

"You said tonight has been difficult for your school. What do you mean by that?"

"With your pulse on the news, I am sure you are aware we recently had a fire on campus," Thanatos said.

"We did get that report at Fox. Something about your stables?" he prompted.

"Indeed, an unfortunate, though not entirely surprising accident." Thanatos gestured at the large copper lamps that hung in decorative beauty around us. "Gaslight and candlelight are kinder on our eyes than electric bulbs. As you already observed, it has a lovely ambiance, but it is living flame and sometimes volatile. A lantern was left lit and unattended in the barn. It was a windy evening. A gust blew the lantern over on a hay bale, setting the stables afire."

"I hope no one was hurt." I thought Adam looked authentically concerned.

"Our Horse Mistress and a fledgling had some minor smoke inhalation damage, and the human in our employ as a stable manager suffered burns, mostly on his hands. He will recover fully. I must tell you for the record that our Travis Foster is something of a hero. He made sure all of the horses escaped."

"Travis Foster is a human?"

"Completely, and a valued employee and friend."

"Fascinating," Adam said. His gaze shifted around. I could see when his eyes lit on the distant pyre, which had smoldered down to an orange glow. "Please correct me if I'm wrong, but I don't think that burning pile is part of the stables. During my research I read that vampyres burn their dead on pyres. Have I chosen a bad time for this interview?" He asked the question in a considerate tone of voice, but I could see the curiosity that was bright in his eyes.

"You are not wrong. That is the remnants of a funeral pyre. We have, indeed, suffered a grave loss at the House of Night that had nothing to do with the stable fire. Our Sword Master, Dragon Lankford, was recently killed in a tragic accident on a lavender farm that adjoins the national preserve known as the Tall Grass Prairie." I closed my mouth, wondering how the heck Thanatos was going to turn Dragon's murder into a "tragic accident" that could be explained to the human public. "A large male bison escaped the confines of the preserve. Several of us were completing a lovely cleansing ritual at the lavender farm, and the beast must have been confused by the sage smoke and our circle. The creature attacked us. Our Sword Master protected our fledglings, losing his life doing so."

"That's terrible! I'm so sorry." Adam looked upset. Actually, we all looked upset, which was hiding our shock at Thanatos's big, giant lie.

"Thank you, Adam. Though it was a horrible accident and a terrible loss to our House, our Sword Master died as he lived, an honorable Warrior who protected our young ones. Because of him no one else was harmed, and the ritual was even completed. We shall all remember Dragon Lankford's bravery for centuries to come." She dabbed at her eyes with a lace handkerchief she'd pulled from within her sleeve. It was a really moving moment. Adam stood there, looking empathetic, as the cameraman swiveled the lens from Dragon's pyre to focus on Thanatos's grief and her very human struggle to pull herself together.

It was really well staged. She made me wonder how many acting classes the High Priestess of Death had taken when she was a fledgling.

Thanatos finished wiping her eyes and drew a deep breath. "And to answer your other question, no, this is not a bad time for our interview. We invited you, remember? We are happy to welcome you to the House of Night, even during our sadness. So, let us officially begin. Is here by the bench a good place?" Thanatos gestured at one of the long stone benches that lined the entranceway to the school lobby. During a regular school day, kids would be clustered around them, doing homework, flirting, and gossiping. Tonight they were completely empty.

"Perfect," Adam said.

While he and the cameraman set up, Thanatos took her position in the center of the bench. Quietly she said, "Zoey, Stark, beside me here." She pointed to her right. "Aphrodite, Stevie Rae, and Damien, over here." They settled on the bench to her left.

When Adam returned and officially began filming, I felt a flutter of nerves. Even my old friends at South Intermediate High School would see this!

"Thanatos, I was wondering if you could elaborate on the comment Neferet, the ex–High Priestess of this Tulsa House of Night, made about you last night. She said Death was the new High Priestess here." Adam paused and smiled. "You don't look like Death to me."

"Have you seen her often, young Adam?" Thanatos said in a soft, joking voice.

"No, actually, I've never died," he joked back.

"Well, Neferet's comment can be easily explained. I am not Death herself. It is simply that I have been gifted with an affinity for aiding the dead to pass from this realm to the next. I am no more Death than you are Humanity. We both are just representations of the two. It might help you understand if you would think of me as a very accurate medium."

"Neferet also mentioned a new type of vampyre—a red vampyre, and suggested that they might be dangerous." I watched the camera shift from Stark to Stevie Rae. "Could you elaborate on that, as well?"

"Certainly, but first I feel I need to make one point very clear. Neferet is no longer in the employ of the Tulsa House of Night. In truth, the way our society works, once a High Priestess loses her job, she has lost that position for life. She will never serve as High Priestess at any other House of Night. As you can imagine that can be a difficult and often embarrassing transition for the terminated employee, as well as for her employer. Vampyres do not have slander and liable laws. We use the oath and honor system. Obviously this time that system did not work."

"So what you're saying is that Neferet is . . ." His word trailed off, and he nodded, encouraging Thanatos to finish the sentence for him.

"Yes, it is a sad but true fact, Neferet is a disgruntled ex-employee with no whistle to blow," Thanatos said smoothly.

Adam glanced at Stark, who was standing beside me not far from Thanatos. "That ex-employee made some disturbing comments about one House of Night member in particular—James Stark."

"That's me," Stark said right away. I could tell he was uncomfortable, but I don't think anyone else, including the TV audience, would see anything except a very cute guy with red facial tattooing that looked like opposing arrows.

"So, Jim. Is it okay that I call you that?" Adam asked.

"Well, it is, but it'd be cool with me if you called me Stark. Everyone else does."

"Okay, Stark, Neferet said you killed your mentor at the Chicago House of Night, and she implied that you're a threat to the community here. Would you care to respond to that?"

"Well, that's a bunch of bullpoopie!" I heard my mouth saying.

Stark grinned his cocky half smile and took my hand, threading his fingers through mine for all of the video audience to see. "Z, don't almost cuss on film. Your grandma might hear and that wouldn't be cool."

"Sorry," I muttered. "How about I just let you talk."

Stark's grin got bigger. "Well, that'll be a first."

Annoyingly enough, my friends all laughed. I scowled. Stark kept speaking, even though I considered smothering him with a pillow next time we slept.

His voice was hesitant at first, but the longer he talked, the stronger and surer he became. "My mentor, William Chidsey, was awesome. He was nice. And smart. I mean, *really* smart. And talented. He helped me. Actually, he was more like a father than a mentor to me." Stark paused and wiped his hand across his face. When he started talking again it was as if it were just him and the reporter, alone, like he'd forgotten that the camera was there at all. "Adam, I found out pretty early, when I was what humans would call a sophomore in high school, that I'd been given this *gift*." Stark enunciated the word, not sarcastically, but not like it was an awesome thing, either. His voice said his gift was a responsibility, and not a cool responsibility at that. "I can't miss my mark. I'm an archer," he explained when Adam gave him a questioning look. "You know, bow and arrows. Well, whatever I aim at—I hit. Unfortunately, it's not as literal as that. Think about it—there's lots of wiggle room between what you're looking at, and what you're really thinking about, and what you're aiming at. Here's a simple example: imagine taking a bow and arrow and aiming at a stop sign. So, you draw the bow, point the arrow, and sight the middle of a big red sign. But what if, inside your head you're thinking, 'Okay, I want to hit that thing that stops cars.' Next thing you know your arrow has found its way smack through the radiator of the next car that drives by."

"Well, I see how that might cause some big problems," Adam said.

"Yeah, big as in epic proportions. It took me a while to figure it out and to be able to control it. Between then and now, I made a really terrible mistake." Stark paused again and I squeezed his hand, trying to telegraph my support through it. "And because of that my mentor died. I won't let it happen again. I've given my oath on it."

"And that is why James Stark is here at the Tulsa House of Night." Thanatos took up the thread of conversation, and the camera followed her. "We believe in second chances in Tulsa." Her gaze shifted to Aphrodite. I had to make my mouth *not* flop open as she continued smoothly, "Would you not say that this is an excellent place for second chances, Aphrodite LaFont?"

I shouldn't have worried. With the camera rolling Aphrodite was totally in her element. She walked forward, toward the camera (of course), then sat at Thanatos's side. "I couldn't agree with you more, High Priestess. I was a fledgling for almost four years, but Nyx, our benevolent Goddess, chose to take my Mark from me and to replace it with a prophetic gift. My parents agree with my decision to remain at the House of Night. Actually, we've talked about the possibility of me serving an internship with the High Council in Venice when I graduate from here. My mom and dad are super supportive." She grinned into the camera. "You can tell that if you pull our credit card bills for the last few months. Wow! I have such awesomely cool parents!"

Okay, seriously. That was such a load of stinking, festering bullpoopie that I couldn't even speak. Thankfully, Stevie Rae was not so mute.

"Speaking of amazing parents, my mom, Ginny Johnson, is gonna make the best chocolate chip cookies in the known universe, and bring them to the open house and bake sale we're havin' here real soon, right, Thanatos?"

Thanatos didn't miss a beat. "You are absolutely correct, Stevie Rae. This coming weekend, should the tempestuous Oklahoma weather allow, we are planning a campus open house. We are hoping that Street Cats will be here with cats for adoption. Actually, I'd like to announce right now that all proceeds from our bake sale"—she smiled in Stevie Rae's direction—"will go to benefit our local charity, Street Cats. In addition, the grandmother of our fledgling High Priestess, Zoey Redbird, is going to have her lavender products for sale on our grounds."

"Don't forget the job fair."

Everyone, including the cameraman, turned at the sound of our Horse Mistress's voice. Lenobia was standing there, leading her beautiful black mare, Mujaji, who looked like an absolute dream.

"Professor Lenobia, how good of you to join our press conference," Thanatos said.

"Wow! What a gorgeous horse he is!" Adam gushed as the cameraman did a close-up on Mujaji.

Damien touched Adam's arm and grinned. "Honey, that's a she, not a he."

"Oh, my mistake." Adam took it all in stride, smiling with a cute flush to his cheeks. "The guy-girl thing never made much difference to me."

"Because we're all the same." I heard the words coming from my mouth, and silently thanked Nyx for them. "Guy, girl, human, vampyre, what difference does it make? We're sharing Tulsa, and we love it. So, let's just all get along!"

Thanatos laughed, and the sound was like music. "Oh, Zoey, I could not have said it better myself. And Lenobia, you were correct to remind me. Adam, I would like to announce this evening that during the open house and Street Cat benefit, the Tulsa House of Night will, as the first House of Night in our written history, be taking job applications for human professors. We will be interviewing for professorial positions in our drama department, as well as in our literature department." Thanatos stood and opened her arms, looking benevolent and wise. "The House of Night welcomes Tulsa. Until Saturday we wish you all merry meet, merry part, and merry meet again."

CHAPTER FOURTEEN

Neferet

Neferet would not have seen the press conference had she not called room service to her penthouse suite. The pleasingly subservient blond boy was almost young enough to interest her. The last bellboy who had had the good fortune to answer her summons would be calling in sick for the next several days. Weak and bruised, he would not remember anything except a fascination for her beauty and a series of dark, erotic dreams. Fever dreams, his doctor would no doubt call them. Humans were such frail creatures. Such a shame that she constantly needed to find a new plaything.

Neferet studied this bellboy. He was tall, and he looked extremely nervous. His skin was bad. He practically oozed virgin from his over-sized pores. Thinking that virgin blood would mix nicely with the chilled bottle of champagne he was carrying past her, she motioned to her sitting room.

"Please, bring the bottle inside my suite," Neferet purred.

Virgin blood was so very sweet that a bad complexion and sweaty palms could be easily overlooked. After all, she was not going to touch him. At least not very much . . .

"Is right here fine, ma'am?" His eyes kept flitting from her breasts to her mouth and then back to the bottle he was opening, all the while he reeked of sexual desire, fear, and fascination.

"Right there is *perfect*." Neferet ran a long, pointed fingernail down the low bodice of her silk robe.

"Wow," he gulped, working the gold foil off the top of the champagne with inexperienced, shaky hands. "I hope you don't mind me sayin' this, but you're way prettier than those other vampyres on the news."

"Other vampyres? News?"

"Yes, ma'am. They're on Fox 23 late night right now."

"Turn it on for me!" she snapped.

"But the champagne's not—"

"Leave it! I am fully capable of opening it myself. Put on the news and go."

The boy did as he was told and then slunk out, still casting longing glances at her. Neferet paid him no mind. She was utterly engrossed in the scene unfolding before her on the large flat screen television. It was Thanatos, Zoey, and several of her group. They were outside at the House of Night, clustered together and talking easily with the reporter. Neferet scowled. They all looked so *normal*.

Her lip curled as she heard Thanatos explain away Dragon Lankford's death as a tragic bison accident.

"That wretched Aurox," Neferet muttered. "Imperfect, inept Vessel! All of this is *his* fault."

She kept watching the interview, smirking at Stark and Zoey, only concentrating when she heard her name mentioned. Neferet pressed the volume button and Thanatos's voice blared, "... *Neferet is a disgruntled ex-employee with no whistle to blow* ..."

Neferet's body became very cold.

"She dares to name me an *employee!*" Neferet continued to watch. Her anger built to such intensity that the glass door to the penthouse balcony burst open, raining shards of crystal across the marble floor.

"*We're sharing Tulsa, and we love it. So, let's just all get along!*" Zoey's ridiculously cheerful voice grated up and down Neferet's spine.

"I will not allow you to undo what I have begun, you obnoxious child!" Neferet seethed. When Thanatos announced that the Tulsa House of Night would be taking applications for human professors her mouth gaped along with the reporters. After the new High Priestess's benevolent, *merry meet, merry part, and merry meet again,* Neferet watched in disbelief as the news anchors chattered inanely about how interesting all the vampyre interaction was and how great the open house and job fair would be for the city as a still shot close-up of Zoey's smiling face decorated the screen. She punched the power button, unable to bear one more instant of Zoey Redbird.

From the clever little alcove that was tucked between the living room and the dining room, Neferet's computer began to ring. On the screen the silhouetted figure of Nyx's upraised arms flashed and beside the icon were the words: VAMPYRE HIGH COUNCIL.

Neferet walked slowly over to the computer and clicked the mouse to answer, automatically activating the video camera. She smiled coolly at the six somber High Priestesses seated on their carved marble thrones. "I have been expecting your call."

Duantia, the senior member of the Vampyre High Council, spoke first. Neferet thought she sounded very, *very* old. There certainly seemed to be more silver than brown in her long, thick hair, and Neferet was sure she could see bags under her dark eyes. "You were summoned to appear before us, yet there you are in Tulsa, and here we are in Venice. What has delayed you?"

"I am busy." Neferet pitched her voice to sound more amused than annoyed. Or afraid. She must never allow them to believe she feared them, or anyone, at all. "It is not convenient to make a trip to Italy at this time."

"Then you force us to pass judgment over you in *absente reo.*"

Neferet scoffed. "Save your Latin for vampyres too old to live in the present."

Duantia continued as if she hadn't spoken. "Our sister High Priestess, and the seventh member of this Council, Thanatos, has produced irrefutable evidence though a reveal ritual witness by High Priestess Zoey Redbird, her—"

"That insolent child isn't a High Priestess!"

"You will not interrupt me!" Even through the Internet, thousands of miles away, Duantia's power was palpable. It was only

with a supreme effort that Neferet didn't cringe from the computer screen.

"Say what you must. I will not interrupt again," Neferet said emotionlessly.

"The reveal ritual over which Thanatos presided was witnessed by the young High Priestess, Zoey Redbird; her circle, each member of which has been gifted by Nyx with an elemental affinity; as well as several Sons of Erebus Warriors. During this ritual the earth gave record that you murdered a human, sacrificing her to the white bull of Darkness, who appears to be your Consort."

Neferet watched the High Council members shift nervously, as if just hearing the word Consort associated with the white bull was difficult for them to bear. That pleased her. Very shortly the High Council would have to bear more than simple words.

"Neferet, what do you say in your defense?" Duantia concluded.

Neferet drew herself up to her full height. She felt the threads of Darkness rustle around her, lapping at her ankles and slithering around her calves. "I need no defense. Killing the human was not an act of murder. It was a sacred sacrifice."

"You dare call Darkness sacred?" the Council member named Alitheia shouted.

"Alitheia, or Truth, as we would say in a language that isn't dead, I will impart a little of your own to you. The *truth* is that I am immortal. In a little over a hundred years I have attained more power than all of you in all of your centuries have managed to acquire. The *truth* is that in another hundred years, most of you will be dust, and I will still be young, powerful, beautiful, and a goddess. If I choose to sacrifice a human, no matter for what purpose, it is sacred and not sin!"

"Neferet, is Darkness your Consort?" Duantia's question shot through the silence following Neferet's shout.

"Conjure the white bull and ask Darkness yourself. But only if you dare," Neferet sneered.

"High Council, what is your judgment?" Duantia asked. She held

Neferet's gaze as each of the High Council members stood and, one at a time, pronounced the same word, over and over, "Shunned!"

Duantia stood last. "Shunned!" she said firmly. "From this day forth, you will no longer be recognized as a High Priestess of Nyx. You will no longer be recognized as a vampyre at all. Henceforth you are dead to us." As one, the High Council members turned their backs to Neferet, and then the screen bleeped the CALL ENDED sound and the picture went blank.

Neferet stared at the black screen. She was breathing heavily, trying to control the tumult within her. The High Council had shunned her!

"Horrid old crones!" she ranted. Too soon! Neferet had, of course, intended to break with the High Council, but not before she had divided them and set them at each other's throats so that they would be too busy with the destruction happening within to meddle in the world she was fashioning outside their cozy little island. "I almost accomplished it before—when Kalona was posing as Erebus at my side. But Zoey ruined that by forcing me to reveal him as a fraud." Unable to quiet her frustration, Neferet stalked from the room, her stiletto heels crunching on the broken glass. She went out on the balcony, pressing her hands against the cold stone balustrade. "Zoey caused Thanatos to be sent to Tulsa to spy on me. And it was Zoey's mother who was too weak, too imperfect a sacrifice. Had Aurox not been a cracked vessel, the reveal ritual would have been stopped by Rephaim's death. And now I am shunned by the High Council and viewed as a domesticated ally by Tulsa humans." Neferet raised her arms to the sky and shrieked her anger. "Zoey Redbird will pay for what she has caused!"

Neferet reached down and ripped the silk robe from her, baring her body to the night. Naked, she threw out her arms and tilted back her head so that her long hair veiled her like a dark curtain. "Come to me, Darkness!" She braced herself, ready for the painful pleasure of her white bull's icy touch.

Nothing.

The only movement in the night was the restless, dark tendrils that had become her constant companions.

"My lord! Come to me! I am in need of you!" Neferet called.

"Your call is not a surprise, my heartless one."

Neferet heard his voice in her head, as always, but she did not feel his awe-inspiring presence. She dropped her arms, turning, searching for him. "My lord, I cannot see you."

"You need something."

Still not understanding why he had not appeared to her, Neferet did not allow her confusion to show. Instead she responded seductively. "What I need is *you*, my lord."

Instantly, the thickest of the snake-like minions of Darkness detached itself from the others that slithered over her ankles. It whipped around her waist, slicing through her smooth skin and drawing a perfect circle of scarlet. The other tendrils crawled up her legs, moving to feed from the warm wash of her blood.

Neferet was very careful not to cry out.

"Lying to me is not wise, my heartless one."

"I need more power," Neferet admitted. "I want to kill Zoey Redbird, and she is well protected."

"Well protected and the beloved of a goddess. Even you are not ready to openly destroy one such as her."

"Then help me. I beg it of you, my lord." Neferet cajoled, ignoring the razor-like thread that continued to cut into her skin and the other tendrils that were feeding from her.

"You disappoint me. I expected you to call me and beg for aid. You see, my heartless one, I should not be able to predict your actions. That bores me, and I have no desire to waste my powers on predictability and tedium." The voice battered relentlessly at her mind.

Neferet did not flinch.

"I will not ask you to forgive me," she said coldly. "You knew what I was when first we came together. I have not changed. I will not change."

"Indeed, and that is why I have always called you my heartless

one." The voice was less of a violation. Now it was tinged with amusement. *"You remind me of how well we began. You were such a delicious surprise. Surprise me again, and I will consider coming to your aid. Until then, I grant you control over the bits of Darkness that choose to remain with you. Do not despair. Many will choose you. You feed them so well. I will see you again, my heartless one, when . . . if . . . you pique my interest enough for me to return . . ."* His voice faded as the thick tendril encasing her waist detached itself and disappeared into the night.

Neferet collapsed. She lay on the cold stone balcony, watching the threads of Darkness lap her blood. She did not stop them. She let them feed from her as she stroked them, encouraging them, taking stock of how many remained true to her.

If the bull would not help her, Neferet would help herself. Zoey Redbird had been a problem for far too long. For far too long she had allowed that child to interfere with her plans. She would not kill her, though. That would bring down the wrath of Nyx too soon. Unlike the Vampyre High Council, a goddess could not be ignored. *No,* Neferet thought, *I need not kill Zoey. All I need do is create a being to do the job for me. The Vessel failed once because of an imperfect sacrifice. With the perfect sacrifice I will not fail.*

"I am immortal. I do not need the bull to create. All I need is a sacred sacrifice and power. I have learned the spell. Aurox was only the beginning . . ." Neferet stroked the threads of Darkness and allowed them to continue feeding from her.

Enough, she assured herself, *there are just enough left.*

Zoey

"Goddess knows I hate to say it, but I was wrong. This is like watching *The* stupid *Bachelorette*." Aphrodite shook her head and rolled her eyes. She, Stevie Rae, and I were walking slowly to the parking lot and the waiting bus full of kids. We were moving slowly because we were super busy gawking at Damien and the reporter guy, Adam. The two of them were standing by the Fox 23 news van smiling and chattering.

"Shhh!" I whispered at Aphrodite. "They're gonna hear you and that will embarrass Damien."

"Oh, please," Aphrodite snorted. "Gay boy's all atwitter, or atitter, or whatever. He's not paying any attention to us."

"I'm just glad he's flirting," I said.

"Look! They're takin' out their phones!" Stevie Rae gushed in a whisper that was too exclamation pointed to be whispery.

"I was wrong again," Aphrodite said. "It's not like watching *The Bachelorette*. It's like watching the National Geographic Channel."

"I think he's a cutie patootie," Stevie Rae said.

"The guy talking to Damien?" Shaylin asked as she joined us.

"Yeah. We think they're makin' a date," Stevie Rae said, still gawking.

"He has soft, pretty colors," Shaylin said. "Actually, they go real well with Damien's."

"What, are their rainbows merging?" Aphrodite snorted sarcastically.

Shaylin frowned. "They don't have rainbow colors. That's such a horrible stereotype. They have summer sky colors—blues and yellows. Damien also has some billowy white stuff that looks a lot like cumulus clouds."

"Oh, for shit's sake, it has no sense of humor at all," Aphrodite said.

"Aphrodite, you gotta stop callin' Shaylin *it*. It's not nice," Stevie Rae said.

"So, for future reference, how not nice is it on the retard-mean-word scale?" She lifted a questioning blond brow at Stevie Rae. "Is it more asstard, fucktard, or old school, hardcore, retard not nice?"

"You're the High Priestess, but I say answering her at all just encourages her. You know, like what happens when you pick up a screaming toddler—they keep on screaming," Shaylin said, sounding very matter-of-fact.

All I could think was *holy crap, Aphrodite is going to yank her hair out by the roots.*

Instead Aphrodite laughed. "Hey, it made a joke! It might actually have a personality."

"Aphrodite, I think you might be brain damaged," Stevie Rae said.

"Thank you," Aphrodite said. "I'm getting on the bus. And I'm timing Gay Boy. If he flirts for more than five more minutes I'm going to—" Her words stopped when she turned toward the bus. My eyes followed her gaze. Shaunee and Erin were standing just outside the bus's open door. Shaunee looked upset. Erin's face had no expression on it whatsoever. I could see that they were talking, but we were too far away to hear what they were saying.

"There's something wrong about her," Shaylin said.

"Who her?" Stevie Rae asked.

"Erin," Shaylin said.

"Shaylin's right. There's something wrong about Erin," Aphrodite said.

I couldn't tell which shocked me more, what Aphrodite and Shaylin were saying, or that they were agreeing.

"Tell me what you're seein'," Stevie Rae spoke quietly to Shaylin.

"Here's the best way I can describe it. There was this culvert that ran behind the house I lived in when I was a kid, just before I lost my sight. I used to play by it and pretend that it was a bubbling, beautiful mountain stream and I was growing up in the Colorado Rockies, 'cause it was clear and even kinda pretty. But the second I got too close to it I could smell it. It stunk like chemicals and something else, something rotting. The water looked good, but under the surface it was dirty, polluted."

"Shaylin." I was seriously at the edge of my patience. I felt like I was listening to one of Kramisha's poems—and that's not necessarily a good thing. "What in the hell are you saying? Erin is the color of polluted water? And if she is, why didn't you say something before now?"

"She's changing!" Shaylin yelled. When faces on the bus, along with Shaunee and Erin, turned their heads toward us, she added, "Winter seems to be changing to Spring! Isn't it a beautiful night?"

Kids shook their heads and squinched their foreheads at her, but at least they seemed to quit listening.

"Oh, for shit's sake. You are no good at espionage at all." Aphrodite lowered her voice and huddled us up. "Z, get a clue. It's simple. What Shaylin is saying is that Erin looks like she used to—pretty, blond, popular, perfect. You know, typical. But the truth is that under the surface, there's something rotting. You can't see it. I can't see it. But Shaylin can." Aphrodite glanced over at the bus. We all looked with her in time to see Shaunee shake her head no, and disappear quickly up the black, rubber-treaded stairs while Erin stood there looking beautiful but very, very cold. "Seems like Shaunee might be able to see it, too. Not that we'd believe her. We'd believe she was just pissed at Erin because the Dorkamise Twins have been surgically separated."

"I think that's pretty harsh," I said.

"So do I," Stevie Rae said. "But my gut's tellin' me it's the truth."

"Mine is as well," Damien said, walking up to us. His cheeks were still flushed, and he waved gaily as the Fox 23 van pulled away, but his attention was focused on Erin. "My gut's telling me something else, too."

"That you and News Boy are about to become butt-buddies?" Aphrodite's voice was perky and polite, which was in direct contradiction to what she'd just said.

"*That* is none of your business," Damien said, then transitioned smoothly to, "And you may want to pay attention, Aphrodite. What I'm getting ready to say is going to rock your world."

"That's a seriously old saying," Aphrodite said.

"Old doesn't equate to inaccurate," Damien said. "You translated what Shaylin envisioned. That means you're acting as an oracle."

"I'm not an effing oracle. I'm a Prophetess." Aphrodite really looked pissed.

"Oracle—Prophetess," Damien held up first one hand then the other, as if he was measuring something in each palm and equaling them both out. "Seems the same thing to me. Check your history, *Prophetess*. Sibyl, Delphi, Cassandra! Do these names not ring a bell with you?"

"No. Seriously. I try not to read too much."

"Well, I'd start if I were you. They are just the top three of many that come to my well-educated mind. Some name them Oracle. Some call them Prophetess. Same thing."

"Can I get the short version from the Internet?" Aphrodite was trying to sound like a smartass, but her face had lost all of its color and her eyes looked giant and even more topaz blue than usual. And scared. She looked super scared.

"Okay, well, lesson learned. I say, well done, us!" I piped in perkily. When everyone just stared at me I attempted an explanation. "Thanatos said we had to practice our Gifts. I think what just happened is, like, extra credit for us. How 'bout we get on that bus and go back to the tunnels and watch some *Fringe* reruns?"

"*Fringe?* I'm in," Shaylin said, and started off toward the bus.

"I like Walter," Aphrodite said. "He reminds me of my grandpa. Well, except Walter's a little smarter and is high and crazy versus drunk and sociopathic. Yet oddly they're both likeable."

"You have a grandpa? And you like him?" Stevie Rae beat me to the question.

"Of course I have a grandpa. What are you, a biology moron?" Then Aphrodite shrugged. "Whatever. My family is kinda hard to explain. I'm going to follow *it* on the bus." And she did. She followed Shaylin.

Stevie Rae, Damien, and I were left alone.

"Crazy Town," was all I could think to say.

"Indeed," Damien nodded.

"All right, well, do you think everyone else is on the bus?" I asked.

"I hope so. I know Rephaim's there, and we only have a couple of hours until sunrise. I can pretty much be sure he's never seen any episodes of *Fringe*, and I think he'd like them. Watchin' DVDs curled up with him sounds real good right now, even if we do have to do it with Crazy Town Aphrodite." She grinned at me. "Can we order Andolini's pizza?"

"Totally," I said.

"Hurrumph..." Damien cleared his throat with staged precision.

"Yes?" I asked.

"Do, um, you guys think it's awful if I, um, maybe, meet *someone* for coffee. Late. Tonight. At The Coffee House on Cherry Street?"

"Are they still open?" I asked, glancing at my phone. Jeesh, it was almost 4:00 A.M.

"They've started staying open 24/7. The ice storm killed business for weeks and they're trying to make up for it by catering to the, well, *night-time* crowd," Damien explained.

"Seriously? They're staying open for us?" I so remembered their awesome deli sandwiches and the beautiful local art they displayed. "They used to close at 11:00 P.M.!"

"Not anymore," he said happily.

"Wow, that's cool. I mean, I've never been there, but it's awesomesauce that a coffee shop is stayin' open in Midtown so that we can hang out there," Stevie Rae said.

"How about tomorrow we have Darius detour the bus there on the way back to the depot?" I followed my gut. *It's normal for a group of high school kids to want to stop off at a coffee shop after school.* "Damien, if you went tonight would you ask whoever's working if they'd be okay with us coming by tomorrow?"

"I would definitely reconnoiter for you!" Then Damien's expression dimmed. "So, what do you think? Would Jack hate me?"

"Oh, honey, no!" I said quickly. "Of course he wouldn't."

"Jack would understand," Stevie Rae added. "He wouldn't want you to be sad and lonely while you waited for him to come back around."

"He will, won't he?" Damien stared in my eyes. "Jack will come back around, right?"

Their souls are meant to meet again . . . the words whispered through my mind. Recognizing the wise, familiar voice of Nyx I smiled, twining my arm through Damien's. "He will. I promise. And so does the Goddess."

Damien blinked tears from his eyes. "I have a date! And I'm going to be happy about it."

"Yeah!" I said.

"I'm so happy I could just spit! Even though that's kinda gross," Stevie Rae said, taking Damien's other hand.

"It is a weird saying," Damien observed.

"Totally," I said. "You know it was disgusting during the *Titanic* movie when Leonardo did that whole spitting scene with Kate."

"Never would have happened," Damien agreed. "It was the only flaw in that movie."

"Well, that and Leo turning into an attractive Popsicle," I added.

Damien and Stevie Rae made noises in absolute agreement with me as we approached the bus. I could see the kids' faces in the windows. It looked like it was full, which made me feel a giant rush of relief because I was more than ready to go home. Stark was there, standing at the top of the stairs beside Darius. His eyes found me and his gaze made my skin feel tingly and warm. Rephaim was sitting in the first seat, right in front of Kramisha, and I could practically feel Stevie Rae vibrating with joy as she waved at him. Shaylin and Aphrodite were climbing the stairs. I couldn't see Aphrodite's face, but the toss of her hair said she was already flirting with her Warrior.

Okay, Darkness was a pain in the butt and hard things happened to us, but at least we were together and we had love. Always love.

"I need to talk to you."

Erin's emotionless voice was like ice water on my happy shower.

"Okay, sure. Hey, I'll be in the bus in a sec," I told Stevie Rae and Damien.

"I'm staying." Erin spoke the two words as soon as we were alone.

"Staying? You mean here?" I knew what she meant, but I needed to stall, to buy some time to try to wade through the questions in my mind. I mean, I'd stopped Shaunee when she'd tried to break away from us and move back to the House of Night right after she and Erin had started having problems. Shouldn't I stop Erin, too?

"Yeah, of course I mean here. I'm sick of the tunnels. The humidity is frizzing my hair."

"Uh, there's product for that. Aveda makes it. We'll pick you up some from the Utica Ilhoff salon tomorrow," I said.

"Okay, so, it's not just my hair. I don't want to live in the tunnels. This is where I live. This school. I don't want to be bussed in. It's stupid."

"Erin, I know taking the bus is stupid. Hell, it was stupid before I was Marked. But I think we need to stay together. We're more than just a group or a clique, we're a family."

"No, we're not a family. We're a group of kids who all go to the same school. That's it. The end."

"Our affinities make us more than that." She was shocking me—not just by what she was saying, but by her attitude. Erin was so damn cold! "Erin, we've been through too much together to ever believe that we're just a group of kids who happen to go to the same school."

"What if that's how you feel, but not how I feel? Don't I get to choose? I thought Nyx was all about free choice."

"She is, but that doesn't mean we can't say something when someone we care about is messing up," I said.

"Let her go."

Erin and I looked up to see Aphrodite standing on the bottom stair of the bus. She was leaning against the doorframe with her arms crossed. I expected to see the familiar Aphrodite Sneer on her face, but she didn't look mad. She didn't sound sarcastic. She just seemed very sure of herself. Behind her I could see Stevie Rae and Shaylin. Each of them nodded, and that unspoken support for Aphrodite tipped me over as I realized that my Council had ruled—they'd decided what was best for all of us, even if it wasn't what was best for Erin.

"Thanks, Aphrodite. Who knew you'd be the one to agree with me?" Erin laughed, sounding petulant and childlike in the wake of Aphrodite's calm maturity.

"You know what, Erin, I'm glad you *and* Aphrodite reminded

me," I said. "Nyx does give us free choice, and if you choose to live at the House of Night, then I'm going to respect that. I hope that doesn't change things with our circle. You're still water. Your element and you are still important to us."

Erin's lips smiled, but the expression didn't reach her cold blue eyes. "Yeah, of course. I'll always be water, and water can slide around from anywhere. Just call if you need me. I'll be sure to get right on it."

"Sounds good," I spoke quickly, feeling super awkward. "So, well, I guess we'll see you tomorrow."

"Yeah, right. I'll see you guys in class." With a flippant wave of her hand, Erin walked off.

I climbed the stairs into the bus asking Darius, "Are we all here?"

"All present and accounted for," he replied.

"Then let's go home." We all scattered to our seats—Stevie Rae beside Rephaim, Aphrodite in the first seat right behind Darius as the driver. Stark was waiting for me in the next seat back, and I leaned down, kissing him quickly and whispering, "I'm gonna go check on Shaunee, then I'll be back."

"I'll be waiting. Always," he said, touching my cheek gently.

I lurched in time to the potholes in the parking lot as Darius made a big U-turn and headed toward the school's long driveway, making my way to the back of the bus where Shaunee sat by herself.

"Mind if I sit down for a sec?"

"Sure, yeah," she said.

"So, you and Erin aren't so much talking anymore?"

Shaunee chewed the side of her cheek and shook her head. "No."

"She's pretty pissed." I was trying to figure out something to say that would help Shaunee open up.

"No, I don't think she is," Shaunee said.

I frowned. "Well, she seemed pissed."

"No," Shaunee repeated, staring out the window. "Go back and think about how she's been acting for the past couple of days, but especially today. Pissed doesn't describe her."

I did think about it. Erin had been cold. She'd been unemotional.

And that's about all she'd been. "Well, you're right. Now that I really think about it she hasn't been much of anything except detached, and that feels weird," I said.

"You know what's weirder, she's showing more feeling than Erin." Shaunee pointed out the window at the little professors' courtyard not far from the edge of the parking lot. A girl was sitting beside the fountain there. As we drove past there was just enough light to glimpse that she had her face in her hands. Her shoulders were shaking as if she was bawling her heart out.

"Who is that?" I asked.

"Nicole."

"The red fledgling Nicole? Are you sure?" I rubber-necked, trying to get a better look at her, but we were already heading down the tree-lined driveway and my view of the girl was completely obscured.

"I'm sure," Shaunee said. "I saw her there on the way to the bus."

"Huh," I said. "Wonder what's going on with her?"

"I think things are changing for a bunch of us, and sometimes that just plain sucks."

"Anything I can do to make it less sucky for you?" I asked.

Shaunee looked at me then. "Just be my friend."

I blinked in surprise. "I *am* your friend."

"Even without Erin?"

"I like you better without Erin," I said honestly.

"I do, too," Shaunee said. "I do, too."

In a little while I went back to my seat beside Stark and let him put his arm around me. I rested my head against his shoulder and listened to his heartbeat, leaning on his strength and his love.

"Promise me you won't freak out on me and become some cold, distant stranger," I said softly to him.

"I promise. No matter what," he said with no hesitation. "Now, clear your mind of everything except the fact that I'm going to force you to try a different pizza tonight."

"No Santino? But we love that pizza!"

"Trust me, Z. Damien told me about the Athenian pizza. He said it's the ambrosia of pizzas. I'm not sure exactly what that means, but I'm thinking it's better than good, so we're going for it."

I smiled, relaxed beside him and pretended, for the short ride from the House of Night to the depot, that my biggest problem was choosing to expand my pizza horizons.

CHAPTER FIFTEEN

Grandma Redbird

Sylvia greeted the sun with joy and thanksgiving and a heart that felt lighter than it had for years—lighter even than it had the morning before when she'd faced Aurox and chosen love and forgiveness over anger and hatred.

Her daughter was dead, and though she would feel Linda's loss for the rest of this lifetime, Sylvia knew that she was finally free of the wasteland her daughter's life had become. Linda rested in the Otherworld with Nyx, content and pain-free. The knowledge made the old woman smile.

Sitting at her crafting desk in the workroom of her cottage, she hummed an ancient Cherokee lullaby as she chose from the various herbs and stones, crystals and threads, picking a long, thin blade of sweet grass to wrap around a bundle of dried lavender. This dawn she would sing to the sun while the cleansing smoke of sweet grass and the soothing scent of lavender mixed and bathed her along with the sunlight. As she created the smudge stick Sylvia's thoughts turned from her biological daughter to Zoey, the daughter of her spirit.

"Ah, *u-we-tsi-a-ge-ya,* I do miss you so," she said softly. "I will call you today when the sun sets. Your voice will be good to hear." Her granddaughter was young, but she had been specially gifted by her Goddess, and even though that meant Zoey had unusual responsibilities to bear, it also meant she had the talent to rise to meet the challenges that came with those added responsibilities.

And that had Sylvia's mind turning to Aurox—the boy who was a beast. "Or is he a beast who is a boy?" While her hands worked, the old woman shook her head. "No, I will believe the best of him. I name him *tsu-ka-nv-s-di-na*. Bull instead of beast. I have met him, looked into his eyes, watched him weep with regret and loneliness. He has a spirit—a soul—and therefore a choice. I will believe that Aurox will choose Light, even if Darkness resides within him. None of us is entirely good. Or evil." Sylvia closed her eyes, breathing in the sweet scent of grass and herbs. "Great Earth Mother, strengthen the good within the boy and allow *tsu-ka-nv-s-di-na* to be tamed."

Sylvia began humming again as she finished fashioning the smudge stick. It was only when she'd completed the weaving of grass and lavender that she realized the song she hummed had changed from lullaby to a much different tune: "Song for a Woman Who Was Brave in War." Even though she still sat, Sylvia's feet had begun to move, beating out the strong rhythm to accompany the rise and fall of her voice.

When she realized what she was doing, Sylvia went utterly still. She looked down at her hands. Woven within the sweet grass and lavender was a blue thread that was strung and knotted with raw turquoise. With a jolt of clarity, Sylvia understood.

"A Goddess Bundle." Sylvia spoke the words reverently. "Thank you, Earth Mother, for this warning. My spirit heard you, and my body obeys." Slowly, solemnly, the old woman stood. She walked to her bedroom and took off her sleep shirt. Opening the armoire that rested against the raw pine walls, Sylvia took out her most sacred regalia—the cape and the wrap skirt she had made when she first learned she was pregnant with Linda. The deerskin was old and a little loose on her slight body, but still smooth and soft. The green that Sylvia had spent so much time mixing and then dyeing had remained the color of moss, even after three decades. Not one of the shells or beads was loose.

As Sylvia began to braid her silver hair in one long, thick rope, she began to sing the "Song for a Woman Who Was Brave in War" aloud.

She looped silver and turquoise earings through each earlobe.

Her voice lifted and fell in time with the beating of her bare feet as she strung necklaces of turquoise around her neck, adding one on another, so that their weight felt familiar and warm.

Sylvia circled her thin wrists with cuffs of turquoise and smaller, thinner ribbons of silver and turquoise—always turquoise—until both forearms were almost entirely filled, wrist to elbow.

Only then did Sylvia Redbird pick up her smudge stick and a long box of wooden matches, and walk from her bedroom.

She let her spirit guide her bare feet. Her spirit did not take her to the bubbling stream that ran behind her house where she usually greeted the dawn. Instead Sylvia found herself in the middle of her wide front porch. Continuing to follow her instincts, she lit the smudge stick. With graceful, practiced movements, Sylvia began circling herself with the scents of sweet grass and lavender. It was when she was engulfed in smoke, foot to head, and singing a Wise Woman's war song, that Neferet stepped from a pool of Darkness, materializing before her.

Neferet

Sylvia Redbird's voice sounded like chalk screeching on a blackboard. "By your own belief system it is impolite not to welcome a guest." Neferet raised her voice so she could be heard over the old woman's horrible song.

"Guests are invited. You have no invitation to my home. That makes you an intruder. According to my beliefs I am greeting you appropriately."

Neferet curled her lip. The old woman's singing had ended, but her bare feet still beat out a repeating rhythm. "That song is almost as annoying as that smoke. Do you really think the stink of it will protect you?"

"I think many things, Tsi Sgili," Sylvia said, still wafting the thick wand of herbs around her as she danced in place. "At this moment I am thinking that you broke an oath you made to me when my *u-we-tsi-a-ge-ya* first joined your world. I call you to task for that."

Neferet was almost amused by the old woman's insolence. "I made no oath to you."

"You did. You promised to mentor and protect Zoey. Then you broke that oath. You owe me the price of that broken oath."

"Old woman, I am an immortal. I am not bound by the same rules as you are," Neferet scoffed.

"Immortal you may have become. That does not change the Earth Mother's laws."

"Perhaps not, but it does change how they are enforced," Neferet said.

"An oath-breaking is only one of the debts you owe me, witch," Sylvia said.

"I am a goddess, not a witch!" Neferet felt her anger rise and she began moving slowly closer to the porch. The tendrils of Darkness slithered with her, though Neferet sensed their hesitation as wisps of white smoke drifted down, seeming to melt around them.

Sylvia continued dancing and waving the wand around her. "The second debt you owe me is greater than an oath-breaking. You owe me a life debt. You killed my daughter."

"I sacrificed your daughter for a greater good. I owe you nothing!"

The old woman paid no attention to her. Instead she paused in her dance long enough to bend and place the smoking herbs at her feet. Then she lifted her face and opened her arms, as if embracing the sky. "Great Earth Mother, hear me. I am Sylvia Redbird, Wise Woman of the Cherokee, and Ghigua of my tribe, that of the House of Night. I beg mercy from you. The Tsi Sgili, Neferet, who was once a High Priestess of Nyx, is forsworn. She owes me an oath-breaking debt. She is also the murderess of my daughter. She owes me a life debt. I invoke your aid, Earth Mother, and call both debts due. The payment I demand is protection."

Ignoring the tendrils of Darkness that were cowering around her, Neferet approached Sylvia, climbing the steps up to her porch as she spoke. "You are vastly mistaken, old woman. I am the only goddess listening. I am the immortal to whom you should be begging protection."

Neferet stepped onto the smoke-filled porch when Sylvia spoke again. The old woman's voice had changed. Before it had been powerful as she evoked the one she called Earth Mother. Now her voice had gentled, become softer. Her arms were no longer spread. Her face no longer raised in supplication. Instead her dark eyes met Neferet's gaze steadily. "You are no goddess. You are a mean-spirited, broken little girl. I pity you. What happened to you? Who broke you, child?"

Neferet's anger was so intense that she felt as if she would explode. Threads of Darkness forgotten, she struck out at Sylvia, wanting to connect flesh with flesh—to gouge and cut and bite this insolent hag.

With a movement so quick it belied her age, Sylvia lifted her arms defensively before her face, meeting Neferet's blows.

Pain burned through the Tsi Sgili's body, radiating from her hands. Neferet shrieked and jerked back, staring at the bloody marks left on her fists, burned in the exact shape of the blue stones in the bracelets that circled her withered arms.

"You dare to strike out at me! A goddess!"

"I strike at no one. I only defend myself through the stones of protection the Great Mother has gifted me with." Never breaking her gaze, and keeping her turquoise and silver swathed arms raised, the old woman began singing again.

Neferet wanted to tear her to shreds with her hands. But as she circled closer to the Cherokee she could feel the wave of heat that radiated from the blue stones in which she was covered. It was as if they pulsed with a fire equal to her own fury.

She needed the white bull! His frigid Darkness would extinguish the old woman's flames. Perhaps the odd energy she wielded would surprise him, and he would, again, lend Neferet his alluring might.

Controlling her anger, Neferet stepped back, outside the ring of smoke and heat that engulfed Sylvia. She studied the old woman, watched her dance, listened to her song. Old. Ancient. Everything about Sylvia Redbird said she, and the earth power she was wielding, had been here for a very long time.

The white bull was ancient as well.

This Indian would not surprise him.

"I will deal with you myself." Still meeting Sylvia Redbird's gaze, Neferet lifted her hands and, without so much as flinching, used her sharpened fingernails to gouge the wounds already formed by the old woman's protective turquoise. Her blood flowed freely, spattering the porch. Neferet shook her hands, raining scarlet through the smoke cloud, dispersing it, and painting the old woman with bright dots of red, which were a garish, stark contrast to the earthy greens and blues she wore. Then Neferet turned her hands, cupping her palms and letting her blood pool there. "Come, my Dark children, drink!" The tendrils were hesitant at first, but after the first taste of Neferet's blood, they were emboldened.

Neferet watched Sylvia's eyes widen and saw fear shadow them. The old woman's gaze did not waver, but her song faltered. Her voice began sounding old . . . weak . . . tremulous . . .

"Now, children! You have tasted my blood and Sylvia Redbird has been anointed by it. Entrap her—bring me the old woman!" Neferet's voice changed, and became rhythmic. Darkly she mirrored Sylvia's earthy war song.

> *"You need not kill.*
> *You need only sate my rage.*
> *You drank your fill.*
> *Now create for me a cage.*
> *I'll make old new.*
> *You'll feast on youth, vibrant, strong.*
> *To me be true.*
> *And kill this old woman's song!"*

The tendrils obeyed Neferet. They avoided the old woman's turquoise stones. They wrapped around her naked, unadorned feet, halting her rhythmic dance. Like the floor of a jail cell, Darkness formed from her feet, spreading, and then growing up and up and up, caging Sylvia, and finally, finally her song was silenced, replaced by an agonized scream as they lifted her and, moving through shadow and mist, carrying the terrible cage and its prisoner, Darkness followed their mistress.

Aurox

Aurox waited until the sun was high in the winter sky before he climbed from the pit again. The morning had dawned cloudy and gray, but as the endless hours passed the winter sun had broken through the mist and shadows. At noon, when the sun was highest in the sky, Aurox emerged.

He did not allow the sense of urgency that skittered under his skin to make him careless. Aurox used the sinuous muscles of his arms to hold firm to the roots and hang, partially belowground, partially aboveground. He used all of his paranormal senses to seek. *I must get away without being seen,* was foremost in his mind.

The school was not as silent as it had been the day before. Human workmen were busily repairing the damaged section of the stables. Aurox saw no vampyres, but the human cowboy, Travis, seemed to be everywhere. Yes, his hands and forearms were still swathed in white gauze bandages, but his voice was so strong that it drifted across the school grounds to Aurox. Lenobia did not show herself in the noonday sun, but she did not need to. Travis was there for her, and not simply with the workmen. The cowboy interacted freely with the horses. Aurox watched him move the huge Percheron and Lenobia's black mare from one makeshift round pen to another.

He does not merely work for Lenobia. She trusts him. The realization surprised Aurox. *If a High Priestess can trust a human so much in times of stress and tumult, perhaps there is a chance that Zoey can—*

No. Aurox would not allow himself to indulge in such a fantasy. He'd heard what he was. Zoey had heard what he was. They all had!

He had been formed by Darkness through the lifeblood of Zoey's mother. He was beyond her trust or her forgiveness.

There is only one person on this earth who trusts me—only one person who forgives me. It is to her that I must go.

Aurox hung there, peering through the roots and the shards of bark, waiting . . . watching . . . Finally the humans began to meander from the stables, talking about how glad they were to be within walking distance of Queenies so they could have the Ultimate Egg sandwich for lunch, and laughing. Friends always laughed.

Aurox longed to share the laughter of friends.

When their backs were to him and their voices faded, the boy pulled himself fully from the pit and, monkey-like, scaled the felled tree to where it rested against the wall of the school, and then vaulted over it.

Aurox wanted to sprint—to call the beast and tear the soil and run with all of his otherworldly might. Instead he forced himself to walk. He brushed the dirt, leaves, and grass from his clothing. He ran his fingers through the matted mess that was his hair, breaking apart the clumps of mud and blood, and combing it into some semblance of normalcy.

Normal was good. Normal was not noticed. Normal was not apprehended.

The vehicle was exactly where he'd left it the day before. The keys were still in the ignition. Aurox's hands trembled only a little as the engine turned over and he made his way from the rear parking lot of Utica Square and headed southeast—to sanctuary.

The drive seemed to take only a moment. Aurox was thankful for that. As he turned the car down Grandma Redbird's lane, he rolled down his windows. Even though the day was cool, he wanted to drink in the scent of lavender, and with it accept the calm it offered. Just as he accepted the sanctuary Grandma Redbird had offered.

When Aurox parked before her wide front porch, everything changed. At first he didn't understand it—couldn't process it. The scent hit him, but he fought the knowledge he breathed in with it.

"Grandma? Grandma Redbird?" Aurox called as he got out of the car and jogged around the side of the little cottage. He expected to find her beside the crystal stream—she belonged there. She should have been humming a joyful song. Peaceful. Secure. Safe.

She was not there.

A terrible premonition washed over him. Aurox remembered the fetid scent that had drifted to him amidst the lavender air when he'd parked before Grandma's home.

Aurox ran.

"Grandma! Where are you?" he was shouting as he rounded the side of the cottage, his feet sliding in the loose gravel that paved the small parking space in front of the home.

Aurox grabbed the railing of the porch, and took the six stairs in two wide strides, stopping in the center of the wide, wooden deck, just before Grandma's closed front door. Aurox yanked the door open and ran inside.

"Grandma! It's me, Aurox, your *tsu-ka-nv-s-di-na*. I have returned!"

Nothing. She was not here. It felt wrong, so very wrong.

Aurox retraced his steps, moving to the middle of the porch. The scent was thickest there.

Darkness. Fear. Hatred. Pain. Aurox could read all those emotions and more from the blood that spattered the porch. As he stood there, breathing heavily, taking in the terrible knowledge of violence and destruction, the smoke came to him. It lifted from around his moccasin-clad feet in swirls, carrying wisps of information. Imprinted in the gray mist was an ancient song that lifted around him, feather-like. Within it Aurox could hear the echo of a courageous woman's voice.

Aurox closed his eyes and breathed deeply. *Please,* he pleaded silently, *let me know what has happened here.*

Feelings assailed him—hatred and anger. Those feelings were easy to understand, familiar. "Neferet," he whispered. "You have been here. I scent you. I feel you." But after the familiar emotions came those which knocked him to his knees.

Aurox felt Sylvia Redbird's courage. He knew her wisdom and determination, and finally her fear.

He fell to his knees. "Oh, Goddess, no!" Aurox cried to the heavens. "This is Neferet's blood, drawn by Grandma Redbird. Did Neferet kill her as she did her daughter? Where is Grandma's body?"

There was no answer except the sighing of the listening wind and the annoying clicks and croaks of a huge raven that perched at the edge of the porch.

"Rephaim! Is that you?" Aurox ran his hands through his dirty hair while the raven stared at him, turning his head from side to side. "I wish the Goddess would take the bull within me and make me a bird. If she did I would take to the skies and fly forever and ever."

The raven croaked at him, then spread his wings and flew away, leaving Aurox completely alone.

In equal parts Aurox wanted to weep in despair and frustration, as well as to call the beast to him and attack someone, anyone, in anger and fear.

The boy who was also a beast chose to do neither. Instead Aurox did nothing—nothing at all, except think. He sat on Grandma's porch for a very long time, and amidst the residue of blood and smoke, fear and courage, Aurox reasoned his way to truth.

Had Neferet killed Grandma Redbird, her body would be here. She has no reason to hide her deeds. Her crimes have already been discovered. Thanatos made sure of that. So, what is it Neferet wants more than death and destruction?

The answer was as simple as it was horrible.

Neferet wants to create chaos and one very easy way to do that is to cause Zoey Redbird pain. Aurox knew the truth of it as the thought came to him. Grandma was unique among mortals—she was a gifted leader—beloved of many. And powerful. Grandma was powerful.

Sylvia Redbird would make a more perfect sacrifice than her daughter had made.

"No!" Aurox's mind skittered away from that terrible thought. It was also true that by capturing Zoey's beloved grandmother, Neferet would ensure the fledgling would come after her with all of her very impressive might. In doing so she would also fragment the vampyre community and wreak havoc locally.

"Whether she is used as a sacrifice or as a hostage, as long as Neferet holds Grandma Redbird, and Zoey tries to save her, Neferet gets what she most desires—chaos and vengeance. Well, then, someone else must save Grandma."

Aurox made his decision quickly, though he understood it could very well be the end of him. The drive back to Tulsa seemed to take an unusually long time. Aurox had time enough to think. He thought about Neferet and her callous disregard for life. He thought about Dragon Lankford and how he'd fought and vanquished the loneliness and despair that had tried to swallow his life. Aurox thought about the courage of those who stood against a foe so great that just the memory of the white bull made his insides shiver. And Aurox thought about Zoey Redbird.

It was well past sunset by the time Aurox returned to Tulsa. He did not drive to the obscure back lot of Utica Square. Instead, Aurox drove past the closed shopping center, heading east on Twenty-first Street. He turned left at the Utica Street light, and then left again a block later, entering through the front gate of the House of Night, parking not far from the empty small yellow bus.

Aurox drew a deep breath. *Be calm. Control the beast. I can do this. I must do this.* Then he got out of the car.

Aurox had thought a lot on the way from Grandma Redbird's empty home, but he hadn't actually considered the specifics of what he should do when he reached the House of Night. So, letting his instincts guide him, he simply began walking through campus.

It was obviously lunchtime. The scents that drifted from the cafeteria part of the main building made his mouth water, and he realized he hadn't eaten in an entire day. Automatically, his feet moved toward the center of campus, following the food.

Just as he stepped on the sidewalk outside the entrance to the dining hall, the big wooden doors opened and a group of fledglings poured out, talking and laughing in familiar, easy voices.

Zoey saw him before anyone else did. He knew it because her eyes widened with surprise. She'd begun shaking her head and was opening her mouth as if to shout at him when Stark's voice shot across the space between them like an arrow.

"Zoey, get back inside! Darius, Rephaim, to me. Let's get him!"

CHAPTER SIXTEEN

Zoey

"I need to talk to Zoey!" Aurox shouted, and then Stark punched him squarely in his mouth and he was too busy spitting blood and falling to his knees to shout anything else.

"Stark! Holy crap! Stop it!" I tried to grab my Warrior's arm.

"I said, get back inside!" Stark was yelling at me as he shook me off like I was an ant. He and Darius had thrown Aurox off the sidewalk and tossed him out into the school grounds and the waiting thicket of oaks where the shadows were deepest.

They're going to beat the crap out of him!

"He's not fighting you, Stark. He's not hurting anyone." I jogged after Stark and Darius, hating the muffled sounds of pain Aurox was making as they pulled him across the grass. I tried to reason with him, but Stark was seriously not listening to me. Darius didn't even glance at me.

Then I felt Stevie Rae's hand on my wrist. "Z, let the guys handle this."

"No, but he's—"

"He's not going anywhere." Stark kicked him and Aurox rolled into the shadows at the base of a big oak. "Even if he changes into that creature." Stark sounded as dangerous as he looked. He'd pulled his bow from the sling across his back and had notched an arrow, pointing it directly at Aurox.

"I don't want to change. I'm trying not to." Aurox struggled to his knees. His head was bowed and blood spilled from his mouth onto his shirt. "If you won't let me speak to Zoey, get Thanatos."

"Do it," Darius told Rephaim. "Get Kalona as well." Rephaim took off as Darius walked up to Aurox. Aurox lifted his head. His eyes were glowing and I could see that his face was flushed. He started to stand, but Darius backhanded him, knocking him down again. Then the Warrior pulled a thin, dangerous looking knife from inside his coat and stood over him.

Aurox's face was pressed against the pavement and I heard a terrible groan escape from him.

"You change and I will kill you," Stark spoke slowly and clearly.

"I am trying not to!" The words sounded strange, as if they had been forced from Aurox's throat. He turned his head then, and I could see that his face was totally contorted and his eyes were glowing. His skin was twitching and rippling like dozens of bugs were skittering around underneath the surface.

It looked disgusting and made my stomach roll. *This thing cannot be my Heath. The Seer Stone was wrong.* I put my hand over the stone and pressed it against my chest. Nothing. It wasn't even warm. *I'd made a mistake. It had all been just another mess up by me.* I could barely think through the rush of sadness I felt.

"Try harder!" I was blinking at Aphrodite in surprise and wondering what the hell was going on, when she marched past me straight up to Aurox.

"Aphrodite, get back! He may—" Darius began, but Aphrodite interrupted him.

"He's not gonna do shit. Bow Boy will shoot his ass. Then you'll slit him open from crotch to throat. I couldn't be safer if I was teaching kindergarten. Well, I'd be totally nauseated by the brats surrounding me, but you get my meaning."

"Aphrodite, what are you doing?" I found my voice again.

She pointed a manicured nail at Aurox. "As long as you don't attack anyone, there's nothing here for you to fight. So control that shit that's going on inside you. Now." She glanced over her shoulder at me. "Get closer. We don't need the whole damn school gawking at us like a train wreck." Her gaze took in my circle, my friends who had closed ranks and were hurrying up behind me: Damien, Shaunee, Shaylin. Their presence along with Stevie Rae's began to calm me, and helped me to think as she continued, "Okay, Shaylin says he's the color of moonlight, which made me think of Nyx, which then had me realizing that anyone, even someone as disgusting as this boy-bull-thing, who makes me think of Nyx should probably be allowed to speak. That's all. The end."

"Yeah, sorry." Shaylin moved closer to me and said softly, "I know it's not what anyone wants to hear, but I totally see silver moonlight when I look at him."

"It's what I want to hear." Aurox's voice was more normal. His skin had stopped doing the nasty bug twitchy thing. His mouth was still bleeding, and the side of his face had a bright red skid mark from where he'd hit the sidewalk when Stark had punched him, but he looked like a regular kid again and not like something out of *Resident Evil*.

"Don't you fucking move," Stark ground between his teeth. "Aphrodite, for once listen to Darius and back off. Do you not remember what he changed into?"

"He killed Dragon. He could kill you," Darius said.

"I did not want to! I tried not to." Aurox's gaze found mine. "Zoey, tell them. Tell them that I tried to stop what was happening. I don't know what happened. You believe me. I know you do. Grandma Redbird said you protected me."

Stark took a step toward Aurox. "Do *not* talk about Zoey's grandma!"

"That's why I'm here! Zoey, your grandma's in danger."

I felt like Aurox had punched me in the gut. Stark was stepping on the back of Aurox's neck, forcing his face into the ground and yelling something about Grandma. Darius was shouting, too. Damien had started screaming. Aurox's face had begun to ripple again and suddenly Kalona was there. He picked up Stark in one hand and Darius in another and tossed them away. Wings fully spread, he stood over Aurox, fists closed, face looking like an immortal Hulk. He was totally going to smash Aurox into nothingness.

"Don't kill him!" I shrieked. "He knows something about Grandma!"

"Warrior, stand down!" Thanatos didn't raise her voice, but the power of her command rippled across Kalona's skin. He twitched like a horse trying to dislodge a fly, but he lowered his fists. The High Priestess of Death skewered me with her dark eyes. "Call spirit. Strengthen the good within Aurox. Help him not to change."

I drew a shaky breath and closed my eyes so that I couldn't look at the thing that was Aurox—the thing that I'd thought was Heath—the thing that might have hurt Grandma. "Spirit, come to me," I whispered. "If there is good within Aurox, strengthen it. Help him to stay a boy." I felt the element I considered my closest affinity whisk around me and heard Aurox's gasping intake of breath as it moved to him. And then, for just an instant, I felt my Seer Stone heat up.

I opened my eyes and the Seer Stone went cold. Aurox was sitting on the ground, leaning heavily against a big oak, bleeding and bruised, but completely a boy again. Darius and Stark had picked themselves up and, scowling, were moving back to our group. Kalona looked pissed, but he'd stepped aside.

"Stevie Rae, summon earth. Deepen the shadows beneath this tree. Damien, call on air. Make the breeze blow hard enough to muffle our words. Our fledglings do not need to witness more violence and chaos. What happens here remains private," Thanatos commanded.

Stevie Rae and Damien obeyed the High Priestess, and in moments it felt like the group of us was standing in a little oak-scented bubble as wind whipped around us, carrying away our words.

Thanatos gave the two of them a nod of approval. Then she turned to Aurox. "Now, what do you know about Sylvia Redbird?" Thanatos shot the question at him.

"Neferet has taken her."

"Oh, Goddess!" I staggered and Stark caught me before I could fall. "Is she dead?"

"I-I do not know. I hope she is not," Aurox said earnestly.

"You don't know? You hope she's not dead?" Stevie Rae sounded super pissed. "Was this somethin' you did again, but tried not to do?"

"No! I had nothing to do with it."

"Then how do you know about it?" I managed to ask, even though my voice was shaky and I felt like I was going to puke.

"I went back to her home and she was gone. There was blood on her porch. It was Neferet's. I know it. I know her scent."

"Was Grandma's blood there, too?" I asked.

"No." He shook his head. "But traces of her power lingered in smoke and in the land, as if she had been prepared for battle."

"You said you went back to Sylvia's home. Why?" Thanatos asked.

Aurox brushed some of the blood from his mouth. His hand was trembling. Actually, he looked like he was going to burst into tears.

"She found me yesterday morning, after that awful night. She forgave me. She said she believed in me, and then she offered me sanctuary. She talked to me, like I was normal. Like I wasn't a monster. She named me *tsu-ka-nv-s-di-na*." Aurox met my gaze.

"Bull," I said, recalling words recited from my childhood lessons. "That's the Cherokee word for bull."

"Yes, that's what Grandma said. She offered me sanctuary, as long as I didn't hurt anyone else, but I left." He shook his head. "I shouldn't have! I should have stayed there and protected her, but I did not know she was in danger."

"I am not blaming you. Not at this time," Thanatos said. "You say you left yesterday, and then returned today?"

Aurox nodded. "I left because I needed to figure out who I am— what I am. I came here. I hid under the shattered tree." He looked beseechingly at Thanatos. "I heard what you said at Dragon's funeral pyre about what I am. I couldn't bear it. All I could think was that I had to get back to Grandma Redbird—that she would help me figure out a way to undo whatever was done to make me."

"The killing of her daughter made you, Vessel," Kalona said, his voice cold. "You expect us to believe you were granted sanctuary by the woman whose daughter's death created you?"

"It is unbelievable. I know that." Aurox's strangely colored eyes found mine again. "I do not understand how Grandma could be so kind, so forgiving, but she is. She even fed me chocolate chip and lavender cookies with milk." He pointed down to his shoes, which I recognized as hand-stitched moccasins, the kind Grandma liked to make for Yule gifts.

"No human is that forgiving. Even a goddess would find it difficult to forgive one such as you," said Kalona's cold, dead voice.

"A goddess forgave me," Rephaim said softly. "And I have done worse things than Aurox."

"Grandma named him bull. She makes chocolate chip and lavender cookies," I said. "And those are her handmade moccasins, too."

"Which means you have been at her house, and that she talked to you," Stark said. "But it doesn't mean you didn't do something terrible to her and then steal her stuff."

"If that's true, then why would he come here?" I heard myself asking.

"An excellent point," Thanatos said. She turned to Shaylin. "Child, read his colors."

"I already have. That's why Aphrodite stopped Darius and Stark from beating him up," Shaylin said.

"His aura is made of moonlight," Aphrodite took up the explanation. "Which is why I stepped in and used a PAUSE button on the testosterone."

"Explain, Prophetess," Thanatos commanded.

"If he's the color of moonlight then I have to believe he is, somehow, connected to Nyx because the moon is her main symbol," Aphrodite said.

"Well reasoned," Thanatos said. She studied Aurox. "Even before Zoey strengthened your spirit you were controlling the metamorphosis that was trying to change you."

"I wasn't controlling it very well," he admitted.

"But I could see you were trying." Her gaze went from Aurox to me. "Would your grandmother forgive him, even after witnessing what he can become?"

I didn't hesitate. "Yes. Grandma is the kindest person I've ever known. She is our Wise Woman, our Ghigua." I walked up to Aurox. "Where is she? Where has Neferet taken her?"

"I do not know. I only know that Neferet battled with her. Grandma Redbird drew her blood, and now they are both gone. I am sorry, Zo."

"Don't you ever, *ever* call me that again," I said.

Beside me, I could see Stark had narrowed his eyes and was studying Aurox like a fly he wanted to pull the wings off of.

"You are *not* Heath Luck," Stark said. He kept his voice pitched low, but it was obvious that he was ready to explode.

Aurox shook his head, looking utterly confused. "I am Aurox. I do not know this Heath Luck."

"Damn right you don't," Stark said. "So, like Zoey said, don't ever call her Zo again. You couldn't even wipe the shoes of the guy who used to call her that."

"Does Heath Luck have something to do with Grandma Redbird?" Aurox asked.

"No!" I cut off whatever pissed-off thing Stark was getting ready to say. "And we really need to focus on finding Grandma."

"I may know where Neferet has taken Sylvia Redbird," Kalona said. We all stared at him expectantly. "She has a penthouse suite at the Mayo Hotel. The entire balcony is hers. The walls are solid marble and leak no sounds. She has all the privacy that her wealth can purchase. She could have taken Sylvia Redbird there."

"How could she have done that?" I asked, even though I wanted very much to believe finding Grandma was as easy as following Neferet to her penthouse. "Grandma wouldn't have just walked in there with her, and even though the mayor and City Council seem to be kissing her butt, no way is the staff of the Mayo going to ignore the fact that she's dragging an old woman through their lobby."

"You have seen her move silently, invisibly. I daresay you can appear and disappear fairly easily yourself, Zoey Redbird," Thanatos said.

"Well, yeah, I can. Sorta. But I don't think I can make someone else invisible."

"Neferet can," Aurox said solemnly. "That and much more. Your goddess has gifted her with power. The white bull has gifted her with power. And what power she hasn't been gifted with, she steals through pain and death and deception. She is bloated with it."

"It would be a mistake to underestimate Neferet," Thanatos agreed.

"Then we need to go to her penthouse and make her let Grandma go," I said.

"Hang on," Stark said. "How do we know he's not making this all up as a way to get us to go after Neferet?"

"I am not Neferet's creature!" Aurox cried.

"You sure as hell were two nights ago. Dragon Lankford is dead because of it," Stark shot back at him.

"Stark has a point," Stevie Rae said. "Try callin' your grandma."

Glad I had something to do, I pulled out my phone and punched Grandma's number. As it rang, Thanatos said, "If she does not answer, sound normal. Leave her a message about the open house. If Neferet has taken her, she may have access to Sylvia's phone as well."

I nodded and felt my stomach sink when she didn't answer and Grandma's familiar voice said she wasn't available, but that she would call right back. I took a deep breath, and after the beep tried to sound as normal as possible.

"Hey there, Grandma, sorry to be calling you so late. I'm glad you have your phone on silent, though, so I'm not waking you up." My voice started to shake, but before I could fall totally apart and burst into tears Stark's strong arm slid around my shoulders. I leaned into him and spoke quickly, hoping I sounded perky and not hysterical. "I don't know if you saw the news yet, but Thanatos announced that we're having a big open house and job fair and basically inviting all of Tulsa. It's a charity for Street Cats, too, and a way to make Neferet look as crazy as she is and us look, well, *not crazy*," I added, thinking *so there, you hateful hag!* "Anyway, it's this coming Saturday, and Thanatos asked me to ask you if you'd help us coordinate with Sister Mary Angela. I told her I thought you'd be totally cool with that, so call me as soon as you can and I'll give you the details, 'kay? I love you, Grandma! I really, really love you! Bye."

Stark took the phone from me and pressed the END call button. Then he pulled me into his arms as I did, indeed, burst into tears.

During my shaking and snotting I felt another hand touch my back and recognized the calm presence of earth. Then another hand touched me, and air brushed softly against me. Yet another hand joined the others, and fire warmed me. Spirit, that was already present, settled within me, calming my tears and allowing me to pull back from Stark enough to smile shakily at my friends.

"Thanks, guys. I'm better now," I said.

"Well, you will be after you blow your nose," Stark gently kidded as he handed me a balled up tissue from his pocket.

"You're a mess, Z. That's for damn sure," Aphrodite said. She was shaking her head, but she was also standing shoulder-to-shoulder with the rest of my circle—showing solidarity—showing support.

"I am not lying." I looked from my friends to see that Aurox had stood. He was facing Thanatos. Darius and Kalona had positioned themselves protectively between him and the High Priestess. Aurox turned his head and his eyes met mine. I was shocked to see tears standing in them. He looked almost as devastated as I felt. Then he faced the High Priestess and begged, "Chain me up. Lock me away. I will take whatever punishment you mete out to me, but please, for the sake of Sylvia Redbird, believe me. I am not in league with Neferet. I despise her. I hate that she created me from death and pain. In order to control me, she must have Darkness take over my body and awaken the creature within. High Priestess, you know that is true."

"From what evidence we have uncovered it would seem that is the truth," Thanatos said.

"Then listen to me. I give you my oath—Neferet has taken Zoey's grandmother."

"You only have this one chance." I stepped from the circle of my friends and walked over to Aurox. "If you are lying to us. If you have anything to do with Grandma being hurt I will use all five of the elements and all of my Goddess-given powers to destroy you, no matter what you are. No matter who you are. You have *my* oath on that."

"Accepted," he said, bowing his head to me.

"Bound," Thanatos said. "All beings with spirits have a choice. I hope you are making the correct one, Aurox."

"I am," he said.

"Yes, we have your oath on that," Thanatos said, then she gazed around at the rest of us. "We need to get into Neferet's penthouse."

"I can go," Aurox said.

"No!" Stark, Darius, Kalona, and I yelled together.

"I can get into her damn penthouse," Aphrodite said. "That bitch believes I'm as big a bitch as she is, and while in some ways that might be semi-true, Neferet measures everyone's loyalty by her own, which is non-existent. She's always wanted to use me, *and* she can't hear my thoughts. I can get in."

"She may let you in, but she would never allow you to see whether she has taken Grandma Redbird prisoner," Aurox said.

"He speaks the truth. She would cloak her prisoner's presence from Aphrodite," Thanatos said.

"Not from me. She would never believe it necessary. Neferet will be angry at me for failing to stop the reveal ritual, but she will allow me in at least long enough for me to discover if she holds Grandma Redbird," Aurox said.

"Or long enough to manipulate you," Darius said.

"And wake up that thing that sleeps inside you," Stark added.

"Aurox, you cannot control the beast. Not if Neferet sacrifices to awaken it," Thanatos said.

"That may be why she captured Zoey's grandmother," Darius said, sending me an apologetic look. "Perhaps she needs a greater sacrifice than a Warrior's cat to regain control of Aurox."

"No! I, no . . ." Aurox said brokenly, his shoulders sagged and he put his face in his hands.

All I could do was shake my head back and forth, back and forth. Stark took my hand and squeezed it. "We won't let that happen. We're going to get Grandma back."

"But how?" My words came out between sobs.

"I will go." Kalona was staring at me as he spoke. "I will not simply enter Neferet's home. If she is holding Sylvia Redbird prisoner, I will find her and rescue her. Darkness cannot cloak itself from me; we have too long known one another. Neferet thinks herself invulnerable because she has become an immortal, but she has only a child's experience compared to my vast centuries of power and knowledge. I cannot kill her, but I can steal an old woman from her."

"Well, maybe. *If* she lets you in the front door," Stark said. "Last time I checked, she doesn't like you much."

"Neferet loathes me, but that does not change the fact that she desires me."

"Really? That's not how it looks to everyone else. Neferet's moved on," Stark continued. "Her Consort's the white bull."

Kalona smiled sardonically at Stark. "You are young and know little of women."

I felt Stark bristle and quickly wiped my eyes and my nose and pulled myself together. "You're going to have to make her believe you're betraying us to her—that your oath to Thanatos is a fake."

"Neferet does not know I have sworn to Thanatos," he said.

"Uh, I think she might," Shaunee said.

I glanced at her in surprise.

"I'm not saying this to be mean, and I really don't want to go into details, so I'm asking you to just trust me—but it's pretty safe to say that whatever Erin knows about us, Dallas knows," Shaunee said.

"Holy crap!" Stevie Rae said.

"Dallas talks to Neferet," Rephaim said.

"Huh?" I'd practically forgotten Rephaim was there, and then I felt guilty as hell when he shrugged and explained, "I'm not used to talking a lot. I don't say much, so people ignore me and then I hear things."

"I don't ignore you," Stevie Rae said, tiptoeing to kiss his cheek.

He smiled at her. "No, never you. But Dallas does. He was near me when his phone rang between classes today. Twice. It was Neferet both times."

"And I'm about ninety-nine percent sure Erin would tell Dallas anything he wants to know about us," Shaunee said.

"Erin remained here at the House of Night when the rest of you returned to the depot yesterday," Thanatos said.

I met Shaylin's gaze. "Tell her."

The fledgling didn't hesitate. "Erin's colors are different than they used to be. I noticed it a couple of days ago."

"She's changing," Aphrodite said. "Shaylin and I both believe it. That's why we advised Zoey to let Erin stay when she told Zoey she wanted to."

"Then I agree with Shaunee. It is very possible that Neferet knows everything Erin knows," Thanatos said.

"Here's what I think," Aphrodite said. "I think we all need to keep our mouths shut about what's going on with Grandma Redbird and Aurox and our business in general. If you're not part of this group, then you don't know shit. Erin's just one kid, but what she knows could definitely mess us up."

"Prophetess, it sounds as if there is a lesson to be learned in what you're saying," Thanatos said, and the rest of us nodded.

I glanced at Kalona. Including him in our group felt really weird, but I couldn't tell if that meant we should or shouldn't trust him.

Weirdly echoing my thoughts, Thanatos asked Kalona, "Do you still believe she will trust you?"

"Neferet? Trust me? Never. But she does desire me, even if it is only my immortal power after which she lusts. And, as Aphrodite said, she measures everyone's depth of loyalty by her own," Kalona said.

"Neferet is only loyal to herself," Rephaim said.

"Exactly," Kalona said.

"Well, let's hope you're not that shallow," Stark added, sounding like he believed the opposite.

I just stood there, staring at Kalona, remembering what a lying, manipulative killer he had been, and thinking *that's who's going to save my grandma?*

I was blinking back freaked-out tears when Rephaim whispered my name. I looked over at him. He smiled and mouthed two small words: *people change.*

CHAPTER SEVENTEEN

Shaylin

"Here. Now." Aphrodite crooked her finger at Shaylin, motioning for her to follow. She did her twitchy walk, cutting across the grass and heading in the general direction of the fledglings' dorms.

Shaylin sighed, squelched her irritation, and followed the annoying blonde. As she caught up with her, Aphrodite was already talking. "Okay, you need to reconnoiter."

"Okay, you need to grow some manners," Shaylin said.

Aphrodite stopped and narrowed her eyes to blue slits.

"You should know that look is unattractive *and* it causes crow's feet," Shaylin spoke quickly before Aphrodite could say something mean and smart-assy.

"You've been talking to Damien, haven't you?"

"Maybe," Shaylin answered vaguely, not wanting to get Damien in any trouble. But, yeah, the truth was she had been talking to him. Actually, she'd really started to like Damien, as well as Stevie Rae and Zoey. Aphrodite, though, *she* was a different story. "Aphrodite, really, it looks like you and I might have to work together, or whatever you'd call this Prophetess stuff. So, it'd make both of our lives easier if you could, at least, be polite to me."

"No, it would make *your* life easier. Mine, it wouldn't change at all."

Shaylin shook her head. "Really? Why don't you run that attitude past Nyx? We have major Darkness to fight. Zoey's mom was just killed and now her grandma's in serious danger. Correct me if I'm wrong, but isn't Zoey a friend of yours?"

Aphrodite's eyes narrowed again, but she only said one word: "Yes."

"Then how about you do everything you can to help her."

"I am doing that, bitch," Aphrodite snapped.

"How can you be so sure? Did you ever consider the small fact that maybe, if you were less hateful, you'd have access to more of your Prophetess gifts?"

Aphrodite's eyes un-narrowed. Slowly. She even looked a little surprised. "No. I've never considered that."

Shaylin threw her hands up in frustration. "Jeesh, were you raised by wolves?"

"Sort of," Aphrodite said. "But they had money."

"Incredible," Shaylin murmured. Then she started over. "Okay, here's what I know. When I read your aura and was bitchy about the little flickering light I saw within you, it messed with my head. The next time I looked at you, it was like your colors were all running together."

"Which, obviously, means you saw me being pissed."

"No, because *everyone's* colors looked all runny and indistinct until I apologized to you. Wait, scratch that. The complete truth is my True Sight was messed up until I apologized to you and *meant it.*"

"Huh. That's almost interesting."

"I'm not getting through to you at all, am I?"

"As much as anyone can," Aphrodite said. "So, back to reconnoitering."

"Fine. Yes. What do you want me to do?"

"Find Erin. And Dallas. If I'm correct, which, just FYI for future reference, I almost always am, you're going to find them together."

"And that would be bad, right?"

"Are you brain damaged?"

"I'm not even going to answer that," Shaylin said.

"Good. We don't have time for connect-the-dots. It's going to be dawn in a couple of hours. The bus will be heading back to the depot and Kalona will be heading into Neferet's nasty lair."

"Yeah, Kalona waiting until dawn so she'd be weakened by the sun without it being totally obvious that he was waiting until she was weakened by the sun doesn't look like it's going to work," Shaylin said, looking skyward.

"What in the hell are you talking about, fucktard?"

Shaylin pointed up. "Rain clouds. Lots of them. I really wish they'd clear out. They blanket the sun and its weakening effect. Now who's the fucktard?"

"Do not call me a fucktard," Aphrodite said.

"Well, then don't call me one," Shaylin said.

"I'll think about it. Back to my original point—before we go back to the depot and Kalona takes off, I want you to check out Dallas and Erin's colors. Any additional info you can give us about Erin, especially about whether she's a traitorous, skanky ho—yeah, I'm paraphrasing Shaunee—would be a good thing. I have a feeling about them, and it's not a warm, fuzzy one."

"All right, yeah, sounds good, but I have no idea where they might be. Do you? Is that one of the gifts you have?" Shaylin asked.

"Goddess, you are brain damaged. No, I don't have a GPS inside my head. I *do* have a brain inside it, though. It tells me that if Erin and Dallas are doing the nasty, it makes sense to start looking for them in Erin's dorm room—the dorm room she *doesn't* share with Shaunee anymore."

"Oh. Yeah. That does make sense." Shaylin hesitated. "But I don't know which dorm room is hers."

"Third floor, number thirty-six. When they shared a brain, they used to say it stood for their chest size. I said it was their combined IQ."

"Of course you did," Shaylin said.

"See, you do understand me!" Aphrodite said with fake enthusiasm. "I'll meet you back at the bus. Soon." Aphrodite started to walk away, paused and added, "Please."

Shaylin's eyes widened.

Aphrodite rolled her eyes and opened her mouth, obviously preparing to say something hateful. Then she stopped, stared above her for one long moment, before glancing at Shaylin and saying, "Looks like you're getting your wish. The rainclouds are clearing." Then Aphrodite tossed her hair and twitched off.

Shaylin shook her head. "Total nutjob," she muttered to herself as she made her way to the girls' dorm. "Nyx, I don't know you very well, and I don't want you to think I'm rude or blasphemous or anything like that, but Aphrodite as your Prophetess? Why?"

"No one knows, and I think that includes Aphrodite herself."

Shaylin jumped in surprise as Erik Night stepped from the shadows of a nearby oak tree.

"Erik! What are you doing out here?" Shaylin's hand went to her throat. She imagined Erik could see how hard her pulse pounded there, and not just because he'd startled her. Her first view of him was always the same—his absolute, total, tall/dark/handsomeness was obvious and distracting. But then she got a glimpse of his colors and they weren't nearly as attractive. Shaylin had decided he was like one of those gorgeously painted pieces of pottery that you'd like to use to toss a salad in or whatever, but if you flipped the piece over you'd see the *WARNING: DO NOT USE TO SERVE FOOD* label.

"Sorry. I didn't mean to scare you. I'm out here procrastinating." His smile was a zillion-watt lightbulb. Shaylin could see why almost one hundred percent of the fledgling girls were in love with him. The problem was, she could also *see* more than his gorgeousness.

"I didn't mean to interrupt you. I'll let you get back to your procrastination. See ya."

"Hey." He touched her arm, just for a moment as she walked past him, coaxing her to pause. "I thought we were friends."

Shaylin studied him. When Erik had Marked her his colors were mostly made up of an indecisive, pea green that overshadowed the bright flashes of something that might have been golden, like the rays of the sun, but were too fleeting for her to be sure. Other than that he'd just been kinda foggy and wishy-washy. She hadn't paid much attention to his colors the past few days, so when she focused,

Shaylin was surprised to see that, even though his green was still there, it had lightened and now it didn't bring to mind mushy peas. Instead it reminded her of turquoise, like pretty sea foam green turquoise. And all around the green-blue the foggy mishmash of gray had lifted, revealing a solid tan, like the sand of a beautiful, untouched beach. Feeling a little like she'd fallen into deep water, Shaylin tried not to look nervous and blurted, "Yeah, we are friends, but that's all."

"I didn't ask for anything else, did I?"

Shaylin met his eyes. They were bright and blue, and spent way too much time wandering south to her boobs. Of course, saying something like "you totally want to be friends with benefits" sounded way too much like something Aphrodite would say. So instead she chose a nicer answer. "No, you haven't *asked* for anything else."

He smiled again. "So, we can be friends?"

It was hard not to smile back at him, and truthfully, she couldn't think of a reason not to. Shaylin grinned and nodded. "Yep, friends."

"Awesome! How about I walk you to wherever you're going? I can procrastinate just as well with you as I can by myself."

"What are you procrastinating about?" Shaylin avoided the question of where she was going and just kinda meandered in the general direction of the dorms. Slowly.

"Lesson plans," he said with a sigh. "I really hate writing them. You know, I never meant to be a professor."

"Yeah, everyone knows that. You were meant to be a movie star," Shaylin said. She spoke in an offhand manner. She hadn't meant to be patronizing or sarcastic, but the hurt in his blue eyes said she'd probably sounded both.

"Yeah," he repeated in a clipped voice, turning his gaze away from her and stuffing his hands in the pockets of his jeans. "Everyone knows that."

"Hey, but this Tracker thing is just a little speed bump in the road to Hollywood, right? What are you, twenty-one?"

"Nineteen. I just completed the Change a few months ago. Why? Do I look old?"

Shaylin laughed. "Twenty-one isn't old."

"It is if you have to add four years onto it, and I've just started a four-year Tracker job."

"Does being a Tracker mean you have to stay at the House of Night in Tulsa?"

"Trying to get rid of me?" He only sounded about half kidding.

"No, of course not," she assured him. "What I meant is, can't you transfer to the West Coast and still be a Tracker? There must be a House of Night nearer to Hollywood than this." As they talked, Shaylin realized that Erik didn't sound like a pissed-off, spoiled brat. He just sounded tired and frustrated and maybe even kinda depressed.

"I already looked into it. The answer I got was weird and a little creepy." He paused and sent her a sideways glance. "Well, probably creepier for the kids who are being Tracked than for me."

"Been there—done that. It wasn't so creepy. Actually, you were kinda funny," she said.

Erik frowned. "I was supposed to be powerful and confident and maybe a little scary."

"So, you want to be creepy?"

That made him laugh. "No, not really. And the actual Marking isn't the creepy part anyway, or at least it's not supposed to be. The part that's definitely *not normal* is that there's something in my blood that keeps me anchored to this place. Yeah, I can travel, but only if it's because my blood's calling me to Mark a kid who belongs at this House of Night."

"So, you're kinda like a GPS."

"I suppose." Erik didn't sound thrilled about it. "Hey, but enough about me. Where are you going?"

Shaylin swallowed around the dryness in her throat and said the first lie that came to her mind. "I'm going to the dorm. Aphrodite asked me to pick up some of her stuff from her room."

"She asked, as in *please would you?* Or she commanded, as in 'Get my stuff or I'll rubber band your hands together and shove you in a boiling pot like my mom's chef would cook a lobster!'"

Shaylin giggled. "Your acting skills either went way up or way down in my opinion, because you sound entirely too much like Aphrodite."

He shuddered. "I'll try not to do that again."

"But in answer to your question—it was more like the second example than the first."

"Big surprise. So, I'll walk you to the dorm. Okay?"

Shaylin met his eyes. *What could it hurt?* "Okay," she said.

Erik

"I think I agree with you about the lesson plan stuff. It must be super boring to have to figure out what you're going to teach—write it down—turn it in—then teach it. Talk about overkill," Shaylin said.

"Tell me about it," Erik said dryly. "We're going into Shakespeare. I love the plays, but it was a lot cooler when I just got to act and didn't have to be a damn robot for the school's High Council. Yeah, lesson plans are boring. Writing them sucks."

He had to keep reminding himself to stop looking at Shaylin's boobs. Okay, but in his defense, she was wearing a white T-shirt that was sheer enough that it was obvious she had on a hot pink bra under it. And that bra had little black bows in the middle part and on the straps.

"So, which play will you teach in the Shakespeare class?" she was asking him.

Look at her face and concentrate! "Shakespeare class?"

She gave him a look that said she thought he was an idiot—and he had to agree with her because when he forced himself not to glance at her pink-bra-ed boobs he got all distracted by her thick mane of dark hair that curled and waved and looked like it would be soft as silk if he just—

"Oh, yeah, Shakespeare class. Definitely a comedy. There's way too much tragedy in the world today."

"Which one?"

She looked honestly interested, so he heard himself admitting, "I'm torn. My favorite is *The Taming of the Shrew*, but when you think about it and really look at Kate's last speech, it doesn't go with the matriarchal belief system of the House of Night, and the last thing I need is to piss off Thanatos. So, I'm thinking about doing *As You Like It*. Rosalind is one of the Bard's strongest heroines. That shouldn't cause me any hassles with the administration."

"Isn't that kinda like caving, though?"

"Probably, but teaching isn't as easy as you'd think. There's a bunch of crap that goes on behind the scenes, and that's not counting the battle with Darkness that seems to be, like, never ending and the annoying fact that professors keep getting killed, *and* more and more fledglings are getting Marked, so we're short staffed."

There was a long, uncomfortable silence, then Shaylin said, "Yeah, it must be real inconvenient for you that professors have been disemboweled and decapitated and gored. Not to mention all the new red fledglings you have to teach because we haven't died for real. Yet."

Erik frowned. He hadn't meant it like that. Not really.

"I think that came out wrong," he said.

"And I think I need to remember that peas do not turn into pretty turquoise sea foam and an untouched beach."

"What's that supposed to mean?" She was really hot, but Shaylin totally messed with his head and confused him.

"It means I needed a reality check. Thanks for giving me one." Shaylin picked up the pace, and Erik was still trying to figure out the peas and turquoise comment when they were suddenly stepping from the winter grass of the school grounds to the sidewalk that ran into the front of the girls' dorm.

"Um, you're welcome?" he offered as they came to the wide cement stairs that led to the porch of the dorm.

Shaylin was still a little ahead of him, so she reached the first step before him. Standing on it, she was almost at eye level with him, which was weird because she was so little.

"No, you don't need to 'you're welcome' me," she said, sighing.

"I really wasn't thanking you. I was just reminding myself of something."

"Of what?" he asked, honestly interested.

She sighed again. "Of the fact that what the eye can see is not what's actually the most important thing about a person. The most important thing is what's hidden inside."

"Only with you, it's not really hidden at all, right?"

"Right." She spoke softly.

"I really didn't mean what I said before. I was just venting. You know, girls do it all the time," Erik said.

"Erik, you're not making it any better by being a misogynist."

"Misogynist . . . that's bad, right? Nothing cool, like a gynecologist?"

"Erik, maybe you should try not to speak." Shaylin sounded annoyed, but he could see that she was struggling not to laugh. And then a little giggle did escape from her pretty pink lips. "Gynecologist? Did you really just say that?"

"I did, and I'm proud of it." Erik put on his best good ol' boy Okie accent. "I do 'preciate me a career that's all 'bout them thar girl parts."

"Okay, that's enough for me," she said, still giggling. "I gotta go before—"

Shaylin moved back and completely missed the next step. She was absolutely going to fall right on her cute, round ass, but Erik was faster than gravity and, almost like a superhero, he caught her around her waist, keeping her from hurting herself.

And then there they were. She was standing on a step above him and he had his arms around her waist. When she was falling her arms had flailed out, and as he caught her they'd automatically wrapped around his shoulders. So she was pressed against him so hard he could feel the black bows on that pink bra.

"Careful," he spoke softly, gently, like she was a frightened bird. "I wouldn't want anything to happen to you."

"Th-thanks. I almost fell."

Shaylin gazed at him and he got lost in her big, brown eyes. She smelled as incredible as she had the night he'd Marked her—sweet, like peaches and strawberries mixed together. He'd never wanted anything as bad as he wanted to kiss her. Just once. For just a second. He bent. It seemed she was tilting her lips to his. He bent some more, pulling her closer.

And that's when she whacked him in the chest.

"You're trying to kiss me now? *Really?*" Shaylin shook her head and shoved, pushing him off his step.

Erik staggered back. He was trying to figure out exactly what had gone wrong when he heard the mocking laughter. Feeling like shit, he looked up to see Erin and Dallas standing at the top of the dorm stairs just outside the wide doorway.

"Damn, talk about mixed messages," Dallas said. "First she's all over you, then she's shoving you away. That just ain't right."

"Yeah, when a girl says yes she should mean yes, and not 'hey, I think I'll tease you and then reject you.'" Erin air quoted.

"You two don't know what you're talking about." Shaylin had one hand on her hip and her chin raised, but her face was flushed. Erik thought she looked cute, but not tough at all.

Dallas slid his hand around Erin's waist, and she leaned against him as they walked down the stairs to Erik, laughing at Shaylin the whole way.

"Hey, man." Dallas chuckled. "Don't worry. My mermaid and I will let everyone know what a dick tease she is." Erik tried to interrupt him, but Dallas just kept on talking. "No, you don't need to thank me. Just consider it a favor from one vamp to another."

Erik glanced up at Shaylin. Her face had gone from pink to white. He did consider it—just for a second, though. It'd be easier to laugh and walk off with Dallas and Erin. It might even make him feel as cool as it used to feel when he was the hottest fledgling at the school—when he could have any girl he wanted. Then he realized what he was thinking and felt sick to his stomach.

"No." Erik met Dallas's gaze. "Shaylin was right—you don't know what you're talking about. What you saw was me trying something stupid. Shaylin didn't ask for it."

"Ah, come on. You're Erik Night." Dallas's voice was still all friendly, but his gaze had gone hard.

"Yeah, I am. And I'm telling you that you're wrong. Shaylin isn't a tease. I was being a dick. If you two have to talk about her, that's what you should be saying."

"You expect people to believe a little freak like her turned *you* down?" Erin didn't even try to cover the spitefulness in her voice.

And I used to dream about being the center of a Twin sandwich. Goddess, I am a dick.

"What I expect is for you two to either tell the truth or shut up," Erik said.

"Well, this wasn't fun at all." Shaylin walked down the stairs quickly. As she passed Erik, she paused. "I've changed my mind about getting stuff from the dorm. Aphrodite can run her own errands." Shaylin looked from him to Erin. "I guess this means you won't be catching the bus back to the depot again tonight."

"I've ridden the short bus for the last time, but you go ahead. It fits you better than me, anyway."

"You tell 'em, mermaid," Dallas said, rubbing his hand over Erin's ass. "Water needs to be free to go wherever it wants."

"Yeah, and it's time for us to go. I'm bored," Erin said.

"I got somethin' for that!" Dallas bit her neck. Erin's squeal turned into a throaty laugh.

"And I won't be saying yes-no, yes-no. I'll just be saying yes-yes!" Erin sneered at Shaylin, grabbed Dallas's hand, and they walked away, laughing sarcastically.

Erik stared after them. "When did the two of them happen?"

"Right after Erin and Shaunee un-happened," Shaylin said. "And it's as bad as Shaunee thought it might be."

Erik's eyes widened. "You didn't come here to get Aphrodite's stuff, did you?"

"Nope."

Understanding hit him. "Ah, shit! Erin's changed sides, hasn't she? And that means Dallas and his group will know everything Zoey's group knows."

"Looks like it. I gotta go tell Z and Stevie Rae that Erin and Dallas really are together." Shaylin hesitated, then she added, "Thanks for standing up for me. I know it wasn't an easy thing for you to do."

"You really do think I'm a jerk, don't you?"

Shaylin didn't respond right away. Instead she studied him as if she understood how important her answer would be to him. Finally she said, "I think you have the potential to become more turquoise green than pea green."

"And that's a good thing?"

She smiled. "Even better than being a misogynistic gynecologist."

He laughed. "Okay, good. Hey, can I walk you to the bus?"

"No, not this time. But ask me again some time. For the record, when I say no I mean no, and when I say yes I mean yes."

"I pretty much already knew that about you," he said.

"Good, then next time you can wait until I say yes to kiss me. See ya later, Erik."

As Shaylin walked away Erik's smile got bigger and bigger. It wasn't his one hundred watt smile—that one was *acting* happy. This smile was better—it was *feeling* happy. And for the first time in a long time, Erik Night realized feeling was way better than acting. . . .

CHAPTER EIGHTEEN

Kalona

"The clouds clear from the sky. I believe it is a good omen," Kalona said. He spoke to the High Priestess of Death, who was standing before the busload of fledglings and vampyres who still had not left for their depot home.

"Yeah, okay, we hear ya. We really gotta get our butts back to the depot," Stevie Rae said. "But we all wish you good luck. I just know if Neferet has Grandma Redbird, you're the right guy to get her back!" She smiled that innocent, joyful smile of hers at him, and his son waved in happy agreement, then the bus's doors closed and Darius drove away.

Zoey said nothing before they left. Nothing at all. She'd just sat on the bus while everyone else talked and collected their schoolbooks and finished loading the bus. But he could feel her eyes watching him. He felt her mistrust through them. He also felt her hope. *I am her only chance at getting her grandmother back alive,* Kalona thought as the school bus disappeared down Utica Street. *She could have at least wished me luck.*

"Nyx, I ask that you watch over my Warrior, Kalona."

Hearing the Goddess's name startled Kalona and he refocused on Thanatos. The High Priestess was standing before him, arms raised, face lifted to the pre-dawn sky.

"He has chosen to bind himself to your path through me, your loyal High Priestess. He is my sword—my shield—my protector. And as I have been given dominion of this House of Night, Kalona has become its protector as well."

Thanatos's voice was rich with power and as it brushed over Kalona's skin, he trembled. *She is invoking Nyx! And the Goddess is responding!* He held his breath as she continued.

"Thus, I beseech your aid, benevolent Goddess of Night. I ask that you strengthen him should he be weakened by Darkness and its trappings. Allow his choice to shine and, like moonlight through the grayness of mist, let his purpose part the shadows of that which might cloud his judgment and distract his intent. Do not let him fall prey to Darkness as long as his choice is for Light."

Kalona fisted his hands so that Thanatos would not see how they had begun to tremble.

Nyx did not appear, but her listening presence was tangible. He could feel the sweet goodness that stirred the air in the wake of the Goddess. It had always been so. Wherever Nyx turned her immortal attention, there followed magick and Light, power and laughter, joy and love. Always love.

Kalona bowed his head. *How I have missed her!*

"Kalona, go with the blessing of Nyx!"

The swirl of energy that followed Thanatos's invocation washed against them both. Kalona lifted his head to see that the High Priestess was smiling beatifically at him.

"Nyx heard you," he said, grateful his voice did not sound as shaken as he felt.

"She did indeed," Thanatos said. "And *that* is most certainly a good omen."

"I will not disappoint either you or the Goddess," Kalona said, then he sprinted and launched himself into the air, thinking, *not this time—I will not disappoint her this time.*

Kalona flew straight and true. The balcony of the Mayo was wide and high. He dropped easily to its cold stone surface from the plum-colored sky. He folded his raven-colored wings against his naked back. Yes, he'd come to her with his chest bared. She preferred him that way.

"Goddess, your Consort returns!" Kalona called, thankful for who or whatever had shattered the glass of the penthouse's doorway. It saved him having to awkwardly break it open should she not welcome him as he expected.

"I see no Consort, only a winged failure." Her voice came from the shadows behind him in the far corner of the balcony, well away from the entrance to her penthouse.

He turned slowly to face her, allowing her time to take in the sight of his naked chest and his powerful wings. Neferet was a lusty creature. She craved men, but even more than the physical pleasure she took from a man's body, Neferet craved lording dominion over men. The white bull could give her power, but a bull was not a man.

"During the eons of my existence I have, indeed, failed at some things. I have made mistakes. The greatest of both was leaving your side, Goddess," Kalona spoke truthfully, though the Goddess foremost in his mind was not Neferet.

"So now you call me Goddess and you crawl back to me."

Kalona took two strides toward her, allowing his wings to stir. "Do I appear to be crawling?"

Neferet tilted her head. She hadn't moved from the shadows and all he could really see of her were her emerald eyes and the flame-colored shimmer of her hair as the sun began to rise behind her.

"No," she said, sounding bored. "You appear to be flapping."

Kalona unfurled his wings and opened his arms. His amber eyes met her cold, green gaze and he focused his will on her. Neferet had not long been immortal. She would still be susceptible to his allure.

"Look again, Goddess. Gaze on your Consort."

"I see you. You are not as young as I remembered."

"You forget to whom you speak!" He tried to temper his voice, but she stirred his anger. He had forgotten how very much he had come to loathe her cold sarcasm.

"Do I?" Neferet glided from the corner of shadows. "It is *you* who comes to *me*. Did you actually believe I would welcome you?"

The sun had lifted above the distant horizon, and as she approached him, Kalona was finally able to fully see her. Neferet had continued to change. She was still beautiful, but anything soft, mortal, *human* about her had been lost. It was as if she were an exquisite statue that had been given the breath of life, but had been animated without a conscience, without a soul. She had always been cold, but until now Neferet had maintained the ability to mimic kindness and love. No longer. Kalona wondered if he was the only one who could see so clearly that she was becoming a conduit for evil.

"I did not believe it, but I did hope it, even though I have heard rumors that my place at your side has been usurped." He hoped she would misjudge the shock in his voice for jealousy.

Neferet's smile was reptilian. "Yes, I found something bigger than a bird, though I do admit your jealousy is amusing."

Swallowing down the bile that rose in this throat at the thought of touching her, Kalona closed the distance between them. He commanded his wings forward so that the cold softness of his feathers stroked her skin.

"I am something bigger than a bird."

"Why should I take you back?" Neferet's voice sounded emotionless, but Kalona could feel her skin tremble in anticipation under his caress.

"Because you are a goddess and you deserve an immortal Consort." He moved even closer to her, knowing she could feel the frigid power of his moon-blessed immortality.

"I already have an immortal Consort," Neferet said.

"Not one who can do this." Kalona enfolded her in his wings. Slowly, he knelt before her, his lips inches from her quivering flesh. "I will serve you."

"How?" Her voice betrayed no feeling, but her hand lifted to stroke the inside of his wing.

Kalona closed his mind to everything except sensation and moaned.

She continued to stroke him. "How?" Neferet repeated the question and added, "Especially now that you serve another mistress."

He had expected her to know about his oath to Thanatos and he had an answer ready. "The only mistress I can truly serve is a Goddess, and if my Goddess would forgive me, I would do anything she asks of me." Kalona had thought his continued play on words would be amusing. Neferet would believe he spoke of her, and actually he could be talking about any of the female deities. But the moment he said the words, the truth of Kalona's statement rippled through his body, causing him to gasp and lurch away from the creature who stood before him. The games he had been playing with himself for eons ended with that one sentence. *I was created to serve one Goddess and one Goddess only.* Neferet embodied the opposite of everything Nyx represented. With his back to Neferet, Kalona buried his face in his hands. *How could I have ever thought she, or any other woman, could supplant Nyx's place in my heart? I have spent centuries as a broken shell of myself, attempting to fill what was missing within me through violence and lust and power. Nothing! Nothing has worked!*

He felt her hands on his shoulders. They were soft and warm and seemed to radiate kindness. Gently, ever so gently, she turned him, coaxing Kalona to face her. When he lifted his head his body went very still. Neferet had not followed him. She had not moved. She could not have touched him. Neferet had *never* touched him with such kindness.

But Nyx had.

Kalona's face felt wet. Absently he brushed away the tears.

"Hmmm..." Neferet was tapping one long, sharp fingernail against her chin, studying him from across the balcony, showing no sign that Nyx had just been present before him.

Had he imagined his Goddess there? *No! I remember her touch— her warmth—her kindness.* Nyx had been there. Kalona willed himself to believe it.

"Kalona, I cannot say that I am unmoved by your supplication. You seem to finally be learning how to speak to a real goddess. Perhaps I will forgive your betrayal and allow you to love me again. Under one condition."

"Anything." Kalona spoke the word to his invisible Goddess, hoping that she was still present, still listening.

"This time you will have to bring me Zoey Redbird. Though I don't want her killed, at least not yet. I've decided tormenting her would be far more amusing." Neferet walked slowly to Kalona and let her fingernails scrape across his chest, breaking his skin and drawing thin lines of scarlet. Neferet turned her hand so that his blood dripped down her fingers and into her palm. Cupping the blood in her hand, she leaned forward, licking his chest and closing the wounds. Smiling, Neferet continued past him. "I had forgotten how delicious you taste. Follow me and we shall see if the rest of you is still as pleasing."

Feeling utterly numb, Kalona did not move. In the wake of Nyx's touch, he had forgotten Sylvia Redbird. He wanted nothing except his Goddess.

I cannot bear Neferet's touch. I cannot, even in pretense, open myself to a perversion of Nyx ever again.

It was the croaking of a raven that returned his focus. He glanced behind him. The sun had risen fully, silhouetting the bird perched on the edge of the stone balustrade. It watched him with knowing eyes.

Rephaim? Kalona mentally shook himself. *I swore not to disappoint Thanatos or Nyx, and I will not disappoint my son, either. Yet I cannot bear the touch of this twisted version of my Goddess.*

Kalona couldn't move. He was confused. His mind was a battlefield; his thoughts enemies of themselves.

"What is wrong with you?" Neferet was standing just inside the shattered glass door to her penthouse. Her eyes were narrowed with suspicion. She lifted her hand. Her palm was still cupped—still holding his blood.

"Come, a few of you. Feed. I may need you to show Kalona how very much I have changed. I no longer tolerate disobedience."

Kalona watched the snake-like tendrils of Darkness slither from a corner of the main room. They engulfed Neferet's hand, appearing to absorb it as well as his blood. Kalona knew the tendrils must be causing her pain. They pulsed and writhed as they fed, but Neferet stroked them with her other hand, almost lovingly.

Kalona looked away. Neferet disgusted him.

He heard the moan then. At first he believed the sound came from Neferet, but when he glanced back at her, she was still smiling and stroking the threads of Darkness. The moan sounded again. Kalona looked around the room. Neferet had no electric lights on. The floor-to-ceiling windows were thick stained glass and, though the penthouse was on the top of the tall building, they let in little light. Neferet had lit a few thick, white pillar candles. Their flickering flames served as the only real illumination in the suite. Kalona peered within, but saw nothing except shadows and Darkness.

Another tendril quivered from an especially dark corner of the main room, causing a break in the inky shadows. Something within the blackness stirred. There was a slight glint of silver momentarily catching and reflecting the candlelight. Kalona blinked, not certain he could trust his vision. The immortal focused on the darkness and it took form. It seemed to be shaped like a cocoon hanging from the ceiling. Kalona shook his head, not understanding. Silver within the darkness flashed again, and Kalona saw something else reflecting light within the cocoon-like shape. Eyes—a human's open eyes. Everything came together for Kalona when he met her eyes.

The winged immortal stepped into the room.

Sylvia Redbird shifted and, in a whispery, tremulous voice mumbled, "No more . . . no more . . ." as the tendrils reshaped, curling around her, cutting into her skin. Her blood dripped to join the pool that had already formed below her cage. Oddly, the tendrils of hungry Darkness did not feed from the ready feast below them. As Kalona watched, Sylvia shifted her body again, this time pressing outward with her arms. When her forearms, which were ringed with turquoise stones and silver bracelets, came into contact with a tendril, the living strand quivered and pulled back quickly, giving off black smoke and shriveling so that it released and another tendril slithered to take its place.

"Ah, I see you've discovered my newest pet."

Kalona made himself look away from Sylvia Redbird. The tendrils of Darkness were done feeding, but they were still wrapped around Neferet's hand and arm, grotesquely mimicking Sylvia's protective bracelets.

"You will, of course, recognize Zoey Redbird's grandmother. Pity she was ready for me when I came for her. She had time to gather her ancestors' earth power in a protective spell." Neferet sighed, clearly irritated. "It has something to do with the turquoise and the silver. It's proving an impediment to reaching her, though my lovely children of Darkness are doing some damage."

"If nothing else, the old woman will bleed to death," Kalona said.

"I'm sure she will. Eventually. Pity that her blood is good for nothing. It's absolutely undrinkable. No matter. I'll wait her out."

"You intend to kill her?"

"I intended to sacrifice her, but as you can see that has turned out to be more difficult than I anticipated. No matter. I am a Goddess. I adapt easily to change. Perhaps I'll keep her, make her my pet. *That* would truly torture her granddaughter." Neferet shrugged. "No matter—kill her or use her. It will all end the same. She is, after all, nothing but a mortal shell."

"I thought the Aurox creature was your pet." Kalona forced himself to sound only vaguely interested. "Why would you abandon such a powerful creature for an old woman?"

"I did not abandon Aurox. The bull creature is flawed and has not been as useful as I had hoped he would be. A little like you, my lost love." She caressed a pulsing tendril. "But you already know that, don't you? You are Sword Master for the House of Night in Dragon Lankford's place. Surely you know how your predecessor was killed."

"Of course. Aurox killed him." Kalona began to move slowly toward Sylvia's cage. "And I have only taken Dragon's place so that I can gain the confidence of Thanatos and the High Council."

"Why would you want to do that?"

"For us, of course. They have shunned you, unanimously. You can no longer cause dissention among them, so I thought to cause it for you. Thanatos is beginning to trust me. The High Council trusts her. I have already begun whispering dissent to Death."

"Interesting," Neferet said. "And so considerate of you, especially as the last time we parted we did so as sworn enemies."

"I was wrong to so hastily leave you. I only realized how wrong when I learned that you had taken another as your Consort. I do not enjoy being made to feel jealousy." Kalona paced as he spoke to her. He hoped to appear frustrated at her questioning. In truth he made quite certain that his pacing kept bringing him closer and closer to Sylvia Redbird's cage.

"And I do not enjoy being betrayed. Yet here we are."

"I am not betraying you." Kalona said the words honestly. He was not betraying Neferet. He owed her absolutely no allegiance.

"Oh, I believe you are doing much more than betraying me. I believe you have also betrayed your own nature."

Her words halted his pacing. "You make no sense."

"How is your son, Rephaim?"

"Rephaim? What has he to do with us?" Kalona felt his first sliver of worry at the mention of his son's name.

"I saw you. I watched you grieve over his loss. *You care for him.*" Neferet spat the words, as if they had a foul taste. She took a step toward him. He backed one step away.

"Rephaim has long been by my side. He has done my bidding for centuries. I missed his presence as I would any dedicated servant."

"I believe you lie."

He made himself chuckle. "And by believing so, you prove that immortality does not equate to infallibility."

"Tell me you have not allowed feelings and sentiment to make you weak. Tell me that you have not chosen, like a pathetic lapdog, to chase after a Goddess who already rejected you."

"My feelings do not make me weak. You are the one torturing an old woman to torment a child."

"You dare to speak to me of Zoey Redbird! You, who knows how much pain she has caused me?" Neferet was breathing hard. The tendrils of Darkness that slithered around her writhed in agitated response.

"Pain Zoey caused you?" Kalona shook his head in disbelief.

"You leave chaos and pain in your wake. Zoey does not antagonize you—you attack her. I know. You have used me to hurt her."

"I knew you lied. I have always known you've loved her—your sweet, special little A-ya reborn."

"I do not love her!" Kalona almost blurted the truth: *I have always and will always love Nyx!* A moan from behind him changed his words. "But I do not hate her, either. Can you not consider that you might find contentment in fragmenting the High Council and ruling those vampyres who choose a more ancient path from your island castle on Capri? Your red vampyres in particular would worship you and be eager to breathe life into the ancient vampyre ways. I will aid you with that path, be your Consort, do your bidding," Kalona spoke in a calm, reasonable voice. He also moved another step backward. Farther from Neferet. Closer to Sylvia Redbird.

"You want me to leave Tulsa?"

"Why not? What is here? Ice in winter, heat in summer, and narrow-minded, religious humans. I believe we both have outgrown Tulsa."

"You make an excellent point." The tendrils of Darkness, still swollen from Kalona's blood, quieted as Neferet seemed to consider his proposition. "You would, of course, have to swear a blood oath to serve me."

"Of course," Kalona lied.

"Excellent. Perhaps I did misjudge you. I do have the perfect creatures to aid me in casting such a spell." She stroked the snake-like tendrils fondly. "Shall they mix my blood with yours and bind us together forever?"

Kalona tensed his muscles, readying himself to spring the few feet that now separated him from Sylvia Redbird. He would command the strands of Darkness from her, and then fly her to freedom as Neferet was slicing open her skin and conjuring a dark spell that would never be cast. Kalona smiled. "Whatever you wish, Goddess."

Neferet's full, red lips were beginning to turn up when the raven croaked its dismay. Neferet's eyes narrowed and her attention shifted to the bird, still perched on the balustrade, a clear target in the morning sunlight. She pointed one slender finger at the bird and commanded,

> *"With immortal blood you've been fed.*
> *Now make the Rephaim bird dead!"*

The tendrils that had been wrapped around her body released and shot like black arrows at the raven.

Kalona did not hesitate. He hurled himself between the raven and death, absorbing the blow meant for his son.

The force of the impact lifted him from the penthouse and flung him out onto the balcony, throwing him against the stone balustrade. As pain exploded in his chest, Kalona shouted at the unmoving bird, "Rephaim, fly!"

He had little time to feel relief as the raven obeyed his command. Neferet advanced, tendrils of Darkness slithering in her wake. Kalona stood. He ignored the terrible pain in his chest. He spread his arms and wings.

"Betrayer! Liar! Thief!" Neferet shrieked at him. She, too, spread her arms wide fingers splayed. She combed the air and gathered the sticky tendrils that multiplied around her.

"You think to battle me using Darkness? Do you not remember you attempted to do so not long ago, and I commanded them away? You are as foolish as you are mad, Neferet," Kalona said.

Neferet's answer was in the singsong words of a spell:

> *"Children, you know my need!*
> *Make this immortal bleed!*
> *Then you may feed and feed and feed!"*

She hurled the tendrils of Darkness at him. Kalona brought his hands forward and spoke directly to the snake-like minions the same words he'd used mere weeks before when Neferet had first dared to challenge him when he was whole, undamaged, and free from the suffocating confines of the earth. "Halt! I've long allied with Darkness. Obey my command. This is not your battle. *Begone!*

Shock hit him at the same time the tendrils sliced into his body. *The tendrils did not obey him!* Instead they cut his flesh, ripping and tearing and drinking—like toxic leeches. The immortal pulled one of the pulsing creatures from his chest and hurled it to the balcony floor. There it shattered, only to re-form into dozens more of the razor-teethed horrors.

Neferet's laughter was manic. "It seems only one of us is allied with Darkness, and that would not be you, my lost love!"

Kalona whirled, ripping the creatures of Darkness from his body and as he fought his mind became very clear. He realized Neferet was correct. The tendrils did not obey his commands anymore because he had truly chosen another path. Kalona no longer trafficked with Darkness.

CHAPTER NINETEEN

Kalona

It came back to him swiftly, like a lost friend returning to break bread once again. Kalona had been Nyx's chosen Warrior. He had spent lifetimes battling Darkness more fierce than this.

Yes, they multiplied when shattered, but break their necks and they could not instantly regenerate. They were lesser minions.

Kalona laughed as he whirled and struck and fought. It felt so good to be doing what he'd been created for again! In the midst of battle, he saw Neferet silently watching.

"You think to defeat me with puppets? For centuries I battled such as these in the Otherworld. You shall see that I can battle them for centuries once more."

"Oh, I am quite certain you can, betrayer. But *she* cannot." Neferet pointed her long finger at Sylvia Redbird who was still trapped and suffering within the cage of Darkness.

> "With Kalona's blood filling you
> Obey me, be faithful and true
> The turquoise will no longer save her life
> His power will be my avenging knife!"

The tendrils instantly obeyed Neferet. They released their suction-like hold on him and, bloated with his immortal blood, swarmed Sylvia Redbird. She screamed and lifted her arms, attempting to block their onslaught. The stones she wore still slowed them, that was obvious, but not enough. Through power stolen from Kalona's immortal blood, several tendrils were able to withstand the protection of the turquoise. They sliced into the old woman's flesh. Then, as the tendrils weakened and smoked, they slithered back to him to feed. Kalona fought them anew, but for every two he stopped two more broke through his defenses long enough to cut his flesh and drink his blood. Refortified, they returned to attack Sylvia.

Sylvia Redbird began to sing. Kalona did not know the words, but he heard the intent clearly. She was singing her death song.

"Yes, Kalona. Please do remain and battle Darkness. You serve only to feed Zoey's grandmother's tormentors. They will eventually break through her protection, but with your *help* her end will happen sooner rather than later. Or, perhaps, once the protection of the turquoise is broken, I won't kill her. Perhaps I will keep her and make her truly my pet. How long do you believe one old woman's sanity will withstand the torments of Darkness?"

Kalona knew Neferet was right. He could not save her—he could not command Darkness away from her. Instead Darkness would use the power in his blood to torture her.

"Go! Leave me!" Sylvia paused her song long enough to shout the words to Kalona.

He knew she was right, but by leaving the old woman there he would have to return to the House of Night having been defeated by Neferet. *But he had no choice!* If he remained and battled Darkness all that would be left of Sylvia Redbird would be her mortal shell. Neferet would not be able to control her anger. When the turquoise no longer protected the old woman, Neferet would destroy her. Though it wounded his pride, to be victorious, Kalona had to retreat and then return to fight another day. The immortal spread his mighty wings and launched himself from the balcony, leaving the tendrils of Darkness, Neferet, and Sylvia Redbird behind.

Kalona knew where he must go. He flew high and fast, and then dropped with inhuman speed, landing in the center of the House of Night campus, directly in front of the life-sized statue of Nyx. Kalona knelt, and then he did what he had not allowed himself to do until that moment. Kalona gazed up at the marble likeness of his lost Goddess.

No, he corrected himself silently. *It was not Nyx who was lost, but me.*

The incarnation of Nyx that the sculptress had chosen to capture was, indeed, lovely. The Goddess was naked. Her arms were upraised, cupping a crescent moon. Her marble eyes stared straight ahead. She looked beautiful and fierce—magnificent and powerful. Kalona would have given anything if she would simply touch him again.

"Why?" he asked the statue. "Why did you accept my oath and allow me to walk your path again at the moment it cost me dominion over Darkness? Now I have had to allow Neferet to defeat me. I had to leave a kind old woman entrapped and tortured. I failed! Why accept me just to allow me to fail?"

"Free choice." Thanatos's voice carried the power of authority and command. "You know even better than I what that means."

"Yes," Kalona continued to gaze up at the statue as he spoke. "It means Nyx does not stop us when we make mistakes, even if it costs us, and those around us, dearly."

"Being immortal you might not have realized this, but life is a lesson," she said.

"Then I will forever be in a classroom," Kalona said bitterly.

"Or you could look at it as an unending chance to evolve," Thanatos countered with.

"Into what?" He stood and faced his High Priestess. "Did you not hear me? I failed. Sylvia Redbird remains entrapped by Darkness over which Neferet holds dominion."

"First you asked into what you could be evolving. My answer is: choose. You are definitely a Warrior. But what type is your choice. Dragon Lankford was a Warrior. He almost chose to become bitter and hard, an oath breaker and a betrayer. All because his love was beyond his reach. You may do the same."

"You know." Kalona said.

"That you love Nyx? Yes, I do," Thanatos said. "I also know she is beyond your reach, whether you want to admit it or not."

Kalona pressed his lips together. He wanted to cry out his rage—tell Thanatos that he believed the Goddess had touched him—that perhaps she was *not* beyond his reach. But he remembered how the door to the Goddess's Temple had solidified under his hand, barring his entrance. His certainty faded.

"I admit it," he said shortly.

"Good. As to your second question: yes, I heard you. You could not rescue Sylvia Redbird because you no longer command Darkness."

"Yes."

Thanatos's gaze went to the slash marks that covered his body. They were healing, but they still wept with blood. "You battled Darkness."

"Yes."

"Then you did not fail. You fulfilled your oath."

"And by fulfilling it, I could not do what you asked of me," he said. "It is a disturbing paradox."

"It is, indeed," Thanatos said.

"What now? We cannot allow Neferet to torture the old woman. She plans to control Zoey through her grandmother. Zoey would be a powerful ally for Darkness to gain, even if she was being used against her will."

Thanatos shook her head sadly. "Warrior, all that you have said is true, but you have missed the point."

"The point?"

"Neferet cannot be allowed to torture an old women because it is inhumane. If you understood that, Nyx would not be so unreachable."

"I understand it!"

Kalona and Thanatos turned as one to see Aurox. He had been sitting on the stone steps of Nyx's Temple, silent and watching, unnoticed by either of them.

"Why is he not under guard? Or at least locked in a room?" Kalona said.

"I do not need a guard or a prison any more than you do! I chose to come here—to turn from Darkness—just as you did!" Aurox shouted at Kalona. "And if I'd gotten to Grandma Redbird's home sooner, or not left at all, I wouldn't have let Neferet steal her away. I would have fought harder for her!"

Kalona strode to him, grabbed him by the scruff of his shirt, and tossed him to the ground at the statue's feet. "You could not even stop yourself from killing Dragon. You attacked Rephaim. You cannot fight Darkness, you foolish creature. No matter what your brave words and your oh-so-noble intent, you were created from Darkness!"

"And yet I do not have to be told that an old woman's life is not only important because of how her granddaughter could be used!" Aurox hurled back at him.

Kalona reached for him, wanting to shake Aurox by the scruff of his shirt again, but Thanatos interceded. "No, the boy is being truthful. He does care for Sylvia."

"He is also a creation of Darkness!"

Thanatos's eyes widened. "Yes, he absolutely is. And that, Warrior, may very well prove to be Sylvia Redbird's salvation." The High Priestess began walking quickly away, leaving Kalona and Aurox staring after her. "Well, what are you waiting for? Come with me!" she called without pausing.

Kalona and Aurox shared a confused look, and then did as their High Priestess commanded.

Zoey

I couldn't sleep. All I could do was worry about Grandma. I tried not to think about everything that Neferet could be doing to her, but my mind was filled with images of Grandma being hurt—or worse.

Neferet could have killed her.

"Stop thinking that!" Stark had told me sternly when he and I curled up in bed together. "You don't know that's happened, and you're driving yourself crazy thinking it."

"I know. I know. But I can't help it. Stark, I can't lose her. Not Grandma!" I'd buried my face in his chest and hung on to him.

He'd tried to reassure me, to comfort me, and for a while I had found comfort in his touch. I'd focused on his love and his strength. He was my Guardian, my Warrior, and my lover. He grounded me.

Then the sun rose and he fell asleep, leaving me alone with my thoughts. Not even Nala's purr machine could turn my mind off. Seriously, all I wanted to do was to curl up in the corner and cry into my cat's soft orange fur.

But that wouldn't get Grandma back.

I knew my restlessness would wake up Stark, and while the sun was up that wasn't a good thing, so I kissed Nala on her nose and tiptoed quietly from the room. My feet automatically took me to the kitchen where I foraged for a can of cold brown pop and a bag of nacho cheese Doritos. I sat at the table for a while, wishing someone would wake up and talk to me. No one showed up. I didn't blame them. We'd been up early the day before, and everyone was stressed out. They needed to sleep. Hell, I needed to sleep.

Instead I stared at my phone, drank brown pop, and ate a bag of chips.

I also cried.

If Neferet had Grandma it was my fault. I was the one who'd gotten Marked and caused a bomb to explode in my human family.

"I shouldn't have kept in contact with any of them." I hiccupped a little sob. "If I'd broken from them, Neferet would have never known anything about my mom or my grandma. They'd be safe . . . alive . . ." I wiped the Dorito cheese on my jeans and used a paper towel to blow my nose. "I brought all of this vampyre crap on my family." I put my face in the paper towel and bawled like a two-year-old. "That's what I feel like—a damn toddler. Helpless! Stupid! Useless!" I sobbed. "Nyx! Where are you? Please help me. I need you so much!"

Then grow up, daughter. Be a woman, a High Priestess, and not a child.

Her voice filled my mind. I lifted my head, blinking quickly and wiping snot from my face. The earthen walls of the tunnel were glowing. Directly across from me an image began to surface. As if I was looking into a pool of dark water, something started to form and lift from the concave depths. It was the figure of a woman! Under normal circumstances I would have described her as fat. She was naked and she had enormous boobs, wide soft hips, and thick thighs. Her hair floated around her, as full and dark as her body.

She was absolutely and completely beautiful—every single pound and curve of her, which totally made me rethink my idea of "fat."

She opened her eyes, and I saw that they were amethyst crystals, kind and warm and the color of violets.

"Nyx!"

Yes, u-we-tsi-a-ge-ya, *that is one of my names. Though your ancestors would know me as Earth Mother.*

"You're my grandma's Goddess, too!"

She smiled and it was hard for me to keep looking directly at her because she was so incredibly lovely. *I do know Sylvia Redbird.*

"Can you help her? I think she's in big trouble right now!" I clenched my hands together.

Your grandmother knows me well. She may cloak herself in the power of my earth, as may any of my children if they choose to walk my path.

"Thank you! Thank you! Will you tell me where she is and then help me save her?"

You have the means for both, Zoey Redbird.

"I don't understand! Please, for Grandma's sake, help me," I begged the Goddess.

She smiled again, and it was even more blinding. *But I answered you when first you beseeched me. If you are to save your grandmother and, ultimately, your people, you will have to grow up. Be a woman, a High Priestess, and not a child.*

"But I want to be, I just don't know how. Could you please teach me?" I bit my lip to keep from crying again.

How to be the woman you were meant to be is something no one can teach you. You must find the way yourself. But know this: a child sits, weeps, and dissolves into self-pity and depression. A High Priestess takes action. Which way will you choose, Zoey Redbird?

"The right way! I want to choose the right way. But I need your help!"

As always, you have it. What I have gifted I never take back. I wish you, my precious u-we-tsi-a-ge-ya, *to blessed be . . .*

And the Goddess sank into the wall of the tunnel, disappearing in a glimmer of dust that glistened like the amethyst crystals that had been her eyes.

I sat there and stared at the wall, thinking about what the Goddess had said. I realized what I felt was mostly embarrassment. Basically, the Great Earth Mother had just told me to quit whining. I wiped my face again. I sucked down the last of my brown pop.

Then I made my decision. Out loud.

"Time to grow up. Time to stop bawling. Time to *do something*. And that means if I'm not sleeping, my herd of nerds isn't sleeping, either—sun or no sun."

I retraced my path down the tunnel, punching phone numbers as I went.

"What's happenin', Z?" Stevie Rae answered on the third ring and sounded groggy.

"Get dressed, get a green candle, and meet me in the basement," I said, and hung up. Aphrodite was next.

"Someone better be dead," she said as her hello.

"I'm gonna make sure that someone isn't Grandma. Wake Darius up. Meet me in the basement."

"Please tell me I can call Shaunee and Queen Damien and wake them up, too," she said.

"Absolutely. Tell them to bring their circle candles. Oh, and have Shaunee grab Erin's blue candle. You may be standing in for water."

"I have a better idea, but that's nothing new. Anyway, see you soon."

By that time I'd gotten to my room. I didn't hesitate. High Priestesses aren't hesitant babies. They act. So, I acted.

"Stark, wake up." I shook his shoulder.

He blinked, peering up through his cute, messy hair at me. "What's wrong? You okay?"

"What's wrong is we're not sleeping until we have a plan to save Grandma."

He sat up, dislodging Nala from his hip and making her mutter grumpy old lady cat noises at him. "But Kalona went to rescue Grandma."

"Would you trust Kalona to babysit Nala?"

Stark rubbed his eyes. "No, probably not. Why do you want Kalona to babysit Nala?"

"I don't. I'm just proving my point. Here's the deal: I don't want him to be who I trust to rescue my grandma."

"Okay, so what now?"

"Now, we circle." I went to the little table beside our bed and grabbed a lighter and the thick purple pillar candle that sat there, smelling like lavender and my childhood. I breathed deeply. Then I told Stark, "Get dressed and meet me in the basement."

I walked quickly. I didn't want to wait for anyone, not even Stark. I needed some time by myself to focus on spirit—to draw strength from the element that was closest to me. I needed to be brave and strong and smart, and the truth was I wasn't all of those things—or at least I wasn't all of those things at the same time. I remembered that I'd asked Grandma once how she got to be so smart. She'd laughed and told me she surrounded herself with smart people, and she never stopped being willing to listen and learn.

"Okay," I said as I climbed up the metal ladder that led from the tunnels below the depot up to the basement entrance. "I have smart friends. I can listen. And, in theory, I can learn. That's what I'll do."

I walked to what looked like the center of the basement, and then sat, cross-legged, and put the candle on the cold, cement floor. Holding the lighter in my hand, I closed my eyes and took three deep centering breaths, in and out, in and out, in and out. Eyes still closed I said, "Spirit, you are my heart. You fill me and give me strength. I ask you, please come to me spirit!" Then I opened my eyes and lit the purple candle.

The flame turned silver. I felt the inrush of the element and suddenly all of the turmoil and confusion that had filled my mind and soul since Aurox had said Grandma was missing dissolved. I was strengthened by spirit as it rushed around and through me as the silver flame of the purple candle danced in what seemed like joyous response. I nodded. "Okay, now I get busy. First step. Find out what the hell is going on." I pulled the phone from my pocket and punched *Thanatos*. It might be smart to wait belowground for the sun to set so that I had my red vamp backups with me, but that did *not* mean I went to bed quietly like a child scampering home before curfew.

Her phone was ringing as Kalona pulled the rusted grate aside and Thanatos strode into the basement, followed by the winged Warrior and Aurox.

I hit END CALL, and stood. I'd opened my mouth to ask Thanatos what the hell she was doing and why the hell she'd brought Aurox here when my mind caught up with my vision. Kalona was covered with pink slashes and spatters of blood. It looked like someone had been beating him with a whip made out of razor blade.

"Grandma? Where is she?"

Kalona halted in front of me. His amber eyes held mine. As he stood there, several of the pink slashes opened and began to cry blood. *His body is vulnerable down here, down in the earth,* I remembered. *It's difficult for him to heal.* But I didn't acknowledge that he'd willingly entered the earth even though it was obvious he was wounded. He was a Warrior. It was his oath sworn job to protect.

"Where is she?" I repeated.

"Neferet's penthouse. The Tsi Sgili has her imprisoned by tendrils of Darkness," he said.

"Why didn't you get her out of there?" I wanted to raise my fists and beat against his chest and open more of the cuts and make him hurt as badly as I was hurting—as badly as Grandma was hurting. But I didn't. I only wounded him with my eyes and my words. "You said if Neferet had her, you would rescue her. Darkness has been your BFF for centuries! Why couldn't you rescue her?"

"The minions of Darkness no longer obey Kalona. He has truly chosen to return to the path of Nyx, thus he is allied with evil no more," Thanatos said.

"Oh, just fucking great. Talk about shit timing skills, Kalona," Aphrodite said. She and Darius and Stark had climbed up the ladder, followed by Shaunee, Damien, and, I was surprised to see, Shaylin.

"So why did you run? Why the hell didn't you fight the tendrils, beat them, and grab Grandma Redbird?" Stark said. "Supposedly protecting Nyx against Darkness used to be your full-time job before you messed that up. Did you forget how to do it?"

Kalona rounded on Stark. "Do I look as if I ran from a battle?"

Stark didn't hesitate. "Yeah, you're here. Grandma's not. You fucking ran!"

Kalona snarled and took a step toward Stark. Darius pulled a knife from his sleeve and Stark lifted his ever-present bow. Pissed as hell, I stepped between them.

"This is *not* helping, Kalona! Tell me why Grandma's still being held by Neferet," I said.

"I could have battled those puppets of Darkness for days. I would have eventually been victorious over them. It would have cost me little except blood and pain. But their command was not to war with me. They had been commanded to feed from my blood to strengthen themselves so that they could break through the earth power with which Sylvia Redbird has girded herself."

"Go on. Tell me everything." I sounded strong, but I had to press my hand against my mouth to keep from sobbing. *I will not cry!*

"Turquoise and silver—earth power. That protects her, but with my blood filling the tendrils, they were able to begin breaking through that protection. Had I stayed and continued to battle them, I would have been victorious, but Sylvia Redbird would have been dead."

"We must have a creature made of Darkness to break through the cage of Darkness that imprisons your grandmother," Thanatos said.

"That creature is me." Aurox stepped forward.

"Oh, for shit's sake! We are absolutely fucked!" Aphrodite said.

Sadly, I had to agree with her.

CHAPTER TWENTY

Zoey

"I can do it. I was created by Darkness, from Darkness," Aurox said. "The tendrils will not feed from me—it would be like eating themselves. I may even be able to command them. If they will not obey my command, then I will vanquish them and rescue Sylvia Redbird. Zoey, I care very much for Grandma. I can save her. I know it."

"You can't control that shit inside you!" Stark shouted. "Sure, Neferet will let you into her penthouse. Are you kidding, why shouldn't she? She has plenty of blood from Grandma. She'll just use some of it to feed Darkness and control you. Again!"

"The tendrils cannot feed from Sylvia Redbird's blood," Kalona said. "Neferet admitted it, and I witnessed it myself. I can only guess that her blood is protected by the same earth magick that shields her body."

"But you can still be controlled, right?" Damien had walked up to Aurox. His voice was clinical and I knew he was accessing all the biology files he had in his very big brain. "You are a Vessel created by Darkness. So the beast within you, which is basically a creature formed from the evil of the white bull, morphs without a sacrifice. We saw it happening earlier when Stark and Darius hit you."

"The beast feeds on violence and hatred, lust and pain. That is true," Aurox said.

"But you have some control over it. You did not actually change earlier," Thanatos said.

"I try not to change. I try to control it."

"Well, do you have a clue how you've kinda controlled it so far?" Stevie Rae asked, joining the rest of us.

"No." Aurox sounded miserable.

"And that is why we are here. We must teach Aurox to control this change, at least long enough for him to break through the cage of Darkness that binds Sylvia Redbird so that he can throw her from the balcony of Neferet's lair," Thanatos said.

"Throw her?" My voice squeaked, but there wasn't much I could do about that. I felt like my head was going to explode.

"I will hover there and catch her and fly her to safety," Kalona said.

"And how long do we have to figure out how *not* to push Aurox's buttons and grab Grandma?" Aphrodite asked.

"I would not expect her to live another night," Kalona said.

"Well," I said. "Then let's get to work." I looked at Aurox. "Do you really care about my grandma?"

"I do. Very much. I would give my life to save her if I need to."

"You may need to," I said. Then I looked from him to Stark and Darius and Kalona. "Sounds like you need to start causing Aurox a bunch of pain and violence. Now."

The Warriors glanced at Thanatos. "I agree with Zoey. Cause Aurox pain."

Aurox

"I may enjoy this," Stark said, setting his bow and arrows aside and cracking his knuckles.

"As may I," Kalona said, as he began circling Aurox. "I owe you blows for my son."

"And I owe you for Dragon," Darius told him, pulling from his belt loop a small, deadly looking knife.

"You're not supposed to kill him," Zoey said. Her voice sounded cold, emotionless.

That absence of emotion frightened Aurox more than any of the three Warriors.

"I'll bet he's pretty hard to kill," Aphrodite said, crossing her arms and winking at Darius. "So, you go ahead and have some fun with your knives, handsome."

"The beast feeds on anger. Get serious. Get angry," Thanatos commanded the Warriors, and they went silent and closed on him.

Aurox felt the change in their energy immediately. Where before the three of them obviously disliked and mistrusted him, they were not angry. Now tension radiated from them, building in intensity. The beast within him stirred expectantly.

Aurox clenched his teeth and tensed his body. *No, I will not release control. It is* tsu-ka-nv-s-di-na, *not beast. I will tame the bull!*

Kalona struck first. With a movement that was inhumanly quick, he spun and backhanded Aurox across the face, knocking him to his knees. Before he could rise, Darius darted in. He felt an electric line of pain across the top of his shoulder, and then felt warmth as the thin, shallow cut began to bleed. An instant later, Stark punched him in the stomach.

Aurox doubled over. The Warriors were angry. The scent of his blood worked on the two vampyres. He could feel the violence within them build, especially that which rested inside Stark. *Darkness—I can feel it. Stark has known evil, though he has chosen another path.* Aurox was able to gain his feet, where he took a defensive stance just in time for Kalona to send another stinging blow to the other side of his face. Aurox turned, going with the blow, and brought his arm up in time to block Stark's fist.

As he moved, turning, and blocking, the creature within him quivered, trying to break free of Aurox's will. Though his skin twitched and he felt his bones begin the terrible melting change that turned boy to a horned beast, still he remained himself. Still he had control.

"You have to fight back!" Zoey called to him.

Aurox blocked another of Stark's blows. "I cannot!" he yelled. "If I fight—I change."

"Then what the hell good are you?" Aphrodite lifted her hands in frustration. "Neferet isn't going to let you walk in there, tell Darkness to get lost, and then walk out holding hands with Grandma."

"They are correct," Thanatos said. "You must fight back. And you must control the beast as you do."

Aurox nodded and, feeling a terrible dread, he ducked under Darius's knife hand and came up swinging, sending a blow under the Warrior's chin.

Aurox felt the pain and anger explode within Darius. The beast felt it, too. The emotions siphoned into his body, filling the creature within with power. Aurox tried to stop it, tried to control it. But when he whirled and kicked Stark, connecting with the Warrior's stomach and knocking the breath from him, he felt his feet begin to solidify and morph into hooves.

"Think of moonlight!" the True Sight fledgling yelled at him. "You have it inside you. Try to find it."

He thought of moonlight and lavender, of silver and turquoise and the earth around him.

Kalona struck again—another stinging backhand. This time Aurox grabbed his wrist and, using his own inhuman strength, tossed the immortal away from him.

The beast roared.

"He's losing it!" Aphrodite said.

"You guys get back down the tunnel," Stark called. "I don't know how long we're going to be able to control him."

"You better control him because we're not going anywhere! Aurox, hang on!" Zoey shouted.

"I try!" Aurox cried, backing away from the three Warriors, who were breathing hard but not attacking him again. "I control!"

"If you do not. If you harm any of them I will destroy you." Kalona's voice was calm. He did not shout. He did not posture. But Aurox felt the truth of his statement. *The immortal may be able to destroy me.* The thought had the beast retreating, releasing some of its anger.

Aurox stood his ground. "Control! I control."

"That's what I'm counting on," Zoey said. "Guys, stand down for a sec. I have an idea." The three Warriors nodded, but continued to watch Aurox warily. Zoey continued, "Damien, Shaunee, Stevie Rae—take your places. Form a circle around Aurox. The three of them scattered. "Aphrodite, take Erin's candle and stand in for water."

"Better idea." Aphrodite handed a blue candle to the True Sight fledgling. "Go west and think wet."

"Water? Me?" The girl took the candle, but shook her head, looking confused.

Aphrodite pulled a small, handheld silver object from her pocket and snapped it open. Aurox saw light dance across its mirrored surface. She held it up to the girl's face. "Read your own aura."

The fledgling sighed and looked into the mirror. Then her brows went up and her eyes seemed to double in size.

"Awesome! Wow! I never even thought about reading myself. I'm all different colors of blue!"

Aphrodite clicked the mirror closed and put it back in her pocket, looking smug. "Yep, just as I thought. So, head west."

Smiling, the fledgling took her place in the circle.

"That was wise, Prophetess," Thanatos said.

"I have my moments," Aphrodite said. Then she called to Zoey, who was watching, wide-eyed, along with the other fledglings, "You are welcome."

"Okay, well, let's see if I can be as wise," Zoey said.

"How may I help?" Thanatos asked.

"Cast the circle. I don't want to be anything but spirit this time," came Zoey's quick answer.

"Agreed," Thanatos said.

"Aurox, do you have a handle on yourself?" Zoey asked him.

He was still breathing hard, and the beast hovered just below the surface of his skin, but since the Warriors had stopped their attack, Aurox had gained a measure of control again. "I do. For now."

"Alright, here's what we're gonna do." As Zoey spoke, she walked toward him. "Thanatos, cast the circle. We'll manifest our elements and hold them here, ready. Warriors, once all five elements are present, attack Aurox. Aurox"—she'd stopped just a few feet from him and the three Warriors—"I want you to fight back and do your best to control the beast, but when that control starts slipping, 'cause we're all seeing that you can't stop what's happening to you, it'll be our turn to try to help you."

"How?" he asked her.

"I did it a little before. I sent spirit to strengthen you. Imagine that times five," she explained. "You say the beast feeds off of violence and anger and pain, right?"

"That is right," he said, nodding.

"Well, even though the elements aren't good or bad, how they make each of the five of us feel is definitely good. So, I figured if the five of us channel not just our elements to you, but the good way they make us feel, then maybe *you* can grab onto them and get enough positive power to shut down the beast."

"Aurox, if this works"—Thanatos joined Zoey in the middle of the circle—"then it will prove that you are more than the Darkness from which you were fashioned."

"Then it will work because I am not Darkness. I cannot be," he said firmly.

"Prove it," Stark said.

"I will," Aurox replied. He met Zoey's gaze. "I am ready."

"Then we begin with air." Thanatos took the lighter Zoey offered her and walked to Damien. Speaking simply Thantos called, "Air, you are the first of the elements, and I call you to this circle." After she lit Damien's yellow candle, she moved to Shaunee, invoking fire in the same way. When she stood before the True Sight fledgling, she took longer, saying, "Water, you are ever changeable, always adapting. You have been called to this circle and manifested many times for your fledgling, Erin Bates. But that fledgling has, like water, changed and adapted to another environment. This new daughter of Nyx stands here, open and excited to accept your gifts. As High Priestess I invite you to this circle. Come, water, and show Shaylin she may blessed be!" Aurox watched as Thanatos lit the fledgling's blue candle, and then she gasped in pleasure.

"I can feel it! Water is here, all around me!"

Thanatos smiled. "And for that gift we thank Nyx most profoundly." The High Priestess moved to Stevie Rae, invoked earth, and lit the green candle. Aurox could smell grass and earth. He breathed deeply as it reminded him of the morning he'd woken to Grandma Redbird's singing.

I must do this. She believed in me and I will not desert her.

Then Thanatos was standing in front of Zoey. "Spirit, you are the last element to join a circle. You open and close our union. I call you here with a resounding, merry meet! Come, spirit!"

When she touched the lighter to the purple candle, there was a sizzling sound and Zoey's candle flamed a pure, silver color. It grew and flashed, and suddenly the silver flame became a glowing rope, connecting each of them around the circle. Aurox could feel the power stir the air around him. He drew a deep breath and readied himself.

"Let's do this," Zoey said. "Warriors, bring him pain!"

This time Stark attacked him first. Aurox had thought himself prepared, but the vampyre surprised him. Instead of punching, he kicked his legs out from under him. Aurox went down hard. He was trying to collect himself and get up when Kalona kicked him in the stomach as Darius sliced the knife's blade across his other shoulder.

Aurox reacted automatically. He grabbed the immortal's legs and twisted as he turned and struck out with his hand, which was already solidifying into a cloven hoof, and struck Darius in the back. Both Warriors grunted in pain and that pain lit within Aurox like a match on dry tinder. The beast within him exploded to the surface. He roared and charged Stark.

"It's time!" Thanatos said.

"Command your elements to fill Aurox! Show him what it's like to feel the joy of air, fire, water, earth, and spirit!" Zoey shouted.

Aurox could dimly hear Zoey. His head swung in her direction.

The silver flame she held before her caught the beast's attention. He roared, wanting to change course, wanting to attack the flame.

"Watch him, Z!" Stark was yelling. "Over here, you bastard! Don't you fucking look at her!" The Warrior rammed Aurox with his shoulder, knocking him backward. Aurox pretended to stumble, but instead he feinted right and his left fist, now a fully formed hoof, caught Stark in the middle of his gut, doubling him over. Aurox was lowering his head, ready to gore the Warrior when the elements hit him.

This time his stagger was not pretended. He felt spirit first. Felt it deep within him. Something stirred. Something that was the opposite of the beast of Darkness that shared his skin. Joy leaped to life. It was an oddly familiar sensation, and with it Aurox turned his head, his gaze automatically seeking and then finding Zoey. Their eyes met. Hers had tears in them. In one hand she held the silver-flamed candle. Her other hand was pressed against the middle of her chest.

"Don't cry, Zo. You'll get snot everywhere," he heard himself say in a perfectly normal, perfectly human voice.

Then air whooshed into him and he gasped—and laughed. It felt like a mini-tornado. Fire was a sizzling rush, which water cooled. Earth was a fragrant field of lavender, calming and strengthening.

Aurox laughed. He looked down at what had been hooves, cloven and deadly. He had hands and feet again!

"Don't take a victory lap yet. This doesn't mean shit if you can't fight." And Stark punched him. Hard. Blood rained with pain from his nose.

Aurox grunted and threw his own punch, which caught Stark on the side of his chin. "I can fight!" he shouted. Stark went down.

The beast quivered within him, but Aurox thought of the elements and their presence strengthened him, and as it did, he felt the creature shrink and cower.

Aurox was grinning when Darius struck at him. Aurox deflected the blow, knocking the Warrior's wrist so hard that his grip on the knife loosened. The blade skittered across the basement floor. Aurox was still grinning when he kicked Darius's legs out from under him and the Warrior fell back on his ass.

Kalona wasn't so easy. His speed was otherworldly, and now that Aurox didn't have the beast's reflexes, he was only able to block a third of his blows. But it didn't matter. What mattered was that Aurox was still fighting, and he was still a human.

"Okay! That's enough!" Thanatos's command came as Stark and Darius rejoined Kalona and were closing on Aurox. The Warriors halted, though Aurox thought they did so reluctantly.

"Spirit, earth, water, fire, air—I thank each of you for your powerful presence. You may depart now, and until next time, merry meet, merry part, and merry meet again!" Thanatos closed the circle. As one, all of the candles flamed high and then went out.

"Huh, it worked," Zoey spoke into the silence.

Using his shirt, Aurox wiped the blood from his nose and mouth. He didn't actually think about what he was doing—he just followed his legs as they strode over to Zoey. Then his arms were lifting her and his body was twirling her around and around as his voice shouted, "You did it! It worked!"

A burst of laughter escaped from her, but as soon as he put her down she was stepping away from him, moving to stand by Stark's side.

"It wasn't just me who did it. It was all of us." She took Stark's hand and, ignoring Aurox, smiled at everyone else. "You guys were all awesome."

"Okay, yeah, the circle worked," Stark said. "But how does that translate to helping him get Grandma out of Neferet's penthouse? Neferet isn't gonna let you cast a circle up there."

"Well, I didn't think that far ahead," Zoey said.

"Must you see Aurox to strengthen him with the elements?" Kalona asked.

"Actually, no," Zoey said. "It's harder, and I don't know how long we could keep it up, but we don't have to see someone to send our element to him."

"I believe a spell of protection is the answer." Thanatos spoke slowly, reasoning aloud. "Surround the Mayo building. I will open the circle and cast the spell, binding it with salt. Zoey, as long as spirit is at the center of the circle, in the heart of the building, the circle should hold."

"The lobby of the Mayo is big. There's a bar and a restaurant in it," Aphrodite said. "Food's pretty good, and they actually have a decent champagne list, *and* it's dark and romantic."

"I care because?" Zoey asked.

"Because you and I can sit there, in a corner booth. I can sip good champagne. You can read a boringly huge textbook while you really are lighting a smaller, less obvious version of that purple candle and zapping bull boy with all of the elements."

"Where will we be?" Stark asked, not looking happy at all.

"Outside, watching over the nerd herd so that some street crazy doesn't stagger into, say, Queen Damien and cause him to shriek, drop his candle, and fuck everything up," Aphrodite said.

"I would *not* drop my candle," Damien said.

"What if he smelled really, *really* bad and you thought he had lice?" Aphrodite asked.

"Eeew," Damien said and shuddered.

"Told you so," Aphrodite said.

"Aurox, can you do it?" Zoey asked.

He met her gaze and didn't hesitate. "Yes. I can do it. I will do it. As long as the elements can strengthen *me*." Aurox paused and couldn't stop a smile of pure joy. "Me! I am more than a beast. I am more than Darkness." He turned from Zoey to Thanatos. "You said I had a choice. I choose Light and the path of the Goddess."

Thanatos returned his smile. "Yes, child. Yes, I believe you have. I also believe Nyx has heard you."

"Well, he's definitely talkin' loud enough for the Goddess to hear," Stevie Rae said, but she smiled at him, too.

Zoey wasn't smiling, though. She'd turned to Kalona. "Can you really catch Grandma? It sounds ridiculous and super scary. I mean, Aurox is going to throw her off the roof of the Mayo."

Kalona spread his wings. They surrounded the group and brushed against the ceiling of the basement. The immortal's wounds had opened during the fight, and blood ran freely down his body. Aurox thought he looked like an avenging god.

"I will catch her and once I have her, Sylvia Redbird will be completely safe."

Zoey nodded. "I'm counting on that. Okay, then, that's our plan."

CHAPTER TWENTY-ONE

Zoey

Waiting until dusk was hell. Keeping my mouth shut when the rest of the depot fledglings woke up slowly and shuffled sleepily around, taking their time, eating cereal and talking about school and homework and other crap that was totally *not* saving Grandma made my head pound and my stomach clench.

And then, of course, add to everything the fact that Aurox was crouched up in Tower #1, hiding out, waiting until we come back and pick him up right before we start the whole circle-casting-save-Grandma plan because, as Aphrodite said, "We can't let anyone see him. If Neferet gets one tiny word that Bull Boy stuck his face back at the House of Night and we didn't totally fuck him up, well, then paint a giant target on him and call Grandma toast."

So, yeah, I had one humongous headache and I was working on some serious IBS.

"Have a brown pop," Stark said, sliding a chair over next to where I was sitting at one of the kitchen tables.

"Already had one," I said.

"Have another." He leaned into me, kissed my cheek, and whispered, "You're tapping your foot like a crazy person and the other kids are looking at you like you might explode."

"I might." I nuzzled him, using that as an excuse to whisper back.

"Count Chocula, Z?" Stevie Rae asked with exaggerated perkiness.

"Not hungr—" I started, but Aphrodite cut me off.

"She'd love a bowl. Breakfast is the most important meal of the day."

"You never eat breakfast," I said, frowning at her.

Aphrodite raised her half-empty champagne flute and mock toasted me. "I choose to drink my breakfast, and I do that every day. Orange juice is brain food."

"And champagne is brain-cell killer," Shaylin said, through the mouthful of Lucky Charms.

"I like to think of it as a way the Goddess levels the playing field. Consider for a moment how ridiculously much smarter I would be than all of you if I *didn't* drink heavily."

"I think your logic is flawed," Damien said.

"And I think your hair is flawed. Is that early male pattern balding I see?"

Damien gasped.

I sighed.

"Don't be such a meanie pants," Stevie Rae told Aphrodite, and then she handed me a bowl of cereal.

"Speaking of pants, the waist of those bumpkin nightmare Roper jeans you have on today is so high it couldn't pass a drug test," Aphrodite quipped as she refilled her mimosa.

"I think Stevie Rae looks cute," Shaylin said.

"Of course you do. And tomorrow you'll probably be wearing two different shoes, because that's the kind of refined fashion taste you have."

I tried to eat while my friends bickered and Stark stayed close to me, resting his hand on my thigh and giving it a periodic, comforting squeeze.

My mind would not shut up. Okay, I understood why we had to wait until after sunset to go to the Mayo. Two of my five embodiments of the elements would burst into flames if they went outside in the sunlight. And that's not even counting Stark, who would also turn into a crispy critter. I even got that we had to go to school and our first hour, which was taught by Thanatos. She was going to put us into groups and assign us to different jobs, all focusing around getting the school ready for the open house on Saturday. Conveniently, the jobs that she gave to those of us who were going to rescue Grandma were going to be off campus. So, hopefully, Erin and Dallas and anyone else who might accidentally or on purpose come into contact with Neferet would have no clue what we were up to, or that we even knew Grandma was missing.

What was hard was the waiting, especially since the kids—those who weren't in on our plan—knew nothing about what was up, so they were meandering around and taking *forever* to get ready to load into the bus.

Aurox was crouched in a tower on the top of this building. Grandma was being held in a cage created by Darkness. It was hard to pretend like nothing was going on. I wanted to pace. I wanted to scream. Hell, I actually might have wanted to hit something. Or someone. Well, Neferet for sure. But I didn't want to burst into tears, and I thought that was a good sign.

As I was coming to the end of my cereal and my patience, Kramisha entered the kitchen like fireworks. Okay, well, maybe it was just her outfit that looked like fireworks with her butt-hugging yellow skirt, her purple sweater with her silver embroidered fifth former symbol of Nyx's golden chariot pulling a trail of stars blazing on her chest, and her bright red patent leather wedges that almost exactly matched the color of her scarlet bobbed wig.

"The bus is waitin'. An' fine as Darius is, he don't need to be kept sittin' out there wonderin' what's takin' everbody so damn long." She made a shooing motion with her hand at the fledglings. "Go on, scat!"

I could have kissed her. Then she skewered me with her dark eyes and said, "I got somethin' for you."

My stomach dropped when she reached into her giant Louis Vuitton bag and pulled out her purple notebook.

"I cannot tell you how much I hate poetry," Aphrodite said.

"Don't give me none of your attitude," Kramisha told her. "Have you had a vision today?"

"No. Today I'm having mimosas instead of visions, but thanks for asking," Aphrodite said.

"Looks like I be pickin' up your slack, *Prophetess,* so don't be ha-tin' on my poetry." Kramisha made a shooing motion at Aphrodite, too. "Go on. I said this is for Zoey."

"Good. Some people say fuck yoga. I say fuck figurative language. And no, I don't mean that figuratively." Aphrodite tossed her hair and twitched from the room.

"Do you need me to stay?" Stevie Rae asked.

I raised my brows questioningly at Kramisha.

"Nope," she said. Then she glanced at Damien and Shaylin and Stark. "You can go, too."

"Hey, I don't know if I'm cool with that," Stark said.

"You're gonna have to be. I got me a strong *talk to Z alone* vibe, and I'm followin' it." Still clutching what I was starting to think of as The Purple Folder of Doom, Kramisha crossed her arms, and tapped her foot at Stark.

"Go on," I said. "Kramisha's gut has been right way more often than it's been wrong."

"By 'way more often' she means every time," Kramisha said, sounding super impatient.

"Okay, but I don't like it. I'll be waiting in the bus." Stark kissed me, frowned at Kramisha, and left the room.

Kramisha shook her head. "I have three words for that boy: con-trol-ing."

"He's just trying to keep me safe, that's all," I said.

Kramisha snorted. "Yeah, that's what my auntie's second hus-band said before he backhanded her 'cross the room for lookin' at him wrong."

"Stark is *not* going to hit me, Kramisha!"

"I'm just sayin'. Anyway, this is for you. Alone. Don't know why I got this strong feelin' that you gotta hear it, think 'bout it, and keep it to yourself, but I do. You the High Priestess and all, so you can do what you want. But I gotta be honest and tell you every bit of the Juju I get."

"Okay, yeah, I get it. So, let me read it." I reached for the note-book.

"Nope," Kramisha surprised me by saying. "Don't know why, but this is an out-loud thing. All you got to do is listen." When she started reading her voice changed. It didn't get louder, but there was power in the way she spoke, the way she enunciated the words, that made it become more chant than simple rhyming poem.

> *"Ancient mirror*
> *Magick mirror*
> *Shades of gray*
> *Hidden*
> *Forbidden*
> *Within, away*
> *Part the mist*
> *Magick kissed*
> *Call the fey*
> *Reveal the past*
> *The spell is cast*
> *I save the day!"*

She came to the end, and the room seemed very silent.

"Well, that was some weird shit," she said, sounding like herself again. "Did it mean anything to you?"

"I don't know. It sounded powerful, like it was more than a poem," I said. "I like it that it's saying *you're* going to save the day."

"It wasn't meant for me, Z. It's yours. I don't even know for sure what it is 'cause it don't feel like none of my other poems. It feels more like a spell than a prophecy."

"A spell?" I looked around us. Nothing was different. Nothing had happened. "Are you sure?"

"No, I ain't. Take it." She tore out the page and handed it to me. "I know they's somethin' goin' on with you and your circle. I know you'd tell me if you could." She held up her hand to stop what was going to be my non-explanation explanation. "I don't need no explanation. You're my High Priestess. I trust you. I just needed to give you this an' tell you you're gonna need it. When you do, speak it like I just did. There's power in them words."

I took the poem from her, folded it carefully, and put it in the front pocket of my jeans. "Thank you, Kramisha. I hope real soon I'll be able to tell you how much this means to me."

"You will. Like I said, I believe in you, Z. Now it's your turn to believe in yourself."

"Yeah, I know. That's what scares me," I heard myself admitting.

Kramisha pulled me into a warm, tight hug. "Z, if it didn't scare you, then I'd say you had no damn sense at all. Just be strong, and remember—Nyx ain't stupid, and she's the one who picked you for all this stressful shit, and not the other way 'round."

"That actually does make me feel a little better," I told her.

"Well, I ain't Dr. Phil, but I'm smart," she said.

"And your shoes are cuter than his," I said, trying to sound at least semi-normal.

"Yeah, they remind me of Dorothy's ruby slippers, only mine is wedges 'cause I'm more fashion conscious than she was."

Her comment seemed appropriate because I felt like I was following the yellow brick road into some serious flying monkey bull-poopie, which, I suppose, made Aurox Glinda the Good Witch of the West. Me? I was pretty sure I'd be the Cowardly Lion . . .

I thought I was ready to see Erin. I was super wrong. I'd expected her to be distant and cold—she'd been working the cold, distant act for the past several days. I'd even known about her thing with Dallas—Shaylin had told us she'd seen them, and their very muddy, very yucky colors, together the night before. And Shaunee had admitted she'd seen them making out (even though she refused to give us what she called 'the gory details'). Still, I hadn't expected Erin to be so obvious. But there she was, sitting smack up against Dallas in the back of the class with the other hateful red fledglings when we walked into first hour.

"Oh, hell, no," Aphrodite muttered as Erin's sarcastic, oh-my-goddess-I'm-so-sexy laughter bubbled around us sarcastically.

"Don't give her any attention," Shaunee whispered as she walked by us while we all gawked at how far Erin had fallen into the gutter. Okay, all of us gawked except Shaunee. Shaunee didn't even glance at her ex-Twin. She just walked with her head up, like she couldn't hear Erin's immature giggles or feel the nasty looks thrown her way.

"Shaunee's right." I lowered my voice so only my group could hear me. "Erin's like one of those bad kids who wants any kind of attention—positive or negative. Ignore her and the rest of them."

So, we did. I took my seat in the front row with Stevie Rae and Rephaim and Shaunee on one side of me, and Aphrodite, Shaylin, and Damien on the other.

Aurox's unoccupied seat seemed super obvious to me. *What's he doing right now? What's going through his mind as he gets ready to confront Neferet and save Grandma? Is he going to chicken out? He's probably not even going to be waiting at the depot when we go back to get him. He'll probably be, like, halfway to Brazil by then . . .*

Shaylin's voice cut off my internal hyperventilation. "Look over there," She'd leaned forward to whisper to me across Aphrodite. She was nodding slightly to the left of our group at a single kid. Surprised, I recognized that kid as Nicole. She was completely by herself and sitting up toward the front of the class, definitely separated from Dallas and his group.

"Colors?" Aphrodite asked her quietly.

"The red's almost gone," Shaylin answered just loud enough for me to hear. "And the sandstorm brown stuff is turning gold. It's really pretty."

"Huh," I said.

"Weird," Aphrodite said.

"Totally dang weird," Stevie Rae whispered from the other side of me. "And I still don't like her."

I was trying to think of something wise to say when Thanatos entered the room. "Merry meet!" she said.

"Merry meet!" we responded.

Thanatos didn't waste any time, and I was super grateful for that because I was seriously sick of time wasting.

"I cannot ask you to turn in your homework, as I would were this an ordinary school. I am not going to pretend that you haven't lost your leader, Neferet, and that your lives haven't been torn asunder."

Damien tapped quickly on his iPad and lifted it so we could all see: TORN ASUNDER = TORN TO PIECES.

"I want to know who's responsible for the fire at the stables." Erin's question from the back of the room surprised more of the kids than just me. I heard whispers from everywhere. Shaunee's face had gone blank and pale, and even Thanatos took more than an appropriate teacher hesitation before she responded.

"It seems that it was an unfortunate accident," Thanatos said.

"Well, I don't know no accidents that are fortunate." Dallas's voice was just short of a sneer.

"*Any* accidents? Is that what you meant to say?" Thanatos corrected him smoothly.

"Weren't you an accident? I remember you tellin' me your momma and daddy said they were only in Dallas for the weekend, and not for baby makin'," Stevie Rae called back to him.

A bunch of the kids laughed. Thanatos spoke over them. "Sometimes the best things are born from desperate, accidental moments. Wouldn't you agree with me, Dallas?"

He mumbled something no one could understand. I heard Erin's breathy, Marilyn Monroe voice whisper to him before he spoke up again. "So, basically, no one's gonna pay for settin' the stable fire?"

"It wasn't set." Nicole wasn't talking to him. She was looking at Thanatos and sounding like they were alone in the room. "I already told Lenobia. I was there. It was windy and the lantern blew over. It happened real fast. I was walking to the tack room to put up the brushes and stuff I was using to groom one of the mares. I saw it happen. The wind blew a big gust. The lantern fell—right down in the middle of the big mound of hay bales, and they lit up like Roman candles." Nicole turned around then and spoke the rest directly to Dallas. "It was an accident. Period. The end."

"Well, it's a real nice thing you're so trustworthy, or people might think you're lying." Dallas's voice was an insult.

"Yes, it is indeed." Thanatos cut over his sarcasm. "And our Horse Mistress concurs with Nicole's eyewitness. We are all so pleased no one was killed because of the accident."

"The barn is a mess, though," I heard myself filling the awkward silence, doing my best to get us back to some semblance of normal. "So, does that mean our Equestrian Studies classes are cancelled?"

"No, not at all." Thanatos sent me what I was sure was a grateful look. "Continue with your normally schedule classes. If you have an equestrian class, you may be put to work cleaning and clearing debris, rather than riding, though." Then she touched her forehead as if she'd just remembered something. "Except for those of you who I need to help me prepare for the open house on Saturday."

Damien's hand went up.

"Yes, Damien. What is your question?" Thanatos asked.

"It's not so much a question. I was just going to volunteer to help in any way I can."

Thanatos smiled. "I am most appreciative."

"So, are you talking field trip?" Erin's voice sounded so weird coming from the back of the room.

"I suppose some of what I need can be considered a field trip, as it will require you to leave campus. Erin, are you volunteering to help?"

"If it means gettin' out of class, then you have more volunteers than Erin," Dallas said.

I couldn't even shoot Stevie Rae or Aphrodite a sideways look, but from the edge of my vision I was sure I saw Stevie Rae crossing her fingers.

"Dallas, I can use your assistance. I spent many of the sunlight hours today googling charity events in Tulsa. It seems one of the most successful fund-raisers is called An Evening of Wine and Roses. It benefits the Tulsa Garden Center. It seems the Center strings myriads of lights around the Rose Gardens and then has an after-dusk wine tasting and dinner. And that, my interesting young red vampyre, is perfect for you."

"Perfect? I don't like wine much," he said.

I heard Aphrodite snort, but I kept my eyes straight ahead and tried not to even breathe. I knew what Thanatos was setting up, and I hoped like hell it would work.

"No, you mistake me," Thanatos said. "I simply wish to use their lighting template as one for our open house. Dallas, think of how lovely our campus would be if ropes of electric bulbs were wrapped around our ancient oak trees."

"Lots of electricity would be good. I've been sayin' for a while now that this school needs an update on its electricity. It's not, like, 1960. We need real lights here. Our eyes can handle it." Dallas sounded cocky, as per usual.

"Well, I am agreeing with you, if only temporarily," Thanatos said, smiling at him. Again, I marveled at her massive acting skills. Then she turned her attention to Erin. "Erin, as it seems you would work well partnered with Dallas, may I count on you to help guide the decorations for the open house? We do, of course, need exquisite lighting, but we also need tables, covered with fine linens, scattered throughout the central grounds. Can you handle the responsibility of coordinating with local humans, as well as Dallas's electrical expertise, to get this done?"

"I was born to decorate and shop. Give me the school's gold card and I'm on it," Erin said.

"You will have a generous budget," Thanatos assured her. "Especially as the open house is only a few days away. Time is of the essence."

"If I have money I'm good at deadlines," Erin said, sounding totally up Thanatos's butt.

Right on cue Aphrodite waved her hand. "Uh, hello." She sounded bored and bitchy. Even more than usual.

"You have a question, Aphrodite?" Thanatos called on her.

"More like an intelligent statement. If you're going to put someone in charge of getting the accouterments together for a charity event, you should go to the expert: *moi*. I was teethed on what the middle class so barbarically calls *party planning*."

Thanatos's smile and tone were patronizing. "I am quite certain you were, but Erin and Dallas have already volunteered. I do have a job for you, though. I would like you to take a quick trip off campus and speak with your parents about attending the open house. From your comments to the press yesterday, I assume I can count on their support."

"Yeah, whatever. I'll talk to them." Aphrodite was doing an awesome job playing her part. She sounded pissed and absolutely annoyed that Thanatos hadn't fired Erin and put her in charge—which was exactly what we'd wanted. If Erin (and by association, Dallas) believed they were doing something important, and the rest of us were either annoyed or just puttering around, they'd be smug. They'd be obnoxious. *They'd be totally distracted and not reporting anything to Neferet except that Thanatos was depending on them and giving them lots of responsibilities.* Step one was definitely going according to Plan.

Damien's hand went up, straight and strong. When Thanatos called on him he practically gushed, "Could I please go with Aphrodite? I've always wanted to see the inside workings of city politics."

"Barf," Aphrodite said.

"Yes, you may," Thanatos said.

It was my hand's turn to go up. I'd prepared for this, but still it was hard to keep my voice steady. "Um, I've called Grandma about the open house and selling her lavender stuff, but she hasn't answered her phone yet."

"Did you leave your grandmother a message?" Thanatos asked.

"Yeah, I did." I let out a long breath. "And I guess it's not really a surprise that she has her phone off, seeing as we just did the reveal ritual about my mom and all." It was okay for my voice to be shaky then, and I was seriously glad because I was having a hard time keeping it together. "So, do you want me to drive out to her farm and talk to her?"

"Well, perhaps, in the next day or so," Thanatos said, waving her hand dismissively. "But I don't think that's necessary right now. Where I need you today is with me at Street Cats. I would very much like an introduction to the head of the organization, Sister Mary Angela. We are already confident of your grandmother's support, so coordinating with Street Cats is a better use of your time, Zoey."

"Okay, yeah, I can do that," I said.

"Can I go with you guys to Street Cats?" Shaylin spoke up without lifting her hand. "I'd really like a cat to choose me."

Thanatos smiled. "Of course, young fledgling." She turned her sharp gaze to Stevie Rae. "High Priestess, I need you to coordinate with your biological mother. You mentioned her baked goods during our television interview. Well, I believe we will need more than one mother's cookie baking skills to sate Tulsa's appetite come Saturday."

"I could ask my momma to get the PTA moms involved. They bake like crazy for the Henrietta Hens booster club."

"Then I will count on you to coordinate our refreshments," Thanatos said. "So, to recap—those of you I have named leaders: Dallas, Erin, Aphrodite, Zoey, and Stevie Rae—divide up the fledglings most close to you and delegate tasks. Dallas, you strike me as a Warrior in your own right, so you may stand guard over your group. Zoey, Aphrodite, and Stevie Rae, you may include your Warriors when you travel off campus as you see fit. I will trust in your judgment. Be safe and inconspicuous, which means cover your Marks and do not wear any part of our school uniform. We do not need additional human/vampyre tension or attention from the public.

"In addition, do not feel you must meet here for class between now and Monday. Those I've named leaders should come by this room to give me updates and, of course, ask for assistance should you need it. Today I will go with Aphrodite to meet the mayor, then be assured I will return to the House of Night and remain on campus, available to you as always.

"Let us not wait until the bell has released you. You, my special students, do not need to follow the rules so closely. I know you have the good of the school in your hearts. So, go forth with your tasks. I bid you merry meet, merry part, and merry meet again."

Just like that, Thanatos got rid of Dallas and Erin and their group of gawkers and spies. They believed nothing more than that Thanatos was a gullible High Priestess they could manipulate, and they were being given a bunch of responsibility for the school's open house, which, I was sure, they were going to put their heads together with Neferet to totally mess up.

We, on the other hand, were going to save Grandma and kick Neferet's unsuspecting ass. Then we'd have time to fix whatever mess Dallas and Erin and their gang had made of open house. Or at least that was our Plan.

CHAPTER TWENTY-TWO

Aurox

Waiting in the tower of the depot building gave Aurox a chance to relax. It was strange, but ever since he'd been given the responsibility of rescuing Grandma Redbird, the chaos and tumult in his mind had quieted. He was on the right path. He knew it. And when the elements reached within him and strengthened him so that *his* will controlled the beast, Aurox had been elated.

"I am more than a shell fashioned from Darkness." The words bounced from the stone walls of the tower. Aurox smiled. He wished he could shout them from the top of the Mayo. "I will," he promised himself aloud. "When Grandma Redbird is free and safe, I will shout that I have chosen Light over Darkness." Right now it made him feel good just to speak the words, even though he was the only one who heard them.

Unless the Goddess was listening . . .

Aurox glanced up at the night sky. It was clear, and even though the depot was in the heart of downtown, an abundance of stars was visible, as well as a thin, bright sliver of a moon.

"The crescent. Your symbol," Aurox spoke to the moon. "Nyx, if you can hear me I want to thank you. You must have something to do with the fact that I can choose to be more than what created me. Darkness would not have given me this choice—it had to be you. So, thank you. And I would appreciate it if you strengthened Grandma Redbird. Help her hang on until I get there and rescue her." Feeling confident and happy, Aurox leaned against the rounded side of the stone tower, closed his eyes, and with a smile still on his face, fell into a deep sleep.

Aurox wasn't used to dreaming. He rarely remembered anything from his sleeping hours. So the fishing dream was unusual from the very beginning.

Aurox had never fished, but the dock he sat on seemed familiar. The placid lake was topaz blue and tucked within a beautiful grove of ancient looking trees. He'd never held a fishing pole before, but this one felt right in his hands. Aurox reeled it in and then let fly. The bobber plunked out in the lake with a satisfying sound. He sighed and gazed lazily down at the mirror-like water—and felt a sickening jolt of shock.

Aurox's face didn't look back at him.

Another boy's face did. He had messy, sand-colored brown hair, and blue eyes that were wide with the surprise Aurox was feeling.

He lifted his hand and it touched the face.

"This is not me," he told the inaccurate reflection, and felt the jolt of shock again. It was his voice, but it was inside the wrong body! "It is a dream. Simply an image of my sleeping mind." Aurox just needed to awaken. But he couldn't stop staring.

And then the reflection opened its mouth and Aurox heard himself speaking words over which he had no control. *"Hey, get a clue. You only borrowed my choice and my goodness. It's not your own."*

Dread filled Aurox. This boy—this body was speaking truth. In the reflection Aurox watched his head shake back and forth, back and forth, denying what his heart told him.

"No, I chose Light over Darkness. I made the choice!"

"Guess again, dude. I made the choice, you just coat-tailed. So ya can't afford to relax, especially if you're gonna rescue Zo's grandma."

"Zo." Aurox frowned. "I'm not supposed to call her that."

"Well, no shit Sherlock. That's 'cause I used to call her Zo. Anyway, I'm just givin' you a heads-up. Don't be so cocky. It's just not gonna be that easy for you. I'm doin' my best, but there's gonna come a time when you'll actually have to step up to the plate."

Then a fish took Aurox's line, rippling the water, disturbing its mirrored surface, and fragmenting the dream.

Aurox's eyes opened. He gasped and sat straight up. He was breathing hard. His heart was racing—so much so that he felt the beast within him stir. Aurox got to his feet and paced off his anxiety.

He looked up at the sky. The silver crescent had moved. Aurox checked the watch Stark had let him borrow. It was almost 10 P.M. Thanatos would be back for him at any moment. He needed to get himself together and make his way down to the front of the old depot building. He needed to find his confidence again and get ready to confront Neferet and Darkness.

Aurox climbed up the rusted metal ladder and then dropped from the tower to the roof of the depot. From there he hurried to the side stairs. He would be waiting as Thanatos had asked him. She was counting on him. Zoey was counting on him. They were all counting on him.

He would prove they had been right to trust him with Grandma Redbird's life.

"It was a dream. Nothing more," Aurox spoke to the empty night. His voice was reassuring, but his heart hurt as ghost-like doubt slipped within it.

Zoey

"There he is, waiting over there under the darkest part of the over-hang, just like Thanatos told him to." I pointed to the Gotham City–looking entrance of the abandoned depot. Aurox was in the shadows, but his super blond hair, and moonstone-colored eyes didn't exactly keep him camouflaged. Stark pulled close to him and Thanatos opened the back door of one of the school's many SUVs, motioning for him to get in.

"This is not everyone," Aurox said after shutting the door and glancing around the interior.

"Uh, no, of course not," I said, thinking he sounded really nervous. "Thanatos pretended to split us up and send us on different errands so that Neferet wouldn't hear anything that would make her suspicious. Remember?"

"Oh, yes. Yes." He paused and then added, "Merry meet, Thanatos."

"Merry meet, Aurox. Do not be concerned. The rest of our group is joining us across the street from the Mayo."

"Are you okay? You're looking kinda pale." Shaylin spoke up from the backseat.

I craned my head around. "What kind of pale? Is his aura changing?"

"No, his aura's the same. I meant pale, pale. His face is really white," Shaylin said.

"I am fine," Aurox said firmly. "Just anxious to get this done."

"As are we," Thanatos said. "Calm yourself and save this tension for the battle."

Aurox nodded and went silent. I chewed on my lip, thinking about Grandma, and staring out the window. Thankfully, the Mayo wasn't far from the depot. Stark pulled off Fifth Street and parked in the rear of the Oneok Plaza. Another dark SUV was already there. Darius, Aphrodite, Shaunee, and Damien climbed out. Shaunee and Damien were holding their element candles. Aphrodite was holding on to Darius with one hand, and a super thick geometry textbook with her other.

"Geometry? Really? That was best choice for our pretend study session?" I realized I was doing some nervous babbling, but I seriously hated geometry.

"*Pretend* is the key word. We aren't really going to study. We're just *pretending* to study, retard."

"Yeah, okay, fine," I said. "I know we're not really studying. I'm just nervous as hell and worried about Grandma."

"Which is completely understandable." Damien hugged me. "That's why we're here. We're going to get her back." He looked at Aurox. "Are you ready?"

Aurox nodded. I didn't think he looked ready, but then again I probably didn't look ready, either, so I tried not to judge. Shaylin and I were pulling our element candles from our purses when Kalona, silent as the night itself, dropped from the sky.

"What news from the school?" Thanatos asked the winged immortal.

"Dallas and Erin have fragmented the red fledglings. They sow dissention, even within their own kind. They will have to be dealt with when this is over."

"Agreed," Thanatos said. "But the plan worked."

"It did. They are so busy lording the responsibility you have given them over the other students that they care nothing about what Zoey and you, or any of the rest of us, are doing," Kalona said.

"Erin's making a big mistake," Shaunee said quietly.

"I'm glad she's making it without you," Damien said.

"We're all glad of that," I agreed.

My Bug pulled up then, and Stevie Rae and Rephaim got out. "Sorry, y'all," she said, hurrying to us with her green candle. "Erin and Dallas were in a car behind me, so I had to pretend to start drivin' to Henrietta. Jeeze Louise, I was worried they were gonna follow me all the way, but then they turned off the highway and I realized they were just goin' to Garbee's lighting store." She paused and gave me a look. "You okay, Z? You're remindin' me of a deer in the headlights."

I blinked and realized I'd been staring at her. "It's just so weird to see you without your tattoos."

Stevie Rae lifted her hand and touched her forehead, careful not to smudge off the heavy makeup concealer that covered her beautiful vampyre Mark. "Yeah, looks weird to me, too. All you guys do."

"But we're less noticeable, and that's the point tonight," Stark said.

I understood and agreed that we all needed to keep a low profile—hell, even Kalona was wearing a long leather duster that, in the dark, actually mostly hid his giant wings. But it didn't change the fact that minus our Marks we looked strange and ordinary. Too ordinary. Tonight we needed to be powerful and confident and *extra*ordinary.

I tried to focus on the positive and believe we'd all be okay, but the truth was my stomach hurt and I was struggling not to cry.

No. I'm not crying. Weak little girls cry. Leaders act. For Grandma's sake, if not for my own, I am going to act.

"Hey, your Mark is inside. That can't ever be covered or lost or forgotten," Stark said, obviously feeling my tension.

"Thanks for reminding me," I said, touching his temporarily tattoo-free face gently.

"Let us all remember. Our power lies not in the trappings of our kind, but within, through our choices and the gifts given to us by our Goddess," Thanatos said. "And so, we shall begin. The first step tonight is the opening of our circle and the casting of a spell of protection. Once I have set the spell in motion, our circle will be cloaked. As long as the circle remains unbroken, each of the five of you will be safe. Human eyes will not see you. Human hands cannot harm you. But before and after the setting of the spell, you will all be vulnerable."

The little hairs on my forearms were standing up and I had to breathe deeply to keep from freaking totally out. I kept sneaking little glances at Aurox. He had hardly said anything since we picked him up. In my mind, I pictured the Goddess as I'd last seen her— lush and wise and strong—and prayed silently: *Please, Goddess, let him be ready for this!*

"Shaunee, the front of the Mayo faces south. Though it is winter, there are bistro tables outside the entrance. That is where you will position yourself with your candle. Darius, you will join Shaunee. Protect her," Thanatos said.

"I will, High Priestess," Darius said solemnly. "I will also be close enough to protect Aphrodite and Zoey, if need be."

"The tables are part of the restaurant. They're still out there because of smokers," Aphrodite explained. She reached into her purse, felt around, and tossed Shaunee a pack of cigarettes.

"You smoke?" It seemed silly, but after all we'd been through together the thought that Aphrodite was a smoker shocked me.

"Hell no. Do you know how many wrinkles smoking causes?

Hello, beef-jerky-looking skin at thirty. I know about the smoking tables because I've been to the Mayo's restaurant before, so I came prepared." Aphrodite looked at Shaunee. "While Zoey and I are pretending to study, you can pretend to smoke and pretend Darius is your boyfriend. Again, *pretend* is an important word here. Keep in mind I can see you through the picture window and I will kill you dead if you pretend too well. Oh, p.s., order the white chili soup. That, you don't have to pretend to eat. It's good."

"Thanks," Shaunee said. "And even though you're more than kinda hateful, thanks for the loan of your Warrior."

"Don't mention it. Seriously. Ever."

"Damien," Thanatos continued, ignoring Aphrodite like the rest of us, "an alley runs the length of the east wall of the Mayo. It's poorly lit and is where they keep the refuse. You may position yourself there. Stark, you'll be with Damien. Should anyone attempt to interfere with him before the circle is cast and the protection spell is set, you are to use all of your mind control skills to make him or her begone."

Stark nodded. "I understand. I won't let anyone mess with Damien. Just like Darius won't let anyone mess with my Z."

"You have my oath on it," Darius said.

I squeezed Stark's hand. I knew he hated me being separated from him, but like me, he understood why. The circle had to be protected, and Damien's air was the first element to be called, so he'd be there—holding a candle—just hanging out in a cold, dark alley, waiting for Thanatos to walk all the way around the block and set the protective spell in place. Damien was going to be a whole lot more vulnerable than I'd be in a nice restaurant pretending to study geometry.

"Stevie Rae, Damien's alley meets a small servants' entryway in the very rear of the building, just this side of Fourth Street."

Stevie Rae nodded to Thanatos. "That's my north. Rephaim and I will be there."

Thanatos turned to Shaylin. "Cheyenne is the street that follows the west side of the Mayo. There is no adequate hiding place for you. It is simply a sidewalk beside a building beside a street. Water is the third of the five elements to be called. I will not lie to you. You will be alone until earth and fire complete the circle."

"No she won't," I spoke quickly, thankful for the words my intuition was guiding me to speak. "Nyx will be with her. She's already given Shaylin awesome gifts—True Sight, an affinity for water, and the mind power ability all red fledglings have."

"That's right, Shaylin," Stevie Rae added. "You haven't been Marked for long, so you haven't had much time to practice 'cause, well, we've pretty much decided it's not very nice to poke around in the heads of regular people, but you can do it. If someone tries to bother you, just look at them. Make them meet your eyes, and then tell them what you want them to do while you think about it real hard."

Shaylin nodded. She didn't look nervous at all. She looked rock solid. "I'll think *go away, leave me alone, forget you ever saw me!* Is that right?

"Yep, sure is." Stevie Rae smiled. "See, easy-peasy."

"I will watch out for you as well," Kalona said.

"No! Shaylin can handle herself. We all can. You're not supposed to take your eyes from the top of the Mayo and the balcony of Neferet's penthouse. The second you see Grandma, swoop in and save her. That's your only job tonight," I said.

"Not true, young Priestess," Thanatos cut in. "Kalona is my Warrior, and as such he has a responsibility to protect our fledglings, as well as me." She walked to Kalona. "Shadow me as I cast the circle and set the spell. Watch over our people. Be sure that the stage is set for what we mean to accomplish tonight." Thanatos's gaze shifted to me and then to where Aurox stood at the edge of our group. "Until the circle is cast, you are not to enter Neferet's lair."

"I will wait until I feel the infilling of the elements," Aurox said.

"Remember, Aurox, without the strength of the elements, you have no way to control the beast, and it will emerge when Neferet realizes you have come for her prisoner," Thanatos said.

"I will remember," he said.

"And I will be sure your circle is cast," Kalona said. "From the sky

I will watch over you. I will watch over all of you." The winged immortal turned his cold amber gaze to Aurox. "You realize I cannot help you. You will have to battle your way from Neferet's lair."

I felt a little start of surprise. I'd been so focused on getting Grandma safe that I hadn't even considered what was going to happen to Aurox afterward.

"Wait, can't you carry both of them out of there?" I asked Kalona.

"Safely? No. There are some limits to my immortal strength," Kalona said. "Aurox, if I drop you from the sky will you be killed?"

It was so bizarre, listening to Kalona question Aurox about falling from the sky like he was asking him if he liked ham and swiss, or turkey and swiss better.

Aurox made a restless movement with his shoulders. "I believe that would depend upon whether the beast within me has manifested or not. The beast is much more difficult to destroy than am I."

"When Grandma is safe, we'll recall our elements." Now I was sounding as bizarrely calm as the two of them. "Aurox, let the beast take over enough for it to help you fight your way out of there."

"Do you believe that is possible?" Thanatos asked him.

"Perhaps. I think it will depend a great deal upon Neferet. I–I have not considered getting out, only getting in," Aurox said.

"I agree with Zoey. Use the beast. Neferet needed a sacrifice to control it before. She will need to do so again, and we will have taken her sacrifice," Thanatos said. "It can get you to safety. When you come to yourself again, make your way back to the House of Night."

Aurox's face seemed to brighten. "To stay? I'll be able to go to school there?"

"That is a question too great for me to answer alone. The High Council must decide your fate," Thanatos said.

I held my breath, waiting for Aurox to bail out—to realize that he was basically on a suicide mission, to tell us all to go to hell in a handbasket, and take off.

He didn't do any of those things. Instead, he met my eyes and said, "I have a question for you."

"Okay, what?"

"What does it mean to be coat-tailing on someone?"

I couldn't have been more surprised if Aurox had crouched down and given birth to a litter of kittens. For a second, I couldn't even think of an answer, and then I blurted, "It means that you haven't earned what you've been given, but that someone else has, so you're riding his coattails and getting credit that way."

Aurox's face was an emotionless mask. He drew a deep breath and let it out slowly. We were all staring at him, but he didn't say a word. He just stood there, breathing and looking like an almost-statue.

"Okay, so, who are you coat-tailing?" Stark's voice cut the silence.

Aurox turned his moonstone eyes on my Warrior. "No one. No one at all, and tonight I will prove that." Then his gaze found mine again. "When I feel the presence of the elements I will go to Neferet. When Grandma is safe, do as you said. Withdraw the elements. Then flee. I will not chance harming any of you, and I cannot be certain that I can retain any control over the beast. Tell Grandma that I said her sanctuary is more important than mine." His eyes swept our group as he said, "Merry meet, merry part, and merry meet again." Aurox walked away from us, jogging quickly across the street, and disappeared within the front doors of the Mayo.

"This night is gonna suck for him," Stark muttered.

"Hello, understatement," Aphrodite said. "This *life* is gonna suck for him."

CHAPTER TWENTY-THREE

Neferet

"So, old woman, what do you think it is about your blood that causes it to be so rancid that my children cannot feed on it?"

Sylvia Redbird's head turned slowly. Her eyes were glimmering pools within the cage of Darkness.

"Your puppets cannot feed from me because I had time to prepare myself for you."

The old woman's voice was hoarse, but there was a strength lingering within it that surprised Neferet almost as much as it annoyed her.

"That's right. You are oh, so special and beloved by your Goddess. But wait," Neferet spoke with mock shock. "If you are really so special and beloved, why are you here, being tormented by my children? Why does your Goddess not save you?"

"You name me special. I would not call myself that, Tsi Sgili. Had you asked I would have named myself valued by the Great Earth Mother. No more. No less."

"If this is how your Great Earth Mother treats a valued child who is crying out for her help, then may I suggest you consider changing goddesses?" Neferet sipped on her blood-laced wine. She wasn't sure why she felt the need to goad the old woman. Her pain and her impending death should have been enough to satisfy the immortal, but they weren't. Neferet hated that Sylvia did not scream. She did not beg. Since Kalona had fled, Sylvia had even stopped moaning in pain. Now if she wasn't silent, the old woman was singing.

Neferet loathed her damned singing.

"I have not asked the Great Earth Mother for help. I have only asked for her blessing, and that she has gifted me with tenfold."

"Her blessing! You're inside a cage of Darkness that is killing you slowly and painfully. What are you, a Catholic saint? Shall I crucify you upside down and cut off your head?" Neferet laughed at her own joke, but even to her the sound was hollow. *I need adulation and veneration! How can I reign as Goddess without worshippers!*

"You killed the professors."

Sylvia hadn't asked a question, but Neferet felt the need to answer her. "Of course I did."

"Why?"

"To create chaos between humans and vampyres, of course."

"But how does that benefit you?"

"Chaos burns—people, vampyres, society. The victor who emerges from those ashes controls the world. I will be that victor." Feeling smug and empowered, Neferet smiled.

"But you already had power. You were High Priestess of the House of Night. You were beloved by your Goddess. Why cast that aside?"

Neferet narrowed her eyes at Sylvia. "Power does not equate to control. How much *power* does your Great Earth Goddess wield if she cannot do something as simple as control whether or not I take your life? I learned long ago that control is true power."

Sylvia shook her head, finally looking and sounding as weary as she should be. "You cannot truly control anyone except yourself, Tsi Sgili. It might appear otherwise, but we all make our own choices."

"Really? Let us test that theory. I assume you would prefer to live." Neferet paused, waiting expectantly for Sylvia's response.

"I would." Sylvia's words were a whisper.

"Well, I believe I can control whether you live or die. Now, let's see who has the most power." Neferet raised her wrist. With a quick, practiced movement she slashed one pointed fingernail through the vein that pulsed near the surface there. "I grow weary of this conversation." Neferet's tone changed to singsong as her blood flowed.

"Come, children, taste my rage
Use my power to close her cage!"

Her loyal tendrils of Darkness slithered to her, eagerly feeding from her wrist. Refortified, they circled back to Sylvia. The old woman lifted her arms defensively, but as she did so several of her bracelets broke, raining turquoise and silver through the closing bars of her cage, and falling harmlessly in the growing pool of her blood.

When the old woman tried to begin her song again, her words were cut short as pulsing tendrils filled the skin left naked and unprotected on her arms.

Sylvia Redbird gasped in pain renewed. Neferet laughed.

Kalona

Humans don't look up. That was one thing that had not changed as the world aged. Man had conquered the sky, and yet unless there was a brilliant sunset or a full, gleaming moon to gaze upon, humans rarely glanced above their heads. Kalona did not understand it, but he was grateful for it. He circled the Mayo, sighting Damien, Stevie Rae, Shaylin, and Shaunee. Then he returned to the ONEOK Plaza building, landing beside Thanatos.

"The four are in place."

Thanatos nodded. "Good. Zoey has gone within. It is time to begin." She reached within her voluminous velvet robe and brought out a large, dark bag and a long box of wooden matches.

Kalona gestured to the bag. "Salt to bind?"

"Indeed, it is a large building. I need a lot of salt."

The immortal nodded, thinking that he'd actually come to appreciate Thanatos's dry sense of humor. "Let's hope there is some luck in that bag as well."

"Luck? I didn't think immortals believed in it."

"We're rescuing a human, not an immortal. Humans cross their fingers and toes and wish each other good luck. I am simply following suit," he said. "Plus, I believe we can use all the help we can get. If that means a little luck, then I will take it."

"As will I." Thanatos held out her hand to him. "No matter what the outcome of tonight, I know that you will keep your oath to me, and through me, to Nyx. I wish you to blessed be, Kalona."

He grasped her forearm and bowed his head to her respectfully. "Merry meet, merry part, and merry meet again, High Priestess."

Kalona took to the sky as Thanatos crossed Fifth Street and entered the dark alley where Damien, guarded by Stark, waited. Perching on one of the east wall's stone buttress, Kalona watched from above. He was surprised that Thanatos's voice carried so clearly to him—and then his surprise turned to vigilance. The power in the High Priestess's spell was tangible, and if he could hear it, so too might a human.

"Come, air, to this night's circle I call
protect, defend, be present—hear all."

Thanatos struck the match and the yellow candle leaped to life, illuminating Damien's somber face. Stark stood in front of him, bow and arrow in hand. Kalona hovered overhead as the High Priestess retraced her steps, moving quickly out of the alley and to the front of the Mayo. Hand buried in her robes, Thanatos was spilling a trail of salt. The lights on the decorative foyer entrance caught the tiny crystals, and from above it looked as if she were leaving a path of diamonds behind her.

Thanatos walked to the small, round table at which Darius and Shaunee were sitting. The young fledgling had placed her large purse before her, so that it blocked the view of her red pillar candle from passersby.

"Come, fire, to this night's circle I plead
vigilant, strong, to fulfill our need."

The match burst into flame before Thanatos could strike it, lighting the red candle in an audible *whoosh!*

Kalona scowled. It was good that the elements were manifesting, but he wished they would be less noisy about it.

With salt trailing her, Thanatos walked quickly around the building to the sidewalk that ran beside the street called Cheyenne. As on the alley side of the building, there were buttresses halfway up its nine stories, and that was where Kalona perched, gazing down at the small fledgling who sat cross-legged in the middle of a hedgerow. Shaylin had hidden herself so well that Thanatos almost walked past her. Kalona nodded to himself in approval of the child. "Young," he muttered, "but wily. Nyx was not wrong to gift that one."

> *"Come, water, to this night's circle I ask,*
> *Flow, wash, fill, empower—this is your task."*

The blue candle didn't explode to life, as had Shaunee's fire, but it did burn steadily, and Kalona could smell the cool scent of springtime showers wafting up to him.

He took to the sky, once again following the High Priestess.

Stevie Rae waited with Rephaim in the rear of the building. Thanatos had to climb down a steep, dark stairway and pick her way around vans that waited to make deliveries. Kalona hovered, watching closely. *Rephaim protects his Stevie Rae, and I protect my son.* But it seemed such vigilance was not needed. The night was as silent as death herself as Thanatos stepped before Stevie Rae.

> *"Come, earth, to this night's circle I beseech,*
> *Support, ground, hold confidence within reach."*

The green candle sputtered to flame. In its flickering light, Kalona caught a glimpse of Rephaim's upturned face. The boy looked steady and sure, as if he believed there was no possibility of the night's outcome not being positive.

Kalona wished he had his son's faith.

He flew up, keeping Thanatos in sight as the High Priestess completed the circle around the Mayo, cutting down the alley from the rear, and moving quickly and silently past Damien and Stark, fully encasing the building in a trail of salt. When she reached the front of the building again, Thanatos hesitated only long enough to glance up. Kalona met her gaze before soaring to the top of the ONEOK Plaza and perching there. From that vantage point the immortal watched the cloaked High Priestess enter the Mayo. She disappeared for a few moments, and then he caught sight of her dark cloak as she joined Zoey and Aphrodite at their booth near the restaurant's large picture window.

Kalona could not hear her words, but he whispered the completion of the elemental call.

> *"Come, spirit, to this night's circle I cry*
> *Endow, infill, on your might we rely."*

Zoey had carried a tiny purple votive in her pocket to the restaurant. She and Aphrodite had talked about hiding it behind the textbook they'd used as a prop. Kalona's view was not good enough to see the candlelight, but that the circle was cast and the protective spell set, he was absolutely sure. He felt the inrush of elemental power. It tingled across his skin like an electric spark.

No! The winged immortal wanted to shout to the night. *If I can sense the spell, then so might Neferet!* With horrible dread Kalona stared across the space that separated the roof of his building and the rooftop balcony of Neferet's penthouse. He could not see over the thick stone balustrades. Should he fly high and take the risk that Neferet would catch sight of him? *What was happening over there?*

"Hurry, boy. Get up there and keep Neferet distracted so that she does not know they circle below and the vengeance she wreaks falls only upon you. I will be certain they all get away. Steal the old woman before the Tsi Sgili kills you!" That was the unspoken truth. Kalona knew it, and he believed Aurox knew it as well. There would be no escape for Aurox. Neferet was going to kill her betraying Vessel this night.

Kalona felt the heat and knew Erebus had materialized before he spoke, but he did not turn. Did not take his gaze from Neferet's balcony.

"Ready to accept my help, brother?"

"Why would I need your help? I have always been the better Warrior," Kalona said.

"Better Warrior, perhaps, but not the better Consort."

"That was your title, not mine." Kalona refused to rise to his baiting. "Return to your Goddess. I have not the time, nor the patience, to argue with you tonight."

"Darkness cannot feed from the both of us." Erebus's voice was emotionless. "If I flew there with you, we could free the old woman and return her to her loved ones. Neferet could not stop us."

Kalona shifted so that he could glance at his brother and keep watch on the balcony. "Why would you do that?"

"To get what I want, of course," Erebus said.

"Which is?"

"You gone from the House of Night—from *any* House of Night. Vampyres are not your people. Make an eternity elsewhere and leave these children to the Night and her Sun."

"I have sworn an oath to be Death's Warrior, and I will not be forsworn."

"You have already been forsworn once. What does one more time matter?"

"I will not be forsworn ever again!" Kalona's anger caused the air around them to stir with the cold power of moonlight. Mist lifted from his brother's sun-blessed body as it flowed over the heat of his golden wings.

Erebus shook his wings and the mist was burned away. "As always, you think only of yourself," he sneered at Kalona.

Kalona shook his head in disgust. "What would Nyx say if she heard you bartering terms for an old woman's life?"

Erebus snorted. "You speak to me of one old woman's life? How many women, old and young, have you destroyed during the eons of your banishment?"

"Nyx does not know you are here." Kalona turned his back to his brother. "I have been banished. I am an oath breaker. And yet I am wise enough to know that should she find out, your Goddess would despise what you are doing."

"My Goddess despises you!"

Kalona didn't watch him leave. The absence of his heat and his malice was proof enough that Erebus had returned to the Otherworld Realm.

Silently, Kalona continued to stare across the space to the balcony. It wasn't long before Thanatos joined him on his vigil.

"The circle is open. The spell is cast. Now all we can do is wait," Thanatos said.

"And watch," Kalona agreed, adding silently to himself, *and wonder.*

Aurox

He felt the protective spell being cast and knew what it meant. Without hesitation, Aurox rushed into the elevator and pushed the button to the penthouse. "Hurry! Please hurry!" he shouted at the closed doors. *Too slow! I need to be there now! If I could feel the spell, she could feel it as well!* Aurox wanted to bash his fists against the walls of the slowly moving metal box. Frustration filled him, hot and thick. The beast stirred.

Aurox froze. Panicked he slowed his breathing. *Control the beast . . . control the beast . . .* chanted around and around within his mind. It was as the elevator finally reached the top floor and the doors slowly opened that the elements found him. With a surge of energy they filled him with strength and calm, drowning the heat of the beast.

He released a long sigh of relief, and with new confidence stepped within the slick marble entry hall. The scent of Neferet's blood was thick in the air. For a moment Aurox didn't understand. Had Grandma Redbird managed to wound the Priestess?

Then he heard laughter and the familiar rustling sounds the tendrils of Darkness made when they fed. He also heard the terrible moans of a woman in pain. Stealing himself, Aurox drew courage from the infilling of the elements, and he moved quickly and quietly into the main living area of the penthouse suite.

Aurox had thought he was prepared for what he would see. He'd known Neferet had caged Grandma Redbird in Darkness. He'd known she'd be frightened and hurt. It was so much worse than he'd imagined. He spared Grandma only a glance—met her pain-filled eyes for only an instant. It was Neferet on whom he focused his attention.

She seemed to not even know he was there. She was lounging on the large black sectional that formed the shape of a half circle. Her arms were spread, palms up, and she was laughing. Tendrils of Darkness were all around her, seething over the cushions and writhing against one another in their haste to reach Neferet's bleeding wrists to feed. When one mouth would unlatch from her skin, another would take its place. Aurox watched as the bloated tendril slithered to the cage that held Grandma where it joined others of its kind who were steadily slicing the old woman skin with the same razor-edged whip marks from which Kalona had so recently healed. Aurox knew Grandma would not be so fortunate.

He strode to Neferet and dropped to his knees before her. "Priestess! I have returned to you!"

Her head had lolled back. At the sound of his voice, Neferet lifted it. She squinted at him, as if she was having a hard time focusing, and then her eyes widened in recognition. Belying the lethargic appearance of her body, in one swift motion Neferet grasped a newly fed tendril and hurled it at Aurox. The snake-like creature hit him in the middle of his chest, slicing through his shirt and ripping his skin.

"You are late!" Neferet shouted at him.

Aurox did not flinch. "Forgive me, Priestess! I became confused. I could not find my way back to you." Aurox recited the excuse he had decided Neferet would be most likely to believe.

Neferet sat up straighter, brushing the tendrils gently from her wrists and clucking to them soothingly as if they were beloved children.

"You ignored my command. I had to sacrifice to claim control of the beast, and still you failed me." She hurled another tendril at him. It cut a red ribbon across Aurox's bicep.

The pain multiplied. The beast felt it and began to stir. Aurox closed his eyes and pictured the glowing circle, imagining it surrounding him with its protective glow.

The beast reluctantly quieted.

Strengthened, Aurox opened his eyes and beseeched Neferet, "I did not ignore your command! It was the casting of the circle and the invocation of Death that caused my failure. Priestess, I cannot describe to you the influx of Light and power that Thanatos called forth. It affected the beast. I could not call it forth!"

"But I could, and even after that you failed to destroy Rephaim and to break the circle." Neferet flung yet another tendril at him. This one did not simply cut him. It wrapped around his neck and began feeding from him.

Still, Aurox did not flinch but inside him, the beast roared, though the sound was drowned in a cool rush of water and blown away with a powerful gust of air.

"That was the fault of Dragon Lankford. He was protecting Rephaim," Aurox said, holding his body very still as Darkness continued to feed from him.

Neferet shook her head in irritation. "Dragon shouldn't have been there. I thought Anastasia's death had broken him. Sadly, I was mistaken." She sighed. "I still do not understand why you didn't kill Rephaim *after* Dragon was dead."

"It was as I said, Priestess. The spell did something terrible to me. I was not myself. I had no control over the beast. After it gored the Sword Master I could not force it to remain and finish Rephaim. It ran, and I could not stop it. It was only today that I finally returned to my senses. The instant I was myself again I made my way back to you."

Neferet frowned. "Well, it isn't as if you had much sense to return to. I suppose I must expect this type of thing. Imperfect sacrifice—cracked Vessel," she muttered more to herself than to Aurox. "Well, it has not ended so badly," Neferet spoke to him again. "You did put an end to Dragon Lankford's annoyingly honorable life. You did not stop the reveal ritual, and because of that I have been shunned by the Vampyre High Council, but I have decided that I do not mind that so very much. Not when I have local humans and my own little group of vampyres to play with." She leaned forward and offered Aurox her blood-spattered hand. "So, you are forgiven."

Aurox took her hand and bowed his head over it. "Thank you, Priestess."

The tendril that had been feeding from his neck detached its dark maw, dropped onto Neferet's hand, and slithered up her arm to curl next to her bosom.

"Actually, your return has given me a thought. Dragon Lankford was almost completely broken by his mate's death. Pathetic, really, and weak, to allow someone to have that much control over your emotions. But, no matter. Dragon was mature and wise, yet still Anastasia's death nearly destroyed him. Zoey Redbird is neither mature nor wise. When Kalona so stupidly killed her human, she shattered and I was almost rid of her." Neferet tapped her blood-besmeared finger against her red lips. Her gaze went from him to the corner of the room where Sylvia Redbird hung in an ever-tightening cage of Darkness. "Sylvia, can you imagine how devastated your poor, sweet *u-we-tsi-a-ge-ya* will be when you die?"

Grandma Redbird's voice was weak and laced with pain, but she spoke with no hesitation. "Zoey is stronger than you know. You underestimate love. I believe that is because you have never allowed yourself to know it."

"I have never allowed it to control me as if I were a fool!" Neferet's eyes flashed with anger.

Aurox wanted to beg Grandma, *don't antagonize her—be silent until I can free you!*

Grandma did not stay silent. "Accepting love does not make you a fool. It makes you human, and that is exactly what you are not, Tsi Sgili. You only glory in your victory over humanity because what you have become is a thing tainted, and absolutely unlovable."

Aurox could see that the old woman's words profoundly affected Neferet. The Tsi Sgili stood and, with a smile that made her look reptilian, she commanded him, "Vessel, call the beast and kill Sylvia Redbird!"

CHAPTER TWENTY-FOUR

Aurox

Though Aurox needed the command to get close enough to Grandma Redbird to save her, the words made his stomach tense and his heartbeat speed. He stood and began moving toward the cage made of tendrils of Darkness.

"Just break her neck. Don't damage her body any more than my children already have. I want to be quite sure Zoey can identify her."

"Yes, Priestess," Aurox said woodenly.

He did not look at the terrible pool of congealing blood and broken turquoise that had gathered, staining the carpet beneath the cage. His gaze met Grandma Redbird's. Aurox tried to tell her with that one look that she needn't be afraid—that he would never hurt her. He mouthed two words to her, Run—Balcony.

Grandma's eyes never left his. She nodded and then said, "I will miss sunrise, lavender, and my *u-we-tsi-a-ge-ya,* but death holds no terrors for me."

Aurox was almost within reaching distance of the cage. He knew what he needed to do. The tendrils would open to him. Grandma would run. He would give chase, keeping his body between hers and Neferet's slithering children, and catching her outside—on the balcony—where he would hold her, until Kalona lifted her to safety.

Then the elements would abandon him and the beast would have to fight for his own freedom. Aurox had little hope he would win, but he clung to the thought that freeing Grandma Redbird was a victory in itself. Aurox raised his hands to part the threads.

"Why have you not called the beast?" Neferet's voice was inches from him.

Grandma Redbird cringed back, staring over his shoulder.

Aurox turned. Neferet was there, floating on a nest of slithering tendrils. He could not see her feet. From her knees down she appeared to have become a part of the Dark children she had so long fed.

He felt fear then. It shivered through him like winter wind. Within him fire sent a surge of warmth and Aurox found his voice. "Priestess, the beast does not listen to my commands as it did before the reveal ritual. But I do not need it to break one old woman's neck."

"But I do so enjoy beasts. I will help you call it forth." Quick as a striking snake, Neferet slapped Aurox.

The beast quivered and earth soothed the stinging pain, granting Aurox control of the creature once more.

Neferet's brow lifted. "Isn't that interesting? I don't sense so much as the slightest bit of the creature's presence." Her nest of Darkness carried her even closer to Aurox. He could smell her breath. It was rancid as if she had been eating rotted meat. He forced himself not to move as she leaned into him, putting her arms around him as if he were her lover. "But you know what I do sense?"

Aurox couldn't speak. He could only shake his head.

"I shall tell you." She ran her sharp-tipped fingernail down his cheek. Blood welled and the tendrils around them quivered in response. "I sense betrayal." She slapped him again, this time using her hand like a claw and drawing more blood from his face. "You are a Vessel, created as a gift for me. You are mine to command. The beast is mine to call." Neferet struck him again, drawing more blood. The beast stirred, but spirit strengthened Aurox, allowing him to keep control.

"Spirit? How can spirit be present within you?" Neferet towered over him, fury causing her children to multiply and expand. "Strike him!" The Tsi Sgili hurled a thread of Darkness at him. This time Aurox lifted his arm to block the blow. The tendril cut deeply the length of his forearm. The beast quivered, feeding on Aurox's pain.

Instantly, the other four elements joined calming spirit and water soothed, air cooled, earth grounded, and fire strengthened him.

Neferet's rage was terrible. "The elements are with you! Where is that bitch, Zoey, and her circle?"

"Safe from you, witch!" Aurox yelled, then he turned and ripped open the cage of Darkness. Pulling Grandma Redbird into his arms, Aurox ran.

"Strike! Cut! Cause Aurox unbearable pain is my demand!"

The tendrils caught Aurox around his ankles, cutting deep and tripping him. He dropped Grandma Redbird. The old woman cried out, "Aurox!"

He tried to answer her, to tell Grandma to run to the balcony where freedom awaited, but Neferet was quicker, completing the spell in less than a breath.

"Fashioned from Darkness, beast come forth! Obey my command!"

Aurox was engulfed in the tendrils of Darkness. They did not simply cut him. They pressed their bodies against him. His skin rippled and began absorbing the terrible, snake-like creatures. Pain seared under his skin. With each beat of his frantic heart, Darkness pulsed through Aurox's body, battering the elements until they fled and waking the beast.

Grandma Redbird was sobbing and reaching toward him. The pain within him was unbearable and with a terrible shudder his body began to shift. "No! Go!" Aurox managed to shout. His voice had changed. It was impossibly powerful and completely inhuman.

The beast came forth, birthed in pain and rage and despair.

The old woman got to her feet and began to limp toward the broken door to the balcony.

"Kill her. Now!" Neferet commanded.

Within what remained of his mind, Aurox screamed as the beast roared and obeyed.

Zoey

I shook my head at Aphrodite as she ordered her third glass of champagne. "How can you drink?"

"By using my fake ID that says I'm twenty-five-year-old Anastasia Beaverhousen."

I rolled my eyes.

"Oh, all right. My fake name is really Kitina Maria Bartovick."

"And that's so much less obviously fake," I said, rolling my eyes again.

"Whatever. It works."

"You missed my point about the zillions of glasses of champagne," I said.

"No, I didn't, but you missed a sense a humor." She sipped the bubbly pink stuff. "By the by, all of a sudden you look like shit. What's up with that?"

I wiped my hand across my brow. It was shaking. My stomach was killing me.

Aphrodite leaned closer to me, pretending to be interested in the open geometry book, and whispered, "If you start coughing blood and die you will seriously screw up tonight's Plan."

"I am *not* dying. I'm just—" My words broke off as I was filled with a surge of energy. "Oh, no!"

"What is it?"

"Spirit. The element's back." I was already punching Thanatos's number on my phone. Through the huge front window I saw Shaunee's shoulders jerk, like something had just slammed into her, too, and I swear the air around her sparkled with fire. She whirled around. Our eyes met. She picked up her red candle.

Thanatos answered on the first ring. "Does Kalona have Grandma?" I asked.

"No. There has been no sign of her. Zoey, you can't—" I hung up on her and grabbed the little purple votive candle.

"She's not safe?"

"No." I was on my feet. "I'm going up there." Without waiting to see if she'd argue with me, I sprinted from the restaurant and across the lobby to the elevators. Shaunee and Darius met me there. She was holding her candle. Its flame was burning a lot brighter than my little purple votive, but both candles were still burning.

"Fire's back," Shaunee said.

I punched the up arrow button. "I know. Grandma's still up there."

Stark ran into the lobby, with Damien close behind. He, too, still carried his lit candle. "Air returned! Fire and spirit, too?"

I nodded. Then faced Stark. "Grandma's not out. I'm going up there."

"Not without me you're not," Stark said.

"Or me." Stevie Rae's face was flushed, but she was cradling her burning candle.

Shaylin looked scared and confused when she jogged into the lobby, cupping her hand around the flame of her blue candle. "Something happened. I have water back and Thanatos didn't close the circle. I figured I better get in here."

"You did good," I said. "Okay, look." The elevator doors opened and I stepped in. "Aurox has lost control. Probably because Neferet did something awful. Stark and I are going up there to be sure that awfulness isn't going to get Grandma killed. You guys stay here. Don't let your candles go out. Keep the circle open."

"Hell, no," Shaunee said, striding into the elevator. "If you go— fire goes."

"We're all going," Stevie Rae said.

"Fuck it. Me, too," Aphrodite said.

And that was it. My friends and I all squeezed into the elevator. I hit the penthouse button.

"You know there's going to be some majorly screwed-up shit going on when these doors open," Aphrodite said.

"Stay inside the circle close to Zoey," Darius told her. He had a knife in each hand.

Stark notched his bow. I put the hand that wasn't holding a candle on his arm. "Don't kill Aurox unless you have to."

"Zoey, it won't be Aurox. It'll be the beast. Remember that," he said.

I nodded. "I'll remember. You remember that I love you."

"Always," he said.

The doors opened to a deserted hallway. As one we stepped out of the elevator, holding our lit candles and keeping our circle open.

The smell of blood hit me. Laced in the terrible seduction of its scent was lavender and something I couldn't identify. Something that reminded me of the bluffs that edged Grandma's farm.

"Turquoise," Stevie Rae said. "I can smell it."

Then I heard Grandma sob Aurox's name, followed by a shout, a terrible roar, and then Neferet's unmistakable command, "Kill her. Now!"

I ran into the penthouse. "Air, fire, water, earth, spirit! Stop the beast!"

There was a blinding flash as Aurox, fully changed into the horrible creature that slept beneath his skin, charged Grandma. The power of the elements encased him, sizzling with energy. The beast roared his rage, spittle and blood spraying from his terrible mouth, while he circled Grandma.

"*U-we-tsi-a-ge-ya!*"

"Get to the balcony!" I yelled. There was a shattered glass door just yards behind Grandma, and through it I could see the starlit rooftop balcony onto which Kalona, wings spread, was landing.

"No! Not this time." Neferet was suddenly there, standing before my group. "Seal the door!" Neferet commanded and a web of black formed across the broken door, blocking Grandma's exit. Then she turned to us. "This time you are in my home, and I do not invite any red fledgling or vampyre within!"

"Oh, no!" Stevie Rae screamed as she, Shaylin, and Stark were lifted from their feet and hurled against the closed doors of the elevator so hard that Shaylin cried out. She and Stevie Rae dropped their candles. The circle was broken.

"Zoey!" Stark shouted, sounding like he was in agony as his body kept being battered against the closed metal doors.

"Make it stop!" Shaylin cried.

I understood what had happened. Different rules applied to red vampyres. The sun burned them. They could control humans' minds. And they could not enter a home without being invited.

Aphrodite knew those rules all too well. She ran to the elevator and pressed the button. When the doors opened, the three of them rushed inside. Stark got to his feet first.

"Get me my bow!" he yelled to Rephaim.

"No. I'd rather you didn't have your bow," Neferet said. She waved her hand and something dark and sticky knocked Rephaim off his feet. "But I would prefer the three of you watch." She flicked her fingers and spiderweb-like tendrils formed around the elevator doors, holding them open. Then she turned to me. "So nice of you to join your grandmother. Let's have some fun, shall we? Vessel, kill the old woman!"

Neferet's command worked on the beast like a whip. He roared and battered against the elemental prison.

And the elements began to give.

I dropped my candle and held my hands out. Damien took my right hand. Shaunee grasped my left hand.

"Spirit, hold him!" I yelled.

"Air, batter him!" Damien shouted.

"Fire, scorch him!" Shaunee added.

The bubble of energy around the beast pulsed, and for a moment I thought it would hold, then Neferet spoke again.

"My children within, made of Darkness divine,
Come forth—absorb, and make vengeance mine!"

The beast's skin shivered and twitched, and while he roared, hideous black creatures spewed from his mouth. They slammed against the bubble of elemental power. I felt the drain as if I'd been punched in the gut. Shaunee cried out. I heard Damien gasp in pain. They both still clutched my hands.

"Spirit, hold!"

"Air, hold!"

"Fire, hold!"

We tried, the three of us, but I knew we were lost. The creatures of Darkness were too many. They were too powerful. A broken circle could not hold them.

"Zoey! Go!" Grandma was huddled on the floor before the web of Darkness that had cut off her escape to the balcony. I could see Kalona on the other side, battling furiously against Darkness. He ripped and tore and slashed. He was making headway, but I knew not quickly enough.

"Grandma, come to me!"

"I cannot, *u-we-tsi-a-ge-ya*. I am too weak."

"Try! You gotta try!" Stevie Rae called from the elevator.

Grandma began crawling toward us.

Neferet laughed. "This is such fun! I never believed I would end so many of you at once. This will even get rid of Kalona. The High Council will be ever so distraught when they hear that he went rogue, attacked me, and when you came to my rescue he killed all of you." She was sitting on the back of the giant round couch with her legs crossed and her hand primly placed on her knee. Her long black dress covered her feet, but there was something wrong about it. Neferet wasn't moving, but the cloth of the dress didn't stay still. I shivered. It was like she was covered with bugs.

"No one will believe that. Thanatos was here. She is our witness," I said.

"So sad that Kalona turned on his High Priestess first," she said.

"You won't get away with it!" I yelled at her.

She laughed again and made a "come here" motion with her finger. The creatures that had come from the beast's body pressed against the bubble with renewed strength.

Shaunee stumbled and her hand slipped from mine. The element power that held the beast dimmed.

"I'm sorry, Zoey. I can't keep it up." Damien let go of my hand and he fell to his knees, retching.

The bubble shivered.

I felt a terrible tug within me and knew I would soon lose spirit, too, and the beast would be free.

"Grow up, Zoey. This time you're not going to save the day," Neferet said.

Stark was shouting from behind me. Darius and Rephaim stood side by side in front of the open elevator, battling the threads of Darkness that kept trying to leak within.

But all of that seemed very far away to me because Neferet's last words kept echoing around, over and over, inside my mind. *I save the day . . . I save the day . . . I save the day . . .*

Then I remembered. *It's not a poem! It's a spell!*

I felt spirit wrench from me and I stepped forward. I pulled the piece of folded purple paper from the pocket of my jeans, and as I did my Seer Stone flamed with heat.

I didn't have time to question myself. I only had time to act. I jerked on the chain that held the stone around my neck and lifted it before me like a shield. Then, in a voice magnified by panic and power, I recited:

"Ancient mirror
Magick mirror
Shades of gray
Hidden
Forbidden
Within, away
Part the mist
Magick kissed
Call the fey
Reveal the past
The spell is cast
I save the day!"

I looked through the Seer Stone and the world changed utterly. I was no longer holding a small, Lifesaver-shaped stone. Before me it had expanded so that it was a slick, round surface. I didn't realize what it was until I saw the reflection of the room glistening darkly on its surface.

"You think to battle me with a mirror?"

I didn't hesitate. I knew the answer. "Yes," I said firmly. "That's exactly what I think I'm going to do." Holding the mirror in both hands I turned so that it caught Neferet in its surface.

She'd gotten up from the couch. The mirror trapped her reflection as she glided toward me. She was laughing cruelly and glancing dismissively into the mirror when her entire body language changed. Neferet's head began to shake from side to side. Her mouth opened and she whimpered, cringing back as if from an invisible blow. Amazed at the difference in her, I craned my neck around and looked at her reflection.

It was a Neferet that I didn't know. She was young—she looked barely my age. She was also pretty, extremely pretty, even though her long, green dress was torn, exposing the fact that someone had beaten her. Badly. Her face was perfect. It had not been touched. But her chest looked as though there were bite marks on her breasts. Her wrists were swollen and black with bruises. Most horrible of all was the blood that covered the insides of her thighs and dripped down her legs.

"No!" Neferet sobbed. "Not again! Not ever again!" She covered her face with her hands, keening with despair. As the Tsi Sgili wept brokenly, the tendrils of Darkness began to dissolve.

"Spirit!" I called to my element, the one that still held the beast in a fading circle of power. "Let him go." Then I walked forward, keeping the mirror trained on Neferet. "Aurox!" My shout had the beast's head turning from where Grandma had collapsed on the floor to me. "Darkness doesn't control you. Come back to us! You can do it!" He shook his misshapen head. I kept walking to him. He began to circle me. I kept looking into his moon-colored eyes. "Spirit! Don't trap him—help him!"

I felt the element enter the beast. He stumbled and went down on one knee. He roared.

"Fight it! You are more than a creature made of Darkness!" I hurled the words at him.

He lifted his head and I felt a rush of hope. His flesh was shivering and twitching. He was changing!

"Zoey, watch out!" Stark shouted.

I looked from Aurox in time to see Neferet closing on me. She was still staring at the mirror I held. Tears of blood streamed from her eyes. She had torn her own flesh with her claw-like hands. She raised them, blood-soaked and deadly. "You bitch! I won't let you bring it all back to me! Nyx be damned—I'll kill you myself!" Neferet rushed me.

Aurox hit her hard. He still was beast enough to have horns, and one long, white tip speared Neferet in the middle of her chest. Momentum carried them forward and together they crashed through the remnants of the web Kalona had been battling. The winged immortal jumped aside as the part beast, part boy carried a writhing, screaming Neferet across the balcony. It took less than a breath for them to reach the stone balustrade. The inhuman power of the beast's body shattered it and the two of them fell off the rooftop.

CHAPTER TWENTY-FIVE

Zoey

I dropped the mirror and ran forward. "Kalona! Save him!" The immortal was in motion before I'd finished the command. Wings spread, he leaped over the broken balustrade and disappeared. I rushed after him, coming to a halt at the edge of the roof. Peering down, I saw Kalona grab Aurox's ankle just moments before the boy, who was now completely human again, hit the pavement.

Neferet wasn't as lucky. I could see her. She'd hit the sharp edge of the building and had tumbled and fallen, landing in the middle of Fifth Street. From this height, she looked like a broken doll. Her neck was twisted. Her arms and legs bent all in the wrong direction. Her head was a dark pool of blood.

Thanatos joined me, putting a strong arm around me as if she was afraid I might fall after Neferet. Then everyone was there, beside me. Stark took me from Thanatos and held me while I trembled and continued to stare down at Neferet's body. Kalona landed on the rooftop with Aurox. Aphrodite helped Grandma. She slipped her hand inside mine.

"My *u-we-tsi-a-ge-ya,* come away from this terrible sight," she said.

Still I did not look away. So when Neferet's body began to convulse I saw it. I watched everything. Her arms and legs flailed. Her hair lifted. Her back arched. And then the Tsi Sgili seemed to dissolve. From within the folds of her blood-soaked clothes, thousands of black spiders exploded, skittering into the gutter and disappearing into the darkness.

Then I looked away. I faced Thanatos. "She's not dead."

The High Priestess of Death answered me, though I hadn't framed the words as a question.

"I do not know." Thanatos looked pale and shaken. "I have never seen, never even imagined, what we all just witnessed."

I felt very quiet inside. I wasn't tired. I wasn't crying. I wasn't pissed. I was just very, very calm. "I think we better get ready. My gut says Neferet is going to come at us again," I said.

"Yes, Priestess. I agree," Thanatos said.

I put my arm around Grandma's waist, and let her lean on me. "You need to go to the hospital," I told her gently.

"No, my *u-we-tsi-a-ge-ya*. I need only to go home."

I looked into her gentle eyes. "I understand completely, Grandma. Stark and I will get you home."

"You have to do something first," Stark said.

"She can kiss you and tell you she loves you later. Let's get out of here. The spider thing was the cherry on this shit sundae of a night. I need a bath and a Xanax," Aphrodite said.

I didn't say anything. I was getting a weird vibe from Stark. "Wait here. Everyone needs to see this." He squeezed my hand and then he went into the penthouse. He came back a second later, holding my Seer Stone from its broken chain.

It was Lifesaver-shaped again, and looked totally harmless. I knew better, so when he handed it to me I handled it gingerly, like the un-exploded bomb it was, and I was stuffing it into my jeans' pocket when Stark stopped me.

"No, don't put it away. Lift it. Point it at Aurox. Say the spell again."

"Huh?" Suddenly I didn't sound so grown and together and brilliant.

"Me?" Everyone turned to stare at Aurox. Well, the kid looked like crap. His clothes were all ripped up and his face and hands were bruised and bloody. "Why me?"

"Because when you gored Neferet I caught your reflection in that magick mirror. Everyone needs to see what I saw," Stark said. "Do the spell thing again, Zoey."

"I don't even know if it'll work again. It's that old magick stuff. It's weird and totally unpredictable," I said.

"Recite the spell, *u-we-tsi-a-ge-ya*," Grandma said.

"I don't have—"

Stark handed me the crumpled purple paper. "Yes, you do."

"Well, okay then." I lifted the Seer Stone, and pointed it at Aurox. Even before I started reciting from the paper I could feel the heat radiating off of it.

> *"Ancient mirror*
> *Magick mirror*
> *Shades of gray*
> *Hidden*
> *Forbidden*
> *Within, away*
> *Part the mist*
> *Magick kissed*
> *Call the fey*
> *Reveal the past*
> *The spell is cast*
> *I save the day!"*

My voice wasn't as powerful as it had been the first time, but the words were strong and clear, and at the end of the spell the Seer Stone changed again, expanding to a reflective circle pointing right at Aurox.

"Holy shit. It's true," Aphrodite said. "That's the weirdest thing I've ever seen, and I've seen some weirdness."

Grandma limped to Aurox. She touched his cheek. He was staring at the mirror with tears in his eyes. He looked from it to her.

"I knew I was right to believe in you, *tsu-ka-nv-s-di-na*," Grandma told him. "Thank you for saving me, child." When she leaned forward he bent and she gave him a soft, mom kiss on the cheek.

"You need to look in the mirror, Z," Stark said.

"No I don't." I felt weirdly numb. "I know what Heath looks like."

Aurox was staring in the mirror again. "So, that is Heath?"

"Yeah," Stark said with a sigh. "That's Heath. Which means somehow you're a friend of mine."

Aurox was still looking at his reflection when his expression changed. He smiled and said, "Good to see you again."

Something about his voice made me shiver.

Then Aurox looked from the mirror into my eyes. "And you?" he asked me. "What was Heath to you?"

Lots of answers flitted through my mind: *he was my problem—my pain in the butt—my lover—my Consort—my rock—my forever boyfriend.*

"Heath was my humanity" was what came out of my mouth. "And now it looks like he's become your humanity."

I dropped the mirror. Before it could shatter there was a little popping noise and it was a Seer Stone again. This time I did shove it into my pocket.

Grandma came to me and I put my arm back around her waist. Stark took my hand, lifted it, and kissed my palm.

"Don't worry," he said softly. "No matter what else, we have love. Always love."

The End
For now . . .

HOUSE OF NIGHT

"TWILIGHT MEETS HARRY POTTER."
—MTV.com

MARKED
BETRAYED
CHOSEN
UNTAMED
HUNTED
TEMPTED
BURNED
AWAKENED
DESTINED
HIDDEN
REVEALED
REDEEMED

AVAILABLE OCTOBER 2014

HOUSE OF NIGHT NOVELLAS

DRAGON'S OATH
LENOBIA'S VOW
NEFERET'S CURSE

THE FLEDGLING HANDBOOK 101

 St. Martin's Griffin